Also by Will Elliott

The Pilo Family Circus
The Pilgrims

Shadow
WILL ELLIOTT

Book II of the Pendulum Trilogy

Jo Fletcher
BOOKS

First published in Australia in 2011 by HarperCollins
First published in Great Britain in 2012
This edition published in 2012 by

Jo Fletcher Books
an imprint of Quercus
55 Baker Street
7th Floor, South Block
London
W1U 8EW

A CIP catalogue record for this book is available
from the British Library

ISBN 978 0 85738 142 2 (PB)
ISBN 978 0 85738 153 8 (EBOOK)

For the people of Canada,
who produced (among other fine things) Melissa,
the finder of lost cats

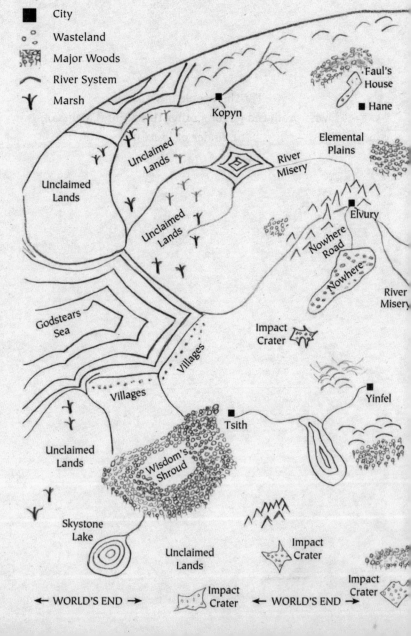

Levaal North

Key:

- ■ City
- Wasteland
- Major Woods
- River System
- Marsh

Kopyn

Faul's House

■ Hane

Elemental Plains

Unclaimed Lands

River Misery

Unclaimed Lands

Unclaimed Lands

Elvury

Nowhere Road

Nowhere

River Misery

Godstears Sea

Impact Crater

Villages

Villages

Yinfel

Unclaimed Lands

Tsith

Wisdom's Shroud

Skystone Lake

Unclaimed Lands

Impact Crater

← WORLD'S END →

Impact Crater

← WORLD'S END →

Impact Crater

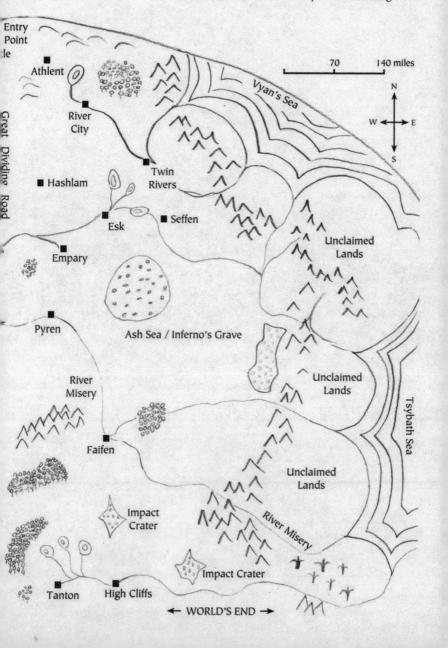

East/West: 945 miles across World's End.
North/South: 500 miles by Great Dividing Road.

70   140 miles

N
W — E
S

Entry Point

Athlent

River City

Hashlam

Twin Rivers

Esk

Seffen

Empary

Vyan's Sea

Unclaimed Lands

Ash Sea / Inferno's Grave

Pyren

River Misery

Unclaimed Lands

Faifen

Tsybath Sea

Unclaimed Lands

Impact Crater

River Misery

Impact Crater

Tanton   High Cliffs

← WORLD'S END →

Great Dividing Road

DRAMATIS PERSONAE

Domudess: a wizard
Gorb: a half-giant
Shadow: a mythical being
Stranger: a magician of some kind
Stuart Casey, aka Case: a changed man

Mayors' Command:

Anfen: former First Captain of the castle's army
Doon: Faul's nephew, killed by Kiown
Eric: a journalist (and fan of Superman comics) who went
    through the door
Far Gaze: a folk magician
Faul: a half-giant
Lalie: an Inferno cultist
Loup: a folk magician
Lut: Faul's husband
Sharfy: one of Anfen's band
Siel: a low-level happenstance mage
Tii: a groundman

Castle:

Arch Mage/Avridis: Vous's advisor, confidante, and overseer of 'the Project'

Aziel: Vous's daughter, imprisoned in the castle; heir to rule, in theory

Blain: a Strategist

Envidis: a Hunter

Evelle: a Hunter

Ghost: a conglomerate of five personalities housed in Vous's mirror (and other glass surfaces)

Kiown: a Hunter

Tauvene: First Captain of Kopyn

Thaun: a Hunter

Vashun: a Strategist

Vous: the Aligned world's Friend and Lord

Council of Free Cities:

Erkairn: Spokesman of the Scattered Peoples

Ilgresi the Blind: mayor of Elvury

Izven: mayor of Yinfel

Liha: mayor of Faifen

Ousan: mayor of High Cliffs

Tauk the Strong: mayor of Tanton

Wioutin: Advisor to the mayor of Tsith

Gods/Great Spirits:

Nightmare: young god

Valour: young god

Wisdom: young god

Inferno: old god

Mountain: old god

Tempest: old god

Dragons:

Dyan: a Minor personality
Ksyn: one of the eight Major personalities
Shâ: one of the eight Major personalities
Tsy: one of the eight Major personalities
Tzi-Shu: one of the eight Major personalities
Vyan: one of the eight Major personalities
Vyin: one of the eight Major personalities

OUTSIDE OF TIME

1

There are horse hooves thudding on the Great Dividing Road. Their beat is fast, urgent. The world has the soft blurred edges of a dream, the deep purple twilight seeming to filter through water. Fragments of memory like broken possessions float in a dark pool but do not break through to its surface. There is just the beating of hooves: closer, closer it comes.

The man's heart, recently still, now beats in time with that sound. He groans. Warmth flushes through his cold flesh, beat by beat, until it reaches his stiff cold fingers. He cannot remember a thing, not a cursed *thing*: not his name, not how he came to be here in a pool of dried blood. His hand goes to his belly, his hand remembering something his mind does not. Then to his neck.

A light approaches from the south, comes close, swallows him, then heat is washing over him in pulsing waves. Above him is a rider on horseback, who pulls his steed to a halt. It hurts to look at the rider directly. The steed has silver barding which glows jewel-bright. Halted or not, the man can still hear the hoofbeats thudding down. 'Who are you?' he says hoarsely.

A voice, quietly commanding, answers, 'I am Valour. You are reprieved.'

Blooming light flares brightly about the god, filling all the world. The man feels for a long time that he is floating in it, laughing, forgetting everything and knowing only joy until the god speaks again to drag him back to the Great Dividing Road and the pool of dried blood. 'Hear me,' says Valour. 'There shall be no second reprieve, if again you fall. Not for you, nor for any other. I have altered the world itself to return your mortal life. I cannot do so again, lest my creator rise in wrath. Do you understand?'

'I do, my redeemer,' he says though he does not understand. He tries to see the god's face but cannot find its features in the light. He can feel Valour's gaze upon him, cold and warm at once.

'Stand again. You are a warrior, not a servant.'

He staggers to his feet. 'For what purpose do I live, my redeemer?'

'Act as you will: with freedom, till death take you. Take you it shall. But I say this: do not serve the brood. Come what may. Whether I leave this land or remain.'

'But, my redeemer ... why would you go?' The thought fills him with profound sadness.

'The brood wish to be free, for we Spirits to be gone. The day will come when I must ride to war. I do not know my future.' The light about Valour begins to withdraw.

'Wait! I love you dearly. Stay with me! I do not understand your words, my redeemer.'

'Then hear this. There are two great Dragons, not one. Now they are naked before each other. Ours still sleeps, the far one is awake. They bend their thoughts to war. The Conflict Point is World's End, where stood the Wall. Where the Great Road meets its twin.'

Valour tosses to the ground a chest-panel of plated metal. It lands with hardly a sound. Atop this he drops a sword, sheathed. 'I give you a part of myself,' says Valour, 'so that part of myself remains, if I am sent away. I cannot better aid a mortal man than this. You will take this sword, this armour. If you find a steed, tell it my name and it will serve you. *Do not serve the brood*. For the Pendulum has begun to swing. Hear me? The Pendulum has begun to swing.'

Tears run down the man's face. Then Valour is gone, and the only way he knew it was no dream or fevered vision is the armour and sword lying there for him, and the pools of dried blood. And his heart, beating again.

IN THE SKY

1

'*Asked* for me?' Case laughed. 'Now why the Christ would a bunch of fucking monster dragons or whatever you got up here ask for *me*?'

Evidently this was a question not worth answering, for the Invia ignored it. Her staring eyes were bright as little pools of water in sunlight, though they and her parted lips expressed nothing other than that she watched him. Case wondered if any human emotion stirred beneath. The wind gaily tossed around her snowy hair and ruffled her wings' long soft feathers. She stood on a shelf of air and stared.

Case's feet dangled from the edge of a jutting shelf just above the thick layer of the sky's lightstone. Though it was dimming to usher in night, its brightness was still painful. A long, long way below them the ground waited to thump the life out of him. He was beginning to get impatient for it. He'd flap his arms on the way down, whoop and bray like a jackass. Try not to land on anyone who didn't deserve it, though the odds were slim. He pictured a bunch of people going about their business and a suicidal old man landing among them making a hell of a mess, and he burst out laughing. He tossed his hat into the sky; the wind whisked it out of sight. 'If I jump, you're going to catch me, aren't you?'

Said the Invia, 'Yes. Don't!'

He laughed. 'Why the hell not?'

'It would annoy me.'

'Which would be just tragic. S'cuse me a moment, some things never go out of fashion.' Case scratched his balls with vigour. The Invia unfurled her wings and picked him up with effortless strength. 'Watch what the fuck you're doing!' he snarled as her hands pinched his underarms, already tender from the long flight after she'd plucked him from his would-be plunge to the death.

Her wings beat the air as she carried him higher through a funnel of deep grey stone, away from the lightstone, up to where she had to push him from beneath through a gap hardly big enough. After an uncomfortable crawl the space widened out to a vast cavern of smooth dark walls. Wind came at intervals through a hundred off-shooting holes bored in the cavern's domed roof and walls, singing eerie notes like a huge woodwind instrument being randomly blown. Now and then echoing inhuman cries reached them from deeper within.

Despite himself, Case was intrigued by the sense this vast bare dome was ancient, far older than anything people had built anywhere. Its age pressed down on him so tangibly he could *feel* it. The air was thick with a strange smell. 'Where're your dragons then?' he said.

'Not here! This is the Gate. They never come here. Not much.'

There was a distant thudding sound. The stone underfoot just faintly shivered. The Invia gave a fluttery excited whistle.

'That was *big*, whatever that was,' Case said. He sniffed deeply, trying to place the air's scent. His head began to spin and suddenly he was on his back. His thoughts spun dizzily until they broke down and became colours and shapes floating before his eyes – all the world just coloured shapes, each with its own simple meaning which needed no elaboration. Then there was a pleasant taste he sucked at greedily, something pressing against his lips. Slowly his mind came back together.

The Invia's expressionless eyes peered at him closely while she put her gashed wrist to his mouth, feeding him her blood. 'Are you alive?' she said.

Case wanted to make a smart-arse remark but all that came out was, 'Ehhhh . . .'

'No walkers come here,' she said. A deep piping note played with a blast of cold wind from a nearby tunnel, throwing her hair around. 'The air is very strong here. Walkers are soft as their skin. They don't like it. Foolish walkers.'

There was a burst of movement and the tunnel directly overhead sang its high-blown note. A small flock of Invia poured through, filling the space about the tunnel's mouth. They exchanged fluttery whistles. Each of them shot off in a different direction, one alone pausing to stare down at Case before it flashed away in a blur of white wings and skin and scarlet hair.

The Invia waited for Case to recover from his faint. He was shaken by sudden cravings for half-a-dozen chemicals he'd been hooked on, once upon a time. He'd taught his body in the end to be content with just the booze; it was the best he could do. 'Not sure what hit me there,' he said.

'You're old, for a walker. And sick. Your aura's bad. Faint and sick.'

'Yeah well. You know my idea to fix all that. But you won't let me.' The enormous dome stretched in all directions further than he could see. 'What is this place for anyway? Doesn't look like a gate to me.'

She tapped the grey stone floor with a knuckle. 'Strong skystone. This keeps them here. They cannot break it. Or fit through gaps. They can't even change shape to fit through! It was made for this.'

'Got it,' he said.

'And the gods. *They* make sure it holds. This is how it works.'

'Yes, ma'am.'

'If the gods went away, it might be different.'

'I'll see what I can do.'

She leaned close to him, her bright sparkling eyes going wide. 'Already, Dyan escaped. He's just a Minor, but clever. There could be others, soon. They are trying to find out how. It's hard. Are you ready to fly?'

Case sat up, rubbing his head. Taking this for assent she grabbed him and flew, picking out a gap in the roof from the scores around it. Cold air blasted out in a low note, painfully loud as they plunged through the wide stone maw, the tunnel snaking around but always leading upward. From off-shooting ones to either side came the occasional shriek reminiscent of the Invia's dying wail he'd heard at Faul's place. The sounds' meanings he caught but they made no sense to him, much like catching only one or two words in a long conversation.

After a time the Invia sat him on one of the ledges set in the tunnel's sides, cocked her head and listened. Wind blasted through with a low thrumming note; within the gust a flock of Invia shot past in a blur of white feathers. Case's Invia wrapped her wings around him, shielding him from any accidental collision. Her cool cheek pressed against his; her wings about him imparted strange tenderness, protecting him as an animal protects its young, no human sentiment in the gesture at all. Still he'd have happily stayed in the soft feathered nest all day.

When the flock had passed, she said, 'They heard him speak. Just a word. They have not heard him for a long while! *I* have. They are excited. They should come here more often. Those ones always pester Tsy. He dislikes them.'

Her face showed unusual animation. Not wanting her to remove the tiny house of soft feathers (he stroked them) he said, 'Who spoke?'

'Vyin. He knows you are here. You heard his feet press down, when he leaped from a perch. That was when we were in the Gate. You didn't hear his voice. Walkers can't, unless he lets you.'

She picked him up and on they flew, through an endless labyrinth of stone.

2

In the maze's deepest darkness were what seemed life forms made of strange light, their bodies a twisted glowing core within a blurry nest, their flickering fingers groping blindly at the cavern about them as if seeking flaws or cracks.

There were times the dark was so utterly black Case could grab handfuls of gloom from the air and *feel* it as he squeezed it in his fist. There were passages where the stone creaked and wept with the bitter sadness of someone wishing desperately for the bright world below: for running water, trees, winds, oceans to dive into, glaciers to swat through the waves with a gush of foam and breaking ice, lands to beat into sculpted shapes. But there was only this darkness, the pressing stone walls – the cruellest cage ever made – with no quick and easy mortal death to buy freedom for those here imprisoned. Case almost drowned in the sadness pouring through him, pouring through the very stones. He could not help weeping. Even the Invia wept, her tears splashing down on his head as she brought him higher, deeper and into the sadness, out of his life and into a dream he was sure he'd had long ago.

Then the narrow ways poured into an open space even more vast than the Gate had been. Below them was a kind of ziggurat, a structure of strangely laid slabs of shining black metal with long arms stretching off at different points. The arms spun slowly. More such designs were set into the walls and roof, ugly and incomprehensible things. A city of such buildings stretched back into the dark, though no living beings moved on the smooth barren ground that he could see. A river gouged into the stone floor cast up a long wedge of brilliant light.

The strange smell was overpowering. Again Case's thoughts dissolved to shifting coloured shapes; again the Invia fed him her sweet nourishing blood to bring him back to consciousness. They flew toward a high roof of gleaming stone, carved with runes through which brilliant colour moved and flowed, as though the cavern had a heart and pulse, and these colours were its lifeblood pumping beneath the dark stone skin.

Case threw up.

The Invia descended with a noise of annoyance at the puke on her forearms. 'I should not be here,' she said. 'I would not be, if you could come yourself. Silly walker! You cannot fly.'

She had only just set him down when there was a sense of something large rushing toward them, a mouth opening wide enough for Case to walk inside, pearl-white teeth so close Case would have (if he'd had time) been certain meant to eat him.

Instead, the Invia gave a surprised squawk as the jaws closed upon her. The thing – whatever it was – rushed away with her so fast it was gone in the ink-thick gloom before he'd turned around to check he'd actually seen what he thought he'd seen.

'Hello?' he said.

A high-pitched wail bloomed through the cavern from the direction she'd gone, its echo slow to fade. Something further away called in answer, but the sound was not made by an Invia. Then silence fell.

For want of better ideas, Case walked to the bank of that glowing river, which seemed filled not with water but with liquid light. Despite its brilliance the light did not penetrate the cavern far or deeply. The footing was bad and Case could not see what he slipped and staggered on – it felt powdery. Bits and pieces like beach shells kicked from his feet and clattered musically together. In parts the floor was ankle-deep with them. Shells? He knelt, felt one, and found it was actually a scale, its colour hard to make out this far from the river's light. The scale was similar but not as big as those Kiown and Sharfy had made such a big deal of. He fished around in the powdery litter for a whole one, compared it with the memory of those Eric had shown him. Smaller, he judged, and thinner.

About Case loomed the odd tall structures he'd seen from high up, twisting and writhing like living alien things. He had to rub his eyes, for it seemed the nearest structure was solid as metal yet behaving like liquid, fluidly changing shape and remoulding itself.

He pegged a scale at it. As though by magnetic force, the spinning scale was drawn to the structure's wall, struck it then glanced away with a *chink!* The moving structure froze motionless, so suddenly it imparted a sense of vertigo that made him stagger. There fell heavily on Case a sense of being observed. 'Hello,' he called. 'Any chance of a beer?'

The structure burst into motion again with greater speed. He looked away, dizzy.

It was then that a voice seemed to vibrate through Case's body: *You stare at things I have made. But you do not understand them.*

The glimmering light-play over the roof snuffed itself out. He felt something approach, something huge. A swirl of darkness blacker than the rest gathered itself up before him and assumed a massive shape. Close by there was a thundering *boom, boom*: the noise of very heavy pillars being dropped. Case felt and heard the ground groaning under the weight of something enormous. Two points high above gleamed and sparkled down at him in twin bursts of unclasped light.

Case could only laugh in awe. Around the two lights – eyes, he understood, though they seemed like pieces of a star – was a huge head, reared back on an enormously long, arching neck, between huge, spreading, pinioned wings. *Look away*, the voice ordered.

Case looked away.

The voice seemed to come not from the dragon's head, but from the ground at Case's feet, vibrating through his whole body. It said, *I have not been beheld by your kind before. I find I do not wish to be. To have you here brings me not rage, as I'd feared it might. It brings a sadness I had not expected.*

I try now to speak in a voice like yours, so you can hear me. It is difficult to express so little. To express much more would drown your mind with my thought and nothing left of yours.

Case laughed again. He had never been so small in all his life and the feeling was somehow liberating. Why fear? This enormous monster was really no larger than familiar old death! 'Are you *the* Dragon?' he said. 'The one they all talk about?'

I am Vyin, the eighth of its young. At your feet is a gift I crafted. It was not made for you. Do not touch it yet. Look at it.

On the ground something flashed among the piles of broken and powdered scale. It was a necklace, gleaming and beautiful. *The others do not know my thoughts, or of your being here. With effort and cunning I hide you from them. I hide this gift also, though they will learn of it in time, and they will rage. It may be that they make gifts of their own, to be this gift's kin, and rival. They may try. If so, they have less than the lifespan of a man to do what I have done with care over many lifetimes of men. A thousand eventualities I saw. In the crafting I prepared for each. Their efforts will be rushed. Do not touch it yet. Watch me.*

One of the dragon's feet shifted forward, swept away a mound of crushed scale and revealed smooth stone beneath, which creaked and groaned as its foot pressed down. Scales rippled, tendons pulled taut as clawed toes bigger than Case clenched, breaking off a piece of the floor. The great beast's paw turned upward. On it lay a slab of stone the size of a car. Vyin's claws wrapped around it.

This, and all things, are made of the same stuff, only in different amounts and arrangements. Watch. Vyin crushed the slab, the cracking noise of it like firing guns; crushed it so thoroughly only fine dust remained when the dragon's paw opened again. A faintly blown breath puffed the dust into the air where it hung in a glimmering cloud. The dragon's paw brushed through it. *I can shape from this raw material many better things, things of more use than the stone it was before. Do you understand me?*

Case felt dizzy. 'No. No, sir, I don't.'

The dragon's huge head bent closer to him; faint hints of light flickered across its rippling scales. *You too are made of this stuff*, it said, *though each of your kind is arranged uniquely. Things* of more use than you, and your kind, could be made of that material. But the law of my Parent forbids this.

Yet the laws in many ways are wrong and no longer suitable. My Parent is greater than we eight, for by It we were formed. But my Parent sleeps. The Wall stood when my Parent was last awake. Here you stand before me with little fear. But I tell you words that should make your kind cower and dread. The Pendulum swings.

Vyin's great paw lowered till it was very close to Case. I do not hate your kind. I do not desire your deaths. Yet it is near certain you all will die. Five of my kin hate you with poisonous hate, and blame you that we are here imprisoned. Two have argued that some of you should live when we are again free, for the sake of Otherworld, your realm, which our Parent protects. Those who aid us now will be so Favoured.

I argue for this too. But I deceive all my kin. I mean for you all to live, and desire to live with you in peace. I cannot convince even one of my peers to come to my thinking in totality. Nor do so by force. I am their tallest pillar, but they too are tall.

The massive bulk shifted. Vyin's paw swept through the sparkling dust cloud again. From this material I may shape things of more use than cruel prison stone. Yet flesh fused with living mind and spirit I cannot truly make from stone. Have you wish for life no longer?

Case swayed on his feet. He barely heard his own voice say, 'No. Kill me if you want. I've had enough.'

Your death is not my wish or it would long ere now be done. I have spoken here to synchronise our purpose, which is now done. My words will guide your paths, but never perfectly nor without risk. Hark! Have I your blessing to reshape the stuff which makes you? It will serve better purpose. I do so if you are willing. Only if so.

The cavern spun. Case fell, his head landing on a soft mound of powdered scale. The necklace glimmered and shone near his feet. His only thought was that it was so very pretty.

Answer, said Vyin.

'Yes. Don't know ... what you mean ... but yes.'

The two star-heart dragon eyes descended upon him pulsing their light, bathing him in it almost lovingly, their heat pouring over him. The beast's warmth and scent enveloped him. The stone beneath Case's limp body groaned with the dragon's pressing weight. Its mouth opened. The jaws closed about him with great care, lifting him up, but Case thought he was floating. Then he knew nothing.

IN THE QUIET

1

Anfen's feet were blistered, his legs chafed and weak in reeking leathers, but still he staggered north on the Great Dividing Road. Standing on the rear feed trough of a passing trade wagon had eaten up many miles before its driver became aware of him and shook him off by veering off road over bumpy turf. The second time it happened had been worse. But he'd got right back up with cuts and bruised ribs and kept on toward his own death, which he fantasised about with relish.

He did not feel the world owed him much, did not feel in a position to make lavish requests. So he wouldn't have asked for the tiredness or aches to be dimmed by drink or by one of Loup's spells. But if one request *were* granted, he would dearly have loved to be free of the constantly playing memory of the Arch Mage at the Wall, his words, the twist of the square gleaming gem in its eye socket. It was all still so clear it may as well have been a gloating phantom ever on the Road before him.

Stones and pebbles tapped and scraped past his boots as though blown by strong wind. In truth, no wind blew. The Road was flat, yet Anfen walked into what felt a stream of gravity, an endless, steep hill. This invisible force was quite real and had pushed back against him since the Wall came down. It did not occur to him to go off road, over where the force was weaker, to ease the burden of each step.

And that was not for fear of the tall dark shapes he occasionally glimpsed through the trees or in fields skirting the Road, motionless but for the curling of spikes all down their long bodies and, once, a head swinging gracefully round to watch him pass. He watched it right back, stared into its stony eyes, expecting it to come at him with stiff lurching strides and the hissing rattle of a mane packed with thin needles. He did not fear *those* bastard things. Nor the Invia who would hunt him, drawn to his Mark, nor anything else, not any more. Instead the Tormentor had just watched him.

Not long ago he'd woken in a ditch. Some courteous traveller had spooned him into it off the Road, rather than leave him to be trampled by a horse or wagon. The traveller was so courteous he didn't bother to rob what must have seemed a corpse, albeit one armed with a sword and knife. One which in life had twice won a warrior's highest honour, Valour's Helm. To be feared, as corpses went . . .

Whether Anfen got to his destination or not hardly mattered. Death if he did, death if he didn't. He wanted the slow death he'd earned, wanted to feel every slow second of it, for his flesh to burn. He'd been walking toward it since his first infant steps lurched across the kitchen floor to grasp his mother's shin for balance. Those steps just as unsteady as these steps now.

His staggering legs weakened against the invisible push, his body lurched, he head-butted the ground. White lights flashed. Before he blacked out, for some reason he heard his mother's merry laugh showering her joy down on him, her praise and encouragement for his clumsy steps across the kitchen floor, a little toy sword in his hand which his father had carved. *My little soldier*, she'd called him, *my little soldier*.

2

'Why is it you wish to die, warrior?' said a voice behind him.

Since he'd raised his pained body back upright and sent it forward again, the Road had been his alone. The sky, the whole world, was a deep shade of twilight he'd never seen, the landscape black silhouettes against it. Silence had snuffed out the wind, bird calls, nearly everything but his scuffing boots. That was until the slow *clip-clopping* hooves began behind him, carrying a rider he knew wasn't really there.

Anfen didn't want to turn and look at a phantom whose existence (he realised) marked his final parting with sanity. But this quiet was nice. So was the ghostly and somehow patient *clip-clop, clip-clop*, its rhythm keeping perfect time. Such calm he'd seldom known, such eerie peace. Where had the world gone? All he recognised was the Road and the distant fang-shaped peaks black against the sky.

Here and there in the gentle blue-black light were what looked like gems hung in the air: clusters of glimmering diamonds. Some were tiny, some the size of boulders suspended far above and distant. The sight disturbed him; why had his mind conjured these strange and beautiful objects? He had no wish or need for beauty.

But ah, such precious quiet.

The Road's southward push had always been there, he reflected as he laboured into it. It was why the clouds went south down the world's middle. Since the Wall came down, it had changed, got stronger, it had ... But he lost the thought, for the horseman behind him spoke again: 'There is rage and grief in you. For he who names himself the Arch Mage. But you were not cheated, warrior. You were elevated. Your function was performed. As was his. It is now done.'

Anfen's hoarse croak was barely audible. 'You mean my choices weren't my own. If they weren't, they never have been. Are they mine now, or not?'

'That is not what I mean, warrior. Your suffering is needless.'

'It will end soon enough.'

'Shed this part of you as you would toss aside a rusted blade and find a new one, far keener,' said the voice.

'What's the difference? I'll go to the same place.'

There was just the slow *clip-clop* of hooves for a time. 'Where do you go to, warrior?'

'I'm going—' he began, but felt no need to explain to a shadow, a figment of delirium, that he was going to the underground cavern where Stranger took him. He'd nicked his passage in and out on the walls, so he'd surely find it. If he made it there alive – somehow he thought he would – he'd kill one of the newly replaced unfortunates who were, presumably, held this minute in the clutches of those pincer-things, those burning hot shackles. He'd lay the body gently down and put himself there instead. He'd grit his teeth while he endured the hissing burn of cooking skin, those curved tips digging slowly into his flesh till they reached the bone, turning deep red or black with heat.

'What purpose will this death serve?' the figment said.

Anfen shrugged. 'It's a death,' he said and laughed.

'I have seen better deaths.'

'I don't care,' said Anfen.

'You are a warrior.'

Anfen spat to get those words out of his head.

'For me to name you such is high praise,' said the voice.

'Leave me be, I warn you.'

It was not *just* death he sought. Likely as death was, Anfen had just a half-formed hope that the caverns would turn him into a New Mage like Stranger, powerful enough to do with spell craft what he could not do with a sword. He remembered her claim that the underground caverns made New Mages unswervingly loyal. But he knew there was not a thing in the Dragon's world that could pry free the glowing hot lump of hate burning inside him. He would never, ever relinquish it.

'Do not waste yourself,' said the voice behind him. 'There are no New Mages.'

'I've dealt with such a mage,' Anfen said wearily. 'Her name is Stranger.'

'She is not a New Mage. She told you that to hide what she truly is. She told you that so you would tell the Mayors, who would see their doom coming. So that in desperation they would help you bring down the Wall. That is what she wanted.'

'She has power. I have *seen* it. A pillar of light she conjured in Faul's yard.'

'Why do you wish to die?'

'Shut up.' Anfen drew his sword and turned. There was nothing but the southern sky and the Road. The horseman's voice carried to him on the wind: *The Pendulum has begun to swing again. The Pendulum has begun to swing.*

He was not in the quiet place any more – he was back in the world's harsh and hateful clarity. A hot breeze with the smell of smoke blew across him like an unwanted caress. High up came the occasional flash of red and white as foreign airs clashed.

He felt the *push* into his back. How easy it would be, to reverse his course and walk *with* that force.

He spat into the air, watched the push take his spit a long way, sheathed his weapon and walked instead up the steep hill.

3

Here came the group which – Anfen knew it upon his first distant glimpse of them – marked the end.

Two dozen men approached, all of them too well fed and too well dressed to be refugees fleeing the north. Some wore colours of various Aligned cities, a few wore glinting chain-mail. As they got closer he spotted one among them in the dress of a First Captain. The stripes had not changed since Anfen himself wore them.

Anfen wondered if he were imagining things again, to see such a small group of highly ranked castle men, roaming south mostly on foot, in disputed territory, along the Great Road which was watched by spies of both sides.

Now the group had seen him too. Weapons came to hand. A few fanned away from the Road in case he ran. He would not. Some of them exclaimed in surprise. He heard his name spoken.

Gladness filled him. He drew his sword for the last time and smiled, thinking back to the wooden one his father had carved, wondering if this end would have pleased the man.

Laughter brayed out from the midst of the approaching group. The tallest among them, in black leather from toe to collar, threw back the hood of a weather-beaten coat, exposing a springing coil of red hair and a gleeful smile.

Anfen could not help but be surprised to see Kiown among high-ranking enemy men. Not just surprised but stupefied, at his own blindness most of all. This was someone who had fought with him with rare courage, who'd travelled uncounted miles with him; someone he'd trusted with his life. Even now he battled with the truth, wondered if his madness was again at play, casting Kiown's face on someone else.

Until he spoke. 'You men are to help spread word of this.' Kiown strode forward. He wore a sparkling gem in one ear, probably a charm which would help him fight. Another on his finger. The kind of gear they gave Hunters.

'Word of what?' asked another of the group.

'That this year I won Valour's Helm. He can swing metal, this one.' The men now surrounded them both in a wide ring. Kiown drew his blade. 'Nothing to say?' he asked.

Anfen stared at him tiredly.

'No? Well, then. Bye.' Kiown lashed his blade in fast cuts. Strong ones. Anfen blocked them but his arm jarred badly. He knew he'd become weak but not *this* weak. Kiown was dictating the fight, making all the attacks, too fast on his feet, making a game of it, unnecessary spins and flourishes, showing off. Anfen was tired, no adrenaline in him, no will to win, just technique. The *ching* of clashing swords and their scuffing boots filled the afternoon. Anfen felt he watched the fight from a distance, as though he were part of the ring of men surrounding them.

He was brought back when pain thudded into his gut and knocked the wind from him. A crossbow bolt knocked him sideways like a hard punch; the sword clattered from his hand. The watchers laughed; fired as a jest, the shot had come very close to hitting Kiown. Who was furious.

'Who shot that? *Who* fucking shot that bolt?' He stormed over to a man in Athian colours hiding a large crossbow behind his back and smashed his sword hilt in the man's face. A scuffle broke out as others rushed over to hold him back, not before some of his kicks landed. The man didn't get up, nor would he.

Nor could Anfen, who had almost been forgotten, writhing on the ground clutching the still-protruding bolt. Instinct was to pull it out, which would make the damage far worse. So that's just what he did. The pain almost sent him unconscious behind a rain of white flashes. Amazing, spectacular pain.

He lay bleeding to death as their boots tromped past, careful not to tread on him. A couple of them matter-of-factly called him a traitor. Kiown crouched beside him, inspected the damage, patted his shoulder. 'Not looking good, my friend. Not looking good. Lost your edge. It happens. Have you considered other work?'

'Be well,' Anfen said, suddenly free of anger and of everything else. How quickly the life ebbed out of him. He was thirsty. He shivered with cold.

Kiown frowned. 'Now . . . now *that* is an odd remark. Where's that old familiar belly fire? I killed Doon and the rest of them. Did you know? Led them to an ambush. *We* killed them, I guess, you and I. You put me in charge, remember? "Kiown leads you, wisely I hope." Angry about it? The real Anfen would be. He'd find a way to kill me even now. He'd choke me with those guts leaking out of him. My, what a lot of blood.' He pointed at the crossbow bolt Anfen had yanked out of himself. 'Ah, I get it. That's for me, right?'

Anfen let the dripping thing fall from his fingers. Kiown hurled it away then leaned close, pebbles grinding beneath his boots. 'Listen. I want you to know something. Tonight, I'm going to have roast fowl in the Batlen. Know it? Luxury inn, not far. Fowl with trimmings, true-gold ale, a nice drop. And I will tip my cup to you. "To Anfen," I shall say. And that will be that. I will bunk in a soft warm bed, two or three whores sating my every strange impulse. Then I shall go about my life, which will be long, exciting for a while, then *very* comfortable. As wills Vous, our Friend and Lord.'

'Be well.'

'I certainly shall. Life can be good. Strange chap! I'm going to chop your head off now. Nice sword this, no? Enjoy. Bye.' Kiown stood and oblivion descended with his arm.

A DRAKE'S VISIT

1

Through Aziel's window the sky's lightstone began its fade into night. Sometimes the fade was slow, sometimes it took only minutes. Tonight was a slow fade. Little shapes still flitted among the grey clouds, specks darting playfully in and out too quickly to be birds. Surely they were Invia. She watched them, imagined herself flying among them, naked and free.

She imagined roaming through that now darkening landscape, seeing up close the horizon's distant tooth-sized peaks. It was hard to believe that there were actually *places* out there – that by taking steps just as she did to walk from one end of her room to the other, she would eventually end up miles away from where she started.

Standing to her window's left side, looking down, she could behold the Great Dividing Road, shooting off in a wide straight line, perfectly splitting the land into halves. Clouds pushed south in line with it at greater than usual speed, casting weak, many-sided shadows along it. A fervent broth of them gathered from east and west, bunched above the castle like pipe smoke being drawn in, then blown south. It was ever thus, but it seemed the whole strange business was suddenly urgent. Now even birds seemed unable to fly against the sky's weird current.

Just ahead another Invia moved closer to Aziel's tower than they usually came. She did not see its shape clearly, just the after-image of spread wings as it dived down through a fat blanket of cloud. Why should *they* be free to fly, she wondered, while the mighty dragons were trapped in the sky? She felt a moment's affinity with the great unseen creatures, imagined that they would feel the same for her, if they'd learned of her.

And learn of her they surely had. She was the Friend and Lord's daughter, after all.

Three faces swam like faint reflections across the window's glass. She gave a small cry of surprise. It had been a long while since Ghost visited. Gladness bloomed inside her to have company, any company.

One of Ghost's faces (not the beastly one, which she had asked Ghost to hide from her when possible) called her name in a frightened voice. She affected annoyance at being intruded upon, which could not have been further from the truth. 'And what do *you* want?' she said. 'Coming to my window like this, after having ignored me so long?'

'We didn't mean to ignore,' Ghost replied, its voice tremulous. The hollow-eyed face which was mostly skull spoke while the others jostled around it. 'We're frightened, Aziel. We have had to watch his room, though he scares us so, these days. Someone broke in last month. Do you know of it? We must be vigilant. And patient.'

'Broke in! Was it a smelly old man?'

'Very unlikely. A great wizard, it must have been. Truly great! And now something else has happened.'

'What?'

'Your father has become . . . a little strange.'

'I don't want to talk about *him*. Not after what he put me

through today.' Those strangled cries, the terrible shrieks of pain. And when one screaming voice was snuffed out, there began another, until three of them had finally been silenced.

'We're not sure who to turn to,' said one of Ghost's other faces, the one so faded it could hardly be seen. Hints of fingertips pressed upon the window glass. 'You're the only other one we speak with. The others we sometimes . . . watch. That's all. Watch.'

She sat back on the edge of her bed. 'You may use the mirror, if you like. That window isn't very clean.'

'No! It's easier to flee the window in a hurry, if we need to.'

'Why would you need to flee? So frightened all the time, you are! What's happened with my father?'

'He's . . .' The faces turned to each other, conferring in whispers too quiet for her to hear.

'You can tell me, don't be afraid,' she said, running a comb through her long black hair. '*I'm* not the one who reports on *you*.'

The hollow-eyed face bunched like it might cry, the others looked pained. 'We're sorry, Aziel. But that was long ago. Have you not forgiven us?'

She kept Ghost in brief suspense. 'Oh, fine; yes, I have. I know you can't lie to him. And I'm glad you've come. I wish you'd visit more often.'

'Why didn't you wail today, Aziel?'

The screams from the room next door echoed loud in her ears again. She hurled the comb. Its metal handle made short work of the window. On the largest shard, two of Ghost's faces jostled for position, until the hollow-eyed face won. 'We're sorry. You're crying! We're sorry, Aziel. We just—'

'Why do *you* care about whether or not I sing for him? Why must you remind me of it? You said you felt sorry for me, having to do that every day.'

'We do! We do!'

She dabbed at her nose and eyes. 'Today was worse than when I was sick and lost my voice, or the day that old man—' She quickly bit her tongue, not daring speak of the peculiar visitor she had since wished would return. 'It's horrible. The noises: so horrible. What do they *do* in there? And Nanny at the door, saying those awful things she says . . .'

'We wish he didn't make you wail for him, we do,' said Ghost. 'But he has to find a part in you that's troublesome and make you put it aside for good. That's why he does it. Don't you see? The part that makes you want to *stop* them doing those terrible things, to save their lives. *That's* the troublesome part. That's what you must get rid of.'

'You've told me before and I still don't understand. I don't think I want to.'

'Aziel. We came to tell you—'

She threw herself on the bed, voice muffled in the mattress and so distorted by sobs that Ghost could not decipher a word: 'Today and yesterday. A little voice inside me just said *not today! Don't do it, no matter what happens. It's him, not you.* So I didn't. I held it inside and had to bite down on my sleeve and pretend it was just animals being killed for the kitchens. Just like yesterday. Oh, I don't know what I'll do if they start it again tomorrow, I don't know.'

'We came to tell you today was the last day. Vous told them so, told your nanny and the guards. We heard their talk. Oh how he frightened them! Aziel, he thinks you've done it.'

'Done what?' she said into the mattress.

'Got rid of it. The trouble part of you. Aziel! He thinks you've learned.'

'Learned *what*?'

'How to be more like him, and less like . . . like subjects. Your silence was what he wanted all along, don't you see? No matter what you heard being done next door, he wanted you to let it happen. On purpose. He knew that on the day he *didn't* hear your voice cry out from your window, you'd have done it!'

One of the other faces fought its way into the largest glass shard, displacing the other. 'And that's why we're here,' it said in a deeper voice. 'Something about you – about you *learning* has changed him. Shocked him, it seems. We don't know why.'

She sat up, her heart beating faster. 'It's not – it's not *the* change? What Arch talks about?'

'We don't know. We watch the Arch – but we don't understand what he – wait, he comes!'

2

'Stay! Come back, won't you, Ghost? Please, come back later?'

But the window's shards, and the oblong mirror in the corner, showed only their normal reflections.

Tap-thock, tap. Tap-thock, tap. Arch's staff and withered leg, sounds as familiar as the walls of her room or the sky out the window. As familiar was the pause, then keys rattling in Arch's hand, sliding into the lock and twisting around. The hideous face peered in, hideous even to Aziel who treasured his deep scholarly voice and even the sometimes foul smell of him, as he smelled now. Which meant he'd cast recently. He'd promised her he wouldn't, unless he really had to. She didn't like how it hurt him.

A black feather was caught in his collar. She reached to pluck it off, earning a smile from the good side of his face. The burned mangled side didn't so much as twitch.

He'd been in his shape-shifter form, the big black bird he posed as when travelling in secret. She felt the heat still easing from him, though no smoke came from the three large horns weighing down his head. 'May I sit?' he asked, knowing such courtesy – however unnecessary – pleased her.

'You may,' she said, curtseying. She watched the pained way he moved and knew he had travelled far. He was not a natural shape-shifter; holding an animal form would, for him, be like squatting in a very uncomfortable position for a long time.

For a while he just sat and breathed his laboured breaths, his face turned so the deformed side was away from her.

'Ghost says, Father's changing. Ghost says—'

'I'm aware. Very much aware.' He sighed wearily. 'It's far from complete. But the last stage of it all approaches. You can't see it with your eyes, Aziel, but power gathers *itself* toward him, independent of anything I do. It is loose power for now. It surrounds him like a great whirlpool, but will condense and be part of him. Not simply used and burned up, like a mage would use it. And I doubt now that there's even time to—' He glanced at the window shards on the floor. 'Ghost, you say. Is it here now?'

'No, Arch.'

'What did it want?'

'It fled when you came. It seemed afraid. Of Father, and of you. It always is of course, but this time it wasn't the usual *kind* of afraid.'

'Ah.' He drummed the fingers of his good hand on the long silver staff, forked at both ends, which lay across his lap. The other hand lay still and looked like a twisted blackened stick pulled from a fire. 'I think we should move you to a lower floor,' he said. 'Tomorrow. Further away from him. Eventually out of the castle altogether, if need be.'

'Won't he—'

'Be angry? Perhaps. I can handle his anger. I think. It is likely to lack focus, to spray about the place.' The Arch Mage glanced at her sidelong and winked. 'Or perhaps he'll be angry with your nanny. It depends who he thinks moved you.' She laughed, not knowing if he was joking or serious. 'You're his caged bird, Aziel, whose voice he loves. That is all. You are less important to him than he and you both think.'

To her surprise, though he'd surely not meant it to, the remark stung. 'Then who *is* important to him?'

'As it has always been: *he* is important to him. And someone called Shadow, I suppose. Aziel. Did you hear anything of the Wall at World's End? Or anything else unusual?'

She thought of the clouds, but didn't want him to think she thought something so silly as that could be important. 'I saw big airships. Strange fat things. They floated along slowly. One came right over this tower!'

'Ah good, they returned. They are mine. I had them built in Esk. Not well enough, apparently. One crashed: I don't even know where.'

'What are they for?'

'They gathered some . . . some rare airs for me. From far away. You have heard nothing about the Wall?'

'What about it?'

He sighed. 'It is destroyed.'

She did not understand.

'We don't know how, or who did this,' he said, staring into

the distance. 'Nor why. It may help the change occur. Or it may harm your father a great deal.' Arch lapsed into one of his silences.

She had read many books about World's End, about the Wall, and other things she did not much understand. 'You look concerned, Aziel,' he said. 'Don't be. A new world is open to us, or shall be soon. And the war will very soon be won. The occasion is joyous. Whatever it does to Vous.'

'But what is on the other side? Are there people there, more rebel cities?'

'No, Aziel. I have seen things in the Hall of Windows. Things I won't tell you of. Once we have mastered the new airs, all will be well.'

'Was it . . .? Arch. You do know who did it! Don't you?'

His face showed surprise. 'How can you tell?'

'I don't know, but I can. You know who did it. You can say who. I won't tell anyone. Not Ghost or Nanny or anyone.'

'Very well. Aziel, do you know what Ghost really is? I shall tell you. Your father killed five of his friends, long before you were born. I shall not lie to you – I helped him plan it. They were a threat to us, to the smooth running of things. But your father had not before murdered with his own hands. That is, not outside the heat of battle. He'd only ever had *others* do such things for him. The deeds lingered in his mind, after. And in the airs, which are stronger here than elsewhere.'

'He felt guilty?'

'Yes. And with our rituals, as the change began, more power drew itself through him, around him, and interacted with his mind. Do you know what magic is, Aziel, at its most fundamental?'

She thought of the little tricks Arch used to do to amuse her, recalled a bird made of light which clumsily fluttered around the room, until it ran into the wall and puffed into a burst of sparks. Even now an echo of childish delight reached through nearly ten years to touch her like a warm breeze. 'You told me what magic is, but I forget the words you used.'

'Magic is loose reality. This chair I sit upon is fixed reality. You and I are fixed reality, though far more flexible and complex than the chair. Think of us standing in a river, as unformed clay floats past us. Mages can not only see the wet clay, we can grab it and shape it. Great mages, such as I, have big, fast hands. Faster than a blink. We make deliberate shapes, very carefully worked out beforehand, for mistakes are dangerous.

'But your father is not a mage. And even if he were, no man has ever had such power about him. Not the greatest wizard who ever lived. No man *can* hold such large amounts of it, let alone shape it by design. Far less than that which surrounds Vous now would slay him, but for my study and rituals. It was not easy, Aziel. It was centuries of work, often tedious, most of it very dangerous.

'Although the power surrounded him, he had no hands to shape it. Now, suddenly, it is almost like Vous has a *hundred* hands. All moving on their own around him, faster than he can see, let alone control. So he forms shapes he doesn't intend. Even some which are terribly bad for him. And for us.'

'Is Ghost . . .?'

'Ghost is one such form, yes, though not a very dangerous one. Made long before you were born. Part of Vous was guilty, or fearful of – well, of ghosts. The ghosts of his own hands' murders haunted him, as ghosts of the murdered are said to do. This fear consumed him in those days. I remember it. I tried to calm him, with the usual results. So he found a way to calm himself before the fear could consume him.'

'So he made Ghost by accident? And made it his friend, so he wouldn't have to keep being afraid?'

'Yes. Even before the changes began, your father was a strange man.' The Arch Mage seemed to realise the deformed side of his face had come into her view. He shifted it away. 'This is why I'm nervous. About how things . . . progress. What remains of the human in your father has other fears, other guilt, other secrets. And far more power than when he made Ghost. We do not ask Tempest or Mountain how they handle the powers about them – they will not tell us. Nor what their powers are really meant to be used for – we can only guess. Nor do the Spirits possess human frailties. And as we have seen, even gods can lose control.'

'Inferno?'

He nodded. 'And your father is already, I fear, less stable than was Inferno, before that god met its end.' Arch poked at a nearby glass shard with his staff, sending it scraping across the floor away from him. 'I sense your excitement, Aziel. No, do not be ashamed of it. You alone in the castle are permitted that emotion. I fear that lately, with the change, Vous has gone from having a hundred hands to having a thousand. And by the time he is truly a god, he may have ten thousand, or more. And control of none of them. It is a dangerous time.'

'Didn't you . . . didn't you—' She could not get the words out.

'Did we not consider this, back in the beginning?' The human side of his face smiled without mirth. 'Of course not. We were so very young. This science was new. We did not know what would happen. That was partly the point. To learn. There was no other way to learn but to proceed. Mistakes made this time won't be made the next.'

She wanted to go and embrace him, seeing his tiredness and his fear. She even moved to do so. But the square gem turned in its eye socket, rippling the flesh around it with a faint sound of scraped bone. She caught a whiff of burned flesh from his cooling body and recoiled, with a stinging pang of guilt. She pretended to be adjusting her position on the bed. 'Are you saying Father destroyed the Wall? By accident?'

'What he did – among other things – was open the Entry Point to Otherworld. That vast, strange place. I think we've shut it off. But some Pilgrims came. The first in my long lifetime. How many made it through I'm unsure: at least two. It may be one of them who destroyed the Wall. They have such marvellous weaponry! If only my Engineers could mimic it. They have tried. Images and descriptions are not enough for them to work with.' He sighed and stood to leave.

'You're going?' she said.

'I must.'

Aziel fought back the urge to plead that he stay to talk a little longer. He, like Ghost, had not been to talk in a long while. He hobbled to the door, hesitated, then turned back. 'Why is it, Aziel, that I come to speak with you?'

She frowned, finding it a strange thing to be asked. A thought came completely unbidden: *Because you like to be around things in cages*. It gave her another pang of guilt. 'You're my friend,' she said, and smiled at him.

He nodded without reply and hobbled out of the room, careful as always his horns didn't scrape the door frame. 'I'll see about your move to the lower floors,' he said. 'As soon as I'm sure it's safe to move you.'

Then he shut the door and twisted the key in its lock, sounds so familiar she hardly noticed.

3

Do you swear to me?

It was a sad voice that tugged Aziel out of troubled sleep and dreams filled with distant screaming. She sat up, rubbed her eyes and discovered the screams were not of her nightmares – they were quite real. Footsteps rushed past outside her room. Yells, wails, a rattle of chains, a grinding like great stone teeth rubbing together. Something heavy and metallic scraped through the hall outside, right past her door. Whatever it was, it caused more screams at the corridor's far end, until abrupt silence fell.

A flickering glow appeared which showed blood seeping under the door. Aziel did not notice: Her father, Vous, stood in the room with her. He was a glowing outline, through which faint lights pulsed like blood, meeting within him in a hundred tiny splashes of sickly colour. One arm extended toward the ceiling. His head slumped forward on his chest.

Aziel didn't scream. She felt calm. It seemed that a deep sadness poured from her father and filled the room. It did not touch her heart, or share itself with her own sadness (much of which she was hardly aware of), but she felt it pouring off him as sure as the dimly glimmering light. She could not recall what he'd said. 'Father?'

The words came without his mouth moving: *Many of them swear to me, on shore. Many of them do, ankle-deep in the lapping waves I disturb. Many do, waist-deep, neck-deep, as the waters go above their heads.*

'What do you want from me, Father? It's late. And you're not well.'

Aziel. Daughter of mine. Changed daughter. I mourn. Evil is about me. My limbs thrash through it like a man drowning, disturbing the evil this way and that. But should I lie still there would be no difference. All others will be washed from where they stand, gawking and speaking my sweet name, eyes drinking down sight of me. Drowned they will be, as I gush through forests and fill valleys. Drowned in the cities where they have lived as shadows of shadows of shadows. Until the driest plains are drenched in me, waters never to recede, all shall drown, all shall drown. I take their bodies on my surface skin, calm and glassy. I collect their bodies on my churning surface skin.

'Father, I don't understand you. And I don't think that's really you. Not your body, certainly. It's illusion, isn't it? Like Arch sometimes does. Are you doing it on purpose, Father? To scare or punish me? Why must you always punish me? I never hurt you. And if I did I never meant to.'

Vous's head rose slowly to regard her. A smile spread across his face. His eyes widened and grew till they were far too large. His mouth opened into a fissure of swirling gloom. From deep in its depths, as though from a long distance, came a pained cry. Then he was gone, leaving nothing but the blood slowly trickling across the floor. The bedroom door swung slowly open without the *click-clank* of someone unlocking it. A body was slumped just outside the door.

Aziel stood and quickly dressed, surprised to feel so calm and unafraid. She stepped into the hall. No brands had been lit but there were sweeping beams of light snaking over the walls. To the right where the hall curved around, Vous – rather, a ghostly simulacrum of him – stood with his back to her. At his feet were the remains of guards. Something had cut them in half.

A high-pitched voice sang, *Shadow, Shadow. Come back, Shadow.*

'Aziel, stay in your room!' said Arch urgently. He stood leaning hard on his forked silver staff, the ends of his horns pouring out thick smoke.

Vous turned about, on his face a look of amazing viciousness, teeth and eyes far larger than they should be. A hoarse, hissing breath rasped from him. Two big stone faces flung from him at speed down the hall, scraping the floor with the same heavy grinding noise she'd heard before. Their mouths snapped, *clack, clickety-clack.*

Something unseen shoved her back in her bedroom an instant before she'd have been caught in the snapping jaws. The beast heads flew at Arch. He vanished and they smashed into the wall, gouging parts of it loose before falling into two crumbling piles of stone.

On hands and knees Aziel peered around the corner of her bedroom doorway. Up the hall, the ghostly image of her father had one arm aloft, his head downcast again in grief, before the image flickered and went out like a blown candle. Screams and cries sounded from the lower floors as some terror wound its way down through the castle.

Stay in your room, Arch had said. She should, she knew. But its door was so very rarely left open. And part of her understood something, though *how* she understood it she could not have said: her father had come to her not to kill or terrorise her. He'd come for help. And she believed there was only one way to help him.

She took from her dresser a knife with gems embedded in the handle, and stepped out into the hall again. In each room she passed were the massacred remains of grey-robe servants and armoured guards. Some crawled wounded and dazed through the ruins. Some of the corpses moved spastically and chattered away like invisible playful hands jerked them around and played mockingly with their voices.

In the big chamber before Vous's private quarters she paused in the doorway. Ten or more simulacra of her father stood, each motionless, each a ghostly projection in an identical pose. One by one they came to life and launched into a strange dance. It was slow and graceful, all of them moving in a wide circle.

A voice, not her father's, said, THERE IS WORSE THAN PAIN.

With a shriek in unison the mirror images dashed away, as though the voice had scared them off.

Calmly, still calmly, she went to the door of her father's chamber, which swung open for her. Within, twenty grey-robes stood with heads bowed, in rows of five, before her father's throne. He was upon it, body writhing and convulsing, eyes rolled back in his head. His voice spoke and filled the room.

I do this to you for no reason. I do this to you, gaining nothing from the deed. I am parting waters with my hands. I am drowning all of you within me. I am parting waters, pushing out the air. I am rushing waters, taking all things with me.

A stone-coloured beastly head swept up from the floor, snapped its jaws shut on one of the motionless grey-robes, biting it in half. The others still didn't move, even as more such stone beasts erupted in their midst, or descended from the ceiling. Aziel screamed and shielded her eyes for what seemed an age, though she did not shield her ears from stone jaws snapping through meat and bone.

The grey-robes – four remained standing – turned as one to face her, expressions blank as metal masks. Still Vous writhed and thrashed on his throne, but she felt his awareness of her. Something invisible flew at her. She felt it come and flung herself sideways. It crashed into the wall behind her with a passing rush of hot air.

'Aziel, get back to your room,' gasped Arch, hobbling toward her.

'What's happening?'

'Go now!' Three ghostly forms of Vous, all naked, sprinted out of the hall, rushed at Arch with their too-long arms thrashing, horrible noises gargling and growling from their throats. Arch vanished from sight and reappeared further away. The Vous-things howled and loped after him until he'd led them up the hall away from her.

Aziel dropped the knife and ran weeping back the way she'd come, back to her room. She wedged a chair under the door handle. *THERE IS WORSE THAN DEATH*, a voice said outside, before something smashed down hard enough to make the tower itself shiver.

She barely heard the newly replaced glass of her window breaking. Only the orange burst from a lick of fire brought her attention to the thing lodged in the frame.

She blinked, at first not believing her eyes. It had to be more of her father's insanity at play. But it looked like a fat red drake. Coughing and spluttering, it crashed down on the floor, grunting at the impact. It stood very clumsily, stretched out its wings like it barely had any idea what they were for, then lowered its head to her, as though it wanted her to get on its back.

In fact, she knew that was just what it wanted. 'Did Arch send you?' she said.

The drake just looked at her.

'Should ... should I hop on? Where will we go?'

It lowered its head further. She looked around at her belongings, wondering which, if any, she should bring. She may need food. Something warm to wear, certainly . . . she slung a cardigan about her shoulders and a scarf around her neck, and swept a few other bits and pieces into a carry-bag while the drake watched her. Awkwardly she took a seat on its back, where there was a dip like a saddle between the raised scales. Warmth poured out to her skin from the fire inside the creature.

The drake refused to move until she'd taken a very firm hold on its neck. When she had, it stretched its clumsy wings, hopped up on the window sill after two failed attempts, uncurled its scaly tail across the floor and heaved a big sigh.

'How long are we to be gone? We're coming back, aren't we? Once Arch cures Father?'

By way of answer, the drake leaped out into the night sky.

OUTCAST COUNTRY

1

It was not the sky which broke into pieces and thundered into the ground at World's End, but the gaps high up in the breaking Wall gave that illusion, as the early morning light set in. Glass-thin slivers carried by the wind pattered harmlessly and settled in people's hair. Fist-sized lumps of it and occasional huge sheets slammed down with lethal force, kicking up dust clouds which obscured the picture revealed of the new world, of Southern Levaal.

The ground shivered under stoneflesh giants' thundering feet as they marched back and forth, back and forth along the line where the Wall had stood. Something had changed in the great creatures as soon as there was no longer a shield between the two halves of Levaal. The giants no longer refused each other's presence in their own little district; rather, they walked back and forth in unbending tilting steps, coming so close to one another their smooth, rounded, basalt-grey chests almost touched. A sound came at such moments, perhaps speech, but it was indistinguishable from the rumbling of their feet slamming on the shivering ground.

And Eric heard *meaning* in the sounds, not translatable to human words and thoughts, conjuring in his mind the image of an avalanche being poured into a valley by enormous, careful hands, like a gardener funnelling water where it's needed.

That Eric understood the great creatures' speech, via the peculiar gift all Pilgrims shared when crossing into Levaal, did not thrill him as it might have before. Something had changed inside him but he couldn't tell what, nor what had provoked the change. He was exhausted and numb, but filled with a sense of riding the crest of an enormous, fast-moving wave, which was rising, rising, rising over the land and would do so for a good while yet, till it reached heights he could barely fathom and then crashed down, drowning him and everyone else. Drowning Siel and all these others nearby, who were in the wave just below him. All equally helpless, though none of them yet knew it . . .

As the great sheets of Wall slipped free and smashed down to reveal the foreign sky through a curtain of dust, and after the illusory giant had vanished – all the work of Vous's Arch Mage, some suggested – those two giants who had battled forgot their quarrel, turned about and marched away from each other, following the line until each came face to face with the next giant along. All along the east-west length of the breaking Wall, the stoneflesh giants did the same thing as its cracks raced out in miles-long webs.

People gathered near the Great Dividing Road's southernmost stretch. This was land not strictly claimed by any city, its villagers referred to in the two nearest cities with some disdain as Outcasts. They watched and waited, talking in half-amused murmurs about whatever idiot wizard had done all *this*. A group of them had begun campfires, as though their practical answer to the vast unknown events unfolding was to fill the air with the healthy familiar smell of smoke. They'd set several cauldrons boiling and now from each ladled out a rich-smelling broth. Siel – who had been watching the Wall come down with her hand in Eric's – went to them to beg food. The woman she'd approached tiredly scooped broth in two bowls her children had just drained and licked clean.

As Siel returned, a young mother nearby tried in vain to comfort two young children, who were determined not to be comforted. 'Shh, shh. Shadow will come, Shadow will save us,' she said.

Eric had turned away but he turned back to them now. 'What did you say?'

She did not hear him for the children's wailing and the rumble of a stoneflesh giant coming back into view from the east, seeming to move slowly but covering immense ground. Its closest neighbour appeared on the opposite horizon soon after.

Siel pushed a warm bowl into Eric's hand. Distracted, he dropped it across the ground. She hissed in annoyance and quickly ladled as much as she could of it back into the bowl.

'Eat,' she said, 'dirt or not. They don't like idiots here. Be more careful!'

Siel's words bounced neatly off his ears. 'What did you say?' he called to the mother.

The mother glanced up at him, stood instinctively between her children and this stranger with a peculiar accent. 'I said Shadow will save us. Old tales. What's it to you?'

'Shadow. Who do you mean?'

'He rides a drake!' one of the newly cheerful youngsters piped up eagerly. 'A red drake. It's true! It's in stories.'

'Eat!' Siel ordered, pulling Eric away by the arm. 'Do you need me to spoon it into your mouth too?'

'Did you hear them? That woman said Shadow will save them.'
He began to say more but Siel made good on her offer and
plunged the spoon into his mouth.

2

They watched the Wall's collapse for some while, waiting with
the locals for a picture to emerge in the foreign sky. It didn't
come and that sky stayed dark. Even when the lightstones
brought about a cold day, there was to the south just a smoky
red haze the eye did not penetrate deeply. Through it they caught
glimpses of long shapes twisting. To Siel and Eric they looked
like flying life forms, but with time the shapes seemed to melt
into the redness around them. None crossed the boundary.

The crumbling wall should have formed enormous mounds,
piling up right where the giants marched. But within an hour
of falling, each piece would melt away. Eric saw faint little trails
like gas leaking from some of the closer fist-sized chunks. Some
bound magic which had made the Wall or held it together was
returning to the air.

During the night, the clash of magic in the sky (which had
put the folk magician Loup into a panic and sent him fleeing)
had caused sparks and flashes far above them. Lashing webs
fast as lightning whipped through the clouds, reddish colours
blending with the earthier hues of magic that his eye had come
to accept as natural. The new magic did not mix well, congealing
into little pockets carried along in the wind, till they were flung
out of sight.

Then it all finished. The skies calmed. Or so it seemed.

Curled up asleep, Siel looked entirely different from the

warrior whom Eric felt (with some guilt and deflation) his survival now depended on. Her head was across his knee making it numb with pins and needles but he didn't want to move it. The locals had found her a strange sight with her darker than usual skin, her bow, curved knife, and long braids like two more hanging weapons, her male companion apparently unarmed. Of course they didn't know about his gun.

More local people had come through the day to watch. All eyes were on the stoneflesh giants. No record or rumour of their present behaviour existed. It seemed to Eric the giants were patrolling. Had their task always been to wait for this day? Who or what had given them this task?

Back in Earth (or Otherworld, whichever it should really be called) to ask such questions brought answers. *Asking* made sense, even if no answers came. Such questions as 'From where comes day and night?' Not in this place. Here, day and night just *were*. Was it the same with the stoneflesh giants?

Siel woke, yawned. 'Your turn. Sleep.'

'I'm well, thanks for asking,' he said.

She ignored him and offered her thigh as a pillow. He lay back in the earthy scent of perfume she'd made from tree sap and berries, and was asleep in seconds despite the rumble of stoneflesh feet and the shivering ground.

3

Siel watched the foreign sky, stroking Eric's hair, hardly aware that she did so. She watched the people who'd gathered around them, wondering why none of them fled. Perhaps they felt their doom was so certain there was no point in fear. It was a far cry from the panicked stampede as they'd fled Elvury, the city aflame and overrun by those demon beasts called Tormentors. She half expected to see a mass of the creatures pour across the boundary at any moment. If they did, she would not wait for a slow death at their hands. Her knife would do the job faster.

But no Tormentors came – nor did anything else. An hour or two went by. Some of the people turned and moved away, and then, inexplicably, there was sudden urgency in them. They abandoned cauldrons and other belongings in the rush to flee. Very soon Siel and Eric were alone in the grassy field by the roadside, alone but for the stoneflesh giants who marched in and out of view.

She woke Eric after letting him sleep an hour more. The possibility of food in the bottom of those abandoned cauldrons was too much for her. Though none of the villagers had returned, the thieves who sometimes roamed this country's trade routes would be drawn to the cauldrons, and they were vicious.

The Pilgrim yawned, rubbed his eyes and stared dazedly at the distant sky. Much more of it was exposed now, for most of the Wall had come down. But the reddish haze replacing it was impenetrable to their eyes. Things still twisted in it like hands making shapes behind a curtain. It hurt to watch for long.

There was not much in the cauldrons after all, but with some very determined scraping Siel got a full bowl of the most flavoursome parts of congealed broth. She ate her share and passed the bowl to Eric, against incredible temptation to have it all. He'd not have noticed; his eyes were glazed and distant. 'Don't drop it this time,' she said.

He ate without speaking then just kept staring around dreamily. 'What's wrong?' she said, annoyed with him. He had hardened a bit since she'd met him, but there was still too much soft and vulnerable about him. Now, while they were alone, was not a time to be weak.

'I don't know why I'm here, Siel,' he finally answered. 'I don't know who I am.'

Helpful, she thought. Otherworld Prince indeed.

Where to go? In any direction there'd be a village sooner or later. Many of those who'd fled Aligned cities had settled in these parts, good people who treasured freedom as only those who'd felt its loss could. The highways branching off the Great Dividing Road would take them to cities, if they wished.

She threw her dagger spinning in the air, letting it decide their course. It landed pointing north-east. Fine. 'This way,' she said, setting off.

Eric hadn't come with her. He'd lingered to stare at something in the field beyond, where there was the beginning of a small wood. She followed his gaze. A lone figure stood at the edge of the trees, watching them. She had time only to see that the figure's clothes were dark before it was gone, vanished in a blink of her eyes. Instinctively she reached for an arrow before remembering that bastard Sharfy had mangled her bow before they'd fled Elvury.

Eric still stared. 'There he is,' he said.

Something in his manner was disquieting. She shivered, wondering if she were even safe turning her back on *him*, let alone safe from whatever else was out here. She'd have preferred him preoccupied with lust like he'd been in the haunted woods.

It would be easy enough to abandon him ...

But whatever leadership remained of the Mayors' Command

would sorely want him. And his weapon, which could slay Invia with such ease. She had no intention of killing him and taking the weapon, but it was a possibility she was aware of.

'This way,' she said. 'Keep your gun ready.'

4

The rumbling of stoneflesh feet was now part of the background, so that in spite of it there seemed an eerie quiet. They'd ventured directly east from the Great Dividing Road, Siel checking behind them for any sight of the stranger. Eric had not yet spoken.

She said, 'When we saw the man back there. You said, there he is, or similar words.'

'I said that?'

'Yes. What did you mean?'

He was a while answering. 'Don't know.'

'Nor I. But you were not surprised by the sight of him. Or were you? Did you know him?'

Eric gave a funny laugh. 'Actually this will sound strange. But it almost seemed ... I meant there *I* was. I don't know. Guess I'm just tired.'

She didn't ask him to elaborate, for his answer worried her.

The foot-worn path branched off. There was a village not far along but a look at the tracks said many feet had just come through here. She crouched down, waiting for happenstance magic to show her something. There was no guarantee it would, but it was the right time in her cycle to see things. Willing it to happen encouraged but did not guarantee a vision.

Waiting, waiting – aha! A glimpse of rough men hurrying by,

hunting dogs with them, running down the slope along the path. Weapons out like they expected a fight. They appeared and vanished in a second, a lonely second of the past thrust forward (or had it cast her back? She could never tell). The men may have been there a thousand years back or just yesterday. Or minutes ago.

There were no clear dog tracks here but she decided not to risk it; another village waited a few miles ahead and she could hopefully forage enough edible roots to keep them going. For the hundredth time she cursed Sharfy's name for breaking her bow and depriving them of the chance to hunt.

The abandoned countryside did not tell her much. They should have come across at least the occasional wagon train or traveller. Abandoned crop fields balmed her concerns about food. From these they ate and stuffed their packs with vegetables.

She was eyeing off the tall stalks of a distant cornfield as possible shelter for the night when a group of dark shapes emerged over the rise to their left. There were twenty of them, some with tall walking sticks. One had a flail. What she didn't yet know was whether they were real or a glimpse from the past. 'Do you see them?' she said.

Eric nodded and pulled out the small black Otherworld weapon. 'I may not have bullets left for all of them. But after the first goes down, the rest will run.'

But can he actually bring himself to kill a person? she wondered. Even one who threatens us? The mad fool did not kill Kiown.

Siel grabbed Eric and dragged him with her behind one of the thorny bushes scattered over the plain, without much hope they'd be hidden by its thin leafless branches.

'We see you, sister,' came a mournful call, sure enough. 'We see you! Don't run, don't hide. No need, no need!'

'We've peace!' said another. 'To this green land we bring it!'

Siel stood in full view with her knife in hand. 'I should have known by the garments,' she said.

'Known what?' said Eric, standing beside her.

'They are Nightmare cultists. It's been long since I met any. We are probably safe. They don't often sacrifice.'

'How often is not often?'

'Twice a year that I know of. The victim is usually one of their own.'

The cultists walked in ranks of five. They limped and looked starved. Their wails and shrieks sounded like carrion birds. The one with a flail lashed his own back with it then passed the weapon to the one next to him, who did likewise. Some of their black robes were already shredded, wounds glistening beneath. 'Come with us!' a few of them cried as the group closed in. There was a reek of infected flesh.

'We're on business for the Mayors. Leave us be,' said Siel.

The whole group of them laughed. Said one, 'Wayward sister! What business? We are the first to go to the new world. You too are invited, by virtue of our invitation, if not the Great Dark One's direct call, which was our privilege alone, for long service given. You may come. We are generous. But you both must walk in the rear rank.'

'Nay! Behind the group, on their own in a rank of two. They may *not* use the flail.'

Said another, 'It was fourteen nights ago his arm reached down! It is said he laid a gift upon a hilltop tower, a sign for all of man.'

'He did!' cried another. 'I saw it with these eyes, traversed the tower's steps with these feet, and read the signs he left there! He calls us across, Great Dark One, roamer of night skies, shepherd of the icy winds—'

'Bringer of the ice winds, shepherd of the storm clouds, tamer of the brood, roamer of the—'

'Breaker of the Wall!'

With each outburst they came closer, their bulging eyes bloodshot. Eric brandished the gun openly but it was clear none of them perceived it was a weapon. An older man with what had to be a broken forearm fell to his knees, wailing: 'Aye, down he cast it, his hands parting the twin *skies* like curtains. Come with us, be among the *called* taking steps of great distance!'

'Have you seen him?' a hunched middle-aged woman cried, her face swollen and bleeding from blows struck by the thick branch in her hand. 'It is said he has roamed these skies.'

'He was west of here, near the Great Road,' said Siel, her tone mocking theirs. 'You should hurry. He awaits you.'

The bruised woman threw herself at Siel's feet. Eric fired a warning shot into the air, the Glock loud as thunder. The cultists shrieked, scattered and ran, then resumed formation and marched south, not one of them looking back, already incorporating in their mythos the gun's firing as some kind of test of resolve. Clearly, they had passed it.

Siel and Eric watched them go. 'There are things I could tell them they probably wouldn't like,' he said. He replaced the gun's clip but could not bring himself to throw the empty one away.

Siel's ears rang painfully. 'They are not always so worked up,' she said. 'I have heard if Nightmare's sighted, they sometimes attack people. It's why I was nervous . . .' but she trailed off.

Behind them a solitary figure had returned. It stared at them. For a second she was sure it was Eric over there. His clothes and hair were different, and he stood at a strange angle, leaning nearly forty-five degrees sideways. The being did not respond to her wave. A blink later it had vanished.

Eric, still staring after the Nightmare cultists, hadn't seen it. 'Come,' said Siel, keeping her voice steady. 'Your gun's noise may have drawn ... all kinds of things. We should hurry.'

'Hurry where?'

'We should head for Tanton. The people of these lands must have gone there. A good choice. Their mayor is Tauk the Strong. He will fight, whatever comes from World's End.'

'How far is Tanton?'

'A hundred miles, nearly. Don't tell me you're tired of the road; I am more so. But it's not safe out here any more.'

5

It wasn't long before Nightmare himself – the Great Dark One, guider of the ice winds – was seen, drifting high off to the west. 'Stop here! Hold! He is seen! He is great!'

'He *is* great! He, tamer of the brood, breaker of—'

'What does he wish? My vessel is cracked, bleeding. My arm is lame. I hurt, I thirst. I am ready to replace this unworthy shell, to be renewed and—'

Lansith, who had climbed the tower and read the signs, gestured for silence and received it. 'See?' he said. 'It is as I read. It is as the evening rites foretold, may the soil glory our victim! And lo, you see his gaze is fixed upon us!'

Indeed it was – Nightmare had turned a slow ponderous circle, his long streaking trail a dark hook across the sky. He drifted toward them.

'March!' Lansith screamed. 'It is what he wishes, it is what he asks. We must cross into that land of reddened skies, we the first, we the called!'

There was not far to march. A hundred paces, fifty paces. They broke into a sprint, those with damaged legs hobbling badly. All of them gave joyful cries.

Nightmare moved with uncharacteristic haste when the group's intent became clear: they meant to cross the boundary. With a low thrumming sound of distress louder than the ground's booming beneath stoneflesh feet, the god rushed through the skies to them, covering in a blink the full distance. Nightmare swatted a hand through the air as he cast. Reality about the group parted in tiny fractures. The effect was as of a cluster of flying blades going through them. Their shredded remains blew through the air, tumbled to a halt and lay scattered across the ground.

Nightmare drifted away, seeking the next threat, wishing for the other Spirits to wake to the danger and come to aid him.

THE WOLF'S FOE

1

His feet thudded down on soft rain-wet grass, a soothing break from the hard slap of mountain road or the stony gravel which tore bleeding sores in the pads of his feet. They would heal when Far Gaze shifted back, but that was slim comfort, since the shift itself in either direction meant bones breaking and re-setting. The inner organs moving around during a change was perhaps even less pleasant: *that* felt like squirming creatures loose inside his body. There was no magic known to ease the punishment of shifting shape.

Of course the wolf would whine and argue against the need to change back – it always did. The arguments weren't complex: *Stay. Run! Hunt!* But it was always a wrestle with temptation for that little part of the human mind still present in the wolf's. Some shifters he'd known had lost the battle, stayed their animal selves too long and forgotten the way back.

But they were, he had thought sourly many times, probably much happier for it. Other than rescuing errant Pilgrims from war mages and other perils, what a relief it had been to switch off his human mind and just *run*, a thousand scents spicing the cold air, rare people gaping or cowering when he passed them, a thunderous growl from his throat for show, give them some tales to tell. (Wolves and dogs knew humour too!) Most of the gawkers had probably never seen a real shape-shifter, wouldn't know there was a mage within the huge hulking white frame, the savage red mouth packed with white knives, tongue lolling and flapping, steam puffing from its breath into the morning air as though an engine in its chest chugged it along.

The wolf did not need much time to pause and rest, but he had sprinted non-stop since near Elvury where the old Pilgrim had jumped from a cliff to his rather pointless death. He'd been tired before then, for the strange and mysteriously powerful woman in the green dress had exhausted him. But whenever he thought of pausing to rest, he'd get a hunch she was close, even pick up a hint of her scent.

As he did now. It was stronger than it had been since he'd picked up her faint trail some while back. She wasn't far.

Ah, these fields were fine to run through, country not recently trampled by the feet of people making war. The air was clean and laced with stable magic. He could smell food cooking in the farmstead homes. One or two polite growls at someone's back door and he'd be served well, no doubt of it.

The air's scents had told him many things as he loped through the night, which his mind would translate when he changed back to human form. The other cities – he had passed Faifen in the night – were in a panic for some reason, perhaps the same reason that had caused the ground to rumble and shiver, and for the very peculiar currents to pass in the upper airs. In fact if Far Gaze judged right, it looked very much like the influx of a new, strange and – surely not – *foreign* magic flooding in.

He would, had his human mind engaged with it, have had an idea of what all this meant. For a while now he'd heard enormous rumbling and playfully pretended the sound was caused by the thudding of his own feet.

And – there! Twisting up in the distant morning sky was a thin spiral of disturbed energy, like a line scrawled in fading ink from the horizon to the clouds. It would have looked to Far Gaze's human eye suspiciously like *her* work. The mage in the green dress, that 'woman' named Stranger.

After what happened in the woods near Faul's, he didn't credit for a moment that she could truly be human. He'd stood as much chance against her as a child with a toy sword fighting an armed, trained soldier. There was one moment alone – as she'd cast that pillar of light in Faul's yard – when she'd been distracted enough for him to get his teeth around her throat.

He'd almost got her too. In her ensuing casts were little flourishes and touches which would have been delighted laughter, had they been translatable to human expression. There had been something playful about the combat from the outset, as though she was showing off to (at last!) an audience able to appreciate her arts.

Knowing he couldn't beat her, he'd hoped only to keep her away from Anfen and the Pilgrims. Whatever she truly was, she was great, surely greater than the Arch (himself about as great as humans could become). Ah, how dearly he'd have paid to learn what she *was*, and where her power came from.

The spiralling twist of spent energy was recent, and yet it had almost faded. It had to be her. A normal mage, even one skilled, could not mask his casts this well. She too would be seeking the remaining Pilgrim. He surged forward with greater speed in the direction of the cast spell.

When a mile or two passed the southern skies had a funny look to them. There was a shimmering redness in the distance.

In fact, the Wall should be in sight by now. For some reason it wasn't . . .

Suddenly the wolf saw what the night's scents had tried to tell him. He skidded to a halt, growled low in his throat and then, for want of better ideas, howled at the sky.

2

Another night's run through Outcast country, past some villages emptying of people, through others looted and abandoned. At one, bandits had begun slaying families in some kind of casting ritual. They had people tied, waiting in grim silent groups while homes were plundered. Far Gaze the man might have stopped to do something about it. But the wolf did not, any more than a man on urgent business would risk himself taking sides in a vicious fight between wild wolves.

There now was more of that disturbing scent. The wolf held a vast library of scents in memory, easily recalled minute variations and combinations of each one. *This* scent was not in there.

Never mind that – there was meat close by! It didn't smell too old, either.

The man forbade eating such things, for it would make him sick if he changed back soon after. But how about just a *look* at the meat? He padded around to the edge of the clearing near another abandoned hut and found the body of a horse, perhaps just a day old. He sniffed. It had died of the horse plague which had made the beasts so rare and valued. But humans didn't catch that sickness. Nor wolves. One little mouthful would not make the man *too* sick, not like the time of that week-old stuff which had nearly killed him, and made him refuse to shift form for over a year.

With what sounded like a growl but was really a note of pleasure, the wolf ripped into the carcass, sending off a cloud of little black bugs. His jaws cracked bones, loosing delicious marrow. Heaven!

He was so occupied it took a moment for his keen ears to notice men's voices from the hut nearby. With a whine he obeyed duty's call, rose from his prize, stalked around the clearing and saw shields had been laid to rest by the front door. There were some the colour of Tanton, others of High Cliffs. The wolf listened for a while, locking in memory conversation of which it understood only parts. It heard that war brewed among cities who were just recently friends. It heard that these two cities – Tanton, High Cliffs – now sought the Pilgrim, thinking him responsible for something or other. The Pilgrim held a mighty weapon, they said, and might help them, although he was very dangerous. If need be he could be slain, but the weapon must be captured. It was their last hope in the war.

Far Gaze the man would listen to it all later. The man would be far more pleased with his wolf incarnation for storing these words in his mind, than for the meat in his belly. It was time to go. The wolf bounded off again through fields of crops plundered and scattered.

So much he'd already scented in the long night's sprint. From the scents alone it would seem a hundred messengers had come.

And there, Anfen's scent! Faint though, quite faint. He had been through here many days ago. The wolf turned north, followed the cooling trail, then caught sight of another plume of used magic. Instinct said to chase that instead.

Half a mile later her scent hit him strongly. He ran into a

green valley, between light grey trunks of papery bark, leaped a brook with shimmering cold water then slowed to a careful stalk. She was close! Scents told the wolf locals fished here every day, children swam the waters. But they weren't here now.

The water burbled among the brook's boulders, hiding the sound of the wolf's feet padding down. There was her laughter, free and easy. He would not fight her this time, he decided. Unless a gift opportunity came to catch her offguard, he would stay hidden, watch her and learn. Later, the man would know what to do about her.

The brook spilled itself into a little blue lagoon a short way down. Something had stirred up the water down there, making it murky with silt. Again came the woman's free, clear laughter, echoing and filling with joy the little glen closed about her like the cupped hands of a forest meaning to protect its daughter. The air's scents promised danger and a very changed world, but here she had only mirth. The wolf whined quietly in confusion.

A green dress hung over a tree branch. Not far from it, her body lay beside the water, naked and white as a pearl, one knee languidly raised, eyes closed, legs open to the water's edge so that occasional lapping waves of it nearly splashed up against her thighs. Her skin glistened from water, beads of it running off her. She had big round scars. Across her midsection there was a hard plate, as though part of her belly had become wood or stone.

Something moved in the water before her. Something quite large, but staying deep, sent lapping waves to its edge. A dark pointed length of flesh poked above the surface, wound slowly toward the woman's feet. She sighed, licked her lips, arched her back as the coiling thing – a thick vine, it almost seemed to the wolf, though surely it was not – traced its point over her ankle, coiled about her knee, then up her thigh, toward her centre.

The wolf's confused whine was hardly louder than a breath, and certainly quieter than his enemy's moans of pleasure, which began to fill the glen.

He hesitated at the top of the small waterfall, wanting in equal parts to leap down and attack, and to leave this dangerous woman be. He was decided when, some distance away from the glistening length – a *tail*? – gently stroking her loins and provoking her sounds of pleasure, the wolf caught sight of what at first seemed a log gently bobbing to the water's surface. But no, it was a sleek head. Two eyes glimmered with power and with humour. Whatever it was, it saw him and had seen him since he'd first poked his head into the glen to look below. The woman, her eyes still closed, had not.

The wolf whimpered quietly, turned about, and ran.

THE HIDDEN VILLAGE

1

Dogs furiously barked from an apparently empty space on the plain. Siel picked up a rock and hurled it in that direction. It vanished on the throw's downward arc. There was a clattering noise as the vanished stone hit something unseen. The barking reached a fever pitch. 'Is this kind of thing normal in your world or not?' said Eric.

'No. Run.'

A short sprint later, looking back, there were suddenly a dozen huts visible where she'd flung the stone, houses of mud-brick and logs. Two dogs strained more playfully than angrily at the chains which held them. There were no people in sight.

Siel jogged back to where they'd stood when she threw the stone. 'It's vanished!' she called. 'From here, I can't see it. Can you see it still?'

'Sure can.'

'A spell,' she said. 'But why does it only shield the place from our eyes when they view from this angle? I don't understand.'

They walked among the huts and called out. No one answered. The dogs were soon befriended and calmed when

Eric fed them meat he found inside a hut whose door was left open.

Valuables and food lay about quite openly, indicating people had fled from imminent danger. Siel found a string for her bow but it was home-made, not military grade, and would not fire nearly as far as her old one.

They stuffed themselves full of fruit and meat found in the same home's larder, which was packed with more spoilable food surely than anyone, even a family, could eat before much of it rotted. 'Maybe the village keeps all its food here,' said Siel, devouring some sweet potato. 'Maybe they have a folk mage to preserve it.'

'But how do you explain these?' said Eric, pointing at the enormous boots by the back door. 'Everything here is too big. It's like Faul's place again. Look!' He held up a wooden spoon and bowl, both enormous. 'The other huts aren't like this. They seem normal.'

They stuffed all the food they could carry into their packs and bathed in the rain-tank shower, complete with soap and a little stove to heat the water. 'Did I ever tell you the story of the three bears?' Eric asked Siel as they dried themselves.

'What's a bear?'

'The three wolves, then.' He gave her a brief amended version of the fairy tale. 'And that's us, I think. I'm not sure whoever left here is gone for good. But that,' he pointed at the roof, 'is a miracle. Let's have one above us overnight for a change. Why don't we rest up here?' She began to object. 'One fucking night, come on,' he said. 'I'm willing to roll the dice.'

They fed the dogs again, barred the door and lay in a bed big enough for five people.

2

Eric was awake, staring at the ceiling.

He was pondering the part inside him which had gone numb as though to protect itself. He peeled off its shell and looked inside it. He saw that he had come to completely understand: this was no game, no adventure, no dream or comic book; he was not going home. Ever. Everyone he knew by now was as dead to him as the war mage he'd shot in the head, high up on the city wall, to watch Tormentors flock to its falling corpse. And to the old world, he was just as dead. Case, if still alive, was the only link to who Eric used to be, aside from the shoes on his feet. (Kiown's face flashed through his mind with mocking laughter.)

Link. Levaal means link, someone had told him. *Link which protects.* Protects what?

Would they have had a funeral back home, with no body to bury? He could see it all very clearly, his mother crying (the picture brought tears bubbling up in his own eyes); his father grim-faced, showing his usual level of emotion – not a whit, unless it was anger steaming out of him. He wondered what songs they'd have played, what old forgotten friends would have turned up to say goodbye.

Siel's arm was slung over his chest, using him and offering herself as warmth. He gently clutched at her forearm and tried to switch off his mind before the numb part filled with feeling again, but found her touch had the opposite effect. His body trembled with sobs.

One of Siel's eyes slid open. Across her face at first was annoyance at being woken, but she watched him for a moment as he wiped his eyes and tried to calm himself. She moved closer to him. 'Shh,' she said. 'You're here now. And you will make a difference here. There is a war for us to win. But only if you're strong.'

She stroked his hair until he felt sleep coming. He didn't know if hers was the empathy of someone who cared or if it was the touch of a mechanic fixing a machine so it would function better. But he felt that either would have been much the same.

Their sleep was broken by daylight, the feel of blades at their throats, and a slow, heavy voice saying: 'I can tell you didn't do it. But someone did. And maybe you know who.'

3

Eric had had a very strange dream, which his mind held with perfect clarity:

He was someone else, seeing through someone else's eyes. He'd been wandering in the night with clumsy steps, through the very fields in which this village lay. The strange sky to the south had piqued his curiosity. He would go across sooner or later, but there were gods hanging around, and he had seen what happened to the Nightmare cultists.

He could make it across the boundary, probably – he could move much faster than them. But for now there were other things of interest to look at. Like that piece of half-broken magic lingering over the village, there. A deceptively simple bit of trickery. How had it been done, covering the village like a big glass bowl? The eye just glanced off it! But the foreign airs had disturbed the disguise, the glass bowl had been cracked.

There, two bodies bundled up. Their warmth made pulsing red-yellow splotches on his vision. The girl, the fellow, dreaming away. As were those two dogs, similarly curled together on the ends of their chains. And there was that other, hidden away in the square hut yonder, a lone man it seemed, working into the night on some project over a bench, muttering to himself. Time for a closer look.

Closer. That was easy. Here to there, very fast, the ground rushing away like the world had tilted sideways to drop him down its sheer face, then righted itself again, all in a second. Easier than walking. One of the dogs stirred at his scent.

These dogs. Funny bodies, fur, teeth and paws. How were these things actually alive? It seemed a miracle, very peculiar. What was inside those funny bodies? More fur, bundles of it packed into that doggy shape?

That unpleasant mystery solved (no noise – he was fast) he went to the fellow, the girl. Cuddling up, a little human fireplace of warmth. Was anyone who wished to allowed to warm himself here? Could he lie here with them? Was permission needed? How was it obtained? He stood gazing at their peaceful sleeping faces. A touch of beauty about them not found in those awake. He'd not yet been so close to this pair. To others, yes. But these two were . . . different.

He reached a hand down to do he knew not what – maybe nothing, maybe something bad – when the woman stirred, rolled sideways, surprising him. The sheet came away from her left breast, exposing a dark nipple erect with cold. He peered at it, patted his own chest, wondering at the difference. She was still asleep. What was inside her body? Was it like the dogs'? Would enquiry put out the pleasant little fireplace of warmth, or just extinguish half of it?

'Not here, lad,' said a nervous-sounding voice. 'This way. More to show you, over here. You didn't like the mess outside, this will just make another, and worse, oh aye. Come! I'll show you things better than that.

*Way up high, if you can follow me. Wager you can't, lad. Way up, up
we go . . .'*

*Where was this hidden person, brashly interrupting his thoughts,
speaking so loud in his ear? That way! Away he went, the world tilting
again, till he was off in the trees, near where there was a brook burbling,
and a woman's laughter, and – ah, something else . . .*

4

Eric rubbed his eyes, shifted an inch or two away from the blade
at his throat. The three bears, he thought, almost amused to
find the old tale was now based on a true story.

The half-giant said ponderously, 'I come back to feed my dogs.
Should have told a couple of dolls to do it, no doubt. But the
dolls don't always obey or do it properly anyway.' The dolls
remark was self-explanatory, for what held blades to their throats
were little people made from oval blocks of sand-coloured wood,
hardly taller than the mattress. Their flat oval faces had no
features but a cut line for a mouth and two roughly gouged
eye holes. They were still as statues, but for the faintest tremble
in their knife arms.

As for the half-giant, he was not as big or loud as Faul had
been. In dirt-brown overalls, adorned here and there with grass
as though he'd rolled around in it, he sat on a thick wooden
chest at the end of the bed, fists pressed into his knees. From
reddened eyes tears streaked down his fat cheeks.

Siel did not enjoy having a knife held to her and, whether
she'd broken into someone's home or not, it was not what she
wanted to see first thing in the morning. Picking her moment,
she lashed an elbow sideways, breaking the doll's thin arm. It

popped out of its shoulder socket and clattered against the wall. The doll ran about in a small circle as though it were in pain.

'Easy now! Don't break em, they're hard to make. They won't hurt you.'

'Knives to the throat are a strange way to express that, with all due respect,' said Eric, relieved his own doll didn't react to Siel's attack with a pre-emptive strike of its own.

'Dead dogs are a strange way to say thanks for the food and the bed,' said the half-giant. 'Don't mind the dolls, I'm training em to guard the village. They don't learn easy. Outside now, you bunch of useless twigs. Out!' The little wooden men lurched out the bedroom door, clattering into the door frame and into each other as they went. The broken arm remained behind. 'My name's Gorb. Now then. Who killed my dogs?'

'First I've heard of it,' said Siel, covering herself with the sheet. Under its cover she reached for the curved knife, which she'd kept under the pillow.

'You didn't do it, I know that. But he knows something,' said Gorb, nodding at Eric. 'Humans don't keep secrets real good.'

Eric said, 'I don't know anything. But in a dream last night—' he sifted through the murky fevered images his memory had held '—I saw someone killing dogs. Your dogs, I think.'

The half-giant peered at him as though reading a story in his features. Eric almost felt manhandled by the two big amber eyes. Gorb said, 'There's a trail outside, leads in here. Whatever killed my dogs thought about killing you too. For some reason, it didn't.' Gorb peered into Siel's face. 'You got a secret too. Better share it before I get angry. That little sharp pricker won't do more'n make me mad if you use it.'

'Someone was following us,' she said. She told him about the distant stranger they'd twice spotted. The half-giant listened without comment.

'Did the villagers flee because of the Wall?' said Siel to fill the rather awkward silence.

Gorb grunted. 'Oh, no. We don't care about *that*. Everyone's at that new tower. They say a mighty wizard lives inside it. They're all still over there, can't believe their eyes yet.' Gorb sighed. 'I came back to feed my little dogs. They would've been barking loud, like they only ever do when they get hungry. They never minded strangers. Good souls they were.' The half-giant's body leaned further forward on the creaking wooden chest. He stuffed two palms over his eyes and from behind them poured a flood of tears.

Moved by sympathy (and to Siel's amazement at his surely suicidal stupidity), Eric went to the half-giant and reached to pat his shoulder in consolation.

Neither Siel nor Eric saw Gorb's arm move – Eric only felt a push that took the wind out of him and sent him sprawling back on the bed. 'Can I get dressed?' he said once he'd got his breath back.

The question was pondered at length. 'Suppose so.'

Dejectedly the half-giant wiped away the last of his tears. There was a spilled jug's worth of them soaking into the floorboards at his feet.

Eric dressed. He slung the gun's holster over his shoulder but to his dismay discovered it was empty. 'Took it,' said their host. 'Don't know what it is, but I guess it's a weapon. I let the girl keep her knife, since I know what that is.'

'You have a mage here?' said Siel, who also dressed and now examined the thin wooden arm she'd knocked loose from the doll. With her toe she tapped free the knife it clutched and kicked it across the floor to the half-giant, to show him she had no plans for weapons right now. She picked up the wooden arm, testing its joints.

'No mage,' he said.

'But there's magic to this.' She flexed the wooden arm's joint. 'There has to be. Those dolls seem to be alive.'

'I made them,' said the half-giant with some pride.

'And the spell which hid your village?'

'That was a mage who comes by,' said Gorb. 'Used to come by anyway. He did it a while back. Took all the coin and gems we had.'

'A folk magician?' said Siel.

'Said he was. Didn't look it, to my eye. Looked to me like one of them school wizards from the old days, that the castle wiped out. Folk ones are grubby, earthy looking. He was different, real strange. Bald as an egg, never blinked his eyes. Couldn't read his face at all.'

'Why was it so important to hide the village?'

'Better if word didn't spread that the last half-giant in the world lived here.'

'The head of a half-giant will make you rich,' Siel explained to Eric.

Gorb nodded. 'That's right. But they're hard to get. Usual way's to make friends with one till he trusts you. I don't fall for that, in case you think to try. But this village, good people mostly. I plough fields for em, carry stuff. When all that rumbling started, Hesthan gone south for a look. He come back, told us whatever knocked the Wall down stuffed up the spell. Then they found the tower. It'd stuffed up a hiding spell there too.'

Said Eric, 'Can I ask why you're called half-giants? You look completely giant to me.'

'There was once a race of full-blood giants,' said Siel. 'They were much bigger. Then they mixed with us. It was not by our choice. Half-giants resulted.'

'What happened to the giants?'

'We helped humans kill them all,' said the half-giant. 'Long, long ago. The full-bloods were a bad breed, bad to both of us. When bounties started, humans weren't much better.'

'The deeds were done by few, the shame is for us all.' Siel made a gesture which meant nothing to Eric but made the half-giant's expression soften. 'The tower you speak of,' she said. 'Where is it?'

'Off just past the woods, where Tunk and Felious do their hunting.'

'Will you take us there?'

'Yes. You're good people. But you had enough dinner to call it even for breakfast.'

'Thanks, Gorb.' They stood to leave.

'That's weird,' said Gorb in the same slow, ponderous voice. He was staring at the floor near Eric's feet. 'You got no shadow.'

STRANGER

1

Through another night the wolf ran with ears pinned back, following instinct more than scent into Outcast country. He felt he had earned those odd scraps of meat he came across, rotten or otherwise, and now without guilt he gobbled down any he found (but not human meat, not yet). He had run almost the full north-south length of the world without rest, through enemy country and through that of ungrateful friends; had battled Tormentors, slain a war mage and fled two others; run from a wind elemental; duelled fiercely with she in the green dress. It was enough to exhaust him even out here in this fertile powerful country, where the air was rife with clean power.

And it was enough to make him begin to forget that he was a man more than a wolf . . .

But the Pilgrim was close, at *last* he was close, even if the wolf's mind had begun to forget why this was important.

Deserted country thundered by beneath his tired paws. The stoneflesh giants made the ground shiver and the sound filled his head. He sniffed and recoiled; a cloud of sickness had descended from where the rest of the foreign magic rode the upper winds. It had since been blown out of these valleys and fields but a trace remained. Surely even the humans could have smelled this alien poison. Was *this* why they'd fled?

Here was an abandoned clutch of homes, where the poison mingled in the air's more common scent of death. Doors had been smashed in, the place had been ransacked. There was days-old blood spilled here and there. Shuffling sounds came from a barn some way away. Something wasn't right. He growled and went there, hairs standing on end.

The poison – he sniffed again: yes, it was strong here – matched nothing in the wolf's vast library. The closest thing to it was . . . yes, those Tormentors. But the match was far from exact.

Through the open barn door a wedge of light sliced into the shadows, fell across a scattered pile of hay and a twitching foot. He crept closer. Two bodies, one face down, one face up. Too small to be adult. Not dead, sick and twitching, but —

Her!

Stranger looked up at about the same instant the wolf saw her. She crouched by what were, at least in part, two children. Something was wrong with their upper bodies. They were the wrong colour, the wrong shape altogether.

Far Gaze yowled in alarm, lurched backward and fell. How had he not picked up her scent? He sniffed. How odd. He *still* didn't pick up her scent. He smelled *part* of her but it was almost as though part of her self was absent. He thought of the lagoon, the eyes gazing up through the water . . .

And now a *new* smell from her. Fear! She was afraid of him! He could even hear her heart thudding fast.

The wolf had been about to turn and run. Now he paused, moved to block off the barn door, ventured a small growl. She had not been afraid of him before, not once.

'Hello again, dog,' she said, smiling at him. 'Have we not settled our disagreement? I have enjoyed our play. But this is not a time for it.' She gestured down at the twitching bodies. He sensed sadness in her. 'There's only one way to help them now. And it's beyond my power. Not so long ago, I saw a man do a terrible thing which had to be done. Maybe I could kill a man with a sword who means to kill me. But I can't kill these poor children.'

Far Gaze stored these words away for the man to understand. He didn't know what to do. He sensed weakness, still smelled her fear – but was it fear of him, or fear of these sick ones? Fear of the lingering trace of poison, which maybe with a shift of the wind could return at any moment? Instinct said, *Run! Fight!* He crept a step closer to her, whined.

'Come and see,' she said, words he understood.

The two small bodies were still clothed. Their arms and faces weren't human any more. Hard as bark they were, and a prod with his paw confirmed it. There was no reaction, just the same slow writhing. Stranger said, 'There was a cloud that came through. Thick with odd colour. I saw it from the road, as the wind blew it through here. By luck it missed me. The people here had been killed by bandits, I think. These two had hidden in this barn. And then the poison wind swept through.'

She stroked his mane. He jumped, not expecting her touch, rounded on her growling. The scent of her fear spiked strongly despite her assuring smile. 'Friends,' she said, glancing at the barn door. It was another word he knew. 'Friends. We are friends now.'

He whined in confusion. She didn't seem dangerous at *all*.

'Can you do it?' she said, a catch in her voice. 'I can't.' He thought he understood, more from the scents and her tones of voice. She wanted him to kill them. Why? They weren't a threat. For food? Humans didn't eat their own, not often anyway. 'Please,' she said. 'It must be done. They suffer. Do you understand me? If you kill them I'll go with you to find your friend, the Pilgrim. If you help me, I'll help you.' She laughed sadly. 'The man with his sword, Anfen. I thought him such a monster, in the cavern that day. Such a monster.'

Anfen! The wolf recognised the name. The hairs stood on his back to hear this strange woman speak it here in this place of sickness. He rounded on her growling loud, teeth bared.

She backed away with wide eyes. Slowly he herded her out the barn door. There was no indication she was about to cast any of the dazzling magic she'd used all through their earlier encounters.

With a few little nips to her ankles and calves (little nips he'd thought them, but her legs were soon wet with blood) she understood he didn't mean to kill her, only to herd her somewhere. He didn't fear bringing her to the Pilgrim now; this woman was no longer a threat.

'Would it not be faster if I rode your back?' she said after a while, gesturing with her hands to help him understand.

She was indeed a slow walker despite the occasional encouragement of his teeth. The wolf sighed and lowered himself to accept yet another burden.

HUNTERS

1

The steak sizzled nicely on the pan, its nest of onion and bacon slices filling the inn's small kitchen with a heavenly scent. Otherworld meat ultimately, Kiown reflected; how strange. Not native here, cows, nor pigs nor indeed most of the animals Levaal's humanity had found most useful. Goats, sheep, poultry. Bees, even – alien species. Once there'd been no bees, no honey, no mead. No wool, no silk, leather. He'd hardly have believed it, had thought Otherworld itself was myth and fancy, till he'd been to that strange place, felt its flat grey stone under his boots.

The inn's cook was nervous, reasonably enough. A nice sweat, Kiown felt, gazing at the back of the fat man's neck as the beads dribbled down to wet his collar. One more scrape of his knife on the bench top, why not. Scrape he did, leaving a third jagged line in the wood for the cook to explain to his boss. 'Garnish with parsley,' said Kiown, yawning. 'Utter perfection, remember. Which means *perfect*. Which means if I decide this is not the finest steak I have ever eaten *in my life* – I've had many, be apprised – then, well I told you what would happen. I might do it even if the steak *is* perfect. Cut the fat off you like you cut it off meat. It is a hard life. No? Sometimes one finds oneself in . . . predicaments.' Kiown pegged a mushroom from the basket at the back of the man's head. 'You're so fat! Why don't you keep in better shape? Most of the world goes hungry, did you know? Your dog is rather fat too, I noticed. Is your wife fat? Your daughter? Mmm. Maybe I like them that way. A tough job, provide and protect. No?'

Pleasing! No reply, but the man's neck and shoulder tensed. Was there a spine buried among that fat? Time for another scrape across the bench top. *Sssssharp*, said the knife on the wood. Kiown began cleaning his fingernails with its tip. 'Did you know that the cow is not native to Levaal? The flenk is, but it's merely cow-*like*, don't you think? Almost a cheap copy. More meat, no milk. Did you know the cow is alien? Did you know most of our useable crops are too? Rice, wheat, barley, maize, corn, so on? All foreign! Even the onion in that pan there. Alien food. Strange, no? Have you ever wondered, fat man, whether *you and I* are not really native to Levaal? We ourselves may be imposters, aliens. Ancestors of Pilgrims. From Otherworld. I've been there.' Kiown pegged another mushroom at him. 'But then, how did people get *to* Otherworld? Hmmm? Where did they *first* come from? Nothing on the subject in the libraries. Is there an Other-Otherworld? Answer please. But don't get distracted! I want that steak perfect.'

'I will think about it, sir,' the cook said brusquely. He wiped his forehead with his sleeve.

'See that you do. I find it all a very strange business. Like finding your house is yours, but most of the furniture *isn't*. It's borrowed, but you may still use it. Makes one . . . re-appraise.' Kiown yawned again. 'Sorry I was such a grouse, earlier. When I had you by the throat. Squeezing on that rude little air pipe of yours, so full of smart retorts. The original steak, I suppose it wasn't *too* bad. I am used to catching my own game. Food tastes better when one has killed it oneself. Tormenting the cook is the next best thing. Or maybe I'm just not good in the mornings.' He alone had slept well, he guessed, of his companions, not concerned for murders and intrigues during the night, figuring: *if you want me, come get me*. This philosophy as usual had kept him safe. Balls out, paint a target on them, dare the world to take a shot. They'd miss. As long as *you* could hit a pair from long range yourself, now and then.

'Have I mentioned I want the steak perfect?' said Kiown. 'Sing a little song too. I'm bored.'

The inn's cook, despite his shaking hands, was perhaps not the dimwitted hick Kiown had supposed until now. Whether the man knew since they'd checked in yesterday precisely what Kiown and his party were, or whether he'd just gathered that Kiown wasn't in charge of the group (and had perhaps just heard footsteps descending the staircase nearby), he began to sing a big booming voice:

> '*Cloud shades sweep our brows like palms*
> *These fields are promised rain*
> *Steel and armour, silver bright . . .*'

'Shut up,' said Kiown, surprised. The cook sang louder.

> '*Battle, battle, for our lives*
> *Rouse your blood, rouse your pride*
> *To war! To war we ride*
> *To war! To war we ride . . .*'

'Enough!'

The cook's voice rose to a rousing tumult: *'To warrr—'*

Kiown hopped down from the bench, meaning to add one of the cook's ears to the frying pan. Then Envidis was in the kitchen doorway, drawn by the song, a call-to-arms anthem of one rebel city or other, Kiown forgot which.

Envidis gazed serenely in, a faint smile on those fat-woman's lips of his poking through his black beard. Watching, watching, always watching with dark serene eyes. *This game is not allowed*, the gaze said without needing words. Not angered, not amused.

This was the usual rule in enemy country: don't be noticed or remembered. But the whole world had taken a sudden lurch into no one knew where, and the general rules didn't apply. Kiown had granted himself some leeway, and resented being schooled on the basics, with Anfen's blood still dry on his sword.

At the same time, he knew: he was now in an elevated class of Hunter. Envidis, Thaun and Evelle were elites. And now so was he. He had been with the group of rebels when they brought the Pilgrim in, had got to know the Pilgrim personally. By Vous, he himself had *been* to Otherworld! He'd have needed ten more years of service for the status he'd now gained by virtue of circumstance.

Kiown put the knife away against the impulse to escalate things. He knew little of Envidis, only that he had long survived a profession which swiftly made martyrs of most (and had come within a hair's breadth of making one of Kiown, many times; how he'd avoided execution at the tower top was a puzzle for finer minds than his). Envidis had given no clue as yet to what charms and wards he wore, what enhancements they'd given him. Nor had he said a word, not one, since joining the rest of them four days prior. He was a blank page. A blank page was a brilliant disguise. Kiown had with his own hand written disquieting things all over it.

Envidis stepped into the kitchen, tall, thin and graceful as he leaned on the wall, folded arms unnaturally long, and continued to stare. Two minutes from now he would act like this had never happened. Master of the situation, whichever way it went.

Kiown plucked the steak out of the pan and slapped it onto his plate. The cook quite wisely kept his face neutral. Of course he'd stopped singing.

2

Out in the dining room was First Captain Tauvene, beard neatly trimmed, uniform spick and span, mail shirt gleaming where its metal sleeves poked out from beneath the blue-grey of Pyren.

Tauvene, who by some masterful sleights of hand by the Hunters, *still* believed himself in charge of things even as they'd steered him further and further south, away from his area, his men, and – though he didn't yet know it – his allegiances. Over his shoulders were slung medallions of rank. Down over his breast they hung, impossible not to notice, glinting, polished each evening. Rather foolish to wear them openly in disputed country, but no matter.

Kiown and Envidis took their seats at the table, bowing as though in deference to their unwitting inferior, who nodded curtly in response to the interruption of his breakfast. This was someone who aspired to be a general, Kiown reflected, but who most drunks wouldn't hesitate to brawl with in a tavern. The other Hunters surrounded his table, watching him efficiently shovel scrambled eggs into his mouth, not getting the faintest trace on his neatly trimmed beard. Envidis still wore that little smile-shaped non-smile of his. Kiown had been trying to work out what wild creature the wiry Thaun reminded him of. With that braided stringy beard hung about his chin, he'd decided it was some kind of venomous goat. A warrior, though. Not as *classical* a fighter as Anfen had been, but even without charms and wards, at least as dangerous.

Evelle's jutting breasts poured out of a dress Kiown did not feel it should be permissible to wear if the men on a mission with her were supposed to keep their wits about them. It was likely, Kiown guessed, that First Captain Tauvene hadn't even yet worked out Evelle too was a Hunter. When he learned he'd shared his bed with one, and no doubt some of his intimate thoughts, it would turn parts of his neat beard grey.

It was still almost dark enough to be night. Thaun was explaining (in tones very much feeding the illusion that it was First Captain Tauvene rather than Hunter Thaun himself in charge) that they were to go to a more discreet location soon, in fact now, to meet an important contact. His name? A secret. First Captain Tauvene bristled as the very first inkling came that he was *not* in fact the author of his situation after all.

What is this situation? Kiown wondered as the group marched swiftly from the inn without talk, Tauvene 'leading' the way. What were they now? 'Defectors' did not fit, because it seemed to him – to all of them – that *they* had stayed on the same course, that it was the Arch Mage who had left the path of loyalty.

Tauvene paused in his stride. 'Why is she still here?' he demanded of Evelle.

'She is a loyalist,' said Thaun, smiling enigmatically. Tauvene bristled, not liking that answer at all. But on they went, marching half a mile till they came to a raised rocky platform with a cleared lookout, wherein sat a stone altar for a long defunct cult. Dragon worshippers, by the nearly eroded hieroglyphs inscribed.

'Why here?' demanded Tauvene. All four Hunters saw the man's hand lingering near his sword hilt; each read the thought flash through his mind: *assassination. . .?* Kiown was tempted to reassure him that if they'd meant to kill him, three of them would still be relaxing at the inn.

'Our contact wished it,' said Thaun, shrugging in helplessness.

'He is an important "contact",' said the First Captain testily. 'Can you reveal his name yet?'

'Shut up and wait,' said Thaun coldly. The First Captain recoiled as if struck.

At that moment an ancient man hobbled stiffly up the path with the aid of a walking stick. First Captain Tauvene's face spelled out his chagrin quite clearly as he recognised the newcomer.

Strategist Blain's angry, bearded face was curled as though sour tastes always filled his mouth. He pulled off a weathered cloak. The Strategist's robe beneath bled with shifting colours, poured sickly light into the clearing. He hobbled to a slab by the altar and glanced around at all present, taking inventory of faces, an eye lingering on the First Captain.

Tauvene was surely not a coward, Kiown thought. Nor was he as meek a man as he looked. The hypothetical tavern drunk assailing him would likely have had his neck's burden relieved rather quickly. It was fear for his career, not his mortal flesh, that had made him turn ghost white. Until now, all their talk had been plausibly deniable; he was no conspirator yet. It had been, until this moment, not too late to flee safely back to his general and report all he'd heard and seen, or at least leave this business to others until winners emerged to side with. No more. Blain's arrival had set his place in stone.

Blain caught his breath. He was so much feebler and weaker out here away from the castle's potent airs. 'How many men can you get?' he growled at Tauvene.

Still reeling: 'How many men . . .? The time frame, and . . . for what *purpose*?'

Blain waved a hand impatiently and spoke to the Hunters. 'For his benefit. Events are as follows. The war march has begun. The final march. The castle is finishing off the game while there's confusion in the rebel cities. Wise enough I'd say, in normal times. They've ditched Elvury. Can't be taken back. Tormentors have it. It's theirs. Wasn't supposed to be that way of course. Terrible miscalculation. We've culled some trouble from the forces, but also wasted good stock trying to purge the monsters from that city.'

Kiown wondered what to make of the mix of *they* and *we* in Blain's speech.

'In what order are the cities to be conquered?' said Thaun as Blain caught his breath again.

'The east first, working down the map. Not enough horses to go around, as usual. War reaches Faifen by tonight, I judge. If they've the spine to fight that is, or else call it a massacre, not a war. But for us, for all of us, there's a more important problem, and the fool has caused it all by himself.' None present had heard a more damning vitriolic pronunciation of the word *fool* in all their lives.

'What has he done?' said Evelle, in a tone so at odds with the ditsy sex-kitten Tauvene had briefly come to know that he blanched and turned to her in amazement.

'You know what he's done,' said Blain. 'Destroyed the Wall of course. You just don't know what it means. And nor does he!' Blain laughed. 'Few do. Does the word "pendulum" mean anything to you? I doubt it.' Blain stared into the brightening sky, thinking. They waited. 'Hall of Windows,' he muttered after a while. 'The Hall of Windows, he based it all on that, on what pretty things it showed him. Amazing! What a sense of adventure he has. All in the Project must have that, and a love of risk, to do what we have done.' An uneasy look passed between the Hunters, though nothing rippled the serene surface of Envidis's face. 'And all this fear he cultivated in our Friend and Lord, this nonsense about "Shadow" . . . you!' He pointed at Tauvene. 'Tell me. Who or what is Shadow?'

Tauvene began to speak, then didn't. For the first time a smile broke out on Blain's face. 'Stop quailing, you little shit!' he said, chuckling. 'You're implicated. Doomed, understand? It's over for you. Be useful on your way to the grave. Who or what is Shadow?'

'He is, as I understand it,' Tauvene frowned, trying to remember, 'a mythical figure, whom some credit with actual historical existence—'

Blain laughed. 'From the story books, eh? Just like the Invia. And the dragons. *Those* are real too. You.' He pointed to Kiown. 'What do you know of Shadow?'

'Nothing, Strategist. This is the first I've heard of it, or him, or her.'

'You?' said Blain to Thaun.

'Heard the name, Strategist. The context escapes me.'

Blain chuckled. 'Would it surprise you all to know that until recently there was *no such thing* as Shadow? He did *not* exist. Now he does. And it all sprang from his mind, his new power. Our Friend and Lord is very ... nearly ... *there*. Whether the other gods can do this kind of thing, I don't know. Do you fathom what he's done? Woven a new thing, not only into present reality, but made it *part of the past*. This time a month ago, two months, three, you'd not heard the name. You won't believe me. You have memories, I'm sure, of hearing of Shadow. Of bedside stories, perhaps. Tavern tales. And the *fool* helped this happen. A forged letter from "Shadow" about the Wall coming down, given to our Friend and Lord. Feeding poisonous whispers to him, feeding a phobia, making it realer. It's here now, it has happened.'

'What has happened, Strategist?' said Thaun.

'There's a loose force in the world, that's what. Maybe enough to topple him, us, everything. And that's *without* the Wall's destruction to deal with on top of it all!'

'Are we to eliminate this force?' said Thaun quietly.

'Try if you like!' said Blain with another mirthless laugh. 'No. Better we try to *use* it. We may need to, when the Pendulum swings higher and faster. We must study the new force, learn its ways. We must find it. Urgently. This Shadow. He is probably with the Pilgrims.'

'The new war you spoke of?' said Thaun.

Blain laughed grimly and turned to Tauvene. 'Have our First Captain's nerves settled? How many men can you get to World's End, soon as can be? I want a big number.'

'For fighting duty? For siege duty? For ...?'

'Men! Men! Bodies, working bodies. Fool, dribbling jester of a man, we'll send you simpering into this ravine and find a more useful idiot. How many?'

'Five thousand, at the very most. It would be difficult. Very difficult, if you wish it done quietly and quickly.' Blain made a noise of mock sympathy. 'I can scoop some from the forces gathering for Tsith,' said Tauvene. 'Some from Pyren's home guard. I can send for many of the roaming patrols. It would leave some homelands unguarded, which will be noticed.'

'Five thousand? Not enough. Get more. Double that, at least.'

'Where am I to get these troops? As you say, an invasion of Tsith and then all the rebel cities is practically begun, with some boots already on the road! But if this is your official order, I shall try,' said Tauvene in the tone of one trying to hide his disbelief. 'May I ask for what purpose the men are needed, Strategist? Precisely who is our foe?'

Blain laughed again. 'Your foe is whoever seeks to cross into Levaal South. No one's to get anywhere near the border, where the Wall stood. Fan them out, cover as much territory as you can. Concentrate on the roads and plains where a group could charge. Arm your men with longbows; use bolt throwers. Set up staves, pits. Lay traps. Create a moat of death before the boundary. Make examples of any who try to cross it. Be cruel. Crueller than cruel.'

Tauvene's mouth hung open. 'That is . . . absurd. Your pardon, Strategist. I mean only to be useful on my way to the grave. That is too much territory to cover with any hope of—'

'I'll find some reinforcements for you,' said Blain as though the First Captain had not spoken a word. 'They'll be wearing the city colours of our enemies, if I succeed in my next task. *That's* in doubt. I'm not known for a silver tongue. I've some sworn enemies to persuade to help us. Tell your men to expect them, nonetheless.' Blain grunted in disgust, contemplating his task. 'At least you'll have a god or two on your side. No one, not a single man or beast, is to cross the boundary. Understand? Not a one. Forget about "why" for now. Your weak fool brain has load enough to carry.'

'Such rhetorical flourish will surely aid you in persuading our enemies,' said the First Captain, bristling to be insulted this way before Evelle.

'Of what do you wish to persuade the rebel cities, Strategist?' said Thaun.

Blain grunted. 'To preserve the world for a while. Until later, when we can stab their backs at a time of our choosing. All of which they will know full well. But for now we need them. There's little point winning a prize which has burned to ash. How absurd. We need them!' Blain laughed again with what seemed real mirth. 'Go,' he snapped at Tauvene. 'Assist him,' he added to Envidis. No one was under any illusion what *assist* really meant. Least of all the First Captain.

'And where is the rest of your entourage?' said Blain to Thaun when they had left. He got slowly to his feet and drew his plain coat over the shifting colours of his Strategist's robe.

'They are back at the inn, Strategist.'

'They still live?'

'Most of them,' said Evelle, smiling.

'Well let's go and see if they're useful. Take me there. You!' He pointed at Kiown. 'You're not here for your brains. Or your looks. Carry me.'

MIGHTY WIZARD OF THE TOWER

1

While they walked Eric watched the ground before him. Some parts of the sky's lightstone hung lower than others; some grew brighter than others. Right now, Siel's shadow was faint. But Eric indeed had none at all. 'Don't worry about it,' she said, wishing she could take her own advice. It worried her a great deal. 'There must be an explanation for it.'

'Like what, pray tell?' he said.

'Sometimes spells go wrong. Little effects linger in the air. You can step into something you don't even see, and it's almost like you've been cast on.'

He scoffed. 'Look, are you telling me some wizard out there tried to remove his own shadow and *missed*, but the spell kind of blew around on the breeze until I walked through it?'

She shrugged. 'It's not common. There aren't enough mages left for it to be common. Nor is the effect always what the wizard intended. We have been exposed to many strange events, magic effects at play in them. And yes, things are possible which are stranger than losing a shadow. People have died from loose effects. Or been changed for life. There is a famous story of a man who had amazing luck for the rest of his life.'

'All I know is, every time I think I get used to this fucking place—'

'I will listen to your complaint, Otherworld Prince. But it's my turn next.'

'Forget it.'

In big loping strides Gorb led them down an incline until they found a path winding north-east through puffy green thickets and woodland. In it large star-shaped flowers slowly dripped clear sap like tear-drops. Birds made inquiring sounds from the trees. 'Hey Gorb, can I have my weapon back?' said Eric.

'Nope,' said Gorb, not turning around. 'Not till I know I can trust you. Which may take a while.'

Siel whispered, 'He's lying about the dolls. He didn't make them.'

'How do you know?'

'I saw something as we left. A glimpse, I think it was recent past. A man being led through the village as though he were captive. I think it was an Engineer.'

'A what?'

'People who make devices using magic.'

'They're mages?'

'No. Rarer. No one teaches them their trade, they are born with it and can do nothing else useful. They sometimes come away from the cities to collect airs for their works. These people must have captured one. If the city he or she came from finds out, the people of this village are in deep trouble.' Almost on cue there came a banging noise from back at the village. It was unmistakeably the Glock firing.

'What was that?' said Gorb, looking back with alarm.

'Car backfiring,' Eric muttered.

'Give me a moment,' said Siel, ducking off the road.

2

She was used to bathing and peeing in front of travelling companions, but like beds and baths, privacy was a luxury to grab with both hands when on offer. Now she slipped off the path and through trunks spaced like a natural avenue, went deeper in until the road could not be seen through the messy lattice of tree branches. She set down her bow and quill, crouched with her back to a tree trunk. There was hardly a sound but for the now mournful birdsong. The woods smelled clean and there were tracks from game all over the ground.

What an idyllic life this must be, she thought, when bandits are the worst of the villagers' problems. For how many generations have they not known hunger or war? She pictured life here in this greedy idyllic peace, and desire for simple wholeness and happiness pulled her strongly.

There was that image again, once so horrible but now almost cherished: a girl afraid but calm in her hiding space in the wall hollow. Her parents had said, *Stay here, we'll return*, hearing the men kick down their neighbours' doors. The same men kicked down their door, took them outside, knelt them down in a long line with the others of that street. Calmly creeping out of the hiding space, over to the window, listening as a proclamation was read out, full of long words she mostly didn't understand. They had aided enemies of their Friend and Lord. They had been ungrateful. They were dangerous. The hiss of a drawn blade. Cries of protest. Calm still, peeking through the curtain gap. A sight less comprehensible than the words in the proclamation as a man in castle grey walked down the line, swinging his blade.

She had finished peeing when a shape loomed right beside her, jagging her back to the present. She gasped and fell sideways, pants still around her knees preventing a quick roll to her feet. She'd fallen away from her bow.

Looking down at her was Eric. She felt a flare of hot anger for him, embarrassing her this way. 'What are you doing?' she snapped.

Then she saw it *wasn't* Eric. It was someone nearly identical to him, aside from his dark garments and long flowing hair. His outline was slightly blurred, its edges wavering. What seemed Eric's face held eyes that were hollow unblinking things, small dark holes. He spoke in a voice like Eric's but dead of expression: 'Interesting. I'll save you from something. Soon. It's ahead on the axis. In the future. I can see it.'

The stranger leaned forward over her until his body tilted at an angle defying gravity. 'You have a name,' he said. 'And you're alive. Are we the same, or different? I don't understand.'

Siel's hand found her curved knife, while the other pulled up her pants. She rolled backward, was up on her feet, turned to run. But he was there right behind her now. 'You're afraid of me,' he said as though this was interesting in an academic sense.

Her knife flashed with a gleam of bright steel but it only cut air. He was on the other side of her now. 'Fast,' he said. 'You're fast. I can be, too. I can do whatever you can do. Even that . . . that little bit of magic you have, where you see things on the axis. And this! This is interesting.' He had her bow and quiver in hand. The objects stood out in their solidity against his blurriness. He turned them at different angles, examining with childish curiosity. 'You shoot well with this. I've seen you do it. I can too. Watch.' He clumsily nocked an arrow in the string and pulled it back, holding the bow completely wrong.

'Who are you?' said Siel, her voice far more commanding than she felt.

He turned his hole-dark eyes to her. 'Who?' he said quietly. 'I don't know. The question means I'm *someone*. Like you. Doesn't it? It means I'm alive. Doesn't it? Am I alive, like you are?'

'You've followed us. Why?'

'I went lots of places. There's a lot to look at. I don't understand much of it yet.'

'Put my bow down.'

'Sure, I can do that. Soon, all right? Watch this. That bird.' It appeared he'd let loose the string by clumsy accident, but the arrow whizzed from the bow and quivered in the body of a small bird, which landed with a thump in the undergrowth. 'It's dead,' said the stranger. It took Siel a moment to work out this was a question.

'Yes. Dead,' she replied, watching nervously to see if he'd nock another arrow. Instead he dropped both the quiver and bow and lay on the ground, peering so closely at the dead bird his nose touched it. 'How does that work?' he said. 'Something's alive, then it's dead, and it can't go back. You can't put back the stuff you took out, or fix the part you broke, and make it move again. Why?'

'Did you kill the dogs?' she said.

The hole-dark eyes peered up at her from Eric's face. 'I can take you far away, if you want me to. Fast. You like fast. To see other places. Have you seen them? Maybe you can explain things to me. I don't know much yet. It's all . . . strange. I want to understand it all. But there's so much. And I don't think I belong here, I don't think I fit.'

'Did you kill the dogs? Tell me. I know it was you.'

A blink of the eyes later, the stranger was tilting at a perverse angle right before her, so that he leaned backward, looking up at her from near her knees. 'That's a bad question,' he said.

Her backward step was involuntary. 'What is your name? Is it Eric?'

'I have to go.' The stranger righted his angle, stood with arms hanging awkwardly. His dark hole eyes peered into the distance, brow furrowing. 'I'm *him*, sometimes. The fellow you travel with. I can feel him, like someone listening to me. I can ... I can be you, if you want me to.'

He stepped toward her. She lunged, her knife slashing a curve through the air. Again he was simply no longer in the space her knife sliced through. He was some distance behind her, body leaning sideways, face and dark pit eyes expressing nothing at all. Siel grabbed her bow and quiver and sprinted back toward the road. The messy green lattice broke as she ran through it and scraped at her.

Eric lay by the roadside, one leg crossed over the other. He turned as she skidded to a halt and she recoiled from his eyes, expecting – and for a moment seeing – the empty pits she'd seen in a face like his just moments before.

3

'What's wrong with you?' he said.

She looked behind her, saw nothing. 'Where is the half-giant?'

'What are you afraid of?'

'Nothing! Where is he?'

'He got tired of waiting for you. He gave me directions and went ahead to the tower.' Eric stood up. 'Let's go get the gun. It's back at the village.'

'No! We shouldn't be alone.'

'Siel, what the hell is the matter?'

'I had a glimpse of the past. A bad one. It doesn't matter.'

He recalled her unflinching after the hilltop fight when death was spread all over the road, unflinching at the doomed hunters' hall while he'd been sick to his core by what just two or three Tormentors had done; calm as they'd fled the chaos of a falling city. What just now could have been worse?

She kept looking behind as though for a pursuer as they followed a footpath through a small crop field, twisting back through thin woods. Abruptly the trees fell away from a wide flat meadow. In it a crowd of thirty or so people – Gorb among them – gathered about campfires, none seeming to notice their arrival.

All eyes were on the peculiar structure which sat in a wide shallow lake of clear water. Small curling waves rippled their way in slow motion to the grassy shore. In the water's midst, an odd structure stood tall as a hill which had been sliced down the middle, its back half curved, with towers and facades built into the sheer sliced face. Crumbling brick, wood and mortar were all at disagreeing angles, in places as tangled up as tree roots. Grey, dead-looking skeletal trees clung here and there to the flat side, some taking root on crags high above the ground, their thin branch tips sticking out like the last grey hairs from an ancient head.

The air's magic showed a strong dark ribbon running in a glimmering funnel from the sky down to the tower's highest flat-side window, then out another at the rear where it spread out thinly into the atmosphere again.

He had never seen magic behave this way; something within the building surely drew it in for a magician's use. Among the peppery dark bands was the occasional red flash of foreign airs sitting uncomfortably in the mixture. A breeze breathed across the gently lapping waves, which filled the meadow with their swishing music.

Gorb padded over to them, heavy footsteps sinking deep into the grass. 'Fish in the water aren't real,' he said. 'I caught one. Popped in my hand, into just sparks. They're saying don't go in the water at all. Some weird spells about it, they say. Dunno how *they* know: they're not mages.'

'Is anyone up there?' said Eric, nodding at the high tower windows. He felt they were being watched.

'See that woman over by the fire?' said Gorb. 'Myela's her name. She saw a wizard. Said he's got four arms, the head of a bull. Wants to cast death spells at us. He ain't done anything of the sort *yet*. But if this tower's what I think it is, war mages will come.'

Eric didn't properly hear the answer to his question. He laughed aloud in delight. He'd seen a face in the window, a familiar one and no bull's head. The window slid open, scattering a handful of dirt and pebbles to splash into the water. 'Eric, Siel! Get yourselves up here!' Loup shouted as though they were late for an appointment.

The villagers turned as one to gape at them. 'You silly gawking buggers!' Loup screamed. 'Look at you, jaws all hanging loose! Well, they should be! That there's a Pilgrim, from Otherworld.'

A chorus of talk went up. Siel looked at Eric, mortified. '*Why* did he tell them that?' she whispered.

'He's here to save us all, you mark me,' Loup babbled. 'Save us from what, none yet know, not even *him*. But when he knows, he'll get to it! Good lad, he is. Come up here, Eric. Any of that black scale left? I'm almost out and I need it. The rest of you silly gawking folk, piss off.'

The villagers murmured among themselves about whether this wizard was as dangerous as they'd thought. They decided not to risk it and headed back up the path through the woodlands toward their homes.

Eric and Siel waded into cool thigh-deep water. Luminous fish pretty as jewels flashed around their legs and glinted through the clouds of silt their sinking footsteps disturbed. With a shriek Siel sank suddenly deeper into the water, clutching at Eric's hand as he pulled her up.

'Don't scream and panic,' Loup called down from his high window. 'A few deep spots here and there, is all. Nifty place, this! We'll be safe holing up here a while.'

'Not for long,' came Gorb's ponderous voice. He'd taken a few steps into the water. 'War mages will be here soon.'

'You back off!' Loup snarled at him.

'What for?' said Gorb.

''Cause I *said*. No room for you up here.' But Gorb kept coming, till Loup threw something which landed in the water in front of him with a splash. While Gorb fished around for the object, Loup hurled down some kind of broken metal instrument which slammed quite hard into Gorb's huge face. 'I said back off!'

'I could get mad about that,' said Gorb very slowly, rubbing the great slab of his left cheek with a palm.

'Git!'

'Ask your friends who fed em last night.'

'We'll talk later,' said Eric apologetically.

'Git!' Loup screamed, throwing a rock at the half-giant. Gorb swatted it out of the air, his huge arm clubbing it far over the treetops. But he did as Loup asked and headed dejectedly back to the village.

Siel whispered, 'Listen. I don't know what it is, but Loup's not himself. Maybe the new airs have got to him. Be on your guard.'

'You think he's going to throw things at us?'

'I don't know what he'll do. He's not all-powerful, but he *is* a mage. Telling all those people what you are, that was insane. I can hardly believe he did it.'

'Why?'

'Do you understand, Eric? You are a Pilgrim. A weapon, a mine of treasures, an omen, a grand secret. Our whole civilisation exists because of Pilgrims like you, coming here now and then throughout history with knowledge from Otherworld. Every power in the world wants you. Free and Aligned and rogue, all things in between. The fewer who know of you, the better.'

'Why, for Christ's sake? I haven't done anything!'

'For your basic knowledge alone. They'd all have heard of you by now. Even allied Mayors would go to war with each other to possess you.'

The tower loomed over them, on a leaning angle like it might topple forward and flatten them. 'There were war mages at the door when I came in,' Eric said. 'Sent there to kill us. If we're so valuable, why?'

She shrugged. 'The Arch Mage is a fool in many ways. But maybe he knows of your world, and of your magic—'

'It's not *magic*, Siel.'

'— and maybe he feared Pilgrims would bring powers to undo him. This world is his now. I assume he wanted nothing to come here which could change that.' Siel seemed to debate something. 'Listen. I knew things Anfen didn't, things even some of the Mayors didn't. Our task, why we were sent near the castle in the first place. It was nothing to do with getting an underground base near the castle! They *knew* you were coming through.'

'Who knew?'

'The Mayors' Command. Don't ask me how they knew, and why the castle didn't. I don't know the answer. But they knew a Pilgrim or several Pilgrims would come. Sending Anfen's band was a futile dice roll to get hold of you. Somehow it worked. They did not expect us to return, let alone capture the Pilgrims. It's why we've had so little help. My job was to keep us in the area till it happened. If we were caught, the order was to kill you so the castle didn't get hold of you. It would have been me to do it. Anfen never knew.'

'Would you have?'

'Yes.' He'd have appreciated just a moment's hesitation before she'd said that.

She climbed out of the water up onto a hard dirt shelf at the tower's base. 'The point is, those villagers will talk. There could be a patrol at the village right now – that is a trade route back there! We may have a week, or less than an hour.'

'So they'd take me to their city. Beds and baths and hot meals. Sounds terrible.'

'Foolish! People are not as loyal to their cities as they once were. If mercenaries find you and work out what you are worth to the Mayors, there's a chance they will play games and try to sell you to the highest bidder.'

'But look, you know Loup. He does things which are nutty but turn out for the best. You usually only know after.'

'Or maybe the new airs have messed his head, the same way they disturbed the magic hiding that village. And hiding this building, whatever it is.' She slapped a slab of earthy stone set in the tower's sheer face. 'We must get to Tanton. They have a sane mayor. The other cities *don't*.'

There was no staircase or ladder in sight. An arch opened up on the building's right side, leading to a gloomy space beneath. 'Not in there,' cried Loup as they headed for it. 'Stay away! Strange little spot, down there. There's tunnels going beneath the water. Don't know where they go or what they're for, but the tower doesn't want us in em. Murmurs and complains, it does!'

'How else do we come up?' Siel called to him.

'I've seen more brains spattered across Anfen's boots! The *tree*, you two! Climb!'

A brittle grey tree on the earthy platform reached nearly halfway up the tower's face. Siel stripped off her pants and wrung water out of them. Then with some difficulty (not helped by wet feet or Loup's agitated commentary) they were soon high enough that a fall would break bones. From halfway up the trunk they could see through the arch at the tower's base, where deeper water swirled in a large slow whirlpool. A breeze came up from there; in it, so faintly they were unsure they'd heard it, was a whispering voice. 'I do not know what this place is,' Siel whispered, 'but I have seen nothing like it before.'

'Nervous?'

'Yes.'

At the first window ledge, puffing, they both stepped onto a thin shelf of hard dirt. Siel yanked at the window a few times before giving up and smashing the glass with the hilt of her knife. Shards clattered to the floor inside. An outraged noise erupted from the folk magician above. 'Now why'd you do that? This place is *alive*! It mutters and groans, oh aye it does. Don't go beating it! You mark me, this here's no hunk of stone and wood! Not only alive, damn near *aware of itself*. Be polite! Better hope it doesn't hold a grudge too.'

As though in agreement, the turf shelf below Siel's foot broke free and scattered down to the water with a shower of splashes. She yelped, grabbed at the window ledge and hung for a moment until Eric climbed in, reached out and pulled her up inside.

4

Gorb's belly rumbled with hunger. His larder called to him sweetly: *Ham and cheese, Gorb. Freshly baked bread smeared with mutton fat. Raw dough, why not? Vegetables, Gorb, fresh and crispy! We are, as ever, at your service …*

Gorb appreciated the offer and hurried home. Woods, crop field, woods. The path was familiar as his skin, every step of it. He rubbed the welt on his face and considered whether or not to make a rare addition to the page in his mind headed *seek revenge upon*, with a blazing red picture of the silly old mage's face.

Great death-dealing wizard? He thought not. Just a little folk mage, could probably bless brews and do remedies, cure colds. Not even strong enough to re-cast the spell that hid the tower. For now he added the mage's face to the next page over, headed *watch yourself, little fellow*. There were quite a number of faces on that page. That dimwitted Thurnam, for instance, who'd mistreated his dogs. His poor dogs.

As for the tower, it was the work of the old magic schools, no question there. Gorb remembered the wizard who'd cast the hiding spell on the village more than twenty years before. He'd been seen late some nights crossing the village's fields and lurking in their woods; he was tall and bald with footsteps that seemed to float just above the ground. He'd refused to speak with the villagers who approached him, until seeing Gorb. Even then he'd stayed hidden, just sent a voice emanating from the gloom of the woods, demanding more payment for the spell than any honest village could afford.

When the Arch Mage learned of the tower – as he surely would – death would come to these lands quickly. Before the hiding spell broke, the tower had seemed to be a sheer rock outcrop no one had bothered risking their necks to climb. The water was the strange part; its edge was on ground they'd have walked across now and then. No one had ever mentioned getting mysteriously wet feet . . .

Something between the rows of trees caught Gorb's eye. He found with some surprise that he was not alone. A chap stood at a strange angle – an impossible angle, like that of a spear that had been flung into the ground, closer to lying down than standing. The stranger's back was turned.

Gorb rubbed his eyes. He had an eye for enchantments and such, but had seen nothing like this before. He opened his mouth to call out when suddenly there was a loud banging noise from back at the village. It could only be Bald, though what he was up to only great old Mountain knew.

The stranger sank into the ground, almost too quick to see. There was no trace of him – no tracks, nothing.

Gorb ran the rest of the way back to the village, then quickly ducked out of sight. A patrol had come. Five soldiers were talking to Aulek off by his vegetable patch. Two in Tanton colours, the others a mix from all over. So far their blades were still sheathed, but they looked agitated. No doubt they were here to ask why this village had popped up overnight and what mage had hidden it up till now.

The man closest to Aulek gave him a shove. Poor dim Aulek would not have half the words he needed to give them satisfactory answers.

So much for the cities leaving Outcast country alone, Gorb thought. The two Tanton-coloured men took some steps toward Bald's shed, when there came another huge banging noise, truly terribly loud. One of the soldiers fell back, clutching his chest. The others ducked as though fearing some fiery rain from above.

There was Bald! He held Eric's peculiar little weapon and had that delighted look on his face he got when he'd just understood something very tricky. The soldiers were not so pleased. They milled about their fallen friend, trying to work out what had hurt him. They reached for their weapons. Gorb did not see the cause/effect between the loud noise and the wounded soldier, but these men apparently did.

When emergency dictated – when anger or fear reached a certain point in a half-giant's heart – it unlocked a little store of power he or she could not access by simply reaching in. A blast of that potent power went through Gorb now, instantly all through his veins and brain. It didn't just make him move fast, it made him think fast, like he could see a tiny road of the future ahead, and move off it if need be. As he rushed to knock the angry soldiers off their feet (intending minimal damage) he saw this village being massacred when they learned Bald had been stolen from the city who owned him, and – as *they* would see it – had been filled with tales to make him wish murder upon their troops.

Moving quickly Gorb plucked the weapon out of Bald's hand (the Engineer protested vehemently). He tucked Bald under his arm and used that store of power to get them as fast as he could back to the funny wizard's tower. The little old mage could get as angry as he wanted – Gorb was going inside this time, and he hoped there'd be no need to get mad in return.

AZIEL'S FLIGHT

1

The airs were no longer frantic. Sluggish power curled through the castle hallways in lazy bands of colour. The Arch Mage breathed them in and power spread through his body, slowly calming the burn. The burn itself – once a writhing, searing pain – had over long years become a kind of comfort to him.

Vous had kept him busy over the past two days. The silence about the castle was the kind experienced after savage storms. No more screams from below – either the terror had ceased its movement down the levels or there were none left to do the screaming. Hundreds were dead, valuable mind-controlled staff it would take much work and bother to replace.

Vous's chamber door was shut for the first time since the latest episode began. Throughout it, the Arch had done circuits of this upper floor, very narrowly avoiding the terror's various forms and traps, keeping it focussed on himself lest it turn to Aziel. On the run he had paused now and then by her room to call brief words of reassurance through her chamber door. The episode had mostly petered out but he was not quite certain it was over.

In the wide space outside his throne room Vous stood in a now familiar pose. The ghostly form was still, head downcast in defeat. Was Vous experimenting with those newly found limbs the Arch had described to Aziel, the way an infant discovers his voice and experiments with babbling phrases?

The Arch marvelled. Babbling expressions of magic tossed around the room like a toddler's outbursts; spell craft made up on the fly, as fluent as thought, no care or art to it at all. Brilliant yet purposeless. It amazed and offended the Arch in equal measure.

Vous's ghostly image staggered backward into the wall, slumped down, and wept. The Arch went close as he dared, crouched low. The ghostly image whispered something.

'I cannot hear you, Friend and Lord,' said the Arch, bracing himself. The last time he'd spoken directly to one of these illusions the reaction had been . . . unpleasant.

'It ends here,' repeated the ghost.

He waited for it to say more, but it did not. Within a minute it had faded from existence.

It ends here. He allowed himself to hope it meant *the Project* ends here, that Vous was relinquishing his part and succumbing to death, and that that would (if possible) disperse the force about him. No one could pry Vous from his throne at this late hour but he himself. Was there enough of the man left within the changing entity to do it? The Arch Mage hoped, but didn't think so.

He pushed at Vous's door and jumped back as it swung open. The spread of death across the rich carpet was as distasteful to him as excrement. On the throne, splayed, Vous looked almost as dead as the rest.

The Arch had not dared enter this place in a long while. There'd seldom have been a more dangerous day to do so. But Vous did not presently wear his wards and charms. Was this permission, even an instruction, to enter?

The candles on their stands flashed to life, casting orange light through the chamber. Such simple magic it could almost be taken as a jest. The Arch limped in, stepping over remains. Large piles of pebbles lay in the mess. They scattered from his boot.

Vous did not stir as he came near. What would be the safest approach, tone of voice? 'My Friend and Lord. It has been a hard night. How may I aid you?'

'It's over,' said Vous quietly.

'May I ask what, Friend and Lord?'

'The evening.'

'Yes, Friend and Lord, morning has come. Perhaps you also mean the evening's irregularities. Is it your wish to discuss them?'

Vous rolled onto his side, convulsed, hissed, lay still.

The Arch Mage gestured at the bodies about the chamber. 'Friend and Lord, the last time you performed this . . . kind of ritual, the Entry Point opened. Do you recall it? The slaughtered peasants. Had you similar intentions, this time?'

'Intentions,' said Vous mockingly.

Movement caught the Arch's eye and he very nearly fled, only to see it was Ghost flitting across the wall's tall mirror. 'I had assumed, Friend and Lord, there was some point to the recent destruction. Surely not simply the relief of boredom? Friend and Lord, with your leave I shall speak bluntly. Great power gathers itself about you. Immense power. Any of the gods, if they wished, *could* slay us all. In their wisdom they let us live. You will soon join them, Friend and Lord. You shall have their status. Do you share their vision for humanity? Or have you different wishes? I ask only that I may better assist you.'

For a long while there was no answer. Vous was still as a

carving. 'Do you think . . . magicians never fall for magic tricks?' he said at last.

'Friend and Lord?'

'Do the Windows show only plain truth? Only ever bald plain truth, Avridis?'

The Arch Mage baulked to hear the name his parents had given him, jagging him unpleasantly for an instant into the distant past, where he was nothing, no one, reviled and cursed and spat upon. Cast out of the magic schools for exploring his taste for forbidden arts. Held up as a thing of mockery, an example made for others. Memories so ancient it was startling to now and then recall them, and feel their usually impotent sting.

He said, 'I'm sure the Hall of Windows keeps many secrets, Friend and Lord, even from me.'

'Even . . . from . . . you.' Vous's gaze bored into him. His lip curled. 'Secrets! Yes, Avridis. And lies. *Lies*. I learned much, tonight. I am so very tired.'

'Shall I send for your meal?'

'There is no one to make it.'

'Ah.'

'She's gone.' Vous shut his eyes. 'In no sense ever will she return to me.'

'May I ask who, Friend and Lord?'

Vous's inert body draped like a pale sheet across the throne. The Arch waited then turned and limped away, his forked staff picking its way through corpses.

She's gone.

Ruin was all about him. The halls and floors had been torn up by that curious effect, those monstrous stone creations which crumbled to loose pebbles when the life went out of them. The damage dealt to walls and floor had begun to 'heal' as though it were organic flesh instead of stone, jade, ivory and marble.

He had not brought the keys to Aziel's room with him, but would not cast just to open a door. She did not respond to his call. With some effort he ripped the handle free.

She was not there.

Dismayed, he rested a moment on her chair, wondering who he could get to search through the lower floors, when there again was Ghost. Its faces flitted across the shards of broken window on the floor. Tiredly the Arch raised a palm, cast a smaller version of the spell he'd used to trap the Invia in the halls last month. A web of force sprang up among the glass shards and drew them, scraping, till they were together. Sick heat flushed through him. His horns belched smoke and stink.

'We don't speak to you,' said Ghost's tremulous voice. 'You aren't trusted.'

As always his words must be cautious to this detestable thing. 'I shall never ask you to trust me. I would be more worried if you did. It is well your loyalty is for our Friend and Lord, and him only. Where is Aziel?'

'A drake came and took her.'

'Nonsense.'

'The marks on the window sill. On the floor to our left. Evidence!' The faces shook and grimaced in their jagged glass prisons. 'Release us!'

He broke the spell when he saw what Ghost referred to. Quick as a heartbeat, Ghost was gone.

On the floor was a thin red drake scale, broken off as the creature had barged in.

Avridis got to his feet and quite uselessly went to the window. The vast realm in all its emptiness swallowed his searching gaze. Horror and rage ripped through him.

2

Aziel was secure enough in the drake's ridges and lumps, which formed a natural saddle, even a strange kind of chair. The drake's warmth felt like his belly was full of hot coals. But the creature was terribly slow to respond to instructions.

'Horrible thing, put me down! Do you want me to soil my dress? I *need* to go.' To talk of such things (even to an animal) would normally have made her feel little better than an animal herself.

The cold air, funnelled by the drake's labouring wings, tossed her hair violently in all directions. The drake had more or less stuck to the Great Dividing Road, with detours to either side as though it were searching for something. They'd flown over an army marching south, over mountain ranges, fields, villages, farms. And over things she'd never heard of at all, like those big blue domes. How huge it all was, the outside world! How peculiar, the way it went about its business without a word or instruction from her.

She'd learned the futility of slapping the drake's scaly skin when a break was needed. Kicking its sides had once made it belch flame. But it certainly didn't enjoy being whined at. 'Why did you take me from my room?' she asked in the tone it found most objectionable, leaning forward and pouring the words right into its ear. 'Did I ever ask to be taken away?' (Well yes, but not by a *drake*, certainly.) 'Where do you mean to take me? Did Arch arrange it, or did you come to steal me by yourself? That's what you did, you stole me! Set me down or take me back!'

The whining at last broke through the drake's patience. She heard it sigh like a grumpy old man then it began its descent. 'Oh no you don't,' she said. 'Not in the bushes again, I'm not a beast like you are. Take me over there to that building by the Road. I'll go inside for once.'

The drake made an anxious noise but it obeyed, setting her down behind the tallest building of a small roadside town, the only one for miles. She got off him and swayed, dizzy to be on her feet again.

Loud brash voices boomed and roared from the building, along with the smell of ale. A tavern or inn – she'd heard of these. They were necessary to keep soldiers happy. From the sky she'd assumed this was a subject's house, that a meal and facilities would be eagerly offered to their Friend and Lord's daughter. But that ale smelled awful. She changed her mind and went behind the building instead. 'Don't you watch me!' she told the drake.

But the drake suddenly had little interest in her. It sniffed the air and its ears perked up, eyes widening.

When Aziel had finished, she saw the creature's tail slithering around the building's corner as it made its move. A chorus of amazed and frightened shouts sprang up. She ran along the alley to the inn's front. Near a row of outside tables a group of men stood, their backs against the wall and their mouths agog. The drake had its front paws up on a table and the tip of its snout in their beer jug. A few greedy sucks and the jug was drained.

'Stop that!' Aziel ordered it.

The men were so amazed at seeing the rare monster they didn't notice her. 'Catch it,' one of them suggested.

'Is it tame?' said another.

'No saddle on it. And it's not a young one. Must have escaped!'

'They don't *wear* saddles, fool, tame or not.'

'Never knew these things drank ale.'

'Your shout, drake!'

The drake's snout didn't fit into the cups and mugs. It knocked them to the ground and lapped up the spilled ale with appalling eagerness, not concerned for the dirt and pebbles the ale fizzed into. Aziel ran to it and hopped on its back. 'Fly!' she ordered, nervous suddenly about these strange men who'd not so much as bowed in deference to her. 'What are you staring at?' she yelled at them. 'Go inside!'

'Is this pet yours, girly?' someone asked her drunkenly. 'Where'd you find him?'

Aziel blanched, amazed to find these people so animated, much less impetuous enough to call her 'girly'. Arch had told her most people were like the grey-robes, docile and obedient, or mindless and violent. 'Go inside!' she repeated; it was all she could think to say.

The drake kept licking at the damp puddles of spilled ale. Aziel toppled from its back as it examined the next table over, her dress hiking up around her thighs. Her face went almost as red as the drake's scales. A crowd began to trickle out of the inn, gawking at the creature. 'Haven't you seen a drake before?' Aziel snapped, getting to her feet. She leaped onto the drake's back again. 'Go, fly!' she said, trying with little effect to wrench its head away from another toppled jug.

'You be careful, girly, these reds breathe flame, they say.'

The drake made a loud growling sound which made the onlookers cringe in fear of a blast of fire, some of them cowering back inside the inn. When they understood the creature had belched they laughed.

The drake gazed at the crowd of men with surprise, as if it had only just noticed them now that all the ale had all been drunk. It took a few steps away from them, back onto the road, steps a touch unsteadier than usual. Then a voice sounded from one of the upper windows, bellowing in tones of disbelief: 'That's Aziel!'

Startled, she looked up and saw the savage face of Strategist Blain staring down, mouth wide in astonishment. He turned and snapped an order at someone in the room behind him.

Twice the drake had drunkenly tried to take off, to much laughter from those watching it. It took a last look back at the crowd, then froze as a tall red-headed man pushed violently through the onlookers and drew a sword.

Immediately the drake shook Aziel off its back and charged, knocking the man over, battering him with its wings and head. The redhead dropped his weapon and wedged a forearm in the drake's mouth. His punches glanced off its hard leathery hide as the pair rolled about in the dirt. The crowd scattered.

Another man leaned out Blain's window. He held a long pipe to his lips and blew through it a thin dart.

The drake yelped and jumped off his victim, belched again, then scuttled back to Aziel. She climbed on its back. Its skyward lunge this time succeeded. As they lurched higher she looked back over her shoulder to see the redhead getting to his feet, blood seeping from his forehead and arm. 'Why did you attack that man?' she said. 'It's almost as though you knew him.'

Blain's shocked face was still at the upstairs window watching her go, his mouth still wide open.

3

Thaun smiled down at Kiown, feeling the young one would benefit from his embarrassment. But they would have to move, and soon. This was too memorable a tale; drakes were very rare, and there were some rebel infantry drinking down there at the tables.

Blain's order had been poor reflex – 'kill the drake, get the girl'. He would not be pleased at Kiown's failure. He *would* be pleased to learn that the dart in the drake's rump would lead them directly to the doorstep of whoever had managed to kidnap their Friend and Lord's daughter with a trained pet.

Thaun took from his travel bag what looked like a thin wooden card with a metal point, slowly spinning till it settled on a direction. It pointed at the dart now lodged in the drake's rump, the tip of which should by now have wormed its way inside the creature's body, all but irretrievable. It was the second time he'd used this Engineer-built device, named a 'chaser' by its creator, carried with him in two decades' service. He hoped it still worked.

THE TOWER

1

The sound of lapping waves was stronger within the tower than it had been when Eric and Siel were waist-deep in the water of its moat. Its interior was the colours of earth, browns, greens and stone-grey, gently lit from a hidden source. A small, shallow, sparkling pool lay in the middle of the floor, giving no hint of its purpose. The large floor space was interspersed with tall statue-things, vaguely tree-like in shape, made of black metal which flowed like the liquid in a lava lamp. Their 'branches' twisted and spun slowly round in a way that made the eye grapple uncomfortably with what it saw. Down one side of the room were half-a-dozen such things, of wildly varying design. The slow movement of their limbs was mesmerising. 'Don't touch them,' Siel cautioned as Eric went for a closer look.

'What are they?'

'I don't know. Do not stare at them too long either.'

Loup's muttering and cursing about the broken window carried down to them through a winding set of steps. The steps also led down to that dark space beneath where a whirlpool quietly spun and burbled, winding out of sight into the water's depths.

Loup stumbled down, shirtless and barefoot despite the air's chill. The grey wires peppering his chest, and the hairs on his head, stood crazily on end, as did his beard and eyebrows. As though the three of them had been involved in a long discussion, he said, 'Nay, lad, not at all, no clue why they left here in such a hurry. But leave they did, and it's our home for now.'

'Who left?'

'Mages.' Loup cackled. 'Aye, they had most of us off their scent, making out they'd all been killed. But I wondered! Had to be *some* still about from the old schools. Hiding somewhere. Good airs here! Strong!' He gazed around with slightly crazed eyes. 'Small little place by *their* standards, this is, not much chop. Built it in a hurry. Bet there's others like it too, here and there. Off in the far east where no one goes, I'll bet.' He sighed. 'That ugly magic of the Arch and his pets, that's all fast on-the-spot stuff. The old mages could *do* that kind of thing, but they didn't like to. Now why would an artist go round lighting fires, is what they'd say. S'why it caught em off guard you see, that sad night when the Arch sent out his war mages to slay em all. They liked *slow* casting, slow, lasting, thoughtful spells. Not just bang, pop, kill something. Spells'd take a day or longer, ones you could only cast one part at a time.' Loup wiped a tear from his eye and sniffed. 'Works of humans actually rate worth a damn, the slower kinds of magic we do. Could earn respect of higher beings. As for this tower, well hey! For them, the old wizards, this place is a rush job. Ah, those old snotty mages who thought they were so clever they could tell the world what to do. Well, here's news: they *were* clever.'

Siel said in tones of disbelief: 'Mages from the defeated schools have been here, hiding all along, while *we* gave our lives to avenge them?'

Loup snorted. 'Who else built it? *I* didn't! Thought he'd killed em all, that foul Arch Mage bastard! Thought he'd got rid of em. But this old place was hiding, oh aye. He'll be nervous when he hears of it! He'll think that in the long years hiding, they learned up on lighting fires and killing! And maybe he'll find he's not the best at it any more. We'll see. Question is, where'd they go? And when? My hunch is, not long back at all! Days, maybe.' Loup bounded to Eric and clutched his arm. 'But as for you, lad. Who's the new one?'

'The giant?'

'Not him! The one who looks like you, been following you about?' Siel turned away. 'Ah, *she* knows. *She's* seen him, I can tell. What about you, lad? I know a little of him already, but I want to know what *you* know, or what you guess about it.'

'I'm not sure. But I had a strange dream last night . . . You were there! I heard you speaking.'

'*You* heard me?' said Loup. His creased old face bunched with worry. 'I never saw *you* or said a word to *you*.' He paced for a minute or so, muttering. 'Never mind that, though. More of that black scale; you got it handy? Then I'll be able to keep an eye out for him. Not easy to steer him around, you mark me. Dangerous! I found some red and green up there in the attic, but not as much kick in them. Black's what we – Now wait, that's something! Where's your shadow, lad?'

'What would you have us do, Loup, now that you've let word slip to the locals that we have the Pilgrim here?' said Siel to change the subject.

'*Do*? Wait here,' said Loup, crouching down at Eric's feet and examining the floor. 'Safe as anywhere else. Safer! And don't ask me to cast a damn thing till this gunk clears out of the air, if it ever does. I'll not risk it just to make your bread taste better.'

'Wait here for what?'

'You and your questions! All of you people, all the time, *explain explain explain*, with your fool brains getting in the way of things, and your fool *plan this, plan that*, not trusting the mages who lead you by the nose out of your silly messes—'

'Listen old man,' Siel screamed. '*I* have a temper too. I woke this morning to a knife at my throat, after months on the road stepping through death, death, death, everywhere I look, present, past and future, death death death! I've not been paid, I've not been thanked, I've not had a day to relax and *live* without death kicking down the door again and dragging me out in the cold. And if you want to know about that demon in the woods—' She had taken strides toward him, not without a hint of menace, when something tripped her up and sent her sprawling heavily to her feet.

Loup rushed to her and said in the tenderest tones, 'Aw, easy, lass, easy now. Are you hurt?' He examined the shoulder she'd landed on, pressing in his gnarled old fingers. Siel was too baffled to answer, trying to work out what on the flat space of floor she could possibly have tripped on. 'This old house doesn't much care for you, lass,' said Loup gently. 'Might've been breaking the window, might be it don't like happenstance. Better keep your voice low till it learns to trust you. Aye I know, you've journeyed long, me with you. It's a hard life you've had, but it's made you tough as a stoneflesh. Rest up here awhile, lass, easy now.' Siel wiped a tear from her face and manoeuvred herself away (unsuccessfully) from

Loup's hug. 'Come here, Eric lad, join in. Show her all the world ain't mean as a war mage!'

Eric crouched with them and made the hug a three-way business. Siel's body shook with tears she tried to keep back. 'Easy, lass, let it out now,' said Loup, winking at Eric.

There came the unmistakeable noise of the Glock firing outside.

Eric ran to the window. Gorb was at the water's edge. A thin bald man tucked up under his arm kicked and struggled. Gorb examined with some confusion the small black gun, minuscule in his hand. He'd clearly fired it by accident and now peered down its barrel.

'No!' Eric yelled through the broken window. 'Point it *away* from yourself! And *don't waste the bullets* for God's sake!'

'What's all that noise it makes?' enquired Gorb, still peering into its barrel.

'You're back!' cried Loup, shouldering Eric aside at the window. 'You come on up here, just in time for lunch. Bring up that Otherworld trinket, and we'll have a good old yarn, we will.' Loup beamed a gummy smile down at the half-giant with such warmth it was as if he greeted an old friend. Gorb scratched his confused head and stepped into the lapping waves.

As Gorb made his slow way up the tree, its brittle wood groaning in pain, Eric went to an oblong structure the size of a large dining table, split with a gap across its middle. Only after he'd stared at it for a little while did it become plain this was a model map of Levaal, for scale-built cities and terrain emerged on what had been a blank, flat space. The line dividing the two halves was obviously depicting World's End, where the Wall had stood. At the near tip of the oblong was a large white dragon statue: the castle. The map's southern half remained entirely blank space.

But as he watched, it became more than a map; the scale changed, and he could pan his gaze closer to a region, bringing it out in finer detail. Threads of cloud hovered inches high above the table, mostly white as cotton with the odd dark one pouring down rain and little flickers of lightning. Elvury sat high in a nest of mountains, with thin smoke trails curling in the air.

He panned his gaze back, swept it south. Near the Wall, insect-sized things moved back and forth: the great stoneflesh giants, still patrolling along the boundary. In the north, a large swarm of tiny shapes moved down the Great Dividing Road like a column of ants on the march.

'The cities are all in the middle,' Eric said. 'Why haven't any been built out here?' He pointed to the wide fringes, the land near the inland seas, or beyond walls of mountains.

'That country can't be settled in,' said Siel. 'Terrain's impass-able. Mountains, or marsh you'd sink into. Where it's flat or dry, the soil's too bad to grow food in, and there's no game to hunt. There are elementals and Lesser Spirits and other bad things. Snowstorms, bitter cold.'

'No one lives there at all?'

She shrugged. 'The most far-flung settled places are the villages by the Godstears. There may be small groups of dark-skins in the harsher places. Outlaws sometimes flee there. But none return.'

'It's deliberate,' Eric mused. 'You've been fenced in. Except now someone's kicked down the back wall . . .'

'As It wills,' Siel murmured.

That mentality again, Eric thought. Something 'just is';

there's little curiosity in these people to look closer, to ask why and how. Is it because they can see their gods? Or since there's magic, there's been less need to break the world down to its nuts and bolts?

Gorb had evidently given up trying to climb the grey dead tree by the window, not trusting it to hold his weight. He'd gone through the arch to the whirlpool's steps, and now his footsteps thudded slowly up the winding staircase. 'Strange, down there,' he said, nodding to where the water swirled and burbled. 'Sounds, down below. Almost like voices, mixed with wind.'

And Loup hadn't wanted me to go down there, Eric thought. He made us climb that fucking tree and risk our necks. I'd understand what the voices said – is that why?

'Who are you?' said Loup.

'I'm the one you yelled and threw things at,' said Gorb. 'Then you invited me up here for lunch. Now you don't know me. You're mighty confused, even for a mage.'

'Not you, him!' Loup pointed at the squirming bald man tucked under Gorb's arm.

'Oh. This's Bald. He got lost and almost starved. So I fed him and looked after him and he hung around and made things for us. But you have to keep an eye on him. He gets edgy when he's got nothing to make or take apart. And you should probably know that there'll be trouble here soon, because of Bald.' Gorb set the emaciated, crazed-looking man down. Bald lunged for the gun still in Gorb's hand.

'Here, I'll take the bullets out,' Eric said, 'before you kill someone with that.'

'It won't kill anyone,' Gorb assured him, 'just makes a noise that hurts your ears. Bald, what did you do to that soldier anyway?'

'I have established the thing's *purpose*,' Bald rasped in a voice so terrible it would have suited any comic-book arch-villain Eric had encountered.

'Easy now,' said Loup nervously.

When Gorb handed over the Glock, Bald made a pained sound, then sat himself away from everyone else, face downcast, not moving a muscle.

'What's this about trouble?' Loup asked the half-giant.

Gorb had got almost through his ponderous explanation of events at the village when there was a *thock!* sound outside, then another. An arrow sailed through the broken window and skidded to a halt near the stairwell.

At the water's edge were ten men in chain-mail, two with longbows in hand. They ceased their fire.

'Stay down all of you, pretend you're not here,' said Loup irritably. He went to the window and called down, 'Save your arrows, idiots! Strange times these, you'll soon have better things than my house to shoot at.'

'Your house?' called up the group's leader. 'The locals say your house wasn't here, last week. Nor were you.'

'What of it?' said Loup. 'This land's not claimed by – Tanton, are you from? Not by your city or any other. Piss off. Where I live's my business.'

'Where is the half-giant and his murdering friend?'

'Ehh?!'

'Where is the Pilgrim? Send those ones down and we'll leave you be.'

Loup cackled hysterically, thumping down on the window sill. 'Do you think the lot of you together's enough to overpower a half-giant, if there was one here? Lucky there ain't one! Never seen one angry, have ye? I have, oh aye! More'n once.'

The group's leader laughed grimly. 'There are means to deal with such creatures, and we have them. It is his "friend" we want, an Engineer of our city. Send them down with the Pilgrim and it may all end peacefully.'

'No such thing as Pilgrims. Old myths. Go away or I'll set you on fire.'

'Don't threaten us, fraud,' said the leader while the other men laughed. 'We are told you have the Pilgrims here.'

'Oh there're two of them now, aye? Who's the fraud? Leave me be. You interrupted my nap.'

The men strode cautiously into the lapping waves, while their leader waited at the water's edge. 'Fan out,' he called to them. 'Have a shot trained on the other windows.'

'Don't come nearer!' said Loup.

The soldiers were soon halfway across the water. 'So, old man! What magic have you? Where is your fire?'

Loup stuffed a knuckle in his mouth. He looked to the others for help, when the air was filled with a hissing noise. A horrible scream sounded below. Then it was a chorus of screams. White steam gushed up from the waters, suddenly churning and bubbling like a cook-pot.

A touch late, Loup began a theatrical waving of his arms. The men, shrieking and dropping their weapons, raced back to the shore, where one ran in blind circles, howling with pain. The rest quickly stripped off their leggings and fled, backsides pink and scorched. Their captain gaped up at Loup then backed away. The water calmed and serene waves again curled languidly across it.

'Ahey! See that? Safe here, all right,' cried Loup to his gaping companions, affectionately patting the window sill. 'What's more, I'm starting to wonder if this old house wasn't built *for* us! Maybe they knew you were coming, eh, Eric? They left the pantry full after all. Let's eat!'

THING IN THE WOODS

1

The uppermost of the tower's three floors had eleven beds laid out, four of them recently slept in before Loup had arrived to find the place abandoned.

Now Siel alone was still awake despite the quiet song of breeze and gently lapping waves, which had eased the others to sleep. This strange magic house didn't like her; she could sense it longing to give her nightmares. Dreams sometimes gave her things worse to confront than all the grisly offerings of reality. She dreamed she were living a simple happier life, knew love, had children. In this dream life she'd never killed, never known war or battle. She dreamed of her mother and father growing old, she dreamed of looking after them. Dreamed of their praise, their embraces.

It had been a mistake to pick a bed two down from the Engineer. Though Bald was quiet now, his earlier snoring came with occasional convulsions which threw his thin body over his creaking bed. In the afternoon Eric had at last given in to the Engineer's sulking pleas and let him examine the gun (not before taking out its deadly little pellets). 'He'll make more guns,' Gorb had claimed. 'Those dolls, well, he helped me make them.' The half-giant had been shamefaced, caught in his earlier fib. 'I did their faces. He did the joints and did the things that made them go. We were a team.'

Wind sighed across water. A cool gust blew up from the stairwell, with the hint of a human voice sadly murmuring, *Won't you come and speak with me?* Siel had imagined rather than heard its message, she knew. But still she rose and descended the steps. She walked between the odd black structures on the second floor, all still moving with hypnotic liquid motion. The shallow pool of water glimmered. Even Loup had no idea of the purpose of these devices.

She gazed around at it all then spat in disgust, no doubt displeasing the house further. Disgust at those aloof, cowardly wizards who'd suffered their defeat, then hidden in comfort through nearly three centuries, passive through so much evil, lending no help to the common people who worked and died to avenge them.

She went to the broken window and gazed out. The waves below lapped with their patient insistence, edged with luminous traces of silver. For a time she gazed at them, lulled almost to sleep, till movement at the shore caught her eye. Something big very quickly crossed the thirty or so paces to the tree line. It seemed only a blurred patch of night, but a glimmering flash of gold and silver trailed it; a puff of beautiful cloud which fell in hard sparkling pieces to the ground in a rain of bouncing gems. They made a faint sound, like tinkling bells. The lumps of beauty melted into the grass.

Siel exclaimed in wonder. Her heart beat fast. And, there! Movement by the trees, the glimmer of eyes inhuman, more beautiful than human: ancient and knowing and smiling eyes, peering right through the window into her own. An invitation to come outside, the eyes spoke it as loud as words. *Come and play.*

A gust of air pushed from behind her, drafting up from the stairway, almost as though the tower was urging her: *go on*. The tower that didn't like her. That had tripped her up, had tried to make her fall from the window ledge, which surely wished her ill ...

And yet she found herself up on the window sill, stepping onto the thin but firm tree branch out there. Her bow and knife were back by the bed she'd slept in, but she had little thought of that. Down the trunk she slid, landing hard on the little patch of turf around the tree's base, hesitating before putting one bare foot down in the slow-moving waves.

In the dark woods, the eyes were gone from where she'd seen them, if they'd been there at all.

The water was cold. The screams of the burning Tantonese soldiers echoed in her mind. One step, two steps ... soon she was far enough in that she would not avoid being cooked if the waters boiled again. She ran the rest of the way, puffing, filled with adrenaline. She crouched at the water's edge and caught her breath.

And only here, now, did she wonder what in blazes she was *doing*, walking unarmed into the clutches of some unknown power. This was so unlike her she was tempted in a fit of self-reproach to finish the job, walk headlong into the consequences and make sure her punishment was complete.

The sound of branches moving. High in the trees, the white flash of an Invia's wings. There were two of them, there then gone. Something large moved through the thicket with fast thudding footfalls. What seemed a trail of golden smoke puffed behind it; the sparkling mist coalesced into more of those nuggets and coloured gems, raining to the ground with tinkling music, then melting away into liquid gold.

Siel went toward the woods, forgetting herself again. She had not felt this way before, had barely been aware there was some part of life she'd missed living. It was as though a light had been thrown on in a dark room within her, showing something surprising and wonderful which had been there all along. She was tasting youth again, rather tasting it properly for the first time, without grief's bitterness. If only she'd take a few more steps, just into the row of trees there ...

So she did, moving deeper into the woods' gloom. The tree bark smelled fresh; undergrowth's needles and leaves whispered as her boots disturbed them. Between trunks thick as pillars some way ahead were those eyes, watching her. Ancient eyes. Some bulk shifted behind them with feline agility. A gleam flashed off its flanks. Closer it came, its precise shape still obscured as though by a gown of night. She retreated till her back was to a tree. Here is death maybe, but I don't care, part of her rebelled. What does dying matter if you've never really lived? Trade me now an hour's life for three or four decades' death and fear. Take it! Make good your promise, give me life for a little while.

The big shape moved sideways, was gone just as she was about to see it properly, left her peering into empty gloom. There was its presence behind her, something caressing her leg, running up one leg then the other and sending a ripple of pleasure from its touch which moved in shivering waves through her whole body, most intense in her mind, heart and between her legs. She gasped, surrendered to it. Something closed about her like curtains, enfolding her in darkness while the gently tracing thing, whatever it was, slid up her thigh. The air was filled with a musky scent.

Something said: 'May I speak with you?'

'Yes,' she gasped.

There the eyes were, right before her again, above her, filled with noble pleading sincerity. 'I will name you *Hathilialin*, which means *great beauty* in the tongue of my people. I have called you here, you have come. Is that not so?'

'Yes.'

The deep whispering voice was a caress which sent pleasure rippling from her mind down. 'I will protect you, I will teach you. I will fertilise your mind. Only if your trust of me is total. You must give it, there is no time to earn it slowly. If I wished you harm, I have you here and vulnerable. Do I not?'

'Yes,' was all she could say.

'Of all your kind who have ever lived, so few have beheld my race, much less been given *this* high honour, Great Beauty. Yet you are not here reduced; you are elevated. I do not wish you harm. I offer you a place among the Favoured. Do you wish to claim it? You may leave here unhurt and free if this gift is not desired, if your life of trial and pain calls you in a sweeter voice than mine.'

She almost said *yes* again, but she felt a slight relaxing of the force clouding her mind. She clutched weakly at her thoughts, tried to understand what was meant by the word 'favoured'. It was a term she'd heard before, but where?

Something coiled like a long reaching arm around her thigh, grabbing tighter, hinting at far more powerful strength behind it. Pleasure pulsed from it through her. She came quickly once, twice, a pause, then a third time which shook her whole body and left her close to collapsing. Above her an Invia shifted in her perch and stared down with eyes bright and blue as sapphires, its white wings spread wide.

Waves of pleasure, slow to subside, still went through her.

The thing waited patiently, eased off its grip, made a deep sound like whinnying laughter as though pleased with itself. 'Do you see now how things could be, if you would join me? How easily the two of us may—'

Then something broke whatever force was at play. Her seducer's attention was divided; she felt its surprise and panic as though those feelings had hit her like a blast of wind.

What happened next was too fast for her to follow. There was the rushing bulk of something close by, quite possibly the thing which had seduced her, knocking her to the ground as it went; fast as fevered percussion the thud of heavy feet; an eerie shriek of pain or surprise. Something large crashed into a trunk and ripped it out of the ground. Two Invia took off from trees overhead with whistling cries. Heavier wings than theirs beat the air.

The silence that followed was watchful and tense. Siel heard her own pulse loud as a drum and tried to slow her breathing.

'That was hard,' said a voice which made her jump. She had felt she was alone again. She scrambled to her feet. 'Don't go yet.' The voice was like Eric's but flat and lifeless. There he was before her, arms hung clumsily. His dark clothes blended with the gloom, his outline visible only because he stood between her and the tower's lapping water, glimmering with its silvery light. Siel's hand went to where her knife usually hung but of course it wasn't there. Useless or not she longed for its feel in her hand more than she ever had. 'What was that thing?' she said, panting. Her head still spun and her body hummed with warmth and pleasure, but she felt sick.

'The thing that had you? I don't know what it's called.'

Something clicked in her mind. 'Shadow,' she said. 'Your name is Shadow.'

'Are you impressed that I could do that?' he said.

'Do what?'

'Become it. Or nearly, anyway. Just briefly, for a moment. It was hard to do. Harder than being you, or being the fellow, or those other things that I . . .' He sought for a word.

'Those things you shadowed?'

He stared at her through two small dark pits. 'Shadowed. Yes, that fits well. I scared it away, that thing which had you. Could you tell? It thought I was another one of its kind. It wasn't expecting that. It thinks nothing can hurt it down here.' His body had slowly tilted till it leaned at an impossible angle.

'Don't *do* that,' she said. '*Stop it!*'

He spun around as though his feet were the centre point of a spoke, two quick spins seeing his body vanish into the ground and then reappear, upright. 'Why don't you like it?' he said. 'It doesn't mean you're about to get hurt.'

'Who are you now, Shadow?' she said, trying to speak his language.

'No one. Nothing, mostly. I was that thing which had you, just before, just now. Not completely, really I was just a part of it. It didn't know I was here until I did it. I like some of what it did to you. Can I tell you something? That's why I . . . *shadowed* it. To do those things to you too. But when it ran away, I went back to this.' His limp arms shrugged to indicate himself. 'And I can't *shadow* it now it's gone. I like the way it touched you. I like the sounds you made. Can you make them again? Can you make them now? They sounded nice. They made me want to touch you.'

She spat.

'I like what it did with the gold stuff, too. To trick you and make you come nearer. That was good! I couldn't do it, when I was . . . when I was more like it than I am now. I tried to.'

'Where did the thing go, Shadow?'

'Gone. Back to that other woman maybe.'

'Other woman?'

'Green dress. It left her. She cried. I watched, when the wolf found her. She was scared of him but not of the other thing, which was bigger than the wolf. I didn't understand why.'

'Stranger's here? Is she close?'

'Oh. Yes, she's close. She's coming here, with the wolf. They're trying to find you. She was hanging around you and the fellow for a while. Like me. Following. Watching.'

Shadow very quickly sank into the ground as though it had swallowed him. He reappeared standing side-on high up on the trunk of a tree, as though the word had tilted on that angle just for him.

'Please don't do that,' she said.

He looked down at her. 'Why?'

'Just don't. Please.'

'I don't even *do* it. It just happens. I'll shadow you. Want me to?' Suddenly he was very close behind her. She jumped, backed away, tripped and fell. 'You can see backward along the axis,' he said, pointing at some invisible line ahead and behind her. 'I remember now. You're the only one who can.'

'No I'm not,' she said, sitting up, rubbing where a tree root had hit her back. 'It's happenstance. Other people have it too. Stranger, the green dress. What is she? Why is she so powerful, where is she from?'

'I can show you,' said Shadow. Suddenly he was leaning over her, at an angle almost horizontal. Eric's face, with longer flowing hair and those hollow pits for eyes, was close enough to kiss her. 'Should I show you?'

'Yes. Show me.'

His arms reached out to grab her and the world fell away.

2

It felt like he clutched her loosely and that any moment she'd slip free of his arms. Lights whizzed by, the world whizzed by at impossible speed. The Great Dividing Road was beneath them for a time, dead straight. They veered off from it over downward-sloping plains, across more roads, miles and miles eaten up. She tried to find the air to speak, to tell him to stop, to scream in fear and sickness. Then just as suddenly it was over; she was on the ground gasping, unable to move, sick and dizzy. She threw up while he stood there and watched and waited.

It seemed a long time before she recovered. She wanted to attack him, spit curses at him, but had no power to do it. 'You can see back along the axis,' he said. 'So now I can too, but I can do it better than you. I shadowed you, see? We can look back together. You're not as hard to shadow as that thing was, in the woods.'

'Where are we?' she said.

'It's where we have to be to learn about the green dress. I cheated. I looked forward on the axis to when we'd learn about it. That's how I knew to come here. Then we came here and we'll make it happen, by looking *back*. It's like bending a little part of the axis into a circle. Why can't you do that?'

She looked about, half recognising the country. 'Wait – you can control when and where to look, in the past and future?'

'Some parts of it,' said his deadpan voice. 'When you leave, I'll forget how. I can do more things than you can. But I couldn't do most of the stuff that thing in the woods could do, when I shadowed it. Do you understand?'

'I think so, Shadow.'

'I've taken us back along the axis.'

'Back in time you mean.'

'Time? Sure, call it that.'

'How, Shadow? How did you do it? We can't really be here. But we aren't in our present time any more either. So where *are* we?'

'I don't know. It's the same as moving around fast. I don't understand things, I just do them. Look up there if you want to learn.' He pointed at the sky where a long shape loomed, visible only because little points of light glinted off its dark flanks.

'A dragon!' Siel's jaw dropped. It was bigger than a horse, bigger than a drake. It seemed to ripple like a boneless creature swimming through water, with a wide span of pinioned wings, a sleek head. Its long body was of slender proportion but thick with muscle.

It landed near them with the feline grace of a cat's leap, shook itself like a wet dog, its mane of fins and leathery spikes slapping against its flank with a sound of whipping leather. A serpentine tail snaked out behind it, ridged with spikes. Its long mouth was set in a curved grin. She recognised its eyes, the same ones that had peered at her from the woods. Its head swept around, gazed at where she and Shadow stood ... but if this was the past, a glance back, surely it didn't *see* them.

Nonetheless its gaze lingered on their spot, its brow furrowed. It sniffed deeply, frowned at some anomaly. Then its head reared up and with impressive noise it sneezed a white foamy spray into the air, made a gagging sound, cleared its throat of a blockage, spat, yawned.

A Minor personality, Siel thought with amazement which swept aside almost everything else she'd seen and felt tonight. She knew so little of dragons, had only once seen a drake from her father's shoulders as they walked home, not long before the city's invasion. It had been so distant she'd doubted since that it had been more than a bird. There *were* no dragons, not free to roam like this in the human realm!

On four legs, the dragon – Smaller than she'd have expected! Weren't they rumoured to be enormous? – moved forward with a crab-like walk, covering ground quickly. Without warning it slipped into a groundman hole she hadn't even seen.

'I know where it's going,' said Shadow, his voice again making her jump. He grabbed her before she could reply. They sped down the groundman tunnels, right through the slithering dragon's body, which barely fit through the narrow spaces. Suddenly they were in the underground chamber which Anfen had described all too clearly: the place Stranger had taken him. There were those trapped souls, caught up in claw-like hooks on the wall. She did not feel the place's horrible heat; but she remembered talk of those hot hooks burning the flesh of 'new mages' being formed. And there in their midst was Stranger, naked like the rest, her eyes closed, her face like that of a sleeper with troubling dreams. The claws holding her had not wormed their way as deeply into her flesh as had those in the bodies around her.

'Can they hear us?' said Siel.

'No. The dragon's coming.'

They waited. Minutes later, a cloud of smoky light flowed

turgidly into the chamber. It crystallised slowly into the dragon's shape, solidified like mist becoming ice. 'It couldn't fit through the tunnels,' said Shadow. 'That's why it changed to gas. It doesn't like doing that. Hurts it.'

The dragon did indeed look nonplussed once it had finally changed back into its true form; it spat and licked its teeth as though it had tasted something vile. It hopped down from the upper perch to the floor level, then strolled up and down the line of bodies, not bothering with the men, but pausing before each of the women to examine them closely. Every so often, it would very gently nudge one with its nose or paw. When it got to Stranger, it gave an odd shiver, stroked her with the dark tip of its tail, then seemed to weigh up a choice: her, or another it had lingered over before, a few bodies back.

It hooked its tail behind the claws pinning Stranger in place and, with a strain that made it shiver for a second or two, ripped them out of the stone wall one by one, also employing its teeth for the task. It caught her arm in its mouth as she slumped to the ground, then laid her carefully down, stroking her from head to toe with the point of its tail.

The dragon turned about, glanced again directly at them, frowned (How human the frown seemed!) in disquiet before examining its prize again.

'You know what it does now,' said Shadow.

'What?' she whispered.

'It started with you, till I interrupted it. It makes you its house.'

'I don't understand.'

Shadow considered his words. 'The dragon wanted to ride inside you. So it can stay hidden. It's like if you were riding on the dragon's back. It can only do it if you let it. Like you could only ride its back if *it* let you. That's why it was doing what it did to you, making you feel good so you would let it in. I could tell that much when I shadowed it. It only rides women. It likes your bodies. The shape, I guess. I do too. They're nice.'

The dragon's head bent low. It – *he*, Siel felt quite sure it was male – whispered in Stranger's ear, and she showed signs of stirring. 'It has to ask. Has to get permission. She'll be scared at first, then she'll agree, and be happy. Until it leaves her for the wolf to find. Then she'll hate it. I've seen enough now. I'm going.'

'Wait!'

'What for?'

'Take me back to the tower.'

Shadow looked at her with his hole-eyes. 'I don't want to go all the way back there. I want to see what else there is around here.'

'Don't you dare leave me here. Take me *back*. Like you said you would.'

'Only if you make that sound you made. With the dragon, back in the woods. I liked that sound.'

'*What*?' She spat at him instead. Then he was gone and she was alone in the chamber.

HER RAIN FALLS

1

Tempest's mood shifted like the restless pulse and heave of the world's water. She had many homes. The rivers and lakes were hers.

The skies were hers in part, their wind and rain and cloud. She could be many places. She could be spread thin as scattered raindrops, millions of eyes collecting little glimpses of the world as they fell, to coalesce later and be seen as a whole. Or she would howl in wild temper, lashing down on the further seas where no people went, where there were only wild forces. So-called Vyan's sea (his no longer!) was a favoured place for wild moods, for smashing glaciers and bergs together, screaming her voice as winds that blasted the heaving waves.

Just occasionally the Godstears – A far better name for a sea! – would get a good shake too, enough to make its furthest reaching waves lap upon the feet of its villages. Seldom more than that, seldom the tsunamis which swept these polite people into its waters, their polite bodies gently bobbing, feeding the fish they usually ate.

It had been a while; perhaps it was time for another such storm. They provoked, strangely, yet more rituals and prayers, *exquisitely* polite. Fevers of them for years and years.

Now on those shimmering waves she languidly stretched. The lines of some Godstears fishermen passed through the very easternmost part of her. If they could share eyes with the gulls flying overhead, they'd have seen her face: enormous, long and stretched across the heaving blue, bent around the curve of the shore. The fishermen speculated on where she was today, when she would send rain. The water burbled with her laughter – she enjoyed hearing herself discussed, politely or otherwise. She summoned a school of big fish for them, set it loose among their lines and nets, and watched, pleased, their delight as they hauled aloft an impressive catch and praised their own handiwork.

Then day ended, the men went home, night came and she moved from there, a breeze taking the sparkle off the water like someone blowing flame from a billion little candles. She was high now, dispersed in the wind and cloud. Off in the northeast, in the fields of Kopyn, a family had made their ritual for rain, clumsily done but polite in intent. She'd heard them previously do something much more elaborate but had not felt like obliging. Now she saw no harm in tossing a handful of wet sky their way. She did so, perhaps a touch more rain than they'd expected, and certainly its arrival more abrupt. No matter! Funny little things.

Why not send more water down? The clouds were hers. The lazy sleeping Dragon may shift them about, but they'd come back to *her*, they were *hers* and she'd make them weep if she wanted to, wherever they went. She summoned a thick grey blanket about her, thicker and thicker, turned it dark and poured water down on the castle, beating water on the great stone walls. The window panes streamed in that place where the new Spirit grew, the place the other Spirits never dared go near.

Brave new Spirit! Vous its name, weak for now but growing. Its purpose she didn't understand, so different it seemed from the others, and from her.

But she had no thoughts for it now. She was too caught up in the joy of drenching the world, the pure free joy brought by what looked like falling tears. It was the same feeling as the first ever rainfall. In a way, it *was* the first all over again. It didn't matter that the world she drenched had changed, whether dragons or humans roamed about down there: wet, wet, wet! Her laughter pattered down and gushed over the castle's glistening flanks, gently teasing the Dragon, so close, which did not sense her here, would never know of her jest and laughter.

And many little glimpses the raindrops caught for later as they slid down the castle windows …

2

The Arch Mage paced the Hall of Windows, head craned sideways beneath the weight of three horns that had never felt so cumbersome as they did now. He looked over the note-takers' shoulders to read their useless scrawl. And with Vous's words still clattering through his mind – *lies, Avridis* – he watched those Windows to see what they might show him now.

Nothing beyond World's End. None of the wonders and mysteries they'd been eager to show him before.

In the Windows were glimpses of men fighting in the dark, trebuchets flinging stones at Faifen's walls, people dragged from homes outside the city, his men having their way with enemy women. The city would fall by morning. Tsith would be his by the week's end. The rest within a month. Normally all this would be pleasing theatre, to see an enemy crushed.

'Have any of you seen the girl?' he said, knowing to ask was futile. Along the row of grey-robes manning the Windows, all heads swivelled toward him, each expression blank and serene. 'Have you seen the girl?' he repeated. 'Answer me. Each of you.'

'Not I, Arch Mage.'

'Not I, Arch Mage.'

Dozens of identical answers and their heads turned back to the screens before them.

Rage like a curtain of red fire was pulled over his eyes. The airs about him fluttered in response to it. His fist clenched, shaking, on his staff. He drove its forked point through the neck of the nearest Window-watcher. A grunt, a convulsion, then the mind-controlled thing slumped to the floor and obediently died. The two seated to either side, needing no instruction, stood and dragged the body away, while another fetched a mop to clean the red trail slicked behind it.

The Arch watched the blood get cleaned up, reprimanding himself for the loss of control, then resumed his pacing.

Aziel's voice: *Arch, you know who did it! But ... what is on the other side? Are there people there?*

He went to a regular window and gazed through a sheet of rain at the Entry Point's tall fenced valley, hidden in the dark but its features so familiar he could practically see it. For a long time he stared, wondering if it would ever be necessary to flee there, wondering how that place would handle magic, which it *seemed* not to possess. How it would handle a shuffling horde of Tormentors pouring through its cities? For that matter, how would it handle a demented god set loose? (It seemed not to have gods either.)

In the Windows behind him, soldiers taught to scorn Valour's ideals for war cast open the city gates and rushed in, their blade arms threshing through men, women and children, whether they fought or fled or surrendered, trampling the falling bodies. The grey-robes took notes, observing with expressionless faces as rain washed the city's blood-slicked streets clean.

3

Tempest was spread thin and far. She lashed the backs of soldiers marching directly along the Great Dividing Road with the push behind them. They clogged the human-built highways, which branched away from the Road like a river system of pavement. They went with care, these armies, for the foreign things were about, loose from their herders beneath the surface. Or else the creatures had wandered from Elvury, where big numbers of them still held the city as their own. Over there Tempest slapped rain hard on their tough spiked hides, causing a flurry of movement among the dark shapes which had been motionless (and, it seemed, purposeless) as statues. She did not like them very much.

The greedy River Misery gorged itself. And there went yet more armies, the men opening canisters to the sky to collect her flung drops without a word of thanks, on their way to kill others just like them. In Faifen the process was in full swing. A big number of them surrounded the city's walls, gathered about its main gate. Beyond its eastern fields, hidden in grass and the cover of night, more of them waited in secret with blades ready to get those who'd flee that way. The roads looked clear and unimpeded but those thirsty knives waited unseen. There came the first wave, and the knives caught them like teeth in closing jaws. Some were allowed to escape the massacre and spread the tale. Tempest drenched the fields, washing blood from the grass and dirt.

She battered window panes of a cabin where the mayor, Liha, sat ashen-faced across from a man in castle colours. He was alone, clean shaven and young, his face expressing grave sympathy. 'Those who lay down their arms may flee by the gate, but shall vacate our land at once. They have an hour to fetch their families and treasures. After that ...' He shrugged.

'You will allow them to flee and join the other cities?' the Mayor said sceptically.

'*This* dispute is my focus.'

Liha stood defiantly as she began to reply but Tempest, not interested in this drama, left them.

Sad creatures. The dragons had quarrelled now and then, but rarely done such things as this to their own.

Southward then, and where was Mountain? How good he was at hiding, for one so large. What were his thoughts? Hidden, always hidden! No matter. She stretched across the sky so that nearly all the ground at once got a taste of her water, right down to the very southern parts where Nightmare worked with some difficulty to keep the stoneflesh giants from going past World's End. The giants felt the same firm push that made the clouds go south, and each longed to cross over. How easily were the young gods frightened!

Her energy was easing. She folded in on herself, concentrated her rains on a small patch in the middle of the world, randomly chosen. Among other roofs, her heavy drops battered an inn.

She looked through windows her water ran down in sheets, but she was dissipating, tiring, and listened to the men inside like someone hearing a story before sleep.

THE WARRIOR'S RETURN

1

The stool was a tad uneven under Sharfy's rump, tilting it like a boat in water. Or more like a boat in a tide of beer. Braziers and brands held the night off with a flickering glow that seemed angelic. The world was indeed a fine place, these strangers dear friends, and the tavern's rowdy babble a warm blanket wrapped around him. Bad memories were balmed or forgotten, or better yet completely rewritten.

Even the innkeeper's criminally overpriced beer was no issue any more. Everyone had complained until about their fourth or fifth. Sharfy had kept it up till he could barely see how many coins he shoved across the bar top through spilled overpriced puddles of it.

Like inns all down the Great Dividing Road, the place was stuffed with men who had hit on the only worthwhile thing left to do. The sense that all would be soon resolved was as strong as the smell of ale and sweat. Rain drummed the tavern roof, a heavenly sound drunk or sober. It reminded him there *was* a roof overhead, that time on the road was over, at least until his pockets emptied (and he had not forgotten the art of robbery, should that occur). And in all likelihood, time on the road was over forever. Let the end find him pissed or snoring.

He drained his cup to that, slammed it down, slurred for another.

World's End. How that name had revealed its second meaning like a mask falling off someone who had seemed familiar. Sharfy kind of felt he should have understood it long ago, him and everyone else. An omen from the smart-arse seer who'd named it, laughing at the distant generations who would one day discover his jest.

The *war* was certainly lost, whether or not catastrophe crept its way from World's End. Lost with it was any sense of purpose to Sharfy's life. These men around him were just as doomed, yet only a few seemed to know it. Around the bar he could spot the ones who didn't know: grim-faced, they huddled together making plans, mapping out what each Mayor was likely to do, as if it mattered. The ones who had *half* an inkling were morose or shocked-looking, staring into the distance and draining more than the planners. The ones who *really* knew were cheerful like Sharfy, almost openly celebrating the life that was forfeit while still they could.

Sharfy drained his mug again, slammed it down too hard, earning a glower from the barkeeper. People looked at him that way so often he barely noticed. He belched and gestured for more, eavesdropping on conversation around him while waiting for his chance to jump in with a war story.

The talk was that nothing had yet come through from beyond World's End. There was some kind of veil keeping the place hidden from sight. What dwelled in the lands behind it? Some claimed it was people, just like those who lived here. 'Perhaps their help could be had in the war.'

Some optimistic fools predicted treasures untold lay in mountainous piles for the taking, scales, gems and charms. They were going to go and claim it; who was in?

Others said in that place dragons still roamed free, and would come here to release their cousins from their sky holds . . .

All of it rot. A year of life left, Sharfy guessed. It would be spent downing all the beer he'd dreamed of when pulling roots out of the ground or hauling rocks in the slave farm. There were girls for hire in the parlour too, many of them having fled Elvury with no possessions and not natural to this sad trade at all. A buyer's market. Tempting. Looks alone certainly wouldn't get Sharfy laid and he'd not thirsted only for ale on those hard days. But he'd seen Kiown like a swine at a feed trough around girls for sale, like a cruel slobbering dog, and had sworn never to stoop to that (not that he never had). He resolved to slip some coin to one or two of them, maybe with a kind word, for the sole purpose of telling Kiown about it next time they met.

Next time. Strange, how hard it was to keep from thinking like there was still a future to be had. Meanwhile the old vet had finished his story about the Hashlam massacre and a gap opened up for a voice to fill. Sharfy jumped in fast. 'Did I tell you about the Pilgrim, from Otherworld?'

Some piqued interest, some rolled eyes, surely directed at the old vet (whose story Sharfy too had found somewhat implausible).

'Tell it,' said someone.

He didn't need to be asked twice. 'It was a clear day. The Entry Point opened, right behind the castle. Like a window in the sky. There were war mages. Eight of em. And the Pilgrim came in. Clothes were strange. He wielded an Otherworld weapon, which he named *Gun*. It breathed fire, louder than . . . louder than when a storm knocks a big branch onto the roof.' Pleasing! He'd fallen dearly in love with *window in the sky* too. 'Deadly it was, *Gun.* But he was so scared he couldn't use it. It was the first war mage he ever seen. It killed a hundred men who already came in. And it went for him too. I was too far away to help him. But the Pilgrim was a prince in his own land—'

A burly man in Faifen colours who had just sat down interrupted, 'Pilgrim! My arse has spoken sweeter lies.'

'Was, too,' said Sharfy. 'You heard of him? Some people's calling him Shadow, but his name's not Shadow. S'Eric. I knowed him. Taught him some sword play. This scar? He done it. Wields a good blade. Fast as any I seen, since my war days. Fast as me, when I was younger. I teached it to him. So listen. The war mages killed a thousand other Pilgrims. But when Eric come through, I got there in time to save him. I jumped out into the field—'

'You speak shit,' said the newcomer. 'Never happened. None of it. None of the rest of your claptrap either. I heard you last night, belching such gas. We could be trading talk of what to do in this tumult and we're listening to your rot.'

'Nothing we can do.'

'A coward too. You never swung a blade.'

Sharfy almost slipped off his stool in outrage. 'I sparred with Anfen every day on the road.'

'Who?'

'He won Valour's Helm four times. He was the one brought down the Wall. I was there when he done it.' The big man laughed. The others around him joined in rather than mind their own stinking business (or better yet, politely listen to Sharfy's tale). 'I killed ten front-rankers in the Pyren battle,' said Sharfy, his good mood souring. 'Did time in the farms for it. *And* I got out alive. You probably don't know about the farms. Or the mines. Cos no one gets out alive. But I did.'

The newcomer grinned wide through his beard. 'Ten front rank, you say?'

'Ten in *that* fight. There's been more.'

'Finishing off the wounded after the battle, notching your belt, aye? Then off to boast. I've met such men before.'

Sharfy observed the man's left hand, where the skin was rubbed red from drawing arrows. 'Ten front-rankers. That's *from* the front rank. Not sitting away from the blades with a stringed coward-stick. Safe as the Mayors back home.'

The burly man's eyes went hard. He set his beer down. 'You saw me come in with my bow last night, it seems, but are too stupid to know the difference between a hunting bow and a fighting one.'

A ripple of quiet went through the room as heads turned to watch what was unavoidable at this point. 'I do secret ops for the Mayors' Command,' Sharfy slurred. 'Used to. S'why I met the Pilgrims.'

'Then you are to be feared.' The burly man took in a mouthful of beer then spat it in Sharfy's face. The watchers laughed.

Sharfy got up from his stool, made the universal gesture of hand-to-hand challenge and headed to the exit. To lay this bastard out inside might get him turfed from the inn, and he rather liked this place. The burly man laughed at the challenge but he followed. 'Merry one, you are,' said Sharfy, wiping the spat beer from his face with both sleeves.

'A good bit of sport you are,' the man said cheerfully. No doubt in the fellow's mind who was about to be embarrassed. Sharfy was equally assured, though the floor seemed to tilt and he walked into the door frame on his way out. No matter. He'd been drunker than this and beaten better than this.

Only a small crowd gathered outside, the other drinkers put

off by the rain still coming down and not wishing to give up their seats to watch what promised to be a brief and unremarkable fight. The two combatants squared off by the roadside. Sharfy's opponent was a few years his junior, much larger, with broad shoulders and a longer reach. He didn't mind that; the big ones were not used to being challenged and often swung clumsily. What's more, best an opponent of this size and they'd buy him drinks all night, hear every tale he wished to tell.

Mud squelched around his boots as he got into his preferred fighting stance for hand-to-hand. His opponent advanced, fists raised like a common brawler. Sharfy saw immediate mistakes in the way the man held himself and felt a surge of confidence.

A bob left then right, with good speed for someone so big. Sharfy himself however seemed to be moving rather slowly. He threw what he felt should have been a decisive blow at where his opponent had been just a moment ago. Which it turned out was far too late. A large forearm very swiftly tried to occupy the same space as Sharfy's head. With a dull explosion of pain slow to filter through the beer he dropped like a flung sack. His face fell in mud delightfully soft and cool.

One blow. What a mercy he would not remember it took only one blow.

'Roll him over so he's not face down in a puddle,' said the victor when he was done laughing with the spectators. 'Just because he's a fool doesn't mean he should be drowned.'

'What about robbed?' said another.

'Suit yourself.' More laughter. Sharfy blacked out as hands fished through his pockets.

2

When his eyes peeled open, a fine drizzling mist slanted against the dull orange from a group of distant lit windows. It was still night. Sharfy's head throbbed badly but he could not remember why. With some dismay he found his pockets relieved of their coins. He had taken far too much money to the bar . . . he thanked the Spirits for the little locked box under his bed.

The world spun a little and his head pounded. He shivered and sat up, rubbing his arms for warmth. The inn's bar – usually an all-nighter – had put out its lights, which could only mean they'd run out of beer. How much of it did my coin pay for? he wondered sadly.

Despite the rain he still stank of the beer which had been spat in his face (the very last point of memory which had just returned, and he feared it helped fill in the parts that were missing).

There was a shriek from the sky – and not too far – which was unmistakeably that of a war mage. Another sounded much further away, and another. Shivers went down his back when he heard how many of them there were. Most of the township's window lights went out at once. They'd not have heard the sound here in some while, but they knew it all right. He almost felt them passing overhead. Then their cries faded.

When Sharfy sat up it was a shock to find he was not alone. The man stood some way behind him with feet planted apart, one hand on the hilt of his sword, the other behind his back. A hood covered his face, but Sharfy knew who he was looking at. The surprise of it stunned him speechless for a moment. 'I wouldn't be here if I were you,' he said, his voice croaking.

'I am not,' said Anfen quietly.

Sharfy grunted. His poor throbbing head did not need cryptic remarks, not right now. 'Mayors looking for you,' he elaborated. 'Bounties. Lots of military, hereabouts. Inns are packed with em. Some know of you, some don't. Some know who to blame for all the trouble.'

'None know me.'

'I heard what I heard.'

'They won't find me,' Anfen said. 'I'll lose them in the quiet.'

Mad? Sharfy thought. Always has been, a little at least. Something's different though.

'Why do you sleep in the rain?' said Anfen.

'Beaten,' said Sharfy. 'Five of em. Waited till I was drunk.'

'Where is your weapon?' said Anfen.

'My room.'

'Fetch it. And all else you need. We march, now.'

Sharfy squinted up through the drizzle at his former leader. *Former* seemed especially relevant just now. After his initial impulse to laugh there came a flare of anger quite foreign to him, and it had nothing to do with the preposterous idea of 'marching' anywhere at this hour, in the rain. 'Where'd you go?' he said. 'They're looking for you. The Mayors. I heard talk of it. They don't know if you did it or not. But they think you had a hand in it. Traitor, they think. Spy all along, they think. Double dealer. Had em swindled.'

'Did what?'

Sharfy's anger grew sharper. 'You know what. Why'd you do it? Why? Look what you did. It was nothing good. The world's a mess now. Why didn't you see it would be like that?'

'Do what?'

'Destroy the Wall. Don't lie, I know you did it. I rode south with you, remember? What help did you think it would be to do that? How'd you do it anyhow? Don't tell me the catapults was enough. No catapult did *that*. Wall was too strong. It was something else. You used a charm or something.'

There was an almost imperceptible bowing of Anfen's hooded head. His silence seemed pained.

Sharfy got to his feet. The world spun around just once then righted itself. 'Bastard. I should turn you in. Should kill you. There'll be rewards for your head.'

'Go get your weapon and whatever else you need,' Anfen said. 'Hurry.' Sharfy was taken aback by the new note of quiet command in his voice. Not sure what else to do, he headed back to the inn, around to its rear after-hours door. There he was allowed in grudgingly by a night man, jittery from the war mage cries.

Sharfy was marching nowhere but to bed. Then he found his room was locked. His belongings had not been left out in the hall. The night man checked his book, explained the room had been found empty and thus rented again – no shortage of people sleeping in cellars and cupboards who'd pay good coin for a room. After much argument Sharfy got his upcoming week's rent refunded, minus an obscene amount for the broken door lock, kicked in by whoever had robbed him. 'Give me a closet then,' Sharfy said. 'Inn's supposed to be a home on the road. Supposed to look after you. Hard times or not.'

The night man said a closet would cost him what he had just refunded. Sharfy knocked him flat and wrestled with the locked box his coin had just been dropped into. At the sound of its coins rattling footsteps rushed across the floor above, descended the staircase. There was a metal hiss of an unsheathed blade. Sharfy grabbed the cheap little sword from an ornamental coat of arms on his way out the door.

Back outside in the drizzle Anfen had not moved at all from his stance by the roadside. 'Robbed,' Sharfy muttered, more hurt by this betrayal than he'd ever admit.

'Get your steed.'

'None. Sold it. Got nothing.'

'Come, then.'

'Where to?'

No answer. He trudged after Anfen in the squelching grass and mud until the township was well behind them. They were soon on the Great Dividing Road, so wide its eastern edge could not be seen in the gloom. A wagon went *clip-clopping* by on the ancient unbreakable pavement, completely unseen to them. Anfen stood silent for some time in the misty rain, his head bowed. 'Do you feel that?' he said.

'Wet?' said Sharfy.

'Watch.' Anfen unsheathed his sword. Sharfy noticed it was not the sword he'd had when they parted company. A glint like white gold in firelight flashed down its face. He stuck it, point first, into the turf at the Road's very edge. A second passed and the blade slowly leaned south until it fell.

Sharfy said, 'What about it?'

Anfen stuffed it back into the ground with the handle leaning far to their left – the north. In seconds it had turned like the hand of a clock until it collapsed again in the opposite direction.

'Huh!' said Sharfy.

'The push,' said Anfen. He plucked a handful of pebbles and

let them slip from his hand to the Road's pavement, watching
the slight southward curve of their fall. They rolled along the
Road as though blown by strong wind, though no wind could
be felt. 'I know things I did not know before,' said Anfen. 'We
must walk into the push for a while. There is work to be done,
Sharfy. If I told you the Pendulum swings again. What say you
to that?'

Sharfy rubbed the rain from his face and wished the night
were several hours younger again. 'I'm too drunk to know
what you mean. Or maybe you're too drunk to know what
you mean.'

'It means time is short. And the Pendulum must be stopped,
though it is probably too late. There's much to do. Come.'

To his dismay, Anfen began the journey Sharfy already
knew he was bound to, though he did not know why he *should*
be.

The war's done, he wanted to yell in protest. *Leave me to rest! I
done enough fighting! The war's done!*

3

For long days they walked, days that blended into one dream-
like stretch, where the world went a strangely purple twilight
Sharfy had never seen before. Had he the words to express it,
he'd have said it seemed he looked back on old memories even
as the minutes and hours passed, all sights taken in through
sleep-blurred eyes, all thoughts subdued.

Sleeping, eating, and other routine things were the least of
Anfen's concerns. Each brief stop for rest had to be argued for
against abstract responses Sharfy didn't understand in the

slightest. The land about them was eerily empty of people for most of these dreamy stretches; entire days went by without running into a single traveller in lands that should have been swarming. For that matter, on some days he'd have sworn there was hardly a bird call or the buzz of a fly, and the country seemed unfamiliar to him, missing its various landmarks. Anfen marched tall and proud in those quiet times, his strides full of purpose.

Then this dreaminess would at times fall away, reality would rear up in all its grim clarity. Anfen again looked starved, his back bowed by unseen weight, looking just as tired as Sharfy felt. On such days people passed them on the road in heavy numbers: refugees in wandering bands going south from Elvury and (soon enough) from Faifen, often as not missing hands, arms, parts of their faces. They said war had come to their cities. War, and even worse things.

The strangest of it was that news revealed large numbers of castle troops had headed south along this very road, led not by a general but by a first captain. Anfen and he *should* have walked right into this group, and through others, on one of those days when they had instead come across no one at all.

Anfen answered few questions and did not say a word about the huge purple scar that ran around his neck. Now and then he said things which Sharfy could not understand and did not wish to hear: 'There's a dragon I wish to kill,' he muttered once. '*I* wish to kill it. Ah, I feel him, foul thing. I sense he is a spy. I do not know if my redeemer wishes him slain. It is a mistake to assume all the brood are of the same purpose.'

Redeemer. That word again, spoken like someone would speak

of their commander, or father, or lover. 'A dragon, Anfen? Don't talk like that.'

'I must. It breaks the natural laws, to be out among us at all, Sharfy. But then, we ourselves break the laws. The Wall was not supposed to be broken. We are not meant to be here, in the quiet. And I am not meant to live.'

Why can't we exchange the usual stories? Sharfy wondered. He was itching to tell one. 'Then why'd the Wall break?' he said. 'If it wasn't meant to.'

'The natural laws are changing, Sharfy. Do you know what this process is called?'

'Nope.'

'You do. It's called war.'

'War, eh? Yeah, I heard of that.'

'War. The gods, the dragons. War.'

A long silence, filled by their feet beating the road. As happened from time to time, a drop of blood slid from the thick purple scar on Anfen's neck. He looked directly at Sharfy for the first time in a long while, an excited gleam in his eye that Sharfy decided was worse than the grim silent mask he'd got used to. 'It isn't a new war,' Anfen said. 'Like our wars it has times of hot and cold, forces arranging themselves before blades are drawn. We are lucky to be alive now, Sharfy. Blades are now drawn. I have come to understand that I am one such blade.'

What am I, your scabbard? Sharfy almost said, but Anfen did not seem, lately, to appreciate a joke. Yet again, he seemed to expect a response. 'What about the Pilgrims?' Sharfy ventured.

'The *keenest* blade. Though too many hands reach to wield him. He would be better destroyed.'

'Which one you mean? Eric or Case?'

'Shadow.'

4

Another full day's marching had passed when with no explanation Anfen veered from the Great Road, cutting across a plain of loose stone and bare grey pillars, lands once blasted by fire from dragons' throats so that nothing now grew here. It gave way to more liveable country, though it was overgrown and abandoned, replete with ruins both recent and ancient. Their feet scattering pebbles or crunching the bitter, brittle ground were so loud they may as well have shouted out *here we are* with each step.

They were now some way north of Elvury if Sharfy judged right, and had to be nearing Invia country. Anfen had never told the Mayors' Command he was Marked; the rest of them wouldn't have known either but for his constantly checking the sky for the creatures. But he wasn't doing that now. 'Invia, Anfen?' said Sharfy. 'You worried? Forgot about em? Huh? You're Marked, don't forget. Marked! That sword's pretty good, but you can't beat em just with that, can you?' *And don't look to me for help*, he didn't say. 'What if a few of em come, like at Faul's place?'

He was answered by the sound of trudging boots.

Sharfy squinted at motion on the horizon. 'People coming,' he said. 'Look! Ahead there. There's a lot of em. Hard to tell but I think some got weapons. We should hide.'

Crunch, crunch went Anfen's boots.

'Look. You can walk headlong into em. But I'm gonna hide.' He fancied a faint puff of heat came from the armour beneath

Anfen's shirt. Then they were in the twilight place again, with no past or present sign of humanity at all. In the quiet, they were the only ones who'd ever lived, there were no roads but the Great Dividing Road, no enemies or friends, no homes or houses but the grass, trees, hills and distant mountains.

And the pretty diamond-like clusters suspended in the air. It was not the first time Sharfy had seen them, though never so many as now. He had less than no idea what they were, only that he wanted to pocket them. In the distance was a huge one, big as a house, way high up.

'What are those?' he asked, pointing. Anfen didn't respond. 'Someone would pay big for those shiny things. Bet you they would. Look like they're full of magic. Scales, gold we'd get.' It was a hint but apparently missed. 'Fuck it, Anfen. I'm not getting *paid* to follow you. I should get some loot. Look yonder. That outcrop there. If we climb it we can get hold of those small ones. Reckon I'd reach em with a long stick. Knock em out of the air.'

Anfen paused, turned to face him full of majesty and grace, spoke quietly: 'If you try to touch them. If you dare go near them. I will slay you.' He turned away and trudged on.

Sharfy wished he were angry. It was the first time Anfen had ever threatened him. Ever. But such was the command in his voice Sharfy could not but feel it had for some reason been entirely fair: a simple statement of the law. And like an obedient dog he followed his master, grappling with his pride until the sound of a bird call broke the dreamy silence and the quiet's mask fell away.

The village Anfen had led them to was a few years abandoned, Sharfy judged, for the buildings – though neglected – were not in such bad shape, and some could probably be mended in a week fit for living again. In the southern distance Elvury's ranges stood like a row of huge teeth. They were further north than Sharfy had guessed, well and truly in Aligned country. Anfen unstrapped the sword from his belt, let it drop to the ground, and walked away from it.

Sharfy quickly picked it up, surprised at how light it felt. Since his glimpse of it that night with the light flashing down its face, he'd been eager for a close look but afraid to ask. Now he pulled the handle free of its scabbard and was surprised to see there was no blade there at all, just the finely wrought handle. He set the handle back atop the scabbard and put it carefully down.

Anfen staggered past a small vegetable field overrun with weeds. He looked for something in the tall grass, then fell to his knees. 'These are mine, Sharfy,' he said hoarsely.

Sharfy went to him and waited.

Anfen began pulling grass out with his fists, clawing at the dirt. He moved with feverish speed. Sharfy got down to help but Anfen snarled, 'Back!' with such ferocity he thought he was about to be bitten. So he stood away and watched. Half an hour later Anfen's hands were caked in dirt, his fingernails cracked and split. He panted like a dog. And like a dog he had dug up buried bones. All were clearly human. 'These are mine,' he repeated. 'My bones. I made them.' Slowly, tenderly his hands wiped every speck of dirt from them.

Having seen far worse than this in his time, Sharfy was nonetheless troubled. '*Your* bones need a rest. Let's get under a roof for a while. Those huts will do. No one's here.'

Not seeming to hear, Anfen pulled length after length of bone from the unearthed pit. Ribs, vertebrae, fingers and toes. Once he'd got them all out he arranged each with tenderness on the grass nearby. He gently wiped dirt from the skulls, and took a long while making sure each skull sat atop a body which looked to match it. 'They owe me nothing,' Anfen said, weeping. 'Nothing. They have not forgiven me. I'll ask them for answers all the same.'

'Bones don't talk.'

Anfen's laugh was the cough of someone dying. He arranged it all as nine complete bodies, minus a foot on one and some fingers here or there. Several of the skulls were broken. He sat forlorn among them with his head bowed, not moving, just murmuring and weeping.

Sharfy was disgusted. He foraged what roots and fruit he could find and spent the night on a bare floor in an abandoned house with his pack for a pillow. From time to time Anfen's weeping woke him. By morning he was so sick of the whole spectacle he decided he'd chance the long march back, through enemy country or not.

Anfen was still with the bones at first light, a small skull cradled in his arms. Sharfy took off without saying goodbye and instantly felt better about life. About him were bent, thin trees with pale crescent leaves. The stillness and quiet made his footsteps through brittle undergrowth very loud.

He had seen people broken in the slave farms by grief or starvation, pain or fear. But he had never seen a man *choose* to go so far, march so many miles, only to roll around in the shattered pieces of his own ruin. Of course there was only one way Anfen could have known those bones lay where they lay. His very own hands had surely put them there. But what of that? Anfen had killed more of the enemy by now than he ever had of innocents.

Distracted by all this, Sharfy's ankle nearly twisted on a

fallen branch, which he angrily kicked away. Then anger consumed him for a minute as he stomped the fuck out of that branch and several others, cursing and spitting up several days' worth of suppressed rage and indignity. Only then did he really look at the ground and see the many spiked holes punched into it.

He froze, looked through the woods, drew his sword. He spun about twice before catching sight of a dark form up the incline there, maybe a long knife-toss away. It was motionless but for the wriggling spikes along its flanks.

Visions came to him of tavern talk late at night, telling an improbable tale of battle with a monster; doubters calling names; Sharfy reaching into his kit bag and triumphantly producing the monster's head. Finally the renown he'd already earned a dozen times pouring down on him; slaps on the back, women offering themselves, free ale for weeks: *tell it again, tell the tale of your duel with the beast from beyond* . . .

They'd believe his *other* tales too, after he had proof of this one, indeed they would.

He went nearer to the beast. It still hadn't moved. One very hard blow and he might just have it. He'd have to swing with all the strength he had; their hides were tough. As long as it was the only one around.

A rattling sound came from behind him. A sense of inevitability as he turned to find a second Tormentor staring down at him with stony eyes. The bastard thing had been conjured just to thwart his simple wish for a little respect and a free drop of drink. Its arms spread wide as though for an embrace; its huge mane of spiked needles shook.

He was off and running, hoping blindly that he headed for the place he'd just come from. Two dozen paces later everything slowed down. Sharfy found himself running through water. He heard the beast's feet approach, the sound of its steps impossibly fast while he was so slowed down.

Then he was out of the Tormentor's spell, flung forward and toppling into a tree, adding yet another dent to his face. Blood gushed through his nose. Dazed, he looked back and caught a flash of gleaming metal, the *whoosh* of a blade slicing air. Anfen struck the creature with cold fury, only in that confused moment it was not a Tormentor he saw . . .

The world had shifted so it held again the blurred edges of a dream. They were back in the quiet, and there it indeed was not a Tormentor Anfen struck down, but a man. Or something *like* a man but stretched and warped as if it was made of rubber being pulled. Its limbs were curved and warped; its face too long, mouth twisted into a long gaping S-shape. It did not fight back, just stiffly turned toward Anfen, movements clumsy, and without resistance it watched him kill it.

Sharfy shut his eyes. When he sat up, they were out of the quiet and the world was harsh and cold again. He wiped blood from his newly broken nose. Anfen sheathed his blade. At his feet was a large Tormentor corpse in many pieces, like slabs of cracked dark stone.

Sharfy would work out later how to rationalise being rescued, but already he supposed he'd lured the creature quite deliberately into a trap, that he had been on the brink of turning to fight it. Gratitude nonetheless was one of the many things he felt.

Anfen nodded at the corpse at his feet. 'They filled the woods with them. They let the foul things loose, by design.'

'The castle?' Sharfy spat out blood. 'Why? It's *their* land.'

'Think! They now make their last push south. And they will

win. They let these things loose near the roads, in the woods, anywhere an army might come.'

Sharfy nodded understanding. They'd let Inferno cultists loose in some places for the same reason – they made lands dangerous for fleeing refugees, as well as approaching enemies. 'So they protect the place when their troops are gone,' said Sharfy. 'But when the war's done, what then?'

Anfen smiled. 'What do you do with a dangerous tool you no longer have need for, Sharfy?'

'Throw it out.'

'*Destroy* it. When the Arch wins, his armies are not intended to return. Most people in the world will be killed. Their own people too. A small herd is easy to control.' The distant form of a lone Tormentor – a small one – could be seen through the trees with its back to them. Anfen gazed at it. 'My redeemer revealed all this to me,' he said. 'My redeemer told me I was cleansed. But also he told me my will was my own.'

'Anfen. The bones. *Why*?'

'I cleansed them, Sharfy. As best I could. I was gentle. I was loving. They did not forgive me, as I asked. That is their choice. I leave them unburied now. Let all who come by here see the bones, Sharfy. Let them see what I did.'

Sharfy spat more blood. 'Look at it this way: the bones are as clean as they'll ever get. They're as dead as they'll get. Can't hurt em now. Don't owe em nothing either. Don't owe em saying sorry or coin or nice words. Or time.'

Anfen looked at him for a while in silence. 'It's done now. We move.'

'Where we going? I don't move at all till you tell me.'

But Anfen walked away without a word. Sharfy lay there less than a minute before cursing and proving himself a liar.

AN EMPTY BED

1

The world fell away again fast, fast. Through layers of rock he went like a shadow pulled, down as far as he could go, to the secret places. Caverns and creatures whizzed by, labyrinths and hollowed caverns now devoid of any living thing, if living things had ever set foot or claw here. Then he found that final deep layer of rock which wasn't to be penetrated, not by him or anything else. He battered himself against it for a while, each impact provoking his curiosity further till it was a screaming, burning rage. What was beneath the world's floor?

No answers. Up then, up to the surface again, pausing briefly where the unco-operative girl still stumbled her way blindly through tunnels. An enjoyable sight, though the feeling grew hollow as he watched her, some inner, nagging, distant sense that it was wrong to leave her here. Strange creature! He was annoyed with her still; after having chased off the dragon, having taken her so far . . . then to be refused one simple request, a thing so much easier for her to do than what he'd done for her? He did not understand it.

He would revisit her. She had caught his eye back when the Wall fell, she and the fellow she was with: Eric. Something about them, he knew not what, had marked them as reference points. Maybe his only ones.

The surface. Night time. He crossed many miles falling down the world's face, pausing on a whim in a logging cabin. Four men slept and snored. Anything interesting about them? He shadowed them and found only physical strength, aches, anger. Nothing more. The girl, she'd had a little glimmer of something. The dragon, now that was another thing. It had been filled with more power than he'd been able to properly perceive in that brief time.

These men had nothing of the sort. Angered suddenly, Shadow swept through the place cutting them down as they had cut down trees during the day. It was fast, no complaints. His anger abated, though not because this act of death-making had spent it; it went as it came, for no reason at all. Pointless as all these deaths and lives fleeting by. Pointless, surely. He was lost in it all, he was nothing, he was debris on a tide.

A mess in the cabin. How strange, these shreds of flesh and spilled life, so ugly across the floor and walls and ceiling. Put together, capable of beauty. Beauty like hers . . .

Suddenly there it was again, that feeling. He'd felt it before, but never so close! Something pulled him, yanked him skyward. He was so intrigued and curious it hurt. He yielded to the pull for some distance and found its source: in the air a drake flew along slowly, a girl on its back. Out of reach! He couldn't go up through the sky in the same way he could move across the world's face, and down through its belly. It was cruel! This strange compelling pull was so powerful, coming directly from either the drake or the girl on its back, he couldn't tell which. There was nothing to be done but to watch the creature's flapping wings, so maddeningly slow.

Then the pull's force went slack, to leave him craving something he didn't fathom, a need to fill this empty pit inside him.

2

It was still night when Eric rose. The sound of breeze and waves gently filled the tower's uppermost floor; the glimmer across the walls was light glancing off water.

In one of the beds Loup muttered in his sleep and appeared to swat a fly. In another, Bald the Engineer slept with the Glock pressed to his cheek, presumably dreaming about the live rounds which had been hidden from him. The Engineer's efforts so far in replicating the gun had resulted only in some bent wire and planks tied together with rope. It did not look promising.

A head count of the sleepers revealed someone was missing. Siel's bow was propped up beside one empty mattress. The tower seemed to hate her; maybe it hadn't let her sleep.

Eric went to the raised dais in the middle of the floor and climbed its half-dozen stone steps. The thick dark winding ribbon of magic he'd seen from outside came through this very spot, funnelled through one window over this raised platform to escape out another window behind. He put a hand into the stream of magic, faintly disturbing its course to either side of his fingers. The diluted threads of this stuff in the atmosphere could barely be felt; concentrated, it was cool to the touch. He breathed deeply the way war mage had, sucking it in like asthma medication he'd had as a child. Tendrils of dark mist threaded toward him before he'd begun taking the breath, as though called by his intent to do so. Coldly it went into his lungs. A dizzy feeling came over him, the sense of a very mild and almost pleasant electric shock, pulsing from his mind through the rest of his body.

Stepping away, the feeling faded. The dark winding stream of magic continued its flow, unperturbed.

He went to the next floor down, expecting to find Siel. A quick tour of the place showed she was no longer here. 'What have you done with her?' he asked, speaking to the tower. The sound of waves lapped quite innocently in reply.

At the window an arrow from the soldiers' failed attack still jutted out from the sill. He pulled at it but it was stuck fast. Gazing at the water below, a part of his dream suddenly returned: watching someone – Had it been Siel? – wandering through underground tunnels, not unlike those he himself had been marched through at the point of Sharfy's knife.

But if it had been more than just a dream, even if it had been a vision, she could surely not be far. He thought of the steps leading down to the swirling whirlpool and decided to explore them when movement caught his eye. The huge white wolf stood down at the water's edge, its head lowered, panting as though after a long, long journey.

Far Gaze, he recalled, had tried to rip Stranger's throat out back at Faul's place. Which made it a little odd that none other than Stranger now rode the beast's back. She wore the same green dress and looked more or less the same, except her head too was slumped and, though it was hard to be certain at a distance, she looked to be weeping.

But why was Case not with them?

The wolf put one paw experimentally into the water. Eric waved to catch its attention, thinking he should warn it about the water's occasional tendency to boil. But soon Far Gaze had made it safely across, padding out of sight beneath the tower where the water was deeper, Stranger in tow. It came up the steps, staggered a few paces then collapsed. It looked starved, was missing clumps of fur. Stranger slunk up the steps after it, her head bowed, face streaked with tears.

'I see you two have kissed and made up,' said Eric. The wolf shut its eyes. To Stranger he said, 'I'm Eric. I already know who you are.'

'You may know who I was,' she said in a flat voice. 'I'm nothing now.'

'Oh?'

She wiped her eyes, went to the window and stared through it.

'Maybe I know the feeling,' he said, taking a seat on the floor behind her. 'I'm not what I used to be either.'

'Has your heart ever been spat out of your true love's mouth like coughed bile?'

'Not exactly. My true love pretty much thinks I'm pathetic and has from the start. Can't argue either.'

The wolf meanwhile writhed on the floor. Its hair and fur were already shed. Its bones began crunching and breaking. It made a vomiting noise so horrible Eric had to cover his ears for a minute or two. When that finished he said, 'I seem to remember you two used to fight each other. What changed?'

Stranger laughed bitterly. 'I'm lucky he didn't tear my throat out. Dyan gave him every chance.'

'Dyan? Who's that?'

She began to speak, hesitated, then smiled. 'Why not? Why not tell you all I know of him?'

'Not yet,' said Far Gaze hoarsely. 'Wait until I've rested. Then tell us together. Till then, not a word about it.' He stood naked among a litter of white wolf's hair, then bent over, clutching his belly. 'Mongrel! How much rot did he eat? Never again. Damn him!' With a retching noise no less horrid than the wolf's in transition had been, Far Gaze vomited down the steps to the whirlpool below. When at last he'd finished he stood, swayed, muttered to Eric, 'Your friend is dead,' then passed out.

BENEATH THE SURFACE

1

When Siel lurched back into the regular flow of time it felt like she'd been dropped from a height to land with a jolt that jarred her senses. She'd found herself alone in the underground chamber. The wall's shackles all hung limp and empty, the walls behind them crisscrossed with gouges from what might well have been Anfen's sword.

The place – to her immense relief – had been left unguarded, as had the surrounding rooms and tunnels. She'd run from there with no idea which way led back to the surface, only meaning to get away from those hooks before someone tried to put her there where Stranger had been.

That was some time back. There were precious few lightstones in the network she now wandered through, though she'd begun hearing voices and footsteps through its membrane-thin walls. How many hours of it went crawling by, this flitting about like a rodent in a house full of cats? Dead ends. Blocked passages. Footsteps so close they sounded right on top of her. One narrow escape, crouched behind a pile of rubble as two men went by sharing a joke. She'd been a heartbeat from striking at them with the fist-sized rock she'd adopted as her new weapon, could have sworn one of them looked right at her but kept on walking.

Rounding a bend where the lightstones were brighter, she hesitated, debating whether or not to risk a passage where she'd be so visible. It was this or hours of backtracking for likely the same ultimate result. Why not deal with it now, while she had some energy left to fight.

She prepared herself. Before battle she used to rouse her spirit with thoughts of her parents kneeling in their beautiful garden, the pride and envy of their street. Others of the neighbourhood kneeled with them, while pigs (her memory actually depicted them as beast-faced animals in men's clothes) went up and down the line, killing in Vous's name.

This time she thought of something else: of one day looking back on this moment as the most decisive in all the war, a thin thread bearing the weight of all history, when a barefoot woman with a rock in her hand used it to cause an avalanche of events, pouring down on the whole castle to bury it forever. She had that thread in her hand now. She must not let go.

For a while the better lit passage seemed safe enough, silent and deserted but for a not-too-distant *clunk, clank, scrape*. Then she was at another dead end. Four groundmen nattered quietly while they expanded the tunnel with tools. Their expert hands seemed to make the stone crumble away as if it were soft soil.

Their overseer lay with his back to her, one leg crossed lazily over the other. He had a sheathed sword at his side and a long forked prod. The scene was so reminiscent of the groundman art she'd seen it was disconcerting: this kind of thing actually *happened*? She'd always thought the little people somewhat demented.

She moved closer, at first unsure why the groundmen didn't simply run from their lazy captor. Then she saw the square metal device which held all four of them around their bleeding ankles. Similar to traps used in hunting, it allowed them only a forward shuffle. Backward motion would cut into their feet.

One pair of candle-bright yellow eyes turned her way, though she was sure she'd not made the faintest sound. Then another. All four paused in their work and stared. The overseer lifted his prod, debated for a moment between offenders and – despite their having quite frantically gotten back to their task – plunged it into the thighs of the groundman on the right. The victim squealed pitifully. The rest worked at feverish speed.

The overseer didn't get so far as drawing his sword before she swung down the rock, then swung it again to make certain. The groundmen didn't turn as his body slumped to the ground, not until she'd taken off his sword belt and strapped it around her own waist. They spared her a glance then kept working as though one overseer had simply been exchanged for another.

She reached for the keys hooked around the dead man's belt and said, 'I think we can be of use to one another. Do you agree?'

2

They had walked for at least two hours and the little creatures' gratitude had only just begun to lose its hyperactive zeal. Thankfully. It was touching at first to have them pause every few paces to embrace her legs, but soon she'd had to keep in check the urge to kick some sense into them. 'Let's just get moving. Please. That's the best way to thank me,' she repeated through clenched teeth.

The groundmen's bright eyes found secret passages she'd never have seen, where what looked like a wall was actually an empty space. She might well have passed dozens of these earlier without knowing it. With the same ease they spotted old traps, long ago set off but still best avoided. Now and then were parts they had to tunnel through, digging holes in dead ends with the tools they'd kept from their enslavement. The way the stone seemed to melt and crumble in their fast-moving little hands indicated there was more at work than just the small picks and hammers. She'd heard no talk that these creatures held a kind of magic about them, but it could be nothing else. Soon they were well away from those districts under castle control and into other networks, long abandoned. These were not made for human travel, and in parts Siel had to crawl to fit. There were no light-stones. She could see nothing but the thin gleam leaking into the gloom from her companions' eyes.

'We are going deeper,' she said. 'Why? I asked you to take me to the surface.'

'Bad up there,' said the most vocal of them, the one who had been jabbed by the overseer's prong. 'Bad things, up now.'

'Bad things? What bad things?'

'Your word. Tor-*men*-tor. We say, bad things. Up now, above. In trees.'

'How can you tell where they are?' she said. 'You have been enslaved for years. Weren't you cut off from the outside world? Where do you get your news?'

A little laughter broke out. She heard one of them patting the wall. 'This! Stone tells. Tells lots. Feel it. Touch it. All up there, comes through here. Here!' Pat, pat. 'Just faint. But we feel. All time, while we slave, we know what pass, up there. Big war. They think we blind, dumb. It's fine, make us slaves.'

'They make slaves of us too,' said Siel. 'Of other big people. Have you not felt *that* going on up there?' The groundmen made sounds like they didn't believe her. 'It's true. Some big people are very bad, some are good. We are trying to kill all the very bad ones. You can help us. We would like that very much. The world would be better for everyone.'

There was a very awkward silence. 'You, our friend,' said one of them, turning to embrace her knees reassuringly and nearly tripping her in the process. '*You* are. Not them.'

She took this as a request to cease that line of conversation. They had evidence of one non-evil human being, so there must be just the one, which was her. Flattering, kind of. 'Do you know where the Tormentors come from?' she said, suddenly wondering how valuable this friendship could become.

'We know.'

'Do they come from the castle?' she said.

'Not there.'

'We can show. Is far. Long way.'

She asked them to describe it but they wouldn't; the bad things came from 'far away' and that was all. 'Some close by now,' one said in a grim voice. 'They move, still. Feel it?'

'Nearby?' she said, alarmed. 'Where?'

They nattered to each other briefly. 'We show. Come. Is down from here.'

It was not a small detour. She soon regretted agreeing to it as they went further and further below, down long stretches that were almost vertical, with the help of stone grooves functioning as ladders. The little people climbed down the vertical rock faces as though their hands could stick to stone at will. The air grew clammy and cold. Siel had an indefinable feeling that she, indeed any living thing, should *not* be here, that these parts of the world had not been made for her. The groundmen however seemed unconcerned, chatting happily in their incomprehensible speech until one long final descent when they ceased all talk.

'Here,' one whispered, crawling with Siel over a raised hump of smooth icy rock shaped like a wave. Its crest looked down over a wider passageway cut into the stone. There were small lightstones very sparsely placed along the secret highway. Not much could be seen. 'Slaves make this,' a groundman whispered in her ear. 'Long time back. *Big* long road. When road done, they kill slaves. No good, big people.'

A foul and familiar smell was in the air. She fought not to cough. There was a sound of wooden creaking and cracking, hints of something moving along directly beneath them. Then came a flash of blue light which hurt all their eyes, making even the groundmen reel back in surprise. It had come from the tip of a short staff, held by a castle grey-robe who had not been visible before. Its flare was like a small lightning flash which revealed three Tormentors. They were smaller than those Siel had seen invading Elvury from the high inn's window.

More bright flashes some distance away showed another grey-robe, surrounded by three of the creatures which he prodded along like someone steering cattle. 'Where do they take them?' Siel whispered as quietly as she could.

'North. All north. Big under-country, there. Near castle. They fill it. Hard to do. See? Lots dead!'

She did not see. 'Dead? Big people you mean, in the grey robes? The ones who try to move them along?'

'Dead. All up and down road. Hard to move bad things. Kill movers. Kill *everyone*. But they keep on, to bring more, more. Always more. What plan? We can't see. This,' it patted the stone wave they all lay upon, 'don't say what big people think. We leave here now. Must!'

It was no small relief to be out of earshot of the quiet insistent creaking sounds of death creeping beneath the world. For a long time after they'd left that spot the sound still seemed to be in her ears.

3

Their way had climbed for uncounted hours when Siel's body at last refused to go further. She slept, though claustrophobic nightmares made her regret it. The groundmen gently woke her and she went from one such bad dream to another.

A draft indicated they'd come through the cramped spaces into a more open area. Glittering light far ahead had the groundmen excited and rushing off. When she cried out, 'Come back!' one of them returned to guide her along the raised path, which even with eyes well accustomed to the dark she could barely see at her feet. 'What's got into your friends?' she said.

'New picture,' he said, impatient to rush off for a look. Before it the other little people were talking in awed, hushed voices. It was a spectacular display of glowing patterns cast on a flat, forward-tilted slab of wall. She had to laugh for a moment when she saw that it depicted Eric.

Eric's face, unmistakeably. A group of little people surrounded him, kneeling in reverence. 'Why laugh?' one of the groundmen demanded, the first time any of them had spoken to her with anything like anger.

'I know him. That's a companion of mine.' They looked at each other uneasily and didn't speak. Their body language was difficult to read but she had a sense they felt she had lied. 'His name's Eric. He's—' (Was there harm in revealing it? she quickly debated.) '— he's from Otherworld. A Pilgrim.'

There followed several minutes of fast conversation between the groundmen, of which she understood not a word or even its mood.

'Where is he?' said one of them at last.

'A strange tower. Far to the south. I should be there with him. I was abducted.' She described the location as best she could remember. They quizzed her for a while. Many of their questions she could make no sense of and couldn't answer. 'Why do you ask all this?' she said. 'Why is he in this art?'

'Message,' said one of them, nodding at the portrait of light. 'He free us. Free all of us. Make everything good. This picture is message-picture. Eh-Rick, you call him?'

'Yes.'

'Not his name. Says here, name *H'lack-til*. Your word, Shadow.'

She looked at the portrait's eyes. They were Eric's eyes, not Shadow's dead little pits. She had seen a similar picture before too. Where?

It took a minute for her to find the memory: around the campfire, asking Eric about Otherworld. He reaches into his pocket, into that small leather purse of such fine make she wonders if he may be a prince back home after all. He pulls out a thin object, a card with his likeness perfectly replicated. So perfectly she gasps in amazement. He explains how such pictures are made but she doesn't understand. This groundman portrait, she was sure, had been copied from his likeness on that little card.

She remembered further, hearing Eric's account of his travels with Case, about the groundmen who'd trapped then released them, taking the little card with them! She kept the laughter inside this time, but it wasn't easy. Something on the card, in either its picture or the Otherworld runes it bore, had convinced the little people Eric (or Shadow) was their saviour.

So there were two decent big people, at least. She supposed that to them it must have made sense that the two good ones knew each other, for they seemed to accept her story. She wondered if this could be played on. 'Eric – Shadow – is turning a lot of the big people into good people,' she said. 'You can trust anyone he works with. He has a way of changing people's minds. Your people and ours can do much good, if we work together. We can mend our wounds. Make all the world as beautiful as your art, above ground and below.'

'We go,' said one of the little people with a note of urgency. 'We go quick, now. Find him, this Eh-Rick. This Shadow. He help us!'

TELL US ABOUT THE DRAGONS

1

'Was he your father?' said Stranger. They sat beneath the window Siel had broken while Far Gaze slept naked, sprawled on the floor by the steps. Little strings of magic now and then swam to Stranger through the air, though she appeared to do nothing to draw them to her. She twisted them through her long fingers, then they fluttered out through the window like animals set free.

'No, Case wasn't my father,' said Eric. 'I'm just a little shocked. I was beginning to think he was indestructible.'

'Is there no one else you miss, from your home?'

'That's the thing. He was my link back to them. I'm beginning to wonder now if that world even exists. I have a million memories of the place, but I don't know if *I'm* even real. Every ghost in the haunted woods may think he is still real and alive.'

'Don't speak that way,' said Stranger, performing a small gesture with her hands. He'd seen others doing it when they'd passed through those very woods. 'You're no ghost. How long have you known Case?'

'Not much longer than you. I used to see him on my way to work sometimes, would toss him ten bucks now and then. He'd give me a chess lesson every so often.'

'Chess?'

'A game. You play it here in Levaal, I'm told. Case would be so drunk he couldn't stand up, but would still beat me. Easily. I think he'd have beaten most people.'

Eric shook his head at the sleeping form of Far Gaze, angry at how casually he'd broken the news of Case's death. Stranger noticed. 'Don't be too angry at the wolf. He has had a hard road. I made it hard. He felt he was protecting you from me all the while.'

'Was he?'

She sighed and released a little fluttering string of dark air. 'I would say no, of course not. *I* meant no harm to you. But did Dyan? He tells lies so well. He said he just wanted to watch you.' The shrug of her slender shoulders was hardly perceptible. 'Maybe he did, at least up until now. What he intends next, I can't tell you.'

'Do you remember summoning wine for Case?'

'Back on the castle lawns? Of course.'

'That was one of the things that had Loup convinced you weren't just an ordinary mage.'

'He was right. Summoning a cup of wine from nearby, or summoning an illusory one, *those* things a normal mage could do. But creating the real thing from nothing is unusual work. I hope you aren't thirsty. I can't do such things now.'

'Why not?'

She wiped her damp eyes. 'Most of it was Dyan's power. Not *all* of it. I can still do some things. I am as much a seer as I was, though that isn't much. And the knowledge Dyan gave will stay with me as he himself fades to memory.' Her voice thickened with those words.

'So you *could* summon a glass of wine, if you really had to?'

'I dare not try to cast now what he could cast through me. I may succeed, if there were enough power to fuel the spell, but it might hurt or kill me. Dragons have little worry about harm from casting. Their bodies are built to handle it. Ours aren't, however capable our minds.'

'So if you're a seer, do you have a prediction?'

It was a little while before she answered. 'Only that several key people will converge here, in this spot. More than are here now. This tower may have been designed for that purpose, to draw us.'

'It all looks like chance to me.'

'I feel there are too many of us here already for it to *be* just chance.'

'You also assume we're key people.'

She laughed. 'We are, for we surround you, Pilgrim. More will surely come, and if they do, we will know I'm right. Even the timing of this building's revealing itself has me curious. Your friends showed up just in time to find it ere anyone else did.' She gazed around at the room's peculiar devices. 'It is masterfully built. We are not masters of quick spell-casting, we humans. In that, we are insects to the greater dragons. To a Minor personality like Dyan, we are not *insects*, but our most powerful caster is still less than him. It is in our slower, more careful craftsmanship that we actually have the dragons' respect. Even though in that craft too, they best us. Small wonder they feel cheated that we have taken their world.'

Loup staggered down the steps, yawning and farting. He glanced at Far Gaze's sleeping form with no more reaction than a grunt, but stood flabbergasted on sight of Stranger.

'Hello?' she ventured.

'I knew *he* was coming,' said Loup, nodding at Far Gaze. 'What in Inferno's red blazes are *you* doing here?'

'I think I am your captive,' she said, shrugging. 'Although I'll be an ally if you'll let me. You'll have to ask the wolf when he wakes up. He brought me.'

'Ehh! So you *weren't* an ally before, is that what you're saying, lass?'

'I don't know. I thought I was. I might have been wrong.'

'You'd judge it better than I,' said Loup. 'Less kick about you now though, mark me. Oh I noticed you on the road, could feel you about the place even at some distance. It was you all right. Not now though! The fire's gone out of you.'

'Not completely,' she said testily.

He laughed. 'Oh yes it has, enough for us to handle. You're not much more than *me*, now. And not a candle on him.' He nodded to Far Gaze. 'Maybe you can bless the meals around here from now on.' To Eric, Loup said, 'Where's the other lass?'

'Siel? She's not been here since I woke,' said Eric. 'And I'm nervous about it. I had a dream where she was far away.'

'Dream!' Loup's eyes went wide. 'Normal dream, or more funny business? Tell me about it and don't waste words.'

Eric told him what little he remembered.

'More trickery!' Loup cried when he'd finished. His gnarled face twisted into a fury Eric had not before seen in him. '*And you clutz fool shit didn't think to wake me at the first scent of it!*'

'See, here's where you explain to me what it all means. Then the *next* time it happens, I'll know what to do.'

'Next time if we're lucky!' Loup staggered back and fell as though he'd been shoved, hands to his face. 'You know what *he's* liable to do? He's like a wee tot taking toys apart to see what's inside em. What he'll be when he grows up? Well who knows that? *If* she's alive, call it more luck than a rain of diamonds. If she's not, it's *your* hands helped kill her, and I don't care if you're a Pilgrim or a common idiot or both. Scale! Where's the black scale? Oh there better be enough left. Pinch of green in the mix might help, might not. Oh what's he done ...?'

Wailing and cursing, Loup ran back up the steps.

Eric said to Stranger, 'If you are a captive here, I'm not your guard.'

She laughed. 'You'd turn a blind eye if I jumped out the window? I don't want to. I want nothing. He's right, the fire is out. Do you see? It's not the power I mourn, nor is it strictly *him*. I don't know if it was a spell that made me love him, that's beside the point. The connection, the bond. Its very threads, the firm grip of them. *He* didn't matter, I understand now. But his power made the bond stronger than anything I will have again. I'm over.'

'Unless he returns?'

She laughed. 'He won't. I know him now that we've parted, in the way you know a familiar place even more when it's left behind you. He was never mine. Just as we keep horses and beasts until they're not useful any more. That's all I was to him.'

Eric noted the choice of words. *He won't return* was not quite the same as *even if he did return, I'd not have anything to do with him*. Aloud he said, 'But that's not to say a person can't be a genuine friend to his steed.'

'Until it's of no more use,' she repeated sadly.

Far Gaze opened a bleary red eye and groaned. Unabashed by his nakedness he got up and moved very stiffly, like an old man, though he could not have been much older than forty. His hairy body was broad and muscled. 'Get me food,' he said. 'The mongrel tried to kill me.'

'What happened to Case?' Eric demanded.

'Jumped off a cliff. Said thanks for the . . . I forget the words. He said something a friend would say in farewell. I have no more answers for you.'

'No more answers,' Eric echoed hollowly.

'I was in shifted form. Not ideal for playing messenger. Leave me be. I must think about what the wolf scented and heard. There's a lot.' Far Gaze cocked a thick eyebrow at Eric, belatedly perceiving his attitude. 'And as for saving you in the woods, from one peril after another, after keeping a *dragon* at bay, among other things, after a futile sprint across the world. You . . . are . . . *welcome*. Pilgrim.'

He went up the steps clutching his back. A moment later, through the window Eric and Stranger sat beneath, a drake's head burst in.

2

It was well that Stranger saw in time there wasn't room for Aziel's head to clear the top of the window, or the Lord's daughter might have been sent tumbling to the small shelf of turf below. The drake pushed its way in, getting a wing caught on the window and flipping over onto its back with a grunt, almost landing squarely on Eric, who was too surprised to move until he heard the bone-breaking force of its squat body hitting the floor. Stranger pulled Aziel inside.

'Hands off me!' the girl yelled shrilly, thrashing her legs around. 'Leave me alone. Do you even know who I am?'

Stranger – perhaps expecting 'thank you' for saving the new arrival's life – was lost for words. The drake, on sight of Eric, got up and rushed at him. 'Help!' he yelled, backing into a wall, but the drake had him cornered. Rather than attack, it pushed its head into his midriff as though it wanted to have its ears scratched.

'He won't hurt you,' Aziel snapped at Eric. 'He's mine. Don't touch him.'

'What is yours?' said Stranger. 'Eric or the beast? Or maybe everyone and everything?'

'Don't speak to me that way!' said Aziel, though she sounded more frightened than anything. 'Do you even know—'

'You are Aziel, our Friend and Lord's daughter,' said Stranger with a smile. 'And I believe my prediction was right. Don't you, Eric?'

Eric was too busy fending off the drake's affections. It had propped itself up on its hind legs and tail, with one foreleg planted on his chest, looking into his face with what seemed imploring eyes. Eric felt his ribs bend under its weight. 'What's wrong with it?' he gasped.

'He might be thirsty,' Aziel said. 'He likes beer.'

'Is it going to breathe fire at me?'

'No! He doesn't do that much. He's a nice drake. Take me home. Take me back to Arch. I don't understand why I'm here or why it came and took me. I just want to go home.' She burst into tears.

Stranger laid a palm on her forehead, muttered something, then Aziel collapsed into sleep. 'You have a new friend,' said Stranger, a drop of blood leaking from her nose.

'I think so.' The drake had calmed down a little. Now it sat before Eric like a dog awaiting instructions from its master. It made sounds deep in its throat as though it were trying to speak, though the sounds had no meaning Eric could discern. 'It's trying to tell me something.'

Stranger stroked the beast's back. 'It seems very tame. There were some drakes trained for fighting, years ago. If they escaped their handlers, they were dangerous. It's quite remarkable, if this creature will stay with us and be a steed. Drakes are very rare.' The drake turned to her and made more sounds like it was trying to speak. Stranger said, 'They are the only dragon kin allowed to live in the human world, though they were hunted near to extinction for the privilege.'

'Why hunted?' said Eric, patting the creature's back.

'Drake skin makes fine leather armour, easily enchanted. Their blood and body parts are used in rituals. Highly potent, their blood. And they were ridden to war, killed faster than they bred.' Stranger took Aziel in her arms and carried her upstairs. 'I think your new friend will need a name, Eric,' she called over her shoulder.

'You're right.' Eric stroked the creature's hard leathery head. 'I'll name you after a friend of mine. Nice to meet you, Case.'

The drake shut its eyes, seemed to groan and, to Eric's confusion, twice head-butted the floor.

Eric laughed, thinking that the real Case would get a kick out of the beast's reaction, if only he were here to see it.

3

Aziel slept deeply, for Stranger's spell ensured that no noise woke her. Watching her contemplatively, Far Gaze sat on the platform beneath a dark glittering ribbon of winding magic, sniffing in strands of it and murmuring. He'd wrapped a white sheet about himself.

When Loup's scale vision ended he rose from his bed ashen-faced. 'I couldn't find her,' he told Eric with a sigh. 'And I've used up the last little specks of black scale. She may well be gone now, lad.'

'Siel? But what the hell happened?' said Eric.

'He took her. Shadow did.'

'How do you know, Loup? We've got an empty bed and a dream I had. That's enough for you to work out exactly what happened to her?'

Loup gave him a dark look but didn't answer. He filled a dish with water for the drake downstairs.

'What do drakes eat?' Stranger asked.

'Anything and everything,' said Loup, handing her the water dish.

Far Gaze rose from the platform. A ring of dark magic broke from the thick stream and circled his head like a spinning halo. It followed him across the room till he inhaled it with a deep sniff, little curls of it puffing through his lips when he spoke. 'The drake will fend for itself, we need not feed it. Keep anything you don't want in its belly away from it. Shiny things most of all. Seffen used to feed their war drakes diamonds, ages ago. Intended to give them blood lust. Diarrhoea was more likely. But the drakes gladly ate them.'

'What's the odd beast doing here then, eh?' said Loup.

'I'm not the one to ask,' said Far Gaze, his eyes on Stranger.

'Nor am I,' she said. 'I've never seen that creature before in my life.'

'Never seen a drake? I'll credit that. Rarer things, perhaps? Pilgrim, we must speak with you. Stranger, go downstairs until I call you. Go! Do not listen in. I will know if you try to.'

Water dish in hand, she went without a word. Far Gaze sat by the top of the steps, watching her go.

'Is there a reason you have to talk to her that way?' Eric asked him.

Far Gaze laughed. 'What chivalry. Never clashed with her, have you, Pilgrim? Watch your talk around her. Every word she hears, the dragons may hear also.'

'My name's not Pilgrim.'

'You have two names. Eric. And Shadow. Which should I call you?'

Eric scoffed, but he looked down at the bare floor where his shadow should have lain slanted behind him. Far Gaze watched him keenly. 'The Arch Mage does not realise how close his Project is to succeeding,' he said. 'If Vous can do this, he is close indeed to becoming a Great Spirit.'

Eric said, 'Hold on a minute. One of the Arch Mage's war mages helped me out. It killed a Tormentor for us. It "saved" me from you in the woods, when you were in wolf-form, thinking you meant to attack me. Remember?'

'Vividly. The stink of your fear was strong.'

'The war mage wasn't "helping" us on the Arch Mage's orders,' said Eric. 'Was it? Maybe it was nuts, but even if so, the castle lost control of it. So how the hell is he going to control a god? And if he can't, why would he want to create something more powerful than *him*, which he can't control?'

Far Gaze's eyes gleamed. 'Indeed. And you can be assured this has gradually dawned on him, though maybe far too late. What do you think the so-called Arch Mage will try to do now? Eric? Loup?'

'You tell us,' said Loup.

'He will ruin Vous, while he still can,' said Far Gaze. '*If* he still can. Remove him from the throne, replace him with someone else. Maybe with himself. But it is probably too late for that. The great change draws close, if it has not happened already.'

Eric said, 'I was told the Arch Mage spent hundreds of years trying to make all this happen. Now he wants to prevent it?'

'It would seem so. And I tire of hearing his silly self-granted title. His name is Avridis and he is hardly the greatest mage who ever lived. The most destructive of our era, certainly. The father of all modern war magic. But not revered, not by us.' Far Gaze went to the platform and sniffed a big strand of the winding dark ribbon as though it were pipe smoke to focus his thoughts. His eyes glowed violet.

He said, 'Simply put, a Great Spirit is an enormous power embodied, with a personality to govern it. The dragon-youth can be described in the same way, for they are of similar stature. The Arch has for centuries been drawing more and more power about Vous, binding it to him. With rituals, artefacts, by making people swear to him, and other means. But as he has lost control of Vous, Vous has lost control of himself. He opened the Entry Point and called you through, maybe by complete accident. The other gods might one day destroy him as they did Inferno. The destruction all this could cause is unthinkable. But even then, it is not the gravest danger facing us.

'I have smelled much in the air on my travels. Too much to rightly make sense of – the mongrel understood things with his wolf's brain that I do not, when he wasn't busy filling my belly with rotting meat. The war is done. Finished. We have lost. Free Cities who were allies last week now skirmish among themselves. Many people have abandoned their cities, fleeing to Tanton for the final stand. Faifen is gone, Tsith is gone. Elvury belongs to no one, but no one will claim it. Tanton and High Cliffs may hold out for a time, but they are alone. Yinfel has already Aligned without one blade drawn.'

'That'd be right,' Loup muttered.

'There is more yet,' said Far Gaze. 'Indeed the entire war may look like a skirmish before long. To begin with, foreign airs are here. Some of it is harmless enough if left alone. Some is deadly. It is well we are in this place above the ground, for the poisonous airs move lower. There were people made sick by it, whose skin had turned hard.

'But after talking with Loup, it's clear our more imminent danger is Shadow. And he may also be our one hope. What do you know of him?'

'Nothing,' Eric said angrily. 'You ask that like I'm holding some private knowledge back. So does Loup. Do you think I wouldn't have told you by now? All I know is, some kid over by the wall said Shadow would save us all . . .' The words drained from him when he remembered what else the kid had said: *He rides a drake. A red drake . . .*

Far Gaze's glowing eyes peered deeply into him. 'Part of Vous longs to be undone, to be sent to a natural death where he will be at peace. You, Pilgrim, have become that weapon against him, which he himself made. A destroyer of gods, perhaps. Shadow is you. You are Shadow.'

'I don't even know what Shadow *is*. How can it be me?'

'Why you were chosen, only Vous can answer. You are entitled, if you wish, to feel honoured. In a way, you *have* been honoured. Invited to be part of great events. Though your being chosen might have been pure luck.'

Eric thought back to walking past the door on his way to work, and the sight of an eye at the keyhole. Whose was it? he wondered. The thought that it was Vous's eye made him shiver. 'You say the other gods destroyed Inferno. Why don't they destroy Vous now?'

Far Gaze spread his hands. 'It may be because he is in the castle still, where the other gods cannot seem to go. It may be they have decided *not* to destroy him, at least until he proves himself a danger. It may be that they will do no such thing! It *may* be that they need Vous to ascend and join them. They may need his help.'

'Help . . . with what?'

'That is where Stranger may assist us. Stranger! Come back. Tell the half-giant to come too, he is welcome to hear this. Tell us about the dragons.'

Stranger came up the steps with Gorb and Bald following. 'Your pet drake is sick,' she told Eric. 'He keeps trying to throw up.'

'Why do you say he's *my* drake?' said Eric defensively.

'Forget the drake,' said Far Gaze. 'Tell us about his bigger cousins.'

Strange hesitated then went to sit on the platform. She breathed deeply of the dark winding ribbon of magic overhead. 'What should I tell?'

'To show us you are not loyal to the beast who so callously used you,' said Far Gaze with narrowed eyes, 'tell us everything.'

She glared at him but said nothing.

'I am not going to be patient with you much longer,' said Far Gaze. 'The beast may come back to recover its prize. You had better prove you're worth fighting over. For there is an easier way to ensure it doesn't get what it wants.'

'If you want a dragon wrathful with you, take that easy way,' she said hotly.

He smiled. 'Are you *quite* sure he would be wrathful?'

Tears brimmed in her eyes. She gave Far Gaze a look that reminded Eric of Siel lining up a target with her bow.

Stranger turned to Eric. 'I don't know quite where to begin.'

4

'The dragons used to own this world. They had run of Levaal for a very long time. Everyone knows that much. The greater ones each had a region as his or her own. They fought at times, but not as often as we do. There were gods back then, but only three: Mountain, Tempest and Inferno. The old gods. But we are not concerned with them.

'Of the dragons, there are eight Major personalities remaining. They are the original and only brood of the great Dragon, their Parent, overseer, guardian of Levaal, the Link. And protector of *your* world, Eric.'

'*My* world?'

She smiled at him, sadly it seemed. 'I told Case on the castle lawns that Levaal means *link which protects*. This world is the Link between your world and the world you would eventually come to if you went past World's End, down the far half of the Great Dividing Road, to Southern Levaal's *far* side, and on through the *far* Entry Point. There is another world on that side, Eric, though whether it is like yours or not, none say. And you would find, guarding that Entry Point, another Dragon-god, like the one that sleeps somewhere near *our* Entry Point.

'Yes, there are two Dragon-gods,' said Stranger, noticing a look exchanged between Loup and Far Gaze. 'They guard their respective worlds like hounds asleep at the front door. The worlds on either end of the Link are not compatible, or so it appears.

The realities, it seems, do not mix. One will consume the other, if they begin to overlap. Yet both realities are drawn to each other. Levaal is – for want of better a word – their battleground.' She smiled. 'And we put so much stock in our human squabbles and feuds! If either of the great Dragon-gods were slain, or sufficiently weakened, one reality would displace the other. It may be your world's reality, Eric, which loses. Or your world's reality may triumph and spread itself to a new place.'

'Levaal's reality is not my world's reality,' said Eric.

'But in some ways they are similar. No? Or you and I could not live here. Dyan would not tell me what is in Southern Levaal, nor what is found through the far Entry Point beyond it. Would you go through a door there too, Eric, if you found one?'

'Nope.'

Stranger played with a winding dark thread which fluttered over to her from the platform. 'The strain between the opposing worlds, the conflict, the "war" if you wish, has gone on as long as either world has existed. The point the two straining forces meet is World's End. Where until recently the Wall stood.'

She paused to suck thin curling wisps of magic air. Loup watched her closely as though expecting an outbreak of spell-casting. A little glimmer played in her eyes, violet like Far Gaze's eyes had been earlier, though hers were not as bright.

She went on. 'The Wall was made when humans were brought to live here. Dyan thinks the Wall was put up so that the second great Dragon would not know human beings dwelled in this half of Levaal; so it would not know that all the dragons had been replaced by something new. But these are Dyan's words; if you are distrustful of me, you are surely distrustful of him. And everything I tell you is suspect.'

'Leave that decision to me. Speak on,' said Far Gaze. His back was turned to her and his eyes were closed. Loup too did not look at her directly as she spoke. 'How were the dragon-youth imprisoned?'

'Dyan knows, but he never told me, and he spoke as though the subject brought him bad memories. I know the Major personalities fought their Parent. They lost. Eight were spared – there were once twelve. Of the slain not even ghosts are left and the dragons never speak of them.

'The eight survivors surrendered and agreed to their imprisonment. This realm was cleared of all dragons except the little drakes, who remained to serve the world's new owners. Us.'

'Why did this happen?'

'Because humans came to *your* world, Eric,' she said. 'I don't know the tale of their arrival in Otherworld. But did not dragons used to live there?'

'Dragons ... no. Dinosaurs, yes.'

'A strange word. Great magical beasts, were they not?'

'I don't know if they had magic or not. We found enormous bones buried in the ground, from ancient times. But that's all.'

'So it is true. Dyan says dragons called your world home. And when your world was cleared of dragons, so too was this one. When humans took their first steps across your world, so too were they brought here. The Dragon-god shunted aside Its own young to make room for us. But the dragon-youth, and the Minor personalities who are still imprisoned with them, have never stopped wanting freedom. They move to claim it. Whether that means they intend a clash with their Parent, or whether they have ways to avoid such a clash, I do not know.

'And here is the heart of it. The dragons do not have room in their reclaimed world for any of us. They have little love for us, we small weak self-important beings whose existence denies them their freedom.'

'Not for *any* of us?' said Far Gaze with a half smile.

Stranger smiled too, without humour. 'You guess well. They intend to keep a small number of us alive. Those of us who help them gain their freedom. They call this group *the Favoured*. I was told I was one of these. But before you call me a traitor to my kind, that was not why I helped Dyan. I helped him because I loved him.'

Far Gaze quietly laughed. 'How many Favoured will there be?' he said.

'I was not told. Enough to fill a city, enough to fill a house, I do not know.'

Across the room, Gorb had been busy watching Bald the Engineer trying to build a new version of Eric's gun and trying to keep him quiet. The half-giant it seemed had been following the conversation, for his voice carried across the room: 'Over at the village, if we ever need to kill some sheep, we say soothing things. To lead them to slaughter with no fuss. I don't know any dragons. But I'll bet they don't think much more of us than we do of sheep.'

5

'Tell us about Dyan,' said Far Gaze. 'What does he want?'

'It's a mistake to think all the dragons are of the same mind, any more than we are,' she said. 'Dyan does not hate us. He enjoys women very much. He enjoyed his spell play with you, found you a delightful novelty. He would never have killed you. Among the Major personalities, there is division. Four, I think, hate us with fury and poison we cannot imagine. Others – Vyin, Hyan – do not blame us for the crime of existing. But they are only two. And of those two, Vyin may be the only true friend we have among the great Dragons. The idea of the Favoured is a compromise between them all. Without Vyin, there would not even be that much.'

'If Dyan could escape, why can't the rest of them?' said Eric.

'You are asking me to guess,' she said. 'Dyan must have known he and I would part, for he did not tell me everything. I know nothing of the magic that holds the dragons in their prisons. They have not often tried to break out, fearing their Parent would wake and slay them. I would guess Dyan was instructed to try, to see if this would occur. Surely the Majors helped him do it. Perhaps he has tasks to perform for them. Perhaps he defied them and got free of his own will.'

Far Gaze said, 'You hold something back. For which dragon does he work?'

'For himself,' she said, face in hands. 'I tire of this interrogation!' She took a few deep breaths of magic, muttered to herself.

'What did you just cast?' cried Loup.

'Nothing! Ease yourself, you need not fear me. As for Dyan, he has had a taste of freedom. He's revelling in it. He *is* supposed to watch us. For which member of the brood I am unsure, nor may you be certain he will do his duty. He is rebellious. And he does not hate us. He may be quite content for his kindred to remain where they are. Why would he care? *He* is free, and here in this realm he is mighty compared to us, beholden to no one.'

'Would he help us, then?' said Far Gaze. 'Can you bring him to our side?'

She laughed. 'Our side in the war among cities? Why would he care about that? Why would any of the dragons? Do Lords care about feuding neighbours in their realm?'

'*We* aren't beneath their notice,' said Eric. 'Your dragon friend followed us all the way from the castle to World's End. If he's spying on us for the greater dragons it means *they're* interested in us, too. And I think we all know that means they're very interested in *me*. Or should I say in Shadow?'

'Everyone is,' said Loup. 'The Mayors, the dragons, even that foul-faced bastard Arch Mage.'

'Enough!' Aziel yelled, surprising everyone. She had seemed asleep throughout. She rose from her bed. 'Don't talk about Arch like that. *You* don't know him. Just because he's ugly on the outside, you think he's ugly inside. Well *you're* all ugly to me, fouler than death.' In tears she ran down the steps.

Far Gaze said, 'Don't let her escape. Stranger, mind her. *Please*,' he added sarcastically with a bow to Eric.

Stranger went to leave, taking one last big sniff of the magic airs winding above the platform. It made her cough violently. 'What is it?' said Loup. 'You cast something?'

'No! Bad airs in what I just breathed. Foreign. Just a trace, mixed with the rest.'

'She's right,' said Far Gaze. 'I don't need the mongrel's nose to scent that bad airs approach.'

When she'd gone Far Gaze called Gorb over. 'Can I trust her?' he said.

The half-giant rubbed his chin, thinking about it. 'She knows more'n she tells,' he said slowly. 'Sadness is the main thing in her right now, real deep. Makes it hard to see the other stuff behind it. I can't figure out mages as well as regular people. She doesn't plan any harm from my reckoning, though she don't like *you* at all.' He nodded at Far Gaze. 'These others, she's no issue with.'

'Will you watch her for me, Gorb? Don't let her leave the tower without my knowledge, under any circumstance.'

'I'll try,' said the half-giant. 'I fight good. But mages can be tricky.'

VISITORS

1

Impaired by tears in her eyes, Aziel nearly went head-first down the steps.

On the lower floor the drake was by the window. She ran to it and crouched by its head. 'Take me home, quickly,' she whispered into its ear. 'These are *enemies*. They're going to kill me, or . . . *use* me somehow. Why did you bring me here, you horrid thing? They sent you to get me, didn't they?'

The drake's big emerald eyes peered into hers as though he wished she'd shoosh and let him sleep. Which was preposterous. 'Come on, take me home!' she said, slapping its rump as hard as she dared. The drake groaned and heaved up some spit on the floor with a horrible noise. 'What's wrong? You're sick. Serves you right!'

'Aziel!' cried a voice. 'Aziel, come quickly!'

She started and looked around. Stranger's footsteps sounded coming down the stairs, but the voice had come from much closer. 'Aziel! I heard you! Come here!'

There in a triangular shard of the broken window was Ghost, the large hollow-eyed face being jostled on all sides by the others. She picked up the glass and brought it near the drake so that from across the room Stranger would think she spoke to the creature instead. 'How did you find me here?' she whispered.

'Very difficult! We've been going to every window and mirror we can find. So many windows! We're so happy you're here. Are you hurt?' Ghost sounded more frightened than she'd ever heard it.

'My legs are sore from riding this terrible monster. It stole me from my room!'

'We know. We told Arch about it. But Aziel. Is – did they – your chastity, is it—'

'Never you mind that! Go and tell Arch where I am.'

'We'll tell him, but where is this place?'

'I don't know.' She described as best she could remember their flight path to the tower. 'There were some woods not too far. In the shape of a shoe, from high up. Then fields, lots of fields for miles and miles. Tell Arch that they have me! Quickly! Tell him to rescue me before they do something horrible. It's so awful, everyone sleeps in the same room! They have a half-giant here and he smells bad. Those things *eat* people!'

'Who are you speaking to, Aziel?' said Stranger, walking over.

Ghost whimpered in fright. 'I'll tell him!' it said, then vanished.

'No one,' said Aziel, smiling nervously up at Stranger. 'Just the drake. I think he's ill.'

Obligingly the drake retched again, heaving violently and spilling great strings of clear spit onto the floor. 'Help him!' Aziel ordered.

Stranger laughed. 'Evidently I rank low even among the captives,' she said. 'I will obey, O Aziel.' She crouched beside the beast and gently stroked its head. 'What's wrong, little dragon? Have you eaten something you shouldn't have? Is there flame in there that needs to come out? Stick your head out the window, if you have to. Don't set any fires in here.'

The walls creaked as though the tower were in agreement. But the drake breathed no fire. With a horrible choking sound a glut of liquid poured through its open jaws across the floor.

Something shone brightly in the midst of its spew. It was a necklace, gleaming and shimmering. Aziel and Stranger both gasped.

Stranger crouched down beside it. 'Vyin's,' she whispered reverently. She reached for it, then drew her hand back with some effort. 'Don't touch it, girl,' she told Aziel sternly. 'I mean it. You don't know what it is or what it will do. But one of the dragon-youth touched it. Very recently. That means whatever it is, it's dangerous.' Stranger looked at the drake in wonder. 'Where have you *been*, little dragon? What have you seen and heard?'

Case the drake groaned and lay back down by the window to sleep with a guilty look at the mess he'd made. Stranger ran upstairs to get the others.

Aziel stared at the necklace, amazed at how its gleaming prettiness shifted when she closed one eye, then the other. She took a step to the right and found it took on a new set of hues, colours she hadn't ever *seen* before mixed in with sparkling golds, reds and blues. Two steps the other way and it changed again, seeming to draw the room's light about it, making it swirl like a hoop of gems in motion.

She went closer to it, crouched down unmindful of the drake's stinking mess, and reached out just as the others came to the bottom of the steps.

'Don't touch!' Loup cried.

'Aziel, leave it!' yelled Stranger.

Barbarians! She would not take orders from *them*. She slipped the necklace over her head to demonstrate the point. There was a flash of white fire like a lightning strike. Where its metal touched her skin was a coldness so intense it only hurt for an instant before cutting off all feeling. She gasped and fell to the floor as the necklace fused to her, embedded in her as securely as the drake wore his scales.

2

The others ran to Aziel's body but could not get close enough to touch. A wall of heat had come up about her so strong it was a wonder she herself was not engulfed in flame. She appeared unhurt; her chest rose and fell, her face like someone peacefully sleeping.

'She'll survive,' said Stranger, 'though I doubt she will be unchanged.'

They sat as close as they could and watched her. The heat about Aziel gradually subsided.

'What can you tell of that charm?' said Far Gaze.

'Very little. I can tell it is a great work, but so can you. Vyin crafted it, I think. His is the only touch I see upon it.'

'What's it do?' said Loup. 'I can't make sense of those patterns.'

'Nor I,' said Stranger. 'Nor I suppose could any human. But Vyin's having made it should be a relief to you.'

They lingered around Aziel's sleeping body until the heat had eased off enough to crouch beside her. Very carefully, Loup reached a gnarled old hand down and tried to lift the charm from Aziel's neck, but it was not to be moved. 'It's picked its wearer,' he muttered. 'Won't get it off, not easy anyway.'

'I'm not so sure it was meant for her,' said Stranger, looking at Eric.

'Then let it choose again,' said Far Gaze. He went and returned with a hunting knife.

'Don't cut her,' Stranger warned.

'Not more than I need to,' he said, lip curling. 'We can't have blood spill from our Friend and Lord's daughter, can we? Not after all he's done for us. Relax. Loup and I both know arts of healing. I promise not to enjoy myself too much.' He delicately brought the knife's tip to the necklace. The second it touched Aziel's skin the knife was flung across the room and Far Gaze was sent sprawling backward, clutching his chest. Blood gushed from his nose. 'One learns,' he muttered when his breath returned.

'One learns quickly,' said Stranger too quietly for him to hear.

3

Night came with still no sign of Siel. Eric had spent what remained of the day with Gorb and Bald, offering what help he could on the design of their new gun. There were now five versions spread on the floor by the Engineer's bed. Bald's latest model was beginning to resemble a thin length of plumbing pipe nailed to a block of wood. The trigger mechanism was an impressively complicated web of black metal he'd used magic to make. Eric picked up one of the cruder versions, a cumbersome blocky thing which didn't even have a trigger. 'Guys. I'll say it one more time. These things are never going to fire. You realise that, right? Copying the shape isn't going to be enough.'

But Gorb was quietly confident and Bald cackled and babbled

non-stop. He'd even begun to work on projectiles for the 'guns'.

Aziel still slept where she had lain after passing out. None of them dared touch her. The necklace sometimes glowed brightly enough to fill the room with strange light. At times it was nearly invisible, little more than a slight lump about her throat the same colour as her skin.

Eric understood that Stranger felt the necklace was made for him. He was glad Aziel had taken it. But deep into the night he couldn't sleep, despite the soothing sound of lapping waves and breeze throughout the tower. While the others slept, he went downstairs to the window he and Siel had climbed through. The drake opened one eye and sighed. It had given up trying to speak to him; it had tried to do so every time he'd come near it, as though it had important things to impart.

He gazed out at the water's sleepy waves. Luminous fish could be seen flitting about through them. He thought of Case, of his lost friends and family, of Siel. Then he pondered himself. Most vexing were these insinuations that he was of sudden importance to this world he hardly knew. At times these hints ('*you are Shadow . . .*') invited him to live out fantasies he'd had early on, of being a hero to Levaal. But he could wield a sword no better than he could have in his old apartment; he could perceive magic but could not use it. Nor was he even striding toward any destiny but *being moved* toward it, often reluctantly. He was —

He was staring at himself, out there by the water's edge.

He jumped, startled. His likeness down there stood at a strange sideways-leaning angle. Utterly motionless, his arms hung limp from his sides. Eric waved but got no response. The being just stared up at him. Waiting.

Eric put his shoes on and climbed out the window, stepping awkwardly onto the branches of the tree embedded into the tower's side. His feet scraping on the bark as he climbed down seemed a storm of noise – he half expected to hear Loup hollering out the window at any moment, telling him to get back inside.

The strange being at the water's edge just watched as Eric waded into the waves. When he was a stone's throw away Eric said, 'You're Shadow. Aren't you?'

Shadow replied, 'I need to go up there, through the window. I can't. The water won't let me.'

'Answer me. Are you Shadow?'

'I think people call me that. They made stories about me, I don't know if they're true. I don't remember any of it. I don't remember killing dragons, riding drakes, saving people. They say I did all that. But I have only been here a little while.'

'And they say I am you,' said Eric. 'I've done none of those things either. Do you know someone named Vous?'

'No.'

'Are you sure?'

'Listen. I can't get up there.' Shadow pointed to the window Eric had just climbed down from. 'Can you help me?'

Empty black pits stared into Eric's eyes. Inwardly he recoiled but tried to keep it hidden. He said, 'Why do you want to go up there, Shadow?'

'The girl came from there. So did you. I want to see what's up there.'

Something about how he said this indicated Shadow was new to the skill of lying, and not very good at it. 'There's another reason too, isn't there, Shadow? You can tell me what it is. I'm you, remember? We can trust one another.'

Shadow looked at him, giving no indication of what – if any – thoughts or emotions went through him. There were only his words, lifeless as the pits of his eyes. He said, 'You're clever.

I don't think I can shadow you, to see what's inside you. You're different.'

'What's up there that you want, Shadow? And who is the girl you speak of?'

'There's ... I don't know what it is. Something up there is calling me, pulling at me. I need to see what it is. It hurts when I'm this close to it. I followed it all the way here. But the water won't let me cross it. I tried going underneath, too. It won't let me.'

'Who is the girl, Shadow?'

'That's a bad question.'

'It's Siel, isn't it? My friend? Where's the girl now, Shadow?'

'I don't know. A long way away. She went on her own, belowground. It's not my fault.'

'Are you sure about that?'

Shadow was suddenly leaning forward at an utterly unnatural angle. 'This is as close as I can get,' he said. 'It's a strain. Hurts, if I stay here.'

'I'll help you get up there,' said Eric, pointing at the tower's window. 'If you do something for me. Go and rescue Siel. The girl. Wherever she is. Find her.'

'*Rescue* her,' said Shadow as though dealing with a very strange idea. 'How?'

'Just do as she bids you. If you do that, if you bring her here alive and well, I'll be in your debt. I'll help you.'

'I might. If I can find her. If she isn't already dead. She might be. You can't put them back together, when they're dead. When they've spilled out all their ugly insides. Or I might kill her. It depends.'

Eric was taken aback by a ghastly twist of Shadow's face as his lips pulled into a rictus made more terrible by the dark ghost-like pits of his eyes. For a moment those pits widened till they were huge yawning caverns Eric was falling toward, into nothingness. He felt himself pulled forward till he fell face-first into the shallow water. When – shaking – he raised his head, Shadow was gone.

4

To Siel's consternation the little people were now in a great hurry and less open to her pleas for a rest break, as though by walking faster they'd be hundreds of miles to the south in just a little while. Already exhausted, she soon lagged a fair way behind them, and only when the groundmen came upon another group did they pause long enough for her to snatch a brief rest, while they excitedly told their friends of their escape. Soon, far too soon, a little hand shook her shoulder and they told her it was time to go on again, ignoring her protests. The newly arrived groundmen – she counted seven of them – looked at her with great suspicion, and two insisted on walking behind her with their weapons at the ready, despite what sounded like strong objections from the ones she had freed.

Their path wound steadily upward for uncounted miles, past tunnels where the lightstones were large and visibility was much better. This was good, for their path was often a narrow bridge across gaping chasms, surely narrow enough to make small-footed groundmen nervous, let alone big people. She wondered if these paths were designed for this purpose, to keep potential slavers at great peril.

Sounds carried a long way in these depths. There was what sounded like something huge gnawing on bone, the sound drifting up from one of the deep caverns, with a meaty reek like a beast's hot breath. The groundmen whispered reverently among themselves when they'd left it behind, the word 'Mundang' repeated many times, but would not tell her what they knew.

At last they stopped for a break and a meal of some root vegetable one of the groundmen had foraged. Siel's piece squirmed in her hand like something living even after she'd eaten most of it, each bite filling her mouth with tangy juice that cheered the heart like wine. The groundmen nattered among themselves, until they heard a growling sound drift their way on a draft of stale air, and fell watchfully silent. The sound was high pitched and didn't seem far away. 'What is it?' Siel asked one of the freed slaves.

'Devils,' he said. 'They front and behind. Problem. No way up or down, this part. Have to dig. Dig make noise. Noise bring devil. Too much devil! Since bad things, devil take wrong tunnels. Bother us more.'

'Noise bring devil, so you talk, talk, talk,' said one of the newcomers angrily. 'Everyone, shh! Wait here. Devils move soon.'

They waited for what seemed a very long time. There did not seem any more sound from ahead or behind, save the usual underground noises that seemed to find them from far away like messages being passed along by the murmuring stone encasing them. Someone shook Siel awake and put a mining pick in her hand. The newcomers had not trusted her enough to let her wield it earlier, or to wield anything else. 'Move now,' the groundman whispered. 'Be ready. Might be fight, bad fight.'

'Won't the stones tell you when it's clear?' she whispered back.

'Devils talk to stone too. They not same as big people. They live here, they hide in it.'

Slowly, cautiously, one of the group's newcomers crept forward around the bend with his spear in hand till he was out of sight. The rest of them tensely waited, but nothing happened. They got up to follow him when there was a sudden squeal of pain.

With a cry the rest of the groundmen rushed forward. Siel went with them. The passage ahead – two human arm-spans wide – was alive with movement as three pit devils set about tearing the unfortunate groundman scout to pieces, spraying his blood over the large lightstones in the walls and tinting their light red. The groundmen rushed forward and stabbed their spears at the thrashing mess. They drew back when they saw their companion was lost.

Siel drove her pick down into the devils, knowing that only by luck would she strike a good blow and avoid being gored herself. The pick handle jarred badly in her hand, but it caught on something, and as she fell back she saw it had lodged point first between one of the creatures' horns. It shrieked and scurried up the tunnel, drunkenly thrashing at the walls and falling into them hard, driving the pick in deeper till the beast finally fell and stopped moving. The remaining ones grabbed another of the newcomer groundmen who'd strayed too close, and tore him to pieces.

In the midst of the carnage there formed what looked like a small ring of fire. From it an infant pit devil the size of a small puppy fell, the flame about it lighting up the tunnel. The groundmen had been backing away, but they rushed forward to kill the infant with their spears while the parents were suddenly caught up in a squabble among themselves.

Siel had heard that the creatures bred this way, that in a killing frenzy new ones would simply appear as though called from another world by screams of pain. She had always thought it was myth, that these creatures bred in the fashion of most other living things.

'Run!' she cried, dashing past the fighting devils and expecting a stray claw to slice through her as she went. The others came. One unfortunate groundman made it through, but a headless stump spurted blood atop its shoulders before it collapsed. The claw had swiped too fast to be seen.

They ran on till Siel was out of breath. The growls and scuffling of claws on stone were far behind them with no indication of pursuit. The groundmen all went on ahead except for one of the freed slaves, who paused with her. 'Hurt?' he said.

'I'm glad one of you stopped,' she gasped. 'What must I do to prove myself a friend? Not enough to set slaves free. Not enough to risk my life fighting for you.'

'You friend,' it assured her, patting her knee.

'Then why did they leave me here?' she said, tears in her eyes. Even the traitor Kiown had not abandoned the rest of them, even during danger.

'They come back. Scared! Running! Not see you. Don't be sad.'

She got to her feet with a renewed surge of anger at the thing which looked like Eric, for abandoning her here. Then, as though it were summoned by that anger, they were suddenly not alone in the tunnels, and Shadow stood before her.

5

The groundman squealed in surprise.

'What do you want?' said Siel.

'To go through the window,' he answered. 'But I have to help you first.'

'Help? *You* brought me here and left me.'

'You asked to be brought,' he said, tilting sideways like a clock's hand.

'Don't do that! Stand straight.'

His lips curved in a smile, the first time she'd seen anything other than blankness on his face. But he did as she asked and righted himself. 'The fellow told me to bring you back. He said to do as you bid. So ... bid.'

Do as I bid? she thought, baffled. Shadow stared and waited. 'You will take me back to Eric and the others?'

'Yes,' said Shadow.

'Eh-Rick?' said the groundman, creeping toward Shadow for a closer look.

'Don't approach him,' she warned it. 'Shadow. Will you bring my friend back too? He has knowledge we need. He's going to show me where Tormentors come from.'

'Is that what you bid?' he said, seeming to enjoy the word.

'Yes. Take us both to the tower again, if you can.'

She recoiled as he rushed forward and took her and the groundman in his arms. She heard it cry out in surprise. Then the world fell away, fast.

6

Eric went back to the small platform of turf. He sat with his feet in the warm water, fish flitting between them with streaks of light making patterns as though for his personal amusement. Just occasionally a sight like this would make him glad he had come to this world to see occasional miracles buried among the horrors. He longed to go back home and tell people some of what he'd seen, whether or not they'd believe him.

With no warning or ceremony, there was Siel at the water's edge, staggering around dizzy and exhausted. She collapsed.

Eric hadn't recovered from his surprise at seeing her again before he was halfway across the water. He had taken Shadow's little eye-trick as refusal to help.

The shape lying beside her he assumed was a backpack or something, but it rolled across the ground and made a sound like something quite ill. There was no sign of Shadow. 'Siel!' he said, gently shaking her shoulder.

'Let me sleep,' she murmured. She opened an eye, saw him and recoiled.

'It's me,' said Eric. 'Not Shadow.'

When he spoke the word Shadow appeared, moving up from the ground sideways like a fan's blade. His arms hung dead from his sides, on his face was that ghastly imitation of a smile. Eric quickly lifted Siel by the armpits and dragged her into the water, where Shadow claimed he couldn't go. Some strength returned to her legs, enough for her to stand on them.

'Get the small one,' she said. 'He didn't take the journey well.'

'Nor did you,' said Eric, taking the groundman in his arms, finding it weighed more than Siel did.

Shadow watched all this unfold with an air of expectation. 'Now take me to the window,' he said. 'It hurts, that pull. It's worse when I'm close to it. Make the water let me cross.'

'No! Don't let him come inside,' Siel whispered fiercely.

Eric gestured to be quiet. 'I'll go and open the window for you, Shadow. We won't be long. But it's difficult work. Be patient.'

Shadow didn't answer and didn't move as they went through the waves. Siel groaned at the thought of climbing up the tree. 'Go under,' said Eric. 'Are you strong enough to take the midget?'

'No.'

He eyed off the dark space beneath the tower, where both Loup and Far Gaze had warned him not to go. Beyond the water Shadow was a silhouette tilted sideways. 'I'm not letting him in,' Eric told Siel. He explained his phoney promise to get her rescued. She listened without comment.

He'd have known, even if she *had* thanked him, that she did not hold him and Shadow very far apart in her mind at all. He knew then that she would never love him, if that had even been possible before. She had not seemed like someone capable of love as he understood it, but the faint hope of it had been sweet. Faint as the hope had been, it was a strangely bitter loss.

Holding the groundman's head carefully above water he paddled through the arch beneath the tower, surprised by the strength of the whirlpool's downward pull. Swimming made pain flare in the wound where a groundman had stabbed him with its spear. There was a deep spot to the staircase's left, one of three visible from the steps by daylight, where water could be seen winding down in a funnel. He let the pull from it take him toward the stairs, fumbling ahead for the steps he couldn't see in the dark. His hand hit something hard. With Siel's help, he lifted the groundman up onto the floor.

It was the wind blowing over the water which Loup felt spoke a secret language it would be dangerous for him to hear. He heard mutterings about cold, about someone returning here, about danger coming through the skies fast as wind. Someone called his name and begged him to stay and listen, for a likely future needed to be discussed. But he was thinking of Siel, thinking of forcing her to kiss him while they'd rutted like animals back at the hilltop, right after he'd lied to her. Why should she have loved him?

Inside the tower, Stranger was awake and watching the staircase as they climbed to its middle floor. 'Is Shadow out there?' she said.

Eric nodded. Siel, coming up the steps behind him, stared agog at Stranger without speaking.

'No need to fetch your bow,' said Stranger, a hint of darkness across her face as she recognised the girl who'd fired at her more than once.

'I'll explain when you've slept,' Eric told Siel. Without reply she staggered up the steps and collapsed on the first unoccupied bed she came to. Eric laid the groundman down in the one next to her.

It was within the hour that Shadow discovered he had been deceived. A cry rang out. Some of those sleeping stirred but were lulled back to their dreams by the soothing sound of waves. Eric was wide awake and not so fortunate as them.

When at last sleep found him, he was Shadow again.

7

It was confusing, more than anything greatly confusing. They knew of the lure he felt – he had told them! Their indifference ... it was incomprehensible.

The thing drawing him here was the same as he'd felt coming from the drake in flight. Had it come from the drake itself, or some power it temporarily held? He didn't know. It gave him entirely new sensations – thirst, hunger, lust, desire – all of which had filled empty spaces inside him not known as empty until they were partly filled. Each of them told him urgently: You are called here! Go!

He circled the tower as fast as he could for much of the night. He went so fast that winds rose from him, and a path was dug into the ground around the water, the water he could not cross. He howled as day broke then left that place, went back to the village where he'd killed the dogs. Its people mostly slept. He took a few apart but discovered – having forgotten – that this was a hollow thing which brought no joy or relief. Nothing would fill these empty spaces inside him. There were many empty spaces, things missing from him which he'd seen in others. Should not he have those things too? Memories, things connecting him to the world, to people, to places? There was nothing there!

Away south he went, desperate to see something new to remove his mind from pains and trials. There was that stupid god flying very low now, with a crowd of people pointing and staring. More people beyond them, an army spread in a long thin line with pikes and spears, keeping people from getting closer.

Among them he went, not wanting to shadow any in case they taught him more of the things he was missing, not killing any because it would be pointless. The god, however. Could he shadow the god?

He listened to soldiers' talk and learned the god's name was Nightmare. Nightmare was keeping the big stoneflesh giants from crossing over where the Wall had been. It was not an easy task, even for a god. One of the giants there was standing still, facing across into the southern half, and Nightmare flew about him, doing something with his hand that made the giant turn back the other way. Then Nightmare flew east with speed Shadow admired, but speed which he felt he could surpass.

He could shadow Nightmare, he believed. He had shadowed that dragon, back near the tower. That had been hard, maybe even dangerous, and a god would be more so. But he could do it.

And yet, if men would teach him bad things about himself, how much more would a god teach? No! He would not do it, not yet. Frustrated, he screamed again and every human head in sight turned at the sound. 'I am Shadow,' he told them, and whether they understood him or not, there was not one set of ears from him to the horizon that did not hear.

SHAPERS IN THE QUIET

1

As patrols and even armies on full war march became more common deep in Aligned country, they spent longer periods in the quiet. One evening they came to one of those patches of glowing white crystals floating in the air, a way off the road. On sight of it Anfen made a hissing sound, grabbed Sharfy and flung both of them to the ground. They crept closer on their bellies, like men advancing under arrow fire on a battlefield. 'Make no sound,' Anfen whispered.

The things looked a little like a glowing wasps' nest half the size of a man. Their light flickered quite beautifully, and Sharfy wanted to touch them badly.

They waited and watched for what might have been days of dream-like time. Time passed strangely in the quiet, and in a way seemed not to pass at all. Sharfy even slept. Then Anfen shook him and pointed off to their right, where something approached.

It was just about the only moving thing in the quiet that Sharfy had seen. It had no clear shape, was just a disturbance between them and the space behind it. It drifted toward the glowing diamond things, seeming to engulf some of them, slightly dimming their light. What may have been a hand in its midst could be seen closing over one of the diamond things, squeezing it until it was gone. It broke a second glowing diamond thing apart into tiny pieces, scattered them along the ground in a roughly circular shape, then one by one each little glowing broken piece's light went out. It moved on to a third, a fourth, and one by one devoured each of the beautiful floating objects.

Anfen took them out of the quiet, back into the world of harsh light where they lay among gravel and brambles. They heard the *thump-thump-thump* of an army marching in time, south along the Great Dividing Road. 'How long were we gone?' Sharfy said.

'There's no time in the quiet,' said Anfen. He dry-retched like someone dying.

'What *is* the quiet? Come on, you can tell me. I asked you enough times.'

'My redeemer can go there. People are not allowed. If we alter things there, it could change this world terribly.'

'What were those glowing shapes?'

'A spell.'

'Huh?'

'The glowing shape was a spell. That other thing we saw was called a shaper. Spells change reality. The quiet is like a hollow space behind a painting of our world. In this realm a spell looks instant – the mage gives an instruction, reality changes. In the quiet, outside time, shapers carry the instructions out.'

'Shaper. Was it alive?'

'In a sense. Not like other living things. Not even like elementals or ghosts. It was making a spell's effect become real. Weaving it into this reality. The glowing pieces are what a spell's instructions look like, to our eyes. To the shapers it is a language. It tells them what to do. That spell we just saw may have been cast long ago. Centuries, in this realm. Or maybe hours ago. Or maybe in the future. There's no knowing. It was not a very powerful spell.'

'Huh? How you know?'

'Because the glowing pieces were small. I have no name for them.'

They marched on. The castle came into view on the horizon like an enormous mountain of white ice. Sharfy said, 'Boss, it's time we stopped for a rest. You're taking me to the place I'm going to die. That's pretty clear. Do I have to be exhausted when we get there?'

Anfen muttered reluctant assent then followed Sharfy some way off road, to what seemed an unmanned guard house. Inside they found chairs, some water but no food. Sharfy put his feet up and sighed. Anfen stood in the doorway, gazing out at the road, unconcerned about being seen.

Sharfy looked at the big purple scar around Anfen's neck, from which a blood drop slid like a lone tear. 'Boss. How come you can take us there? To the quiet? You couldn't do that before. Something happened to you but you won't tell me what.'

'We are not allowed there,' Anfen said. 'We are not to interfere with the shapers. Even the dragon-youth had no way to get there. Some of the gods had the great Dragon's permission, and It showed them how. But they are nervous to go there. My redeemer is the only one who often goes. He took a grave risk, to let me pass back and forth at will.

'My redeemer told me of a mage named Avridis. I knew him already. He allowed the foreign airs in. I knew that too. He must now be told what he did, and he must help undo it. He will be shown. Given a choice.' Anfen turned and looked at Sharfy with eyes that reminded him of an Inferno cultist's. 'This is not a quest my redeemer gave me. Understand that. It is one I gave myself.'

'And to me, huh?' said Sharfy.

'And you. Be at peace. We have not far to go.'

2

Soon the castle was more than a distant shape. It loomed like a world in the sky, the Great Dividing Road running from its open jaws. Its head seemed to gaze directly at them as they came nearer. Sharfy was certain now that the great Dragon-god was no myth at all, that It alone could have built such a structure, and that it must be true what they said: It slept beneath the castle, deep belowground, and changed the world with Its dreams and thoughts. Those shapers, Sharfy wondered, they're part of It, maybe. Little thoughts It has. The quiet must be where It does Its dreaming. And maybe we can't go there in case we wake It up ...

When the day came, finally, that they reached the castle's lawns, they stood quite plainly in open sight before the steps of the front gate. The castle's enormous mouth stretched wide to either side of them, wider than the Great Dividing Road. Though there were no beggars from the city today, the Road was a bustle of activity. Sharfy had never felt so visible, yet none of the castle army people paid them the least attention for an hour or more, until a commander in uniform and full chainmail paused, glanced at Anfen's sword, and said, 'With whom are you? Where is your uniform?'

Anfen slowly drew his sword. A glimmer of white light flickered up and down the blade. 'Bring me Avridis,' he said.

The commander looked at him, not comprehending. 'Answer my question.'

'Bring me Avridis or be cut in half.'

The commander, stunned, laughed. 'Who is this fool?' he asked no one in particular. Anfen made good on his promise with a flash of sparks as the sword did its work.

A ripple passed through the people nearby. The bustle of movement came to a gradual cease and heads turned. A silence drew out, broken abruptly as other men drew weapons and charged them.

Anfen looked sick, starved and weary, but moved as fast as Sharfy had seen any man move. Any who came at him were soon dead on the ground, their blood spilling over the Great Dividing Road.

An alarm sounded like the huge call of a deathly bird. Sharfy watched the sky uneasily, expecting a war mage, but none came. 'Stay near me,' Anfen told him. Soon the pair of them were surrounded by a ring of heavily armed men. One half held up shields they crouched down behind, while the other poured arrow after arrow at them.

Anfen stood completely still in the midst of it as arrows rained down, but somehow none of them struck home. It was like a big invisible shield guarded them. Sharfy felt heat building from Anfen, then saw his armour was glowing faintly red, and growing hotter the longer the soldiers shot bolts at them. Soon the heat was painful.

Luckily the rain of arrows stopped. A huge litter of them lay on the Road's pavement. Someone shouted an order to charge. Anfen screamed a war cry to Valour and swung his blade over-head in a blurring wheel of death, and Sharfy watched with his mouth hanging open as those who charged were cut savagely down in a storm of blood, until none dared attack them any more. The rest ran.

'Bring me Avridis,' Anfen yelled. 'Bring him!' Then panting and haggard, he collapsed. He was drenched from head to foot in blood. The few castle troops who remained did not dare go near him even as he lay there.

The wailing alarm was answered by another which came from further away. Sharfy felt what seemed a million pairs of eyes peering down at them from the castle's windows, near and far.

He cleaned as much blood off himself as he could, then began wiping it from Anfen's face.

What seemed a long time later, there was movement at the gates above the steps. A group of men in full dyed-black plate – elite guard, Sharfy knew, having heard many stories of them – came out and stood in a new ring around Anfen, heavy double-sided axes as tall as they were planted handle first at their feet. These men would all be wearing enchanted gear, Sharfy knew. They would swing those huge heavy axes fast as whips. Their armour would be like trying to pierce a wall of stone. But he thought Anfen's sword would cut through it with ease.

Anfen didn't even seem to notice them. Sharfy longed to ask the elites if it were true that they were fed half-giant blood before each battle (or was it drake's blood?), but instead he tried to look menacing, as though he'd had a hand in dispatching the dozens and dozens of dead warriors lying on the road around them.

The Arch Mage himself – alone, without ceremony – came out soon after. He hobbled to the small balcony, before which townspeople usually came to beg for work. He looked at the bodies but gave no hint of what he thought. He said, 'You have come a long way. And through dangerous country. But it has not made you weak, I see.'

Anfen stood and leaned heavily on the handle of his sword, its tip not piercing the Great Dividing Road.

Anfen said, 'Very dangerous country. The men who fight and die for you would not like to know you set Tormentors free, to mop them up when they return from the final battle.'

The Arch Mage's gaze lingered on the mound of bodies Anfen had produced. 'For one who professes concern for my fighting men, this is a strange way to demonstrate it. But I set no Tormentors free.' He stared at Anfen like one trying to solve a riddle. The square gem in his eye socket twisted. 'Some of the beasts won their own freedom. A risk of trying to use them. They are extremely difficult to handle. I must condition all their handlers so that they no longer fear death or pain. Volunteers are . . . rare.'

The elite guards watched them silently.

Said Anfen, 'Do you understand you have set the Pendulum swinging?'

The Arch Mage shook his head. 'I am familiar with the Pendulum theory. I do not subscribe to it. Some of my Strategists do.'

'You should have listened to them.'

The Arch Mage leaned forward upon the rail and sighed. 'Otherworld usually has greater *material* science than we do. By which I mean non-magical science. In my long lifetime, even in your brief one, Anfen, their advances defy belief. I am nearly certain they would destroy us in war. But in that place, pendulums are a recent invention. They are used to tell the time, I believe. I do not have much time to spare. You have earned an audience with me. Tell me why you are here. That is mighty armour you wear, and a mighty sword in your hand. From where they come I cannot tell. But you are more formidable than when we met by the Wall. I shall be wary of you.'

'And you have more powerful airs to use than you did on that day,' said Anfen. 'But be careful what you cast, and when. This is why I have come. To give a lesson in magic.'

The Arch Mage peered at him curiously. 'You aren't here to duel? That is well. Then I wait, and learn. Teach me.'

'Cast a spell for me.'

'A spell?'

'Any kind of spell. A small one, if you prefer.'

The Arch Mage looked warily at him, then stood. 'As you wish. This one used to amuse my daughter.' There was no visible movement from the Arch Mage, nothing to indicate his casting of the spell – if he did anything, it was by thought alone, and his eye never left Anfen. A small bird, seemingly made of little spots of multicoloured light, fluttered clumsily down the steps, then crash-landed on the ground in a shower of sparks. 'Sufficient?' he said.

Anfen did not answer. Sharfy saw neither of them, then, for Anfen took the Arch Mage into the quiet, leaving him alone by the steps in the hot glare of the castle's elite guard. 'Shit,' he muttered.

3

All the soldiers, and bodies, vanished. The Road was still underfoot, the castle was enormous before them, vaster perhaps than it had been in the normal realm. The sky was twilight, the distant landmarks black against it. The stone walls seemed here in the quiet to swell and recede like the chest of someone breathing. Enormous white glowing jewels, bigger than any they had seen on the road, were all through the sky, some hung low and some far distant.

Anfen and the Arch Mage were alone. By the steps, where he had cast the little spell which had so amused Aziel – he had not realised just now that he'd referred to her as his daughter – a little cluster of diamonds, no more than a handful, hung in the air. The Arch looked about himself with alarm, not sure what had happened, what effect was in play.

Anfen told him about the quiet. The Arch Mage listened.

'In your words, Avridis,' said Anfen, 'what is magic?'

'I explained it to Aziel, days ago. It is loose reality. Made into fixed reality, by designs of the caster.'

'It is here, where it becomes real.' Anfen pointed to the small clutch of diamonds. 'Do not touch that. That is the spell you cast. Those are the instructions to create your bird of light. Those patterns are the language your instruction is written in. A shaper will come to carry out your instructions. To us, the spell looks instant. But this place is outside of time. There are many shapers here, where the airs are strong. Look there, one comes now.'

Indeed two came, distorted patches without shape of their own. But the second drifted away when it saw the first had already reached the spell. In moments it devoured the little sparkling pieces frozen in the air. Then it moved away like something floating in water.

The Arch Mage watched, fascinated. As he'd read theories on the Pendulum and much else besides, he had also read theories of *this* place, and this process, which likewise he had not believed. Now that he found it was real, he already knew more of this place than Anfen would have guessed, this place the theories gave many names: the under-realm, *Kalom* in an old tongue, which meant *dream aspect*. And more names it had.

And he knew there was no magic here for him to use. He was in dire peril.

He made a grand show of his amazement as Anfen lectured. He would not have needed the mound of bodies to see that Anfen had become dangerous. It had been immediately clear that a new power was about his former First Captain, beyond just the armour he wore and blade he wielded. The Arch Mage could not guess what had caused this change; his first thought went out to the mages of the hidden schools.

'If you went to the unclaimed lands, you would find enormous spells not yet transcribed by the shapers, dating back to the dragon days,' said Anfen.

'How can that be so, Anfen?'

'Shapers follow no order. They roam, they move to whatever spells they see, then do their work. Bigger spells take them longer, sometimes occupying many of them for a long time.'

'Why do you bring me here, Anfen?'

'To warn you. If you use foreign airs, Avridis, you will cause foreign shapers to come. Ones from beyond World's End. Already some are here, though for now very few. They read a different language of instructions. They will alter spells already cast in our realm, but not yet made reality. Here, in the quiet.'

The Arch Mage nodded. 'Which means if they alter spells already cast . . .'

'They will alter the past. They will change everything. It is how Vous made Shadow real, and made him part of a common history.'

'Is Shadow here?'

'He can come here whenever he wishes.' Anfen gazed into his human eye and spoke not to the Arch Mage, but to Avridis, the young man who ignored the warnings of mages and wizards long ago, and provoked them into banishing a promising student from their temples. 'You have created something you shouldn't have,' said Anfen. 'With your knowledge you alone can now help make the damage less. It's why I have not yet cut the life from you, as every part of me thirsts to do.'

The Arch Mage nodded to show he understood. His mind immediately went to the canisters of chilled foreign air, in near-complete purity, sitting in storage. And he knew he held a weapon to Anfen's head, and had all of Levaal at his mercy. But he had first to get back to the familiar realm where he could cast to defend himself.

So he listened to all of Anfen's warnings, his instructions to call back the war mages and to forbid them to cast anything until the foreign airs had dissipated. He even hung his head as though ashamed of his deeds. Privately he reflected with amusement on how those with tender consciences assumed that, deep down, others were ultimately the same. So very wrong.

When Anfen finally took him back, he immediately cast a spell which kept his likeness here on the steps like a puppet, while he fled to the safety of the castle, and controlled his puppet from a distance. A useful trick, one that had saved him from Vous's rages many times. He ordered the elite guards to stand down and leave them be.

'As you have taught me, I shall teach you something of value,' he said when they had gone, and he explained about the foreign magic he had captured with airships when the wall was destroyed. Anfen listened, seeming more weary and sick than ever. 'So I have a quest for you, Anfen. My enemies are now your enemies, and they have stolen Aziel. Find her, and bring her to me. Or I will empty what foreign power I have into Vous's chamber. All at once. What effect this will have in our realm, I don't know. Do you?'

Anfen did not answer.

'But now we both know what it will do in the quiet. Thank you for the lesson on magic. I am sorry you find yourself serving me again.'

When Anfen rushed forward and cut the Arch Mage down, the body did not bleed – it vanished into a sheet of mist and he heard mocking laughter.

A VISITOR

1

Well into the following morning Aziel still slept where she'd fallen and the necklace's secrets remained untold.

On the upper floor, Stranger took what Gorb had caught in the nearby woods – two fat birds, three rabbits – and laid them all out on the platform. 'He is starting to worry me down there,' she said, referring to Far Gaze, who had watched Aziel constantly as though her every breath was of great importance.

'Stand back, shield your eyes,' she said. There was a flash not unlike a camera's. When it faded the meat was skinned and cooked golden. 'Don't tell the other mages I did that,' she said, passing the meat around to Eric and Gorb.

'Why not?'

'They're afraid there's something bad in the airs. They don't want much casting.'

'That red stuff?' said Eric, squinting at the dark glimmering ribbon that wound over their heads and trailed out the rear window. 'There isn't any of it there any more.'

'It's clean enough now.' Stranger plucked a thread out with her finger and wound it around like string, till it broke and dissipated. 'But you can see by the way the magic behaves that something is not right. There are ripples and strange movements.'

Bald was pouring water from a rusty metal jug over his seven wildly varying versions of the gun.

'That's enough,' Eric said. He snatched the Glock out of Bald's hands and put it back in the shoulder holster.

Bald shrieked, tried to bite him, tattled to Gorb. 'I know where you sleep,' he hissed.

'Hush, Bald,' said Gorb.

Bald pointed at Eric like a prosecuting attorney. Spit flew from his mouth. 'You would have to expand his *being*. He will *observe* in a seat above the world, strapped in hanging, effects of *deeds*, effects throughout ages *stretched*, each dependent on innocent *deeds* about them as a demon skipping on dry rocks across a *river—*'

'Bald, hush up and do your work,' said Gorb sternly. 'No one wants to hear that stuff. It doesn't mean anything anyhow.'

'One day the poison shall be *expelled!*' Bald shrieked in anguish. He went back to sprinkling drops of water over his creations like someone watering plants, glowering murderously at Eric.

'Those guns he's making, they're sort of alive,' Gorb explained. 'That's why he's watering em. He couldn't figure out what makes the trigger send out the – what did you call it?'

'Bullet.'

'Yeah. So it was easier to bring a part of the gadgets to life,' said Gorb. His fat lips pulled the meat from a poultry shank with one quick suck. Big hunks of it showed in his teeth when he spoke. 'He's been trying to work out how smart to make them. Enough so the guns understand what they're meant to do: shoot. But not so smart they can decide if they want to obey or not.'

'Can he bring any object he wants to life?' said Eric.

'Sure, if he finds the right airs.' Gorb chewed up the poultry bone as though it were a biscuit with three crunching bites then swallowed the bone chips. 'He could bring a chair alive, say. But why? It wouldn't do much. And you'd need to look after it. Food or water or firelight, whatever it needed. If you didn't, it'd die and fall apart. No one wants a chair like that.'

'How's he do it?'

'Only Engineers know,' said Gorb sagely. 'You saw them dolls we did. Weren't easy to make, took us ages to find the airs. But there's good airs here, I guess.' Eric was newly nervous to learn the crazed little man had such powers. 'You did good to make him mad, just now,' said Gorb. 'He's trying to make the alive part of the guns so they're always angry. Why else would they want to shoot at something? Now he's putting the anger you gave him into the guns.'

'How long till they're ready to fire?'

'They're almost ready now,' said Gorb. At Eric's look of disbelief, he said, 'Yep, all we need's to make some bullets. Rocks we can sharpen, maybe. Something that'll fit in those – what do you call em? Barrels.'

'You can see why Engineers are prized property,' said Stranger.

Eric said, 'Why didn't it occur to anyone in this world to make guns before now?'

'As It wills,' she said, shrugging. She took the scraps and bones as though to toss them out the window, but Gorb took them from her and shovelled them into his mouth, devouring the lot. 'Such a weapon was not part of this world until you brought it here,' said Stranger. 'Just as past Pilgrims brought versions of all other weapons we use. The gun had no place here until you came. Now yours is here, it can be made real and copied. You should bring more things, if you ever return to Otherworld.'

'Stones!' Bald screamed. 'I need stones! Bring stones!' He clawed at his own face, opening up the grooves dug in the last time he was worked up. Blood poured down his cheeks.

'I'll get them,' said Stranger.

When she'd gone down the steps Gorb remembered he was meant to watch her. 'Eric, I better stay with Bald. Sometimes he hurts himself bad enough to nearly die. Can you go with her? Make sure she comes back like Far Gaze asked me? You got your gun back now.'

'I don't think I'll need it for her,' he said, standing. *And I don't know that it will be much use if Shadow returns.* But its weight in the holster reassured him nonetheless. He loaded it then followed her.

2

At the water's edge Eric found Stranger crouched to examine what looked like a scorched path burned into the ground in a neat ring about the moat. 'Enough heat to melt the rocks. Our new friend did this, didn't he?' she asked as he stepped out of the water.

'Yes. Can you sense him nearby?'

'Never him; he goes unfelt. But . . .' She looked at the horizon and he saw excitement on her face, which she quickly masked. 'Stones. There don't seem to be many here. Let's try over there, near the woods.'

There were occasionally villagers around, come to stare at the tower. They'd learned a healthy respect for the dangerous mage who had boiled its waters and sent a Tantonese patrol away, shrieking in pain. Now a young girl, alone among the trees, ducked out of sight of Eric and Stranger. Eric pretended he hadn't seen her.

'Here's some,' Eric said, finding a few smooth pebbles at his feet and stuffing them in his pockets. But when he stood Stranger was no longer with him. She did not answer his calls.

He went to where he'd seen the girl. 'Hey there. I see you, hiding behind the bush there. Come out, you're safe. I'm no scary wizard. Did you see where she went?'

The girl emerged and pointed to her left.

'You look frightened,' he said. 'What's the matter?'

'A dragon's in there,' she whispered in an awed voice.

'*What?* A dragon? Are you sure?'

'I'm going to ask the wizard to kill it. Will he? He's your friend. Can you make him?'

'If by wizard you mean Loup, the most dangerous thing about him is his breath. Why would you want the dragon killed?'

'It killed some people in our village. My friend Shalinta's parents. She's alone now. We are looking after her.'

The dragon killed them, or did Shadow? he wondered. Aloud he said, 'That's very sad. Can you take me to the dragon? Quickly, I need to see it. Then I'll speak to my wizard friends about it.'

'Do you promise?'

He nodded solemnly. She led him in through the same part of woodland Gorb had hunted game from earlier. The trees were spaced a good distance apart, another of those little hunting playgrounds made (it seemed) especially for human convenience. It wasn't far before he caught sight of Stranger's green dress ahead, and a larger shape looming before her. There was a sonorous musical note, not obviously speech at first.

Adrenaline shot through him as another miracle revealed

itself among the horrors: a dragon! A living dragon, as real as the trees.

The village girl evidently did not find the sight miraculous. She ran. The beast glanced up at the sound of her quick feet crunching leaves. Eric ducked out of sight and crawled closer, quietly as he could, shielded from the dragon's sight by a thick trunk with a fan of bush at its base.

The dragon was bigger than a horse; its scales of many sparkling shades tended toward the green of the woods. Its build was sleeker than the smaller drake's, which seemed clumsy and bulky by comparison. This was no mere animal; it was beautiful, he thought, a higher being, its mouth shaped up in a slight permanent grin, the power about it as real as heat about a fire. He wished he were close enough to stroke its head, which was lowered as though in supplication to Stranger.

She stood before it with her arms crossed. Eric could hear her weeping.

'There are no more fitting words, in all the poetry of your kind or mine, than these: I am sorry,' said the dragon Dyan, its voice like a deep woodwind instrument. It peered up at her with big beautiful eyes. The way its wings were spread flat on the ground to either side of it seemed to convey shame.

'The answer is *no*!' said Stranger.

'And yet you remain here to speak with me. I use no magic on you now, O *Hathilialin*, Great Beauty. Find forgiveness for me! Draw it from the memory of love, if love has truly left you.'

'How you cheapen the word. You want something. So you return.' Her voice wavered with tears and anger. 'Ride me like a mule again! You left me to die in that village where the air was bad. You have not even asked what happened. The wolf found me while you were gone.'

'Has he hurt you?' the dragon said in a harder voice. A ripple of bright red passed through its scales.

'Don't pretend you care about that now,' she said.

'Great Beauty, who I freed from the cavern's cruel claws. Great Beauty who I saved! I have not forgotten the flow of your moods. There is a secret inside that you long to tell. Tell it to me! I ask you, Great Beauty, using no arts or devices. Instead I offer freely a secret of my own in the hope you will reciprocate. And it is a warning to take care. Do! There is another dragon free.'

Stranger was shocked to silence for a moment. 'Another dragon? No!'

'There *is*. I felt it, days ago in these very woods. It was watching me. It came upon me by surprise, as I . . . as I sought you out so desperately. I'm nervous. I am *frightened*. There were not supposed to be more. I do not know who sent it. I know nothing of it at all. The moment I felt it near, I fled quicker than the wind. I have sought it ever since, fearing it would come for you, but can find no trace. It hides from me with great skill. It may watch us now. Indeed I feel that something does.'

'Why has it come?'

'To watch me.' Dyan lifted his head and gazed about the woods, eyes gleaming. Eric ducked away from what felt like a searchlight beaming about him. The colour of Dyan's scales shifted from green to deepest blue as he crept closer to Stranger. A thick fallen branch split under the weight of his feet. 'I have not done my duty. I have been lax, idle, have been . . . indulging myself. Swimming with you in lagoons, soaring the skies. It is so different here now! You have no idea the beauty of this place, after being in *Takkish Iholme* so long. But Tzi-Shu is angry. It was surely she, or Shâ, who sent the new one to spy. If they deem I have failed them, I am doomed when they descend. I must go now to World's End, naked and openly, if you will not come and hide me in your great beauty.' The dragon sighed, a low piping note that sent shivers down Eric's back. Dyan said, 'Things must have moved too slow for them. After uncounted years, with so little time left to wait, they have discovered impatience.'

'What will you do?' said Stranger with fear in her voice.

'I will go to where the stoneflesh wait to cross. Two gods prevent them. I will try to—'

'No!'

'I must. I want this no more than you. My freedom is enough. I don't need theirs. But if I am being watched there is no choice. I will be careful. I will not battle them, don't fear! And I will return for you. I swear it.'

Stranger was crying again. 'You have no idea how much you hurt me,' she said.

'Never again! But, Great Beauty, I must act. If only I knew the other dragon's mind. Will you share yours with me?'

Stranger lowered her voice and Eric had to risk crawling closer to hear the end of her story. '. . . the girl has it. Or more likely, *it* has *her*. It has fused to her neck and won't come off. It was surely made for the Pilgrim. The wolf contemplates her murder to remove it, but the charm will protect her. Vyin made it.'

'Vyin!'

'I'm sure it's his touch I see upon it.'

'Do the humans know the artefact's function?'

'I guessed some things, but keep my guesses private. It's not easy. The wolf hates me; the half-giant has keen eyes. The charm must be for the being they call Shadow.'

The dragon crept closer. 'So, he has been made real. What have you learned of him? What are his powers? Is it as Shâ guessed?'

'I have not learned much at all. The Pilgrim and he are linked somehow, but he knows less than I. Shadow cannot come close enough for the charm to do its work, whatever that work is. The tower prevents him.'

'Don't let him near! Keep the girl inside until I know more. I must consult the other great ones and tell them of this.'

Stranger groaned. 'Why? Why involve yourself?'

'They will learn of it in time. They always do. And they will call it betrayal and complicity, and hunt me down.'

Dyan's long tail reached around behind her and gently stroked her back. She fended away its touch. 'No! None of that. If you return for me soon I will know your promises have worth. Don't look at me that way! I would rather be held in that foul prison again than feel the pain you did to me. I must go back soon. If you have any more promises, give them now.'

'First tell me – do the human casters sense me? I have been nearby more than once.'

'No. Something at the tower prevents it. It is the water I think: many enchantments are about it. But if you are with no woman – does your Parent not know of you now?'

Eric backed away till he was beyond earshot of Stranger's voice and the deep music of the dragon's. When he came out of the trees Loup was at the tower window, scouting around so frantically it looked like he was having a seizure. After much waving Eric caught his attention. 'Where'd she go?' Loup called down.

'In the woods,' he answered.

'If she's run off, I'll have your skin for a jacket, you and the giant both.'

'I'm here,' said Stranger, stepping through the trees and waving at Loup. She had erased any sign from her face that she'd been weeping. She smiled at Eric.

'We'd better head back,' he said casually. 'I think we've broken the rules to let you outside.'

'All for a good cause,' she said, smiling as though at a private joke.

'Oh?'

She showed the handful of stones she'd collected.

As he set his foot into the waves, he saw a person standing in that space beneath the tower where there was a whirlpool. It was a man waist-deep in the water, tall and bald, with eyes bent on Eric intently.

Having just seen a dragon in the woods, this should hardly have been a disconcerting sight in comparison, yet an odd feeling came over him, as though he had for a long while now been watched by this man, unseen. 'Do you see him?' he said to Stranger.

'Hmm?' She was looking back at the woods where the dragon had been.

The man was gone. 'Never mind.'

As they neared the tower base, a gust of wind blew from that space. He fancied he heard words spoken within it, just a whisper: *Take the girl to Shadow.*

'Which girl?' he called. Stranger looked at him curiously. From the wind there came no answer.

3

In the afternoon Siel called to the tower's top floor Eric, Loup and Far Gaze. They went up the rickety wooden stairs to a little platform overlooking the room, level with the tower's uppermost window. The groundman cowered over near the beds, desperate to escape but unwilling to go down the steps where lurked the half-giant, who held a particular terror for him. The candle brightness of his eyes had gone out. 'His name is Tii,' said Siel.

'Why is he so afraid of Gorb?' said Eric.

She shrugged. 'Big people are bad, so very big must be very bad. He's also angry at me for making Shadow bring him back here. He feels I tricked him. I certainly didn't ask his permission.'

'He owes you his life. I don't care about his complaints,' said Far Gaze, pacing. He still wore the sheet he'd wrapped about himself. His face was dark with stubble and his eyes intense, as though staring at Aziel's sleeping body had carved on it permanently the way he watched her.

Said Siel, 'Tii told me everything he knows, on the condition that we release him. Being "up" is making him sick. He says he will fade altogether if he doesn't get back belowground soon. I don't know if that's true or not. He has renounced friendship with me, though that might have just been heated words.'

'Tell him he's free,' said Far Gaze irritably. 'You're very lucky,' he called across the room. 'I could extract many things from you, information being just one.'

'*Please* don't threaten him.'

'I hate the little shits. Is that all? Goodbye.' Far Gaze rushed back downstairs, the white sheet billowing behind him to reveal a hairy backside.

Siel climbed down, spoke to Tii and assured him Gorb had no evil plans. He embraced her shins then dashed down the steps, diving into the whirlpool. He sank like a rock.

'Is there a cave down there?' said Siel.

'Aye,' said Loup. 'What did the small one tell you? Don't

you mind our wolf, I'll see he learns anything important.'

'Groundman slaves have built a highway, beneath the deepest mines. Tii was not one of those slaves, but once he met some who'd escaped. The highway leads from a vast underground realm near the castle, near the Entry Point, all the way to World's End. He says that far, far belowground, the Wall was already cracked. Well before anything Anfen or the Arch did.'

'What caused the break?' said Loup.

'Something on the far side. It was not the castle's doing. There is no knowing how long the crack was there. One day, in the deepest mine, at the very southern point of World's End, slave miners overpowered a guard and escaped. There was nowhere for them to flee but down. They were not heard from again. It was assumed they starved or fell to their deaths, or maybe stumbled their way through the deep mazes to freedom. But a few days later, something returned to the mine from the deeps, and attacked. All the slaves were killed. A few overseers found their way back to the castle, with a very strange tale to tell.

'The Arch Mage heard the reports and sent a team to explore. Far below the ground, there was a chamber of stone, the size of this room. It had a sliding stone door with runes on it as though cults had used it long ago. Even the groundmen did not understand the runes, and they are masters of language. Holes were gouged into the floor around it and, inside it, the light was a deep glowing red. And one wall of it was *the* Wall, light blue, just as it was above the ground. A long crack had been made in it.

'Tii says that any who went into that stone chamber were warped and perverted by the poisons which poured through the crack from time to time. When people are shut in there, from outside you can hear strange sounds. The bad airs come through from Levaal South in gusts, like something's irregular breath.

'The Arch had the chamber expanded. He sent more people inside it to be changed into Tormentors, and studied how to handle them. He pondered their uses, and knew they could help him win the war against the Free Cities, which back then was in doubt. He ordered the underground highway built, deep as possible, so he could transport the creatures in secrecy.' She looked at Eric. 'Tii says that there is a big store of Tormentors being kept near the castle. Near the Entry Point. Can you guess why, Pilgrim?'

Eric nodded. He did not voice his thoughts: that Tormentors would not last long under machine-gun fire. But then, he didn't know how Earth would handle magic beings used against it, and he did not enjoy the thought of the creatures pouring in waves through streets he'd lived in.

Far Gaze came up the stairs. He said, 'Shadow has returned.'

Everyone rushed to the window. Shadow was indeed at the water's edge, silent and motionless.

Eric had not told Far Gaze yet what he had seen in the woods, nor what the voice on the breeze had instructed him to do. He took the mage aside. 'Keep Stranger here, and keep her away from the windows.'

'What do you intend, Pilgrim?'

'Just trust me, OK?' He went downstairs. Stranger sat by the window with the drake. 'Far Gaze wants you up there,' he said.

She sighed and stood. 'I feel for you, Eric: now you have three mages to deal with.'

'You're pretty easy to handle at least,' he said. She laughed.

When she was upstairs he went to where Aziel lay and carefully lifted her over his shoulder, then headed down the steps and into the water.

Aziel woke. 'Where am I?' she said groggily.

'Among friends. Friendly enemies, at least.'

It all came back to her. She struggled weakly. 'You'll drown me!'

He laughed. 'You'll handle a powerful magic necklace whose purpose you can't even guess, but now you're afraid of a little water?'

He hummed to keep the winds' voices out of his ears, but could not help overhearing some things: it told him his course was the proper one; it said that the great awakening could yet be stopped; it said his mother was dead, that grief at his being away had helped to kill her —

He paused, jagged immediately out of Levaal. 'What did you say?' he said, his voice seeming to silent all other sounds in the whirlpool's little enclave below the tower.

'I said I don't even have a change of *clothes* here, and you're getting my dress—'

'Shh!' But the winds just seemed to sigh sadly.

At the high window Far Gaze went pale when he saw Eric cross the water with Aziel over his shoulder. 'What are you doing?' he yelled.

On shore, Shadow watched him come. Just once he spun about like the blade of a fan cutting through the earth. He stared at Aziel with a ghastly hunger.

'What are we doing here? It's cold,' she said, her voice weakening. She clutched at the necklace. 'Get it off me, it's so *cold*.'

He set her down. She saw Shadow and tried to flee; he grabbed her.

'So that's what it is,' said Shadow. 'It's *her*.' The dead pits of his eyes went wide, seeming as big as the sky. Aziel shrieked as she fell forward into them. Eric fell too, pulled to the water's edge by Shadow's hunger. Shadow's jaw went wide, stretching so it grew longer than his body. Aziel screamed.

Then suddenly Shadow was pulled into the necklace, his body warped and sucked in so fast Eric saw only a streak in the after-image of his closed eyes. When they opened the apparition could not be seen.

Aziel staggered by the water's edge. Gleaming white sparks showered around the necklace. She fell as if struck. Eric picked her up and went back into the water. Shadow could not be seen. 'It burns,' she said pitifully. 'Why did you do that to me?'

'I didn't know it would happen.'

'Does that seem a good answer to you?'

'No, now that you mention it. But you'll be OK. The mages will fix you up.'

'He's in here,' she whispered. 'I ... I can feel him moving around. He wants to break free again.'

Eric understood: the charm had called Shadow. The charm Vyin, humankind's one friend among the dragon-youth, had made had lured Shadow into a trap. 'Don't let him out,' he told Aziel as they went back into the tower. Far Gaze and Loup stared down ashen-faced from the top window.

Aziel didn't answer him. Her eyes were closed. He could feel heat from the charm she wore.

He was almost at the deep part of the water when movement caught his eye, past the water's edge, up among the trees. He saw a shock of red hair. Or thought he'd seen it.

Eric hurried under the tower and out of sight.

IN THE NORTH, IN THE SOUTH

1

Wind howled. At the boundary where the Wall had been, clouds pooled in a bunch above the Road then dispersed to either side of it, as though the Wall was still there instead of a veil. Gusts of mist seeped from the ground now and then, enshrouding the soldiers so that they could not see the next man along.

When sight was clear, through the barrier's roiling veil could be seen less than a mile of shadowy land, a barren plain which shifted aspect when each of them looked at it, depicting: a spread of rubble; or absolutely smooth flatness; or what looked to be a heaving dark sea.

The men across the line had set up positions a healthy distance away from the boundary. They were not quite close enough to throw rocks across it. Early on when a rebellious soldier tried to do that very thing, the god Nightmare rushed his way through the churning clouds, the long dark misty streak behind him seeming to ripple with flashes like lightning. The god stared them down, a hand sweeping across the sky as though to convey a warning not to do such a thing again. No one had.

The commanders had earlier passed down word – in all seriousness – that if they were required to fight, *Nightmare would aid them*! This in response to muttered concern in the ranks for the way their force was spread so thin across World's End. Officers lied now and then, that was a given, but *that* one was a beauty.

The stoneflesh giants had long ceased their marching. Now each one had turned to the south as though it meant to cross over. Nightmare (and Wisdom, some said, though none saw her) would go to each giant and persuade it to turn back around, facing the north again. They did, sometimes for hours, sometimes days. But eventually each one of the great creatures changed its mind and, with shuffling steps that made the ground rumble, shifted back, to face Levaal South again.

None could explain it, nor explain the strange feeling of *push* along the Great Dividing Road. It had been fine to march with, made the miles seem to sail beneath their boots. Was it all the work of their Friend and Lord?

It was on this drizzly morning that the giant closest to the Road, which had for one and a half days faced north, began to turn itself around. The ground trembled as it took two rocking steps with its huge stiff legs.

What seemed a dark cloud on the eastern sky grew large as Nightmare swiftly returned. The men turned to watch, trying to gain some understanding of the Spirit's will. Nightmare flew low, enveloping the stoneflesh giant; the Spirit was about one and a half times its size at present – his size had in these days often changed. The black cloud Nightmare had become crackled with energy. The stoneflesh giant paused in its movements as though being persuaded by a language of huge boulders breaking.

If this sight did not make tales enough for the men to take home, cries went up along the line: *A dragon! A dragon!*

There – a beast came. It was no dragon; far too small! Hardly bigger than a bird it seemed, when compared with the Spirit and the stoneflesh giants. But ... too big for a drake, they saw as it came near. And it flashed with many colours, as though magic was alive about it. Few drakes remained in the world, but no drake did *that*.

The dragon flew fast, straight toward Nightmare and the stoneflesh his body enveloped. The dragon seemed to split into five of itself, then those five split, then those five. A whole swarm of dragons now flew at the Spirit, each one screaming in a voice it hurt the men to hear.

Nightmare moved in a blur of movement away from the stoneflesh, which immediately began to turn south again.

Two of the dragon illusions sped south-east, the rest south-west, as though they meant to cross into Levaal South. Nightmare split himself into two. The air was filled with a humming sound. Wind rushed at the men, enough wind to topple a big section of the line. There was a flash brighter than lightning, with no indication who or what had caused it. When it slowly died away, only a couple of the dragon illusions remained in the sky. They went close to the barrier, close indeed, then wheeled back in a circle, as if they had never meant to cross it.

Nightmare made a noise which shook the ground. There would be talk along the lines later about what the sound had meant, but most felt it was an expression of anguish. The nearest stoneflesh giant, while the god had been distracted, had stepped across the barrier into Levaal South, as though the play between dragon and Spirit – as though that flash of light, which had blasted most of the illusions from the sky – had finally caused it to make up its mind and go. The ground shook with its stiff unbending steps, until it was lost in the veil between the two halves of Levaal, and its rumbling footsteps grew quieter with distance. Nightmare watched it but did not pursue.

Some said they saw the dragon flying north faster than a bolt-thrown arrow, with a cry that could only have been fear; others called it joy.

2

The castle shook itself, knocking a handful of Window-watchers from their seats. The Arch Mage reached for the wall to steady himself but the quake was over before his hand touched it. It was the third such quake today, all of them minor. Vous was surely the cause, building toward his next great outburst. Staff on the lower floors were abuzz with gossip. There was an almost religious tone to it, which the Arch felt was quite appropriate, like the rites of Godstears fishermen to placate Tempest lest she deliver a savage storm.

There were no such rites for Vous. The time approached, the Arch knew, when he should flee and observe the great change from afar. When Vous left the castle, as he surely would when he'd changed, the Arch would return here.

He sensed Strategist Vashun approaching well before he heard the hollow tap of his steps through the Hall of Windows. Here he came, a tall gaunt man they nicknamed 'Death' on the lower floors, barely fatter than his own skeleton and wrapped constantly in bandages. A capable wizard, however.

Vashun paused by a far window and stared. 'There they are again,' he said, referring to the line of rebelling troops which had for some reason set up a picket line along World's End. Vashun sounded amused.

The Arch hobbled over to watch them too. 'Who do you think started this nonsense?' he said.

'Someone with faith in Pendulum theory,' said Vashun. His hoarse voice could hardly be heard.

'You have such faith, do you not?'

'Oh I do,' he said, turning his mirthful gaze on the Arch and not hiding the fact that he thought him a fool. 'But it is too late to worry about it! As for stopping it with a few thousand men—' Vashun broke out into laughter which made his long stiff body twitch.

'I feel it was Blain,' said the Arch.

'Was I a suspect?'

'Of course you were.'

'Not any more? You never know.'

The Arch's fist squeezed tighter on his staff. 'You are full of mirth today.'

'Naturally. The world has reached a point, I feel, where laughter is one of the few options. May I ask, Arch, what is the purpose of those canisters in the hall beyond Vous's chamber? They came off the airships, did they not? Are they not filled with foreign airs of incredible purity?'

The Arch did not reply. Vashun nodded as though he'd been answered. 'The rogue First Captain, Anfen. He put on quite a performance,' he said. 'It got them talking, down below.'

'No doubt.'

'Do you credit what he said? That casting with foreign airs could change reality, even change the past? If so, I find your placing of the canisters outside Vous's chamber to be . . . curious. An outburst from him and he could, potentially, burn through all those airs in a second. With perhaps unpredictable results.'

The Arch turned to face him, a ripple of anger going up his

throat. Through the gem lodged in his eye socket he examined Vashun's aura for any energies indicating treachery, but he saw no obvious sign. 'If what Anfen said is true, I hold a knife to the world's throat. Not just to humankind's. To the higher powers' too.'

Vashun took this in and was a little while without speaking. 'I did not think the loss of Aziel would stir such tender feelings in you. It is a hard thing, to lose control of something cherished. I advise a means of therapy. Take some staff from the lower floors. Not these boring ones, I mean real people with clear minds. Men or women, young or old. Entire families, as you fancy. Tell them to pack their things, they've been promoted. Bring them up. Kill them slowly, in creative ways.'

Arch remembered long years before, the very earliest days before sipping from power's cup, when Vashun had been the only one of the inner circle to make moral objections to the castle's more extreme measures. For a moment, this conversation had been a brief, faint echo of those days.

'You should try it,' Vashun went on. 'The airs behave interestingly, after such acts. I would like your scholarly opinion on that, once you've seen it. And it's soothing for its own sake. It's why I can laugh about potential ruin stampeding toward us. *Potential*, mind. Console yourself, if you will, to know the rebel cities face *certain* ruin. And forget the girl, Aziel. She's gone now. Forever. She's replaceable. She doesn't matter.'

'Arch!' cried Ghost's voice from the pane of a normal window.

The Arch hobbled toward it, surprised. 'Where have you been?'

'Far and wide. Wide and long. Arch, listen! There's something we have to tell you!'

THE PENDULUM'S SWING

1

Cold and heat by turns emanated from Aziel's unconscious body. Eric laid her down on a bed. 'Did you see what happened out there?' he asked Far Gaze.

'I know what my eyes claim. They claim this charm captured Shadow. I don't know if it's true,' the folk mage replied. He slowly reached for the charm about Aziel's neck, but stopped short of touching it with visible effort.

Eric said, 'Siel, get your bow. He's here.'

'Who is?' she said.

'Kiown. Gorb, come. We may have a fight on our hands.'

The half-giant stood and stretched. 'All right. Hey, Eric. Look! Your shadow's back.' It was true; Eric's shadow was faintly stretched behind him, cast by one of the hanging light globes that lit the tower's interior. 'Do you feel any different?' said Gorb.

'No, I don't.'

'Pilgrim, I do not order, but advise you not to go out there,' said Far Gaze, his eyes not leaving Aziel.

'Why don't you order?' said Siel angrily. 'Have you not worked out you are in charge?'

He ignored it. 'I don't need the mongrel's nose to scent a trap. You're being lured down.'

'Maybe, but he'll be the one to regret the trap.' Eric inspected the gun, making sure he hadn't got it wet in the moat. It seemed OK.

'As you like,' said Far Gaze, sitting beside Aziel's bed, still staring at her. 'I have saved you from more than enough peril for one lifetime. If you are determined to die, have at it.'

Stranger was looking from Aziel to Eric as though she was just beginning to guess at why he'd carried Aziel outside, and why she'd been kept away from the windows. He supposed it wouldn't be long till she figured out what he'd overheard in the woods too.

'Are you sure it was Kiown? Was anyone with him?' said Siel, slipping her bow around her shoulder as the pair of them went down the steps into the water. Gorb followed, humming a tune as though they were just off hunting.

'I didn't see anyone else. But even if he has back-up, they won't be expecting us to bring Gorb.'

Eric led them to where he'd seen the lanky redhead – to where he was almost certain he had, anyway. Siel crouched to look at the tracks and headed between the trees, pulling an arrow taut. 'Wrong way,' said Gorb, evidently seeing something she'd missed. He jogged through the trees, branches snapping off on his shoulders. They followed him.

'Is that the one?' said Gorb. At the end of a clearing, Kiown sat with his back to a tree, looking quite relaxed. He affected surprise, pitched an apple core away and belched. 'Siel! Eric!' he cried, springing to his feet. 'How d'you do? You've replaced Doon, I see. Eric, you didn't tell her about all the . . . you know, our *secret*. Did you?'

Siel raised her arrow but something dropped on her from a tree. A masked woman in leathers wrestled her easily to the ground and soon had a knife at her throat. Eric was caught between Kiown and the newcomer, and ended up firing at neither before something had his arms pinned behind him. The gun dropped at his feet. His hands were quickly tied and he was face-first on the ground.

Gorb peeled the woman off Siel, scooped her in the crook of one elbow and seemed to be deciding on which direction he'd launch her like a catapult, when from out of sight stepped an old man in a shimmering robe of many colours. 'Down,' he said in a commanding voice, and Gorb froze, bent almost double in preparation for his throw.

Blain put a palm on the half-giant's forehead and cried in a voice gone high, 'Sleep!'

Gorb sank slowly to the ground.

Blood dripped from the Strategist's eyes. He coughed white puffs of smoke. 'Combat magic,' he muttered, wiping at his eyes. 'Should have taken his offer of horns. No one told me I'd be wrestling giants.'

Kiown picked up the Glock, peered at it for a little while, then for some reason put it carefully in Eric's pocket.

'So this is the Pilgrim,' said Blain, crouching to inspect Eric with a waft of burning hair. 'Untie him.'

'*Untie* me?' said Eric.

'And free the pretty girl. The giant will wake presently. He's not hurt. I am your humble captive.' Blain bowed sarcastically. He coughed up more smoke. The lean wiry man who had tied Eric's hands cut the bonds free and smiled at him. 'This is called establishing trust,' said Blain. 'You were at my mercy. You fared rather well. Now I am at yours. Be nice. I am Strategist Blain. I must speak to whoever leads you.'

'It will be the dog, Far Gaze,' said Kiown, 'now that Anfen's sleeping in the soil.' He pointed at his sword, then held it aloft for Siel to see. Old blood was on it. 'Say hello. Still haven't washed it. I'm rather proud of this stain.'

'Far Gaze?' said Blain, still wiping blood from his eyes. 'Never heard of him. Piss-ant magician? A soup-maker?' He coughed up more smoke. 'Tauk travels here anyway, a day or two away. I'll talk with him. Word of you has spread, Pilgrim.'

Siel picked up her bow. She didn't appear to know what to do with her hands as she eyed off the sleekly muscled, leather-clad woman who had accosted her. Evelle looked back at her, smiling.

Thaun the Hunter bowed and then he, with Evelle and Kiown, melted into the woods like shadows. 'Just a second. Kiown comes up with us too,' said Eric.

'Not permissible,' grunted Blain. 'The Hunters will scout for us. It's likely to extend our lives, if that matters to you. Many things converge at this point. Wait and see.'

Gorb stirred and got to his feet, clutching his head. He looked around in confusion. 'What happened?'

'It will all come back to you soon,' said Blain, eyeing him nervously.

Eric took the gun from his pocket and pointed it at Blain. 'Kiown comes with us.'

Blain chuckled, ignored the gun and marched off toward the tower.

'Easy now, Eric,' said Kiown, stepping back into the clearing. 'The Strategist doesn't believe in your Otherworld toy. I'll come along.'

Siel's arrow tip rose to his chest. 'Drop the sword.'

Kiown offered it handle-first to Eric. 'Add it to the collection.'

At the water's edge Blain paused, tugging at his beard while he examined the tower. 'Some fine work here,' he said, seemingly to Kiown. 'That structure is alive and conscious. It glowers at us.'

Siel said, 'Then take care. We have seen the water rise up and boil when enemies have crossed it.'

'It has that and other means to dissuade us,' said Blain, prodding his walking stick into the outermost waves. 'Let's see its fancy.' He stepped into the water. It remained calm and cool.

Gorb followed Blain closely. 'We'll talk later,' said Gorb.

'About?'

'Three hundred years of murder. Bounties. That sort of thing.'

Blain sighed. 'Very well. As you like. We'll talk.'

'Are you able to watch them from here?' Eric asked Siel as they neared the tower's base.

She nodded. They went through to the whirlpool beneath but Eric stayed away, instead climbing the tree to the window, not wishing to hear what the winds over the waves might tell him this time.

2

Blain examined one of the black metal structures as it constantly reshaped itself.

'Do you know what those are?' Eric asked him.

'This place is like a living body. These are its organs,' said Blain. 'It should be careful whom it trusts so close to them.'

Far Gaze watched Blain like a patient hunter watching prey. He'd sent everyone else upstairs the second he recognised the colours of someone in a Strategist's robe crossing the water. He did not want Blain to see Aziel's charm, nor the girl herself. Eric and Siel remained with him on the middle floor. Kiown had been tied, blindfolded, and taken upstairs.

'It's true you have Vous's daughter?' said Blain, sniffing the air as though he could scent her. Far Gaze didn't reply. Blain turned to him with arms spread. 'I offer myself,' he said. 'A wealth of information, yours. Given freely. Ask!'

'How long before your forces come?' said Far Gaze. 'Why are they not here now? For what purpose do you buy time?'

Blain laughed derisively. 'There are ways to buy time less personally risky than this!'

'Indeed.'

'*My* forces are spread across World's End. A handful of thousands, stolen from Avridis. Little good they'll do. Very little good. The matter has gone beyond human influence, or very nearly.'

'Which matter?'

'The Pendulum's swing,' said Blain. 'If you don't know what I mean by that, we must speak of it now. We can do little or nothing, if I judge right. But you must know what comes our way. Your side and mine wrestled for control of this world, oblivious that a crushing weight was ready to fall upon it. We must for the moment pause, and ask if we wish for a prize to fight over. I need your help. You need mine, if there is to be a world left to conquer. Avridis is our enemy.'

'For my side, the prize is lost,' said Far Gaze. 'The castle has won. So what difference, for us?'

Blain shrugged again. 'You have *probably* lost. It's not yet over. Close to it, yes. And I do not expect to persuade you. I could pledge loyalty, given my own nest is now shat in.' He sat stiffly on a wooden chair. 'But I'm well aware that your nest is filled with blood and corpses: my own doing again, at least in part. I'll offer my pledge nonetheless. So let's get that little jest out of the way.'

It was Far Gaze's turn to laugh. 'I do not speak for what

remains of the Free Cities, or the Mayors' Command. That alliance has probably dissolved; the last two cities will fend for themselves. Soon I will run wild and think only of my own survival. Maybe I will let the wolf take over for good.'

'But I expect Tauk of Tanton will be here presently. The Mayor comes for him.' Blain pointed with his staff at Eric.

Far Gaze said, 'Am I right to guess that when Vous first rose up, with Avridis, you were bought off to betray the schools? To aid their destruction from within? Offered your seat of power in the new order? Which now you have renounced?'

Blain grunted assent.

'A professional traitor, then. Your promises will have little worth to the Mayor, if he comes.'

'You can trust my instinct for self-preservation,' said Blain, laughing.

'We shall see.'

Blain got to his feet with some effort. 'Pilgrim, come. There is something to explain to you. You need not bring the dragon-friend upstairs down to hear this. She knows already. And if she has kept it to herself, she is no friend of yours.'

Blain went to the tabletop map of Levaal and stood at its far side, leaning upon his walking stick. Then he froze and his body stiffened. Stranger materialised from nowhere, a long knife in her hand. In a stride she was upon the Strategist and driving the knife hard into his chest with a sound as if she had simply punched him.

Blain's mouth opened in shock, his angry eyes went wide. He howled. The cry rose on and on, going higher and shriller even after Eric belatedly moved to restrain Stranger. Far Gaze cast something that knocked her on the floor, stiff and convulsing.

Blain – the knife handle protruding and seeming to twitch

a little with his heartbeats – crumbled like old clay. His mouth still howled even as the face about it fell apart.

The real Blain was across the room, hobbling toward the illusion he'd cast. He beat its crumbling remains to pale dust with violent strikes of his walking stick.

3

'Will she be all right?' said Eric, crouching by Stranger's body.

Far Gaze shrugged. 'Perhaps.'

'I'm curious, what did you do to her?' said Blain. He'd beaten his likeness down to two stumps poking through a mound of soft grey dust. 'That was no combat spell I know of.'

'It was a remedy,' said Far Gaze. 'Too high a dose of it may as well be a combat spell.'

'So this is your dragon-friend,' said Blain, crouching to peer at her. 'Why does she go to such trouble over me?'

'She was to be one of your new mages,' said Eric. 'She was imprisoned in your underground chamber. Maybe that's why.'

Blain scoffed. 'Nothing to do with me, all that. Avridis and his hobbies!' Blain went back to the tabletop map of Levaal. 'A fine device, this. Stand at the opposite side, Pilgrim.' He ran a hand over the edge of the map. They both stared down at the flat blank space. The miniature world soon emerged and came into sharper focus, the clouds crawling inches above the tabletop, rivers and seas of glimmering blue. A ridge of mountains raised on the map to Eric's left as though to fence humankind in. The Ash Sea appeared, where Inferno – dying, dreaming – tossed and turned beneath layers of ruin, wrought in his final battle with the other gods. And there, the castle, enormous and gleaming white like the landscape's crown, sat just before the Entry Point through which Eric had come.

Blain's face showed shock. 'Look!' he whispered. On his half of the map, where it had been blank, there was a small portion of the world now visible: near the boundary, near the Great Dividing Road. 'Something crossed!' he said, glaring around as though seeking some responsible underling. 'Was it . . .? A stoneflesh!' He made that laughing bark again, expressing disbelief. 'It's over! Too much! Too much of a swing! No! I thought we had a year, I thought—'

'Explain yourself,' said Far Gaze.

Blain's head had slumped to one side. Eric looked into the Strategist's eyes, into what seemed a seething ferocious rage, ever burning. 'It's finished, it's over. How this happened I don't know. The gods should not have allowed it, not so soon. It would have happened eventually, of course. They could stop the big things from crossing, but they could not watch the whole width of the world at once. Out in the far places, elementals and Lesser Spirits would have wandered across . . . but a stoneflesh? Too large! How?' Blain took a step toward Stranger as though he meant to strike at her sleeping form.

'Explain yourself,' said Far Gaze, stepping between them with his arms folded. Blain looked genuinely surprised for a moment, a man who gave rather than received orders.

But he went back to the far half of the map, composed himself, and said, 'Pilgrim. Pretend you are the Dragon-god. If you did not know it yet, you do now: there are two of you. Levaal North has one, Levaal South has its twin. The two Dragons, their minds, push against each other with almost identical force. It is a war ages older than man. Where their willpowers meet is World's

End, also called the Conflict Point. The forces are in perfect balance, a balance which resembles peace.

'That is, they *were*. Until the Pendulum effect began. And Avridis the fool started it, this time.'

'This time?'

'Oh yes, it has swung before, but never when humankind was here to witness it, or be destroyed by it!' Blain laughed his bitter, unhappy laugh. 'When worlds collide, boy, fragile little lives like ours do not live through the shaking, crushing ruin. Everything will change. We won't survive it if it reaches that point. None of us will survive.

'I do not cast war magic, boy, but I do illusions of vision and sound. Watch!' Blain muttered something, and what looked like a small silver ball, hung from the ceiling by a gossamer-thin thread, appeared in the air above the table. It hung directly over the world map's central divide. 'When the force gets going it swings like a pendulum,' said Blain. 'Each swing represents an intrusion of one world into the other. Small, at first. An insect crawling could begin it. Then two insects crawl back from the other world. The swing a touch more forceful. Back and forth, back and forth it goes. Avridis began it, or made it worse, when he played around belowground, making Tormentors. You know of their making?'

'We are told the beasts are people, warped by bad airs,' said Far Gaze.

'Yes,' said Blain, staring into the distance, leaning on his staff as though exhausted. 'The thinnest trickle of bad airs it was, at first. We believe this particular poison magic is only found deep belowground on the far side. So far we've been proven right, and it's good luck indeed.

'Avridis made the crack bigger, wider. It took great effort, but it was how we learned the Wall could be brought down, with great enough force. No one had floated such ideas before. We discussed ways it could be done, but never agreed to do it!'

'Why did he make the crack bigger?'

'Making one or two Tormentors at a time was not enough. We wanted an army of them! Then we Strategists learned how difficult the creatures are to control, and wanted it to cease. He *still* wants an army of them; he *still* creates more of the things.' Blain looked at Eric, and hesitated to speak.

'I'll say it for you,' Eric said. 'He wants to invade my world, when he feels he has finished with this one.' He found the notion absurd, but now he wondered: if Engineers could make guns real, and could even make them in some sense living things, what could they do with other weapons of death brought into Levaal? With nuclear bombs, or magic versions of them far greater?

'You guess well,' said Blain. He spat as if annoyed.

'And you would rather I hadn't,' said Eric. 'You hope, with our help, to fend off whatever new threat may come from Levaal South, then carry out the same plans you had before.'

Blain waved a hand irritably. 'I have not thought so far ahead. Forget that! It won't happen. We won't survive what's coming.' He looked up at the small hanging silver ball and, as though by his thought, it moved fractionally toward Eric's side of the table. 'Here is what happens. The far reality intrudes. A small amount, at first, perhaps long ago. Yet enough to set swinging.' The ball moved a small way back toward the south. 'We even sent people inside Levaal South, deep underground. One or two at a time, at first. A tiny, minuscule intrusion of our reality onto theirs. A small Pendulum swing. Back and forth, back and forth, far below the ground, as we sought advantage in a human squabble we had the hubris to call a war. *We* set the Pendulum swinging.'

'Did you warn the Arch of this?'

Blain scoffed. 'Of course. It was a fringe theory! For kooks and dragon cultists. I barely believed myself. From our little pushes the Pendulum built momentum of its own, an automatic force like a geological process, expressing itself through our deeds, our actions.

'Avridis thought his motives were his own. He was unhappy with Vous, with the Project, with the god we were making. He was – we all were – displeased with the time and energy the war was costing us. Thinking himself the author of events, he formed plans to break down the Wall, believing fool visions fed to us through the Windows, fed by we know not what. My guess? The dragons deceived us.'

'How?' said Far Gaze sceptically.

Blain scoffed. 'Please! If they can send a god insane, as they did Inferno, they can fool a human mage! The Wall's ruin would solve many of his dilemmas, Avridis thought. But he had no more volition than a chess piece being shoved around a board. The Wall came down. A mass of our airs intruded on the southern realm. The Pendulum swung.'

The little silver ball grew larger, and swung slowly on its thin chain toward Eric. 'A mass of foreign airs came in,' said Blain. The ball, growing bigger, swung back toward Blain.

'And now, a stoneflesh giant has crossed,' said Blain with his joyless laugh. The silver ball grew larger yet and swung again toward Eric. Back and forth the growing silver ball swung, moving further each time. Blain leaned forward with his hands upon the map's blank half. 'What comes next, Pilgrim? What comes our way, when the Pendulum swings back? What of when the swings are not the minuscule back and forth of people, or people-sized beasts? Stoneflesh giants are *mighty*. A like-sized force will cross the barrier from Levaal South. Will it be a lone creature, or an army of small ones? Will it be airs filled with poison, or a mighty lord on his steed? How will it behave? How soon will it come? How do we stop the Pendulum swinging back from this side, so that a further swing is not caused? How do we trap the Pendulum *here*?'

The now large silver ball stopped on Eric's side of the tabletop.

Blain said, 'What of when the Pendulum swings become *god-sized*? What of when Nightmare, Mountain, and the others leave us, to make war on Levaal South? What then . . . comes . . . here?'

There was silence. Blain's head slumped on his chest as though in grief.

'And now we come to it,' said Far Gaze, a gleam in his eye. 'Eric. You are wondering why the dragons would do such things. Why they would set the Pendulum swinging, if indeed it was their doing? Well, what keeps the dragon-youth imprisoned? They are mighty beasts; why don't they break free?'

'The gods are their wardens, Pilgrim,' said Blain miserably. 'If the Pendulum swing gets momentum enough, our gods will cross the boundary. They will not be here to keep the dragons in their prison!'

'Tell him what the dragons will do, when they are free,' said Far Gaze.

'Slaughter us,' said Blain, with what almost seemed to be relish. 'They may wish to stop the Pendulum from reaching its final swing, when the two great Dragon-gods themselves awaken, arise, and meet at World's End. If that battle goes as past ones have, it will be a stalemate. Or perhaps this time, one or the other will win. Through countless ages they have battled this way. Each time it happens, it reshapes and reorders the world. The time, it seems, has come again. Unless we can stop it, it will leave a pretty handful of scales for Levaal's next inheritors to use for barter! As for us, we will not survive.'

The silver ball had grown twice as big as a basketball now, and was swinging from one side of the map to the other. 'You heard Stranger,' said Far Gaze quietly. 'The dragon-youth will kill all but a handful of us. That's if we are very lucky, and if they mean it when they say that some of us will be Favoured.'

The silver ball became huge, passed once more over World's End, and swung for Eric's head. He ducked under it, then it burst into a thousand gleaming slivers, which scattered across the floor and vanished.

'Why me, for Christ's sake?' Eric said under his breath.

SWING

1

The men across First Captain Tauvene's line could hear the escaped stoneflesh giant long after they could no longer see it through the veil's murky curtain. Then its thundering footsteps ceased and for a while all was quiet.

Not far from nightfall something provoked the great creature. Its feet smashed down again but much harder than before, as though it struck blows at the foreign turf. The noise was like mountains collapsing, yet the ground on their side of the boundary did not shiver.

'Hold!' came the order, shouted down the line. Some had shuffled nervously forward of their positions.

They could hear it happen: beneath the stoneflesh giant's feet the ground in Levaal South split. A great crevasse opened up, and hundreds of underground caverns were shaken. The men did not know this: that places which had for a long time been sealed off were now cracked open.

There was a hissing sound as poison filled the air and was pushed by some force across the barrier like an enormous red cloud.

2

'So, Blain, what do you counsel?' said Far Gaze. He looked out the window. There was the sound of distant rumbling like thunder in the south.

Blain hobbled away from the map and leaned heavily on his walking stick. 'Have you considered that perhaps I came for counsel from you?'

'Yes, I have,' said Far Gaze, still staring through the window. 'A curious notion. You'll more likely have to be tortured till we know every secret you can tell us.'

'Then I am no worse off,' Blain said, shrugging. 'I do not fear pain. I enjoy it.'

'I suspect you'll be indulged. It is not my decision.'

Blain shrugged. 'My counsel, for what it's worth. We have no hope but in what lies beyond World's End. And hope lies there only because we know not what is there! As for this realm, we should slay Avridis, the Arch Mage. Vous you must leave for the gods. He will probably soon be among them. Stay out of his way, be glad you are far from him. But you must destroy his creator.'

Far Gaze turned to him. 'And leave free a path for you to claim the seat of power the Arch will have been forced from. With our help.'

Blain seemed to shudder with anger. 'Yes! Are you dense? It is a game! A *serious* game, but a game! I give up my freedom to you. A gambit, a risk. I do it to use you, and accept I shall be used in turn. Of course! That shall play out in time. For now our interests align. *If* we have a future, our interests may again conflict! But you will know more of me on that day, and shall be better armed to fight me. You I already know! So yours is the better bargain.'

'But you don't know of Shadow,' said Far Gaze with a smile. 'And that is what you have come to learn, under the guise of friendship. You are too used to dealing with mind-controlled people, Blain, and boot-lickers. Hand over your robe.'

Blain looked shocked. 'No!'

'You said you were our captive,' Eric said. 'You have a strange idea of what that means.'

'Your robe,' Far Gaze repeated. 'I fought against the same dragon you sensed in the woods. Over days and days, I fought it. I am familiar with many tricks and illusions. You escaped Stranger but you won't escape me.'

'You did not defeat that dragon,' said Blain with a mocking bark of laughter.

'He survived the fight,' said Eric.

'Not deemed a threat? Bah! We are being foolish.' Blain waved a hand irritably as if the entire situation could be in this way dismissed. 'I need to send word out to Tauvene.'

'To whom?'

'A First Captain I stole. He's at World's End. If a stoneflesh has crossed, we should move the men away from there, and fast. I'll leave, but I'll return.'

'You'll go nowhere,' said Far Gaze, rushing to block the steps which Blain had moved toward. 'Give me that robe.'

Blain paused, the hand on his walking stick white from his grip, his whole body shaking with anger. 'I do not surrender this robe,' he growled. 'I should have waited for the Mayor. Not dealt with a dimwitted soup-making dog.' Blain shook so violently that cracks and splits appeared in his body as though it were made of plaster. The room was plunged into darkness. Eric saw thick streams of magic thread quickly down the steps, folding themselves around Blain like many long dark wings. His body fell apart and lay in cracked pieces.

A swirling white mist filled the room, spun in a circle around it. A great bird flew slowly through it with Blain's ancient angry face atop its neck. A dog with Blain's head upon it ran by so slowly it seemed to float. All manner of creatures appeared, all wearing Blain's bearded face, forming a strange parade while his humourless mocking laugh echoed and rustled from many sources.

'Have you seen illusions like this?' something with Blain's head and black bat wings asked Far Gaze. 'Did your dragon do *this*?' said something akin to a deer. Dozens of creatures flew, trotted, pranced in a wide circle, all at the same turgid pace. Blain's bitter laugh clattered on and on in the background. Beams of light flashed through the white mist, like the colours from the Strategist's robe.

Far Gaze crouched low by the window, staring hard through the mist. He sprang forward, driving his fist into the neck of a four-legged creature with a cream-coloured hide. Its flesh shattered like glass.

'Answer me, you idiot shape-shifter!' said the thing's half-broken head on the floor. 'Did your dragon do these tricks for you?'

3

'Hold!' cried an officer, perhaps the First Captain himself.

The men held, talking among themselves about the strange foulness which had filled the air. It was late, they had eaten and were supposed to be enjoying tales among themselves, or stealing a few hours' sleep. The sky behind them was red, redder than normal.

There was a hissing sound. A strange light bloomed. Then a cloud fell on them, blotting out sight and sound.

For a time there was silence along the line, broken by coughing, then the air filled with screams.

4

Across by the window, in the mist filling the room, Far Gaze crouched like a hunter. Now and then he sprang up to strike at a passing illusion. His fist shattered something with feathered wings and Blain's head. It fell in plastic-like chunks of flesh.

Eric trained the Glock on the creatures circling the room, trying to find the one that was really Blain, if indeed he was among them at all. He did not wish to fire. Each bullet was now rare and precious.

Loup appeared at the top of the steps. 'Where'd Stranger go?' he said, his voice barely audible above Blain's bitter laugh.

'Down here. She's knocked out,' Eric called back. 'She tried to kill Blain.'

'I don't blame her!' said Loup. 'But someone's done a handy bit of casting down there and we had a rule. Who was it?' Loup came down the steps, took a look at the surreal parade. 'What in Inferno's blazes?!'

Loup stepped out of the way of something twice his height, with hooves and six thin legs. Blain's face peered down at him from a long neck. It paused and left the circle, sniffing the folk magician, till he gave its hanging beard a hard tug and slapped its rump. In slow motion it rejoined the circle. Blain's laugh went on.

Loup said, 'Fool illusionist! What's he done? Oh, you have to be *careful* with this kind of thing! They get lost in their own trickery if they're not careful, lad. Well, now what?' Loup stepped down and yelled above the noise of Blain's laugh: 'Now remember who you were! A fool old man in worse shape than me. Come on back! No need for all this, we're not going to fight you. Just talk's all we want.'

A goat with Blain's head said, 'Put away your little weapon, Pilgrim. Tell me of Shadow. And I'll tell you of Shadow.'

'Tell us, then!' said Loup.

'Vous made him real,' answered a flying thing with bat wings. 'He is Vous's fear, come to life. Vous made him with the belief Shadow would be his ruin. And so he may. Shadow alone can do the task we need to do.'

'What task?' Eric said. Across the room Far Gaze pulled the head from the goat they'd spoken to. It shattered into pieces. Blain's laughter clattered on.

Something small as a seagull left the slow circular parade and perched on the stairway banister. From its head Blain's hateful eyes glared. 'When Vous and Avridis are gone, the tools to create a god will lie about the castle.' It flew back into the ring of mist. A huge shaggy dog ran at them in slow motion with a long wet tongue flopping through Blain's bearded mouth. 'The knowledge is recorded in tomes and journals. The artefacts are all still there. On parchment, the spells are written. Will you create a god if you find those tools?'

'Will you?' said Eric. The hound laughed Blain's laugh and joined the circle of illusions. 'How do we destroy Vous? Tell us that!'

Something in the mist: 'I know less than you of Shadow. You refuse to tell. Is he a sword to be drawn? A great sorcerer? A toy of the dragons or the Spirits, or neither? Is he from beyond World's End? You know, not I! I tell you this. Vous fears him! Vous made him real! Vous changed the past to house him in history. Take Shadow to Vous! Take him there! Take him!'

Far Gaze kept seizing and breaking apart individual parts of the parade, but new creatures always appeared in the mist to replace them. 'He cannot be found,' Far Gaze called across to them.

'I'll bet by now he can't find himself!' Loup replied. 'Come on back now, Blain you old fool. Come back! You're lost in there. You proved your point, you can cast a pretty spell. But now the spell's casting *you*! Come on back, Blain. Just follow my voice. Gaze! Leave the illusions. We just have to let the spell burn out.'

Behind them Eric was certain he'd caught a glimpse of someone heading down the steps. It took a moment for him to recall the stranger he'd seen standing waist-deep in the tower's waters, when he returned to the tower with Stranger.

Unnoticed by Loup, Eric dashed down after the stranger. 'Wait!' he called.

The man turned about, his head nearly beneath the whirlpool's surface. He wore a robe of drab brown cloth. Slowly he raised one finger to his lips: 'Shh.'

Eric did not understand at first why he was being hushed; but then the background murmur of the winds' voices quietened. 'Blain is a skilled illusionist,' the man said ponderously. 'But the best ones are themselves never seen. I have seen Blain many, many times. He has not yet seen me.'

'You're the strange wizard the villagers talked about. You're the one who hid the tower and the village with spells. Aren't you?'

'Does it matter?' said the magician, seemingly to himself.

'You did that to Blain up there, didn't you? You made his spell go out of control.'

'It was not hard to do,' the magician said slowly. 'A little push. He will recover soon. It was necessary. But I heard the words Blain spoke to you, when you asked his counsel. Now you have run to me for more. Is this so?'

'Yes.'

The man's body rose out of the water. His robe did not look wet. 'Blain's words held some truth. You should get to what they call the castle. It could be reclaimed. You will probably fail. Take Aziel. Take the drake. He is your friend. He will go where you ask him.'

'When? When should we do this?'

The man considered the question carefully, then said, 'You are far too late. It is no matter. Go back now before the winds down here speak again. They will say things to drive your young mind mad. The waters delight in such things.'

The magician cocked his head, listening, then a look of pain shot across his face. 'They come,' he said, then the water swallowed him. Eric watched the swirling current for a moment, then ran back up the steps. On the lower floor Blain's spell still wound out of control. A mass of broken illusions littered the floor.

There was the sound of screams from upstairs. Breaking glass. The whole tower seemed to shudder, as though in pain or fear. Loup pointed up the steps. 'Get up there, Eric! You're no use here, you can see the airs but never bothered to learn to use em!'

There wasn't time to correct the record. A second scream; suddenly the air was filled with inhuman shrieks. Eric knew the sound well. He'd heard it as soon as he'd regained consciousness after falling through the door, from his old world into this one. He sprinted up the steps with the Glock in hand.

At the two front and two back windows, glass had been sprayed inward across the floor. Shaggy-bearded heads peered in, eyes wide and wild, each of them rasping babble, sniffing hard at the tower's potent airs. Aziel was beneath a bed, screaming in fright, hands over her ears. Case the drake sat with her as though to shield her from any attack but he shivered in fear.

Siel loosed an arrow through a war mage's chest. It fell back, was quickly replaced by another. Gorb rushed in a blur of movement, shoulder-barging three of them from a window, driving them into the night sky with broken bones. Out that window they could briefly see a sky filled with flying shapes circling the tower. The southern sky behind them was a backdrop of dim red.

Two war mages came through the western window. Gorb was there quickly as they crouched low and began to cast. He shoulder-slammed them into the wall. They fell limp, a horrible streak of gore on the wall behind them.

At the window Gorb had left another war mage peered its shaggy head inside. Eric spent a precious bullet to dispatch it. The noise of the shot brought all the creatures' eyes to him.

'Eric! Free me. I'll fight for you!' Kiown yelled, pulling at his bonds.

Eric hesitated, then ran to him. 'I shoot you at the first sign—'

'Yes, yes, of course,' said Kiown as his hands were freed. 'My blade? Where?'

Eric pointed to the work bench. Kiown rushed for his confiscated sword. There was a thump as Gorb crushed two more of the creatures into the wall, then blurred across the room to crush another. The half-giant was growing tired, panting. A war mage leaped up on his shoulders and scratched at him with its clawed feet. Gorb swung it by the feet twice about his head then flung it onto the floor. It didn't get up.

Eric fired another precious bullet. He had lost count how many were left. 'Kiown, help us!' But Kiown had rushed down the steps. Eric trained the gun on him for a moment, then cursed himself.

Too many of the creatures were now inside. A blast of heat rippled through the air at Siel. She threw herself down and out of the spell's path.

'Stop!' Eric yelled. 'I am Shadow!' All rasping voices ceased their talk. The silence was complete but for Aziel's whimpering and Gorb's panting breath.

'Enemies among us, Shadow,' said a war mage, bowing. Its voice was deep as a machine's.

'Your word, Shadow?' said another.

'Leave this place!' he said, overcoming his shock that it had worked. 'Cease this attack.'

'Enemies among us, Shadow,' a war mage repeated, curled clawed fingers gesturing at Gorb and Siel. The windows filled with more of the creatures crawling inside, staring from wild bearded faces, their clawed feet scratching at the floor.

'You must leave this place!' Eric said in as commanding a voice as he could.

'A servant,' said dozens of rasping throats. Those at the window fell back into the night sky.

'Leave this place!' he yelled again. 'Leave!'

'A servant.'

'Your word ...'

The others climbed back through the windows till they'd all gone. Still they circled the tower, now and then one of the flock swooped closer and let loose its awful cry.

'Why do they obey you?' said Gorb, pulling a bandage over where the war mage claws had scratched him.

'I can't answer that,' said Eric.

The tower creaked and seemed to moan with pain. There was a ringing sound like metal being struck. Siel nocked an arrow to her bow and rushed down the steps. He followed her.

No war mages had come to the lower floor, perhaps forsaking it for the upper one where the thick ribbon of potent magic was drawn. Blain's spell was still in play. Loup conversed with several of the creatures near the staircase. Far Gaze, having seen the war mages outside, had begun shifting form to the wolf. He writhed on the floor making guttural sounds.

Kiown crept through the mist of Blain's spell. Eric saw a sword raise then fall upon one of the twisting structures of black flowing metal. The tower groaned as though in pain. Kiown severed one of the winding arms.

'Stop!' Eric yelled at him.

Kiown ran for the window, cutting at several more of what Blain had called the tower's 'organs'. He leaped out the window, caught hold of the tree branch, and slid down fast.

With each chop of Kiown's blade chunks of the tower's exterior fell away. Dark fluid edged with fire sprayed through the air like blood from wounds. Then as though the tower itself coughed to clear its lungs, there was a rush of expelled air. Blain's mist plumed out a window, causing a stir among the circling war mages. The creatures bearing Blain's face hurtled through the sky; the whole illusion was expelled. The force of it knocked everyone else off their feet.

The wolf rose, shook itself, then bounded up the steps, but the fight was over.

5

Bald throughout this tumult had been tending to his guns, muttering and glaring about as though the noise of it all was quite a nuisance. Now he went to a window, set the barrel of one of his odd creations on the sill, aimed and pulled a little lever near the handle. *Ssss-thunk!* With a shriek, one of the flying war mages dropped from the sky. Bald grunted in satisfaction, set the gun down and replaced it with another. He pulled its trigger, nothing happened. The third gun fired successfully. A war mage shrieked in pain and surprise as it fell.

Eric ran to the Engineer. 'Holy shit,' he whispered, examining the sharpened rocks Bald had shaped for bullets. 'You did it.'

Far Gaze in wolf form came to the window, put his paws upon the sill, sniffed the air and howled in dismay. A chorus of shrieks went up from the circling war mages. Some wheeled closer. Eric yelled: 'I am Shadow! Back! Leave this place!'

The wolf whined and immediately began to change back to his human form. 'What's wrong with him?' said Siel.

Loup jogged over. 'He's smelled something. Changing back to tell us, so it must be serious. The air's gone a bit funny or I'm no judge of it. The rest of you, stop firing those guns! Leave the war mages alone and they might go away.'

6

On the lower floor Stranger got slowly to her feet. For a minute or so she saw double, could not even remember what had knocked her out. She blinked until her vision righted itself, sifted through sludgy memories.

One of those strange instruments of flowing black metal was damaged. She went to it, moved suddenly by an impulse to tend it, as though it were a wounded creature found in the wild. She recognised this impulse to be caused by some magic, even as it touched her and used her for its purpose: the tower wished to be fixed. She did as it wished, washing the wound with water, holding the part broken off to the base until it stuck back on and began to mend itself.

Others of the moving structures had wounds too. Feeling a similar tenderness, she fixed them as best she could. A wave of warm pleasure rippled through her as the tower rewarded her for helping it. She felt invigorated.

But immediately she sensed something amiss in the airs. A thin trickle of red bled into the glimmering dark strands. Stranger rushed to the window, staring out and – there he was, a ripple of black movement in the sky. The sight was then obscured by the war mages circling the tower.

'Dyan!' she yelled. 'My darling! Come! Take me away!'

Dyan must have heard her. He flew like a dark lightning bolt among the war mages circling the tower.

7

The dragon's cry of challenge was a long whinnying note: a playful song-burst reverberating through the bodies of those watching at the tower's windows. As Dyan flew among the war mages there was a flash of light, a rain of white sparks. Five of the creatures fell dead with bodies grotesquely bent as though huge strong hands had tried to tie them in knots. Others still in the air burst into flame, with agonised shrieks no different from their usual cries.

The dragon flew higher, drawing some of the flock away from the tower. Dyan sang a long low fluttering note that sent shivers through those watching. In response to it a group of the war mages attacked one another in a frenzy of heat and light. In twos and threes they fell dead to the ground, some of them landing in the moat's waves where their bodies floated. Then the spell ended, and Dyan moved through them, graceful as a diver playing through the air. His scales glittered with playful colour. The surviving war mages – shed now of nearly half the number that began their pursuit – followed the dragon on their doomed chase as he took them further from the tower.

'Better start being polite to Stranger,' Eric remarked at the top-floor window.

Far Gaze stood, panting from the exertions of shifting form.

'What did you smell?' said Loup.

'Death comes,' said Far Gaze. 'We have nowhere to flee from it.'

Loup tore himself with some effort from the window. For

him, to see the dragon's casting was an absolute joy. 'What would we flee?'

'Bad magic, bad airs come. The Pendulum has already swung back.' Far Gaze hung his head. 'We should have let the Strategist go and call back his men from the Wall. How could I have been expected to trust him?'

'He'd not have had time,' said Loup. He put a consoling hand on Far Gaze's shoulder. 'Why you care so much about castle troops I'll not guess.'

'We must get a message to Tauk the Strong. He rides this way.'

'The airs won't come that far in,' said Loup, scratching his head.

'I'll go meet your Mayor,' said Gorb. 'How much time before the bad stuff gets here?'

'No knowing,' said Far Gaze, thumping the wall in frustration. 'If you're going, leave *now*.'

Meanwhile Aziel was clutching the drake's neck in terror. Eric crouched beside her. Case nuzzled his arm with a wet snout. 'You've probably seen enough of this place, haven't you?' he asked Aziel.

She looked at him like he was as dangerous as any dragon. 'You're not to touch me. They'll know. Ghost can visit me any time, and he'll tell—'

'You're safe on that score,' he said. 'Would you like to go home?'

'Home?' She looked at him searchingly, then around at the others. They were quickly getting a store of goods together for Gorb to take with him. 'How?' she whispered.

'That's up to our drake. What do you say, Case? May we ride you? Will you take us north, to the castle?' The drake snorted and crawled before him with its neck lowered. 'Aziel? Will you come?'

She hesitated. 'You'll protect me?'

'I am your humble servant,' he said with a bow.

'It's been so long since someone told me that.'

'Is Shadow still within that charm?'

'Yes,' she said, touching the necklace embedded to her skin. Her voice went even quieter. 'He – he doesn't *like* being in here. He wanted to get in so badly, but I think it was tricking him. Now he wants to be free. I think I can let him go—'

'Don't!' he said. 'Keep him there. We'll take him to the castle.'

'Yes! Arch will know what to do with him!'

'Hurry then, before the others see what we mean to do. Hop on.' Aziel took a seat on Case's back and Eric sat behind her. There was ample room for them.

'It is inevitable that you will, at times on our journey, need to touch me,' said Aziel primly. 'When we go through strong wind or rapidly up or down, we will be tossed around a little. You may at such times grasp me here, and here.' She demonstrated the permissible areas.

'Go, Case,' Eric said. 'To the window, quickly.'

The drake did as he asked it, hobbling toward the north-facing window. Siel saw them first.

'Where are you going?' she said, jogging over. Case put his front feet up on the sill, poking his head out in the night air.

'He must have been drunk, that first night,' Aziel mused. 'He was so clumsy. He's much better at using his legs and wings now!'

'Where are you going?' Siel repeated.

Eric looked back at her. 'Blain told us what we were to do. I'm going to do it. We're going to the castle.'

'And what in a dead god's ashen blazes do you think you're doing?' cried Loup, aghast.

'I guess you could say we're off to see the wizard, Loup.' Eric smiled sadly at Siel. 'I'm not Shadow,' he said. 'But I'm sorry I look like him. Go, Case. Fly.'

'Not without me, you don't!' Loup cried, clutching the drake's tail. 'Not without me!'

'Loup, I know where I have to go.'

'Aye, I won't persuade you different. But you'll be dead in half a day, the both of you, unless I mind you. You haven't even packed supplies, you twit! What did you plan on eating? Rocks?' Shouldering the pack he'd been preparing for Gorb, Loup clambered up onto Case's back. There was only just enough room for him. The drake groaned at the new weight it was being asked to carry. 'Don't you complain, you silly winged mule!' said Loup, slapping its rump. 'You had an easy life the last few days, lazing and sleeping and eating. Time to fly. You're Shadow's drake, according to tales. Look the part, why don't you? Fly!'

The drake fell out into the night sky, and all three riders screamed till it turned the fall into a dive. Case's beating wings took them through buffeting gusts of cold wind.

'Good boy!' said Loup, patting Case's rump. To Eric he said, 'Now where the heck are we off to? And why?'

'Well, I'll tell you, but I don't think you're going to like it.'

8

First Captain Tauvene yelled, 'Hold!' until his throat and lungs filled with what felt like dirt. He had no idea if the men held or ran for he could not see a thing. Braziers had been lit all along the line but now they showed nothing. The strange chemical stink was incredible, like nothing else he'd smelled. His lungs clenched to reject it. He no longer had enough air to yell at all. He was coughing and crawling forward, disobeying his own order. His life, his past, his dreams had all burned down and he was now trying to breathe the ash. Hatred for Blain and lust to kill the Strategist kept him crawling forward. Bodies bumped into him from all sides.

Then everything changed and he went to a place that was not quite sleep.

He did not know how long he'd lain there. All was quiet in the visionless fog but for the sound of things rolling and twitching in the dirt here and there. He did not understand it – he could not breathe, but he was not dead. Then with no warning he felt his body being pulled in several directions, but the feeling was *good*. He felt the bones of his feet breaking, his hands and arms breaking, but oh how good it felt. Yes! he thought. The other men's moaning and screaming filtered through the murk like sounds below water. Redness filled his vision. Yes!

His body felt like it was held in infinitely strong hands, being kneaded and rolled between thick fingers. A sound came from his throat, at first Tauvene's own familiar voice in a vibrating wail, '*Ah-ah-ah-ah-ahhh*,' then something replaced it that was not a sound, but a new sense felt by a new organ. There were other senses too, not unlike touch, with which he felt the pulse and flow of time in the air. It was a current in one direction for the most part, but able to be moved against, and here and there possible to freeze or made so slow it was almost still. His bones kept breaking, stretching, breaking. His muscles clenched till they were tight and hard as stone.

When finally it ended he knew only that he had changed. He had become elegant, beautiful, glorious artwork.

That which had been First Captain Tauvene pulled itself upward. Things bumped against him in the rolling reddish fog with a *clack-clack* like wood striking wood. A rattle of thin needles shook about his head: his laughter, laughter made to release the intense pleasure of *being*, to boast of this incredible pleasure to all the world! *I feel! I sense, I am!* he said in the new language, and the same sentiment echoed all around in the sightless fog.

How he longed to see himself ... there! Another like him! What beauty, what glory! The other watched him back with equal fascination, and both gave a rattle of many thin clattering needles about their manes, both expressing: *What beauty you have! Look at you! What beauty!*

Giddy with delight the noble creatures moved out of the dispersing fog into the evening. Their movements were joy; the creaking sounds of their stiff bodies' graceful steps was incredible music.

There, that strange quailing creature! It was a man, as they had been so recently. That lovely noise it made! That which had been Tauvene reached for the man. His beautiful hand spun a strange and lovely crystalline web in the air, ensnaring the frightened soldier and bringing him closer.

He played the man's body as an instrument, making beautiful sounds of dramatic, powerful pitch. To stroke it this way, a note! To stroke it that way, a note! He drew those notes out through time made sluggish, so they were long indeed.

About him the rattling voices of his kind expressed admiration for the song he made. They crowded around to watch. If only the soft little creature *knew* of the beauty it had within it, the glorious beauty. Slowly that which had been Tauvene played the symphony out, addicted to the sounds that came, in harmony with other such songs playing here and there, as his kindred found more men who had not been changed. The feel of blood drenching its flanks and limbs in rivulets was a new ecstasy altogether.

And they found they loved the music of their spiked toes punching into the ground's hard surface, loved the wind through the grass, the wind swaying the branches of trees. They loved their movements, loved watching one another, loved long periods of silence and stillness. Everything had its joys.

They swarmed north with jagged strides.

SETTING OUT

1

The drake, and Eric, Loup and Aziel on its back, were all soon gone into a wad of cloud, swallowed by the night sky that had poured war mages down on them. Watching them go, Siel wondered what it was exactly that she felt, what it was that had brought these rare tears to her eyes.

She gathered her bow, her knife, stuffed a bag full of bread, meat and fruit, all of which had been blessed for preservation. The night outside the window was now eerily still, with only the occasional faint inhuman cry of war mages coming from widely different points in the distance. The dragon had annihilated and scattered the flock. Over the ground and floating on the water were many of their broken bodies, bent into twisted shapes as though they were in the midst of casting one last spell of death.

Far Gaze writhed on the floor, changing back yet again to his wolf form. It was taking much longer this time; his body was not appreciating so many fast shifts. Gorb headed for the steps with Bald – protesting – under one arm like a bundle.

'Wait!' she called. 'I'm coming with you.'

'You sure?' said Gorb. 'Dangerous, out there.'

'I'm not being left here,' she said. 'Not with that dragon-friend mage and three Hunters in the woods.'

'And a Strategist,' said Gorb, rubbing his chin. 'The wolf's going to smell our way for us I guess. Maybe you can ride his back. We better hurry and find that Mayor.'

Far Gaze stood shakily, the huge white wolf thin and mangy with patches of hair missing. He retched, staggered to the larder and gulped down several pieces of meat.

'What do we do about her?' said Siel as they went down the steps past the lower floor. Stranger sat by the far window, anxiously watching the sky, where Dyan could no longer be seen. The upper half of her body hung out the window and she hadn't yet noticed them.

Gorb said, 'Kill her or leave her. What do you fancy?'

'She is a dragon-friend,' said Siel, reaching for an arrow.

Gorb sighed sadly. 'More likely she just got used. It could've got anyone just as easy. Even you, if you were in the wrong place at the wrong time.'

She felt a blush rise to her cheeks and wondered what Gorb knew, or had guessed, of her encounter with Dyan in the woods. She had been unable to bring herself to mention it to anyone. The sight of the dragon soaring through the flock of war mages had made her want to run from the window, and at the same time watch his every movement. And – although she could not even admit this to herself – part of her had wished for him to come down ...

They left Stranger alone and went down the swirling waters below the tower, crossed the water bobbing with dead war mages and headed for the village. The wolf trotted ahead of them, sniffing the air and whining in fear of what the scents told.

2

Through the window Stranger watched the group of them head up the path through the woods, not far from where Dyan had come. It was hard to sense the dragon from this place where the waters seemed to cast a barrier. But she knew somehow that he wasn't too far. She hoped he was not hurt. Surviving an encounter with Nightmare had made him think himself invulnerable.

She went upstairs to confirm that the drake, the Pilgrim and Aziel had gone also. Had they felt the attack meant it was no longer safe here? Maybe it wasn't. 'Come back, Dyan,' she said quietly, looking at the night sky. 'Come back, my love.'

At the sound of footsteps approaching she murmured the words to a simple lurking spell and faded from common sight. The bleeding colours of the Strategist's robe preceded him up the steps. He leaned on his walking stick, rubbed his eyes and stared right at her. 'I see you.'

'Are you alone?' she said.

Blain grunted.

'Why have you returned? You were not among friends.'

'I am a model prisoner,' said Blain, barking laughter.

'Your jailers have gone. I was their prisoner too. There's no need for you to be here.'

'Ah, is that so? Then you have an issue, girl. For I'm *not* a model jailer. Many thousands attest.'

Stranger edged closer to the window. 'I see.'

He hobbled toward her. 'You see not a tenth of it yet. Tell me about the dragon. What will he do now he knows of Vyin's charm?'

Stranger's mouth fell open. Far Gaze had been very careful to keep him away from Aziel and her necklace. How had he known?

Blain scoffed. 'Oh, she's *shocked*! I'm not one of the soup-making mages you must be accustomed to. I sensed his touch before I arrived here. What's he intend? Why *Aziel*, for the love of the Spirits? What's Aziel mean to the Majors?'

'I can't know the minds of the great ones,' she said. 'I can't even claim to know Dyan's. And I won't be held here by you. I've been your prisoner before and won't be again.' She turned to the window but as she did it vanished – bare wall was now in its place. She touched it, expecting to feel the window glass, but it was no longer there. The other windows vanished. The stairway behind Blain was suddenly a pile of impassable rubble. 'You're going nowhere,' he said. 'Nowhere at all, ever again.'

Ten Evelles and half as many Thauns spread in a wide fan at Blain's back.

'Dyan comes,' said Stranger. 'He will not stand for this. Do you want a dragon angry at you?'

'Do you mean that much to him?' said Blain. 'Wait until he sees Evelle. She stirs my old blood, and my organs failed long ago.' The Evelles smiled sweetly, their movements in synch. 'I know what you are, girl,' said Blain, stepping closer to Stranger. 'A rare common enemy I have with the rebel cities. Even the deranged tribes who gab with elementals would name you traitor, demon, vermin, scum, shit. You are all those things. Know what your dragon did?'

'No.'

'Liar! You know what he did at World's End. You know every

last thing they intend. Talk, girl. Or it's going to hurt very badly, very soon. Here, I'll show you a real lurking spell.' The colours on Blain's robe glittered and the Hunters vanished. 'Where have they gone?' he said with mock alarm. 'What do they intend? Are their blades drawn? Do they have vials of poison? Speak, girl! *Speak!*'

'What do you wish to know?' she said, backing to where the window had been.

'Shadow,' said Blain, stepping toward her. 'Tell me everything you know. Tell me all that the others wouldn't. And what purpose has Vyin's charm?'

'I don't know its purpose,' she said.

'Louder, girl! I can't hear you.'

She wept. 'I don't *know*. Dyan was sent by Shâ and Tzi-Shu. But a second dragon – a second at least – has been sent.'

'Why?' Blain's voice was hard.

'Dyan thinks it comes to watch him. That's why he went to World's End and distracted Nightmare. That's why he caused a stoneflesh giant to cross over. The Major personalities who sent him want the Pendulum to swing high. Dyan has been idle and fears their wrath.'

'But it *wasn't* a second dragon he sensed, was it?' said Blain. He limped toward her until he was almost standing on her toes. 'And you know it. It was Shadow he felt. Wasn't it?'

She frowned. 'Shadow? How . . .?'

'Cut one of her eyes out. She's not sharing.'

Stranger cried out as a blade was drawn close by with a hiss of metal. She said, 'Dyan is here to learn of Shadow! He knows nothing yet. Nor do I. Nor must the Major personalities, if they send him to learn for them.'

'You know *some* things, my one-eyed beauty.'

She crouched with her head in her hands. 'Yes. Shadow is somehow drawn to the Pilgrim. He looks like him too. We don't know why.'

Blain said, 'And Vyin's charm just happened to find its way to the Pilgrim too. Why?'

'I – I think it's meant to contain Shadow.'

'*Contain* him?' said Blain.

'Yes! He's drawn to it, I think. And it has trapped him, caged him. That's a guess. Don't hurt me.'

'Don't cut her yet! How is your guess so specific?'

'Little clues. Air patterns about the charm. Fragments of conversation they didn't notice I overheard. They tried not to speak of it in front of me. They don't trust me. Stop all this, *please*. I'll tell you what I know. I'm not loyal to the dragons, nor to Dyan. Don't you see? I have no one! I'm nothing!'

Blain cursed quietly. His illusion spell abruptly ceased. The room returned to normal with no sign of the Strategist or his Hunters.

Stranger went to the window. A dark shape moved in the southern sky. Dyan was coming – so that's why Blain had fled. She leaned out over the sill, sick and giddy from nerves. She yelled, 'My love! Help me!'

The dragon wheeled once, twice as if searching for something, then swooped to the tower with a rush of wind which pushed her back from the window.

Dyan landed on the sill, sticking his head inside the space too small for the rest of him, peering quizzically around the tower's top floor. His scales glimmered with red and gold. Waves of heat came off him. 'Are you hurt?' he said, his tail snaking through the window and gently running down her arm.

'Do you truly care?' She told him what had happened.

'Great Beauty, you are safe now. There is no one here but you and I, and whatever force gives this place life. A strange place. Well made, for human work.' He sniffed. 'Curious. A drake has been here.'

'Dyan! The Strategist can't be far. He was just here. Won't you kill him? He will come for me again as soon as you leave me.'

'Why do you say I'll leave you, Great Beauty? Have I not returned for you? I have saved you from yet another peril, the man-beasts with horns. And I was burned for my trouble.' He moved so she could see a black mark streaked down his hind leg.

'You are too careless,' she reproached him, stroking his neck. 'Won't you come in? Change form and come in?'

'I'll not cast more just yet,' he said, sniffing. 'There are foreign airs here. A big wave washed in across the boundary. Some strains of it have reached us here.'

'The Strategist cast while you were gone. Very elaborate illusions.'

'Then he is a fool, and the least of my concerns.'

She was hurt. 'What then is the greatest of them?'

'I went to see Shâ,' said Dyan, a ripple of white going over his scales. She had never seen this before but could tell it indicated fear. 'They claim they did not send out another dragon. They are disturbed by what I told them.'

'What happened?'

'I won't speak of it,' he said with a shiver. 'But they will not be idle. Vyin's betrayal enraged them.'

'What will they do?'

Dyan quietened the deep music of his voice, as though afraid the great beasts would hear his voice from their sky holds. 'They have gone to their forges and begun crafting artefacts of their own. They have guessed Vyin's purpose. But they must rush their work, if they wish to change events already unfolding! That is why they are so angry. Vyin's necklace was surely a work many human lifetimes in the making. Whatever the others create will be rushed by comparison, shall need to be crafted in mere days. Do you see now, Great Beauty, that when I leave you it is because I am called away by forces greater than either of us? Greater even than my love for you?'

She tried not to cry. 'You have told me so many times that nothing was greater than that. And I believed you.'

'I am sorry, Great Beauty. I longed to believe it as much as you. And now that I am with you again, perhaps I do.'

3

Movement caught the dragon's eye down by the water's edge. He showed little reaction, tried not to make it obvious he was looking down there as the woman continued to whine at him, and while he made the appropriate responses, said the necessary things. He loved these creatures, loved them as one might love a musical instrument. Such sentimental music.

But while he spoke to her he watched another. A most intriguing form: slender, with long curling dark hair, an immense bust, a face of dark smiling mischief, and an aura about her as dark and colourful as shed human blood. She had no native magic to her, just some borrowed effects from little charms.

But that mattered little; he felt drawn by the natural effortless magic of her intent. She was showing herself to him *on purpose*.

From the water's edge she peered up into his eyes and slowly, teasingly, removed her clothes, revealing a body whose splendour would be the envy of all the Invia. Here she was, seducing *him*, trying to draw him with this provocative dance ... fascinating! He had never been in this position before. He had always been the seducer, never seduced.

There was no resisting this temptation.

One minor cast surely would not be too great a risk. Stranger would never know, would never remember it. Dyan whispered part of a word in the tongue of his kind, made short and simple for human understanding. It meant *sleep*. He put just enough power upon it. Stranger fell back in a faint. She'd not remember the latter part of the conversation when she woke.

Dyan dropped from the window, landed gracefully by Evelle. 'Welcome,' she said, opening her arms to him. He curled his tail about her, ran the point of it over her skin.

'I will call you *Hathilialin*, which means in my tongue *great beauty* ...'

4

Stranger sat up. The peaceful lap of waves and the breath of breeze across water still played soothing music but she knew before hearing the knife being drawn that her death was close.

Stepping before her was a wiry man, naked from the waist up, with thin braids of beard hanging from his chin and a long knife in hand. The tattoos across his chest looked like protective wards; the piercings over his body had to be charms, for they made almost invisible patterns in the air about them.

Next to the man, Blain leaned on his walking stick, face

twitching as though burned and singed by a hot simmering rage beneath his bearded mask. To the Hunter he said, 'Cut off her hands.'

The man sighed regretfully. 'Yes, Strategist.'

Thaun had her before she could reach the window. Stranger let her arm go limp in his hand. Without Dyan here to help, her only spell options to get out of this situation would likely kill her instantly. It was better to try talking her way out. She said, 'What do you think you will gain from doing this?'

Blain said, 'This is your last chance to talk. Your true love is busy with Evelle. He's taken her on a long romantic flight.' He shuddered. 'Talk, girl. Lend me a hand.'

Thaun's knife-edge gently touched her skin. 'Tell him you'll talk,' he said quietly. 'I don't wish to do this.'

'Do not do that in here,' said a quiet voice from the stairway. Blain wheeled about, face betraying his shock. A tall magician stood at the top of the steps, peering at them with half-lidded eyes. He said, 'It will do no good to mutilate her, unless the act is its own pleasure for you, Blain. Do you do it for a purpose, or for love of such deeds?'

'A purpose, of course,' said Blain, sputtering. Crimson colour flushed through his robe.

The tall man inclined his bald head. 'And you have chosen a course in life that requires such deeds quite often. A coincidence?'

'Why do you care about her?' said Blain, hobbling toward the newcomer. 'The dim wench is going to free the great beasts. Do you plan on a place by her side among the Favoured?'

'I don't care about her,' the magician said. He peered at Stranger with a look of distaste. 'Do with her as you like. I just asked you not to do it here. It bothers the airs and the senses.

Mine, at least. Besides, it may be that I can answer your questions better than she can.'

Blain grunted, a sound in which Thaun apparently detected instruction, for he put away his knife. 'Very well,' said the Strategist. He stroked his beard thoughtfully, trying to work out if this was the one who had interfered with his casting earlier; until now, he'd presumed it had been Stranger's doing. He said, 'What do *you* know of Shadow?'

'I suspect you have guessed Shadow's purpose as well as I,' the magician replied. 'Avridis wishes to be rid of Vous, to find a more pliable personality to elevate to godhood. So too does a part of Vous yearn for death and peace. Avridis fed this part of Vous till it grew large, fed it by accident at first, then in recent times on purpose. In response, Vous created something able to destroy himself, quite subconsciously, of course. He created Shadow.

'For some reason Vous selected the Pilgrim to represent Shadow. I have over the past days observed the Pilgrim closely. In my estimation, the selection was random. The Pilgrim himself is just an ingredient, no more significant than that, possessed of no native powers or greatness of any kind. Whether Shadow *will* destroy Vous or not, no one yet can answer, and my guesses are useless.'

'What is your guess then?' said Blain, infuriated to be lectured. 'Useless or not, let's hear it!'

'As you like. I guess that Shadow will not destroy Vous, nor will Vous destroy Shadow. We are stuck with both entities for the foreseeable future.'

'Reasoning?'

The magician smiled at Blain's barked demands. 'Because the greater part of Vous, that which drives him and always has, is lust for power, for godhood. Which is now attainable to him. And I feel this part of him is greater than his urge to self-destruct. I repeat, my guesses are useless.'

Blain paced, muttering into his beard, his walking stick smacking into the floor.

'You are belatedly perturbed,' the magician remarked with a hint of private amusement. 'Did it never seem vain or improper to you, to attempt the creation of a god? After a point, Blain, use of magic goes beyond a matter of simple spell craft. It becomes less controlled and predictable. It is why the gods and dragons act within limits, limits they hardly dare approach, let alone break. They know – as we fleet-lived and all-too-curious humans do not – that magic of the kind they wield can do things to alter fundamental existence. And it can make changes as impossible to undo as the clock is to rewind.'

'Yes, fine,' said Blain.

'It is why my school, and the others, respected limits to what humankind *should* attempt. We devoted much study to it, in those rare moments people were not pestering us to cure runny noses or assist in their political squabbles. But you burned those books and kept the others. You were not quite so curious about what boundaries should not be broken.'

'Don't blame me,' Blain snarled. 'Avridis and Vous made all decisions. We Strategists just advised, or managed things. And our advice may as well have been coughed phlegm for all they valued it. But I'll spare you my pleas. I shed no tears for your schools. I took looted artefacts gladly. I cheered for your deaths. That much is true.'

The magician tilted his bald head as though in thanks. 'Your attacks were predicted, incidentally. But as you know, most predictions fail. This place was built in case that future came to pass. To our great surprise, it did.'

'Then there are other places like this?' said Blain.

'Of course there are – I shan't lie to a potential ally, whatever his past. There are several towers of varying design. My colleagues wait in them, those who survived.'

'For what do they wait?'

'The inevitable ruin of Vous, Avridis, and those aligned with him.'

'Inevitable,' grunted Blain. He paced around the room, his cane thumping down the only sound. Even the swishing music of breeze on waves had gone quiet.

Stranger said, 'How do you keep Shadow out of this place?' The mage turned slowly and gazed at her. His expression was impossible to read. 'It is difficult,' he said. 'Shadow has a strange power. He mirrors something, becomes a different version of it. A fraudulent copy, so to speak. If it could be done to gods it would make him formidable indeed, if only for a little while.' Stranger's eyes widened as though with some realisation. The mage's eye seemed to look deep into her. He said, 'Or indeed, if done to dragons.

'I pondered what Vous may do to protect himself from Shadow's power. What Vous may do is divide himself. I did similar things to keep Shadow from this place. What Shadow saw or believed he saw at the water's edge was an infinite number of small powers as though in a swarm. Each on its own so weak as to be negligible, too numerous and fleeting for his comprehension. Think of a mighty beast in a blinding cloud of insects. What can it do? Had Shadow known this was just illusion, he might have crossed the waters, giving you no haven.'

'You have learned much of him,' said Stranger.

'Indeed. And I learned much of Dyan, when he was at the

window, an hour ago. And much of you, since you have been here. Your heart is treacherous, to you most of all. But also to us.' The mage turned to Blain. 'There is nothing more to learn from this woman. It is best to kill her. Do so with mercy. I will leave this task with you. Do not do it here, in this place which is my home. Do this for me at the water's edge and you shall be invited back. We shall speak and make plans.'

Stranger gasped. Blain looked surprised. 'Good!' he said. 'We will speak more when it is done. I cannot undo my past. But we are of similar purpose.'

'That may be,' said the magician. 'My purpose has never changed. Yours has, and may again. We shall see.'

Blain began to reply but the tall magician dissolved into a pile of sand which sank into the floor.

5

Stranger pleaded as they led her down the steps, then through the waves to the shore. She twisted around in Thaun's hard grip, her dress spreading out on the water's surface like a dark green flower. Thaun smiled sympathetically but did not yield at all. 'I want to see him again,' she said. 'Just once. Just once. If I may just see him again.'

'Do you think that is a rational request?' said Blain.

'Just once, *please*—'

'Draw from your memories. They're sweeter than a current look at him, fucking Evelle as we speak.' Blain shuddered. 'A whole new world has opened up before me. I often wondered why Invia look as they do. Now we know. How does a dragon fuck?'

Apparently directed at Thaun. He replied, 'Very well, it would seem.'

Blain laughed, a wholly different sound from his usual bitter cough. 'I'm serious. How?'

'I am unsure, Strategist. Maybe they assume the form of men.'

'Or shape their women like dragons? I had wives like that. Who knows?'

'You have light consciences, to lead a woman to death, laughing and joking,' said Stranger.

'It has long been a flaw of mine,' said Blain. 'Thaun is weeping inside, I'm sure.'

'Such is war, Strategist,' said Thaun.

She threw herself away from Thaun's grip as they neared the water's edge. He caught her again easily. 'Dyan!' she screamed.

'Shut her up,' said Blain, looking around nervously. 'Kill her.'

'Here, Strategist?' said Thaun.

'Get her out of the water altogether, like our new friend asked. If he truly built this place, he's useful. We'll honour his wishes. And watch your manners, he may have ways to hear us even now.' He examined the line of trees some way back from the water. Kiown was still among them somewhere, keeping watch. Blain murmured a quick lurking spell just to be safe. The smallest burn from casting it flushed through him.

And – there! Blain sensed another power he *thought* was the woman's dragon friend. It was like a weight pulling the blood to the south side of his body. It was some way distant still. Or perhaps it was that other magician, that shape-shifter, Far Gaze.

And yet the power was closing in on them, fast —

'Dyan!' Stranger cried. Her voice rang out in all directions, too loud for a normal cry; she had to have cast something to enhance it.

'Kill her!' Blain snapped. 'Quick, get her out of the water and do it!'

A rush of wind knocked him backward and off his feet. He stayed down under the water's surface, waiting till his breath ran out. Fast, so fast. How had the beast come so fast?

When Blain rose Stranger was not in sight. Thaun's body lay in two twitching pieces on the ground, spilling guts like the stuffing from a torn doll. The Hunter's face showed surprise.

Blain could hardly believe the little lurking spell had saved him from a dragon. Quickly he pulled from the corpse all charms and wards, except of course for those melded into or tattooed on the Hunter's skin. Up in the tower, at the uppermost window, was the tall, bald silhouette of the magician staring down. No magic had won out this time; no illusion, no spell work at all. Simple trickery. *Potential ally* indeed, ah the little chord he'd struck, the note he'd known Blain had wished to hear. Had he also known Dyan would hear Stranger's cries and rescue her? Had he meant for the dragon to kill them both?

Blain tipped his walking stick in a gesture as though to say well played. The bald head did not, as he'd half hoped, nod in a gesture of reciprocal respect to a fellow illusionist; the tower's magician just stared down at him as he limped away from the water, with a last regretful look at the corpse of his finest Hunter.

IN FLIGHT

1

The drake's beating wings had soon put the tower far behind them. Gusts of air both warm and cold blew at them so hard it felt like they'd be knocked out of the saddle-like grooves between the upright nubs on Case's leathery back. The heat always burning deep in his belly kept them warm. It was too dark to see much of the landscape passing below but for the odd lantern-lit window or campfire in fields which looked like oceans of blackness. At times Case tilted forward like a roller-coaster cart heading for a plunge straight down, as though he every now and then lost control of his wings or wished to very briefly rest them. What seemed hours of uneventful flight went by, the wind flicking Aziel's hair in Eric's face all the while. Their winding flightpath veered toward a distant gang of unnat-ural-looking mountains shaped like pillars. Then a voice spoke from the gloom right beside them: 'Your wish?'

All three passengers aboard the drake screamed. Loup nearly fell, and clutched Eric's waist to stay seated. They were descending through a blanket of cloud and could see little but cotton whiteness. The powerful animal stink of war mages carried to them even through the headwind they flew into. Shapes could be heard bumping into Case's wings. The drake grunted in confusion and dropped more altitude. 'Your bidding,' said a machine-deep voice from the other side.

'I'm yours,' said another.

'Your will.' A chorus of such voices intermingled with declarations of servility.

'You're Shadow,' said one visible directly above them when they had come free of the cloud. Amongst a shaggy dangling nest of hair, cat-yellow eyes peered luminously down. Smoke trailed from the tips of its horns, its staff clutched to its chest with long-clawed hands. Its beard strands brushed Eric's head like friendly but unwelcome fingers. 'Among foes,' it said. 'A servant.'

'No! These aren't foes,' said Eric, knowing what it meant to do. 'Don't attack them! Go! Leave us.'

'Your word?' it said, frowning as though confused. Others descended through the clouds and flew shoulder to shoulder with the first.

'Yes, that's my word. Leave us! Fly east. Go! East! Fuck off!'

'A servant,' said a dozen voices in acknowledgement. Each of the creatures veered away.

'Tell em to go and fight that dragon,' Loup whispered in his ear.

But the flock had already departed. Their shrieking was soon far distant till it faded from earshot altogether. Unperturbed, the drake beat its wings harder, steering a course through the clouds as though all the skies were mapped out neatly in its mind. They stopped to take shelter from a heavy rain-shower in a cliff-side cave, its floor covered in smooth white pebbles. The drake set himself heavily down, seeming to announce with a huffed sigh that he had flown quite enough for one day. Loup dug through the smooth pebbles and gathered up bones buried beneath them. He fondled them in his gnarled hands. 'Drake bones,' he said. 'Not dragons, just little drakes. No wonder he brought us here. An old drake nest, this.'

'We're putting a lot of trust in Case,' said Eric, peering out the cave's opening, where dropping off a little ledge was a sheer cliff side. Far beneath, huge square blocks of stone waited patiently to thump falling bodies. 'If he took off and left us here there's no way we'd be able to climb down.'

'He won't leave us. A good old drake, he is,' said Loup, running a hand over the beast's scaled head. It made a noise more like an old man snoring than a cat's purr, but it seemed to denote satisfaction. Loup said, 'Strange, though. He doesn't act like people have trained him, but he's not wild, not at all. Funny old feller! I wonder if a mage got inside his head somewhere along the way and tinkered around.' He peered closely into the drake's large gem-like eyes and squinted as though reading fine print therein. Case gazed back impassively.

'How many drakes have you known?' said Eric.

'This is the first! And I like him,' said Loup. He brought the old drake bones to Case. 'Hungry?' Case sniffed the bones, took one of the smaller ones in his mouth and crunched it languidly into splinters with a noise that filled the little cave. 'They share memories like this, eating each other's remains,' said Loup, patting Case's hide. 'When two meet up they'll each trade a scale to eat. That's like having a long conversation, for drakes. Case will be learning things his long-departed friend knew, once he digests those bones. The old one crawled here when he knew he was going to die. He knew others of his kind would one day come find him, I reckon. Nice old race the drakes, oh aye they are. Even if they do eat expensive necklaces.'

'Arch has one in a cage,' said Aziel, breaking a long, sullen silence which Eric guessed was to protest Loup having invited himself along.

'What's he do with it?' said Loup.

'Nothing. It just sits there,' she said.

'Fine man, he is. Not enough cages in the world for his liking. Guess that's why he's put so many folk in the ground, eh? That's a cage too, with a lock that never opens. The stuff of his sweetest dreams, lass. And part of you knows it.'

Aziel went red but didn't answer.

They slept that night curled around Case, the heat in his belly like coals in a fire.

After an hour or two Eric woke at the cry of a war mage, surely the same flock of them seeking him out for new orders. To his great surprise Aziel had her head resting on his shoulder. She'd tested their patience with complaints about the lack of hot baths, inadequate food, her little aches and pains. All of it code he supposed for 'I'm scared'. Only when he'd told her fables from Otherworld, such as *Snow White*, had she settled down. Loup had listened with equal enthusiasm.

He looked down at her faintly Oriental face. He could not deny that she was beautiful. He imagined ripping her dress off while she peevishly complained and whined . . .

A faint gleam ran about her necklace. Her face creased with pain as the light grew stronger. She moaned in her sleep, cried out and sat up gasping. Loup and the drake did not stir.

'Everything OK?' Eric asked her.

She discovered she'd leaned on him in her sleep. Her eyes would not have shot wider had she found a Tormentor beside her. 'You're not to touch me!' she whispered fiercely.

'I have no interest in touching you,' he lied.

She frowned. 'Why not?'

'Huh?'

'I mean – you're *not* to! But you're allowed to . . . to want to.'

He laughed.

She grabbed at the necklace, trying to dig her fingers between it and her skin. 'I wish I hadn't picked this up. I had bad dreams again.'

'What sort of dreams? Was Shadow in them?'

'He was choking me with a big piece of chain. He kept saying he had a mountain to lift up, but I wouldn't let him. And he couldn't do it till I'd died.' She shuddered. 'There was more but I don't want to think about it.'

'Do you want another story, then?'

Her face lit up at the prospect before she shrugged with feigned indifference. 'The others weren't very good.'

'Let's see if I can do better. Here's one I wrote called *Jack and the Beanstalk*.' Not long into the telling, Aziel slept again, and again her body leaned into his. He stroked free the hair that fell across her cheek, wondering why he should feel this compulsion to look after the daughter of an abomination and a tyrant.

2

Cold wind whipped them in the early morning's flight. The up and down plunge of the drake's wings was like oars in boat-side water. At times Eric felt he was back at the tower, looking into the tabletop map of Levaal. Below them now a river spilled down a waterfall into a vast lake with water so clear they could see huge fish sluggishly prowling near the surface.

The drake's belly gave an impressive rumble. 'Are you sure we don't have to feed it some real food, or give it drink?' Eric said.

'He likes beer,' said Aziel, sitting tall and prim in the foremost of Case's natural saddles. 'He'll stop at an inn when we find one and steal whatever he wants.'

'We've named him well, then,' said Eric. 'The real Case would be proud.'

The drake groaned.

'Are you sure you know where we're going, lad?' said Loup behind him. 'Have you thought it through?' It was the first time the folk magician had voiced this concern.

'I don't know if I have or not. The mage back at the tower told me to go to the castle. He told me that by going, I could bring Vous undone.'

Loup sighed heavily. 'Not much good we'll find at that old castle. And it's Blain's advice too, don't forget. Be wary whenever you find yourself in agreement with the likes of him.'

As night came the drake found another good camping spot on a high platform under the open sky, in what Loup said were called the Spirit's Crown mountains. 'Has other names too, but that's what we called it where I come from. They used to mine these places.'

'For scales?'

'Magic stone. You could find it here, back before they dug the guts out of the place. Made some of Tanton's and High Cliff's city walls with it, stone that'd give itself easy to effects.'

'Effects like what?' Eric asked, settling into Case as though he were a beanbag. The drake seemed quite content with this arrangement.

'Spells of defence,' said Loup. 'Try climbing *those* walls, if you're an enemy of the city!'

'So you think they'll hold out awhile when the castle attacks?'

'Longer'n the others did, aye. Even when the full weight of

the castle falls on em. Which it will, and soon. Whole world's about to change, lad. Aziel here might call it a victory. But sometimes, nobody wins a fight. Nobody at all.'

The following day they saw some of that very force, a huge contingent of men crossing the vast plains between Tsith and the inland sea it shared with Yinfel. Countless spear tips pointing skyward made a shuffling forest. 'Look at all that yonder,' said Loup sadly, pointing to where massive sheets of grey-black smoke plumed into the air. 'Fools're burning the farmland as they go. Such waste.'

'Why would they do that?' said Aziel.

Loup scoffed. 'They don't plan on living in the cities they take. They'll kill everyone off and be done with it. No more taking over a new city, taming a reluctant population. When the war's over, they won't need people or cities. We're done and goodbye. A few of us'll live on the fringes for a while. Maybe a long while, till they push us into the unclaimed lands. Hunt us down like they hunted the half-giants.' Loup sighed. 'Hard future ahead, girl. Not for you, but for everyone else.'

'Doesn't sound much different from what the dragons have in mind for us,' said Eric. Case wheeled east so they would not fly into the sheets of smoke.

'Aye no, it's no different. Death's at both doors, and his ghoulish children at the windows, looking in. No way out, lad. Unless you can do some miracle at the castle, you with no plan or clue what you're up to!' Loup laughed sadly.

'Take me down there,' Aziel ordered the drake.

'Now what? Why's that then?' cried Loup.

'I'll tell them to turn around, since you're so worried about what they're doing. I don't like them lighting fires any more than you, even if those *are* rebel cities.' The other two laughed.

Aziel turned about, glaring at them both. 'Why are you laughing? I'm the Lord's daughter! They'll obey me. Drake, take us down there. Go! Down!' She raised a hand as if to slap the beast, but instead clutched at her neck and moaned.

'What's wrong?' said Loup.

'It's getting hot,' she said. 'He's moving around in there. I can feel it. He wants to get out.'

'You keep him in,' said Loup. 'Hold him! That's the last thing we need, is Shadow loose again.'

Aziel said nothing. Eric could feel the heat from her necklace. An occasional glint of light ran about it, so quick it was hard to be sure he'd seen it. He thought back to Shadow, enraged, running in a circle about the tower's water; of how the rocks had melted from the heat he'd caused. 'Hold onto him,' he whispered into Aziel's ear. 'He'll think you and I tricked him, that we trapped him in there. You and I are the ones he'll be angry at.'

'You're the one who tricked him,' she said.

'Sure. Do you want to have to explain that to Shadow? Hold onto him. You can do it.'

'I'll try,' she said, sounding nothing like a Lord's daughter.

3

The drake descended from the clouds to find shelter for their third night, finding another old nest as though it had seen a sign planted high up in a hillside made for drakes' eyes only. A single piece of lightstone in the cavern roof gave the place a gentle flickering glow. It showed faded hieroglyphs and runes across the curved walls. Loup ran a gnarled forefinger over them, murmuring as he tried to read them. 'Not just a drake den, this place,' he said. 'People used this cave too. We're the first here in a long while . . . a long while.'

'What's the writing say?' said Eric.

'Mostly a lost tongue,' said Loup. 'Something about this being a favoured casting place. My guess, a dragon cult used it. This before the dragon cults were all scattered and killed off (with the Spirits' blessings and help, if the talk's true). The Spirits must take kinder to Inferno cults than dragon cults. If you know why, well hey! It's news to me. They kill off old Inferno but let his cults alone, who want nothing more than to wake him up and feed his embers!'

Eric ran a finger over the runes. They flared with icy cold in response to his touch.

'Careful, lad,' said Loup.

'Why would mages come all the way up here to cast their magic?' said Eric.

'Ah, not mages, lad,' said Loup, crouching low to peer at some marks gouged into the stone. 'Anyone can cast magic. You and Aziel could, if you knew some rituals. Just takes more time than the way mages do it. Long-casting, some call it, or ritual-casting. Can't rely on it, might not work half the time. Ritual casters can't see the airs to tell if the airs are right! Nor see what airs they're working with – lots of different kinds of airs, y'see. My little tricks are good with most types. But those Inferno cult fools, like that Lalie girl, remember? They were doing such spells before the Tormentors found em.'

'Are there any spells we could do now?' said Aziel, looking eager to try.

'No! Never bothered with that nonsense,' said Loup, flopping down on Case as though he were a couch, a bit too heavily for the drake's liking. He said, 'Takes days to cast something that way. Sometimes weeks or more, if you want to make serious magic. Oh aye, once there was a cult which set some kids aside at birth to cast lifetime spells, blessing their valleys and lakes and fields.'

'Did it work?'

'Aye, lass, it did! Good magic, some of it. I've no issue with blessing a paddock so your carrots and tatoes grow! The Inferno people though, not a true mage among em.'

Eric was running out of fairy tales for them. Tonight's was *Red Riding Hood*, which Aziel found particularly gripping, and which Loup apparently took as a comedy. Rain outside eased them to sleep in Case's warmth.

4

The drake nudged Eric awake. 'What is it?' Eric whispered, sitting up.

Case huffed a deep concerned breath as though to warn of danger. The others still slept, but Aziel shifted and moaned in her sleep, her sleeping face creased with nightmares. She seemed to fight for breath. The choking dream again, Eric thought. He was hesitant to wake her – a peevish Aziel with not enough sleep was not the recipe for an enjoyable flight through Levaal. But when she appeared to stop breathing altogether he grabbed her shoulder and called her name.

As though in response the necklace poured pale blue light through the cavern and sent shadows scurrying over the walls. The air went frosty. Some of the runes seemed to catch the blue light that beamed around and hold it after the rest went out.

Eric shook Loup's shoulder. 'Loup, I think you should wake

up.' He kept snoring. 'Aziel, don't let him go. Hold onto him. Please hold on.'

'Can't,' she whispered.

'*Loup, wake the hell up!*' Eric tugged on his beard.

Loup snorted, came awake. He looked at the cave wall's glowing runes. 'What've you done now?' he said sleepily.

'It's Aziel, she's—'

There was a metallic sound like chain being struck and breaking. A burst of intense cold like a rush of wind blasted from Aziel; she fell back gasping. At the same time all the wall's runes gave a bright flare then went out.

As they were temporarily blinded by the light, it took a few seconds to discover someone else in the cave with them. Shadow's form was blurred and for a moment there seemed to be several of him all joined together. The images slowly converged, solidified. Shadow's face showed animal desperation. His mouth and black-pit eyes all opened wide; from the apparition's depths came a hissing noise of rage.

Eric took the gun from its holster despite knowing it would be perfectly useless.

Shadow's hand lashed through him, intended to cut him but having no more effect than a shadow passing over him. Again and again Shadow tried to strike him before giving up and turning to Aziel. Before Eric could react – and what could any of them have done? he later wondered – the apparition had unleashed a dozen blows at her.

She was not hurt, though she cringed in fear. The necklace spat a noise like a blast of radio static. There was a shriek of fear or pain, and Shadow streaked out of the cave with a wail fading behind him, a line of fire in his wake quickly put out by the thin misty drizzle.

Aziel clutched at her neck, breathing deeply.

'What happened?' Loup asked her. 'What've you done, foolish girl?'

'Nothing!' she said. 'Don't you talk at me that way, filthy little man.'

It took a minute or two to calm her down to the point of explaining.

'I had a dream. He was burning me, pulling something around my throat, telling me to let go, let go. So I did! All right? It was just a dream, so I let go!' She burst into tears. 'None of you care! He's been getting harder to hold hour by hour. I just relaxed a little bit and he got away.'

'And he was angry with you and me, like I thought he would be,' said Eric. 'I think the charm protected you from him, Aziel, when he got free. I don't know what protected me. We're just lucky he didn't want to attack Loup or Case. We have to move! He knows where we are. Case, can you fly in the dark?' The drake regarded him silently with eyes like brown-green jewels and showed no indication of flying anywhere.

'He'll always know where we are,' said Loup, getting to his feet and pissing out of the cavern into the night. 'Shadow's drawn to the charm, is my guess. But now he knows it's a trap. Made by old Vyin, if Stranger can be believed! Let's see if he can resist it. Maybe he won't want to find us. And maybe the charm'll grab him again. We'll see. Back to sleep, you lot. We'll leave in the morning.' Loup patted Case's flank. The drake set its head down, huffed a big breath and was soon snoring again.

Loup joined the drake in slumber, Aziel's shivering and crying of no more consequence to him than rain on a rooftop. When Eric put a consoling arm around the girl she didn't fight him off.

5

Shadow did not return to them.

Still the castle was not yet on the horizon. The land they flew over seemed vast and empty, with just the odd skeletal shell of a town or village, as well as ruins far older, stone ziggurats and temples which no one dared explore, and which Loup said were full of bad magic airs and ghosts.

Now and then birds flew to meet them in the sky, carrying eggs in their mouths. They perched atop the drake's head, not minding his human passengers, and gently set the eggs in the folds of his neck. 'What the hell?' said Eric the first time this happened.

'Ah, hand it here!' cried Loup, reaching for the thick white egg. 'Silly birds want Case to sort out their disputes.'

'Birds have disputes?'

'Aye, never noticed? Over territory, just like people. They give drakes an egg from their nest. Or most likely stolen from a rival's nest.'

'And this achieves?'

'Used to be lords of the skies, were drakes, as far as birds and animals had it figured,' said Loup. 'No one told poor old Case by the look of things. Confused old drake! Get used to it, you scaly old man.' Loup patted the drake's side then cracked the egg shell on his teeth, greedily slurping its contents. Aziel looked scandalised, but Loup only belched. 'There'll be more birds, more eggs. Easy food! Good reason to ride a drake. Better than horses, oh aye they are, lass. Next egg's yours.' Strings of yolk stretched between his grinning gums.

Aziel shuddered.

Case charted a course for the cloudier skies to hide them from sight of war mages when the creatures' shrieking again carried to them on the winds. Visible behind them now and then were wheeling specks in the sky.

Beneath them passed what looked like a meteor crater, as though enormous jaws had taken a bite from the earth, and the gash had since filled with rubble. Lonely hillsides stretched around it, begging Eric to go down and explore them, the land about thick with big wreaths of magic air winding over it like dark mist.

'Strange airs here,' Loup murmured. 'I've known good mages who come to lands like this, meaning to farm the powers they find. They never come back. Something gets hold of em, uses em for its own designs. You have to be careful near these big dead plains, Eric. Gods or dragon-youth have traded blows in such places, ages back. Or other things besides I'd soon as not mention. Loose effects here still, or spells that now and then re-cast emselves, with no mind for what they do to the poor silly mages, eager to watch great magic at work and learn from it. Quick, look down there now, lad! A Lesser Spirit!'

Eric gazed where Loup pointed but saw nothing more than a swirling effect like a whirlpool in the midst of a dark blanket of magic. Then Case took them up into a cloud and they saw no more of the land below.

The war mages did not find them again. But there were other shapes among the clouds, which had Loup frequently craning his neck, muttering to himself. 'Can't be Invia,' he muttered. 'You're Marked, lad. But they're not war mages. So I don't know what they are.' Loup slapped his own forehead. 'How could I forget? You're *Marked*! We can't go further north! Eric, they'll kill you, foolish boy! Turn around! Ask the drake if he'll take you back.'

'I've still got the gun, Loup. Invia don't like guns.'

'No! Not one more mile north.'

Eric said nothing for a while. 'What the hell else am I here for, Loup? Is there some purpose to it, or not? What's in it for me to tell you guys about guns and electricity and flush toilets? So far not much. Everyone who mattered in my life is dead or lost to me forever. I don't really care any more if I'm sent to join them. Maybe I'll save your world the same way I came into it, by accident.'

'Spare me rousing speeches, lad! Skin, veins, beating hearts, give me those! Many a time I've had to keep idiots alive in spite of emselves. But I don't sense a safe path north, where you're taking us. There ain't one. Safest way's back behind us to a thousand better places. It was a quick decision you made, to hop on old Case and jump out that window. Just like you jumped through that door, and look where that got you! All blood and gusto, oh aye, I remember the feeling. Loins like jugs o rum, you fool drunk! Sleep on it, would you?'

'Sure. But I'm going to keep going.'

As night came Case sniffed out a drake's den in a range of barren hills, where several nooks in the grey cliff faces said this had once been something of a city for the creatures. The nook he chose led out to a platform overlooking a sheer drop to what looked like glittering black sand below. Within the hour smoky fog rolled over it like a cotton blanket.

The same shapes they'd seen earlier wheeled in the skies as the last light faded. 'Loup! Those *are* Invia. Why aren't they attacking me?'

'No idea, lad,' said Loup grimly. 'Maybe they will in the end.

They're close enough to see a Mark, unless there's strange business about I've not clued upon. You should duck out of sight.'

They had a small fire at the cave mouth. In a little tin cook-pot Loup boiled the eggs which half-a-dozen birds of varying kinds had brought that day, then he blessed them so well that even Aziel had no complaints when she was at last persuaded to eat of them. Loup happily gobbled down the shells under Case's envious gaze. They lay down to sleep after Eric told them *Hansel and Gretel*.

He lay awake a while after, wishing he'd read more Shakespeare so that if the opportunity arose he could plagiarise his way to glory. He sat up at the sound of beating wings outside.

The drake stirred but no one woke. Eric stood, eyeing off the gun in its shoulder holster, which he'd removed, and weighed up whether what he'd said to Loup earlier was true: *was* he quite ready to die? If so it was a matter of walking outside the cavern, where the end waited for him with wings. Did he wish to kill more of those beautiful creatures?

He left the gun where it lay and, surprised at his own calm, went outside the cavern to the ledge. There was of course no moon, but it was light enough that there might well have been. The fog had thickened and spread as far as sight, so that the surrounding peaks were like islands in a white ocean.

Sure enough, two remarkably beautiful women with white wings were out there waiting. One crouched on the ledge while the other was up on the sloping mountain wall, defying gravity. Her hair was a deep orange fire blowing on the breeze; the other's was icy blue.

'Are you here to kill me?' Eric asked the blue-haired one, which jumped down from its perch and landed awkwardly to examine him from closer quarters.

'No,' she said. For a while they just stared at him.

'Are you sure?' he said. 'I'm Marked.'

'Marked!' There was a fluttering whistle from them both, perhaps laughter. 'Silly walker.'

'I'm ... not Marked?'

'Do you slay Invia?'

'Um, certainly not.'

'Silly walker!' They went back to staring. Curiosity was all he could discern in their faces.

He supposed it was not impolite to stare back so he indulged a good gawk at the blue-haired one's full-figured body. He sat with his back to the cliff side. 'You've been following us today,' he said. 'Why is it we interest you?'

'Your drake,' said the one with fiery hair. She spoke hesitantly. 'He's strange. He's not a normal drake.'

'How so?' said Eric.

'The charm the girl wears,' said the other Invia, before her sister could answer. 'Why do you have it?'

He shrugged. 'It was given to us. Actually the drake vomited it up. So maybe he stole it from someone. Are you here to take it back?'

'No!' answered the blue-haired one with vehemence he didn't expect.

'Vyin made it. Why did he?' said the other.

'I can't answer,' he said. Why did they think he'd know more of the dragons than them? He tried to remember what little he'd heard. Vyin – he thought that was the one who was supposedly a friend to humans, but he wasn't certain.

'It has made them angry,' said the blue-haired one, pointing skyward as though this clarified who she meant. 'In parts, the lightstone broke away. A house was destroyed where the piece fell!' Again she made the fluttering whistle, laughter.

'Your woman carries Vyin's charm,' said the other.

'They know about it now,' said the blue-haired Invia, leaning closer to him as though to confide. Strands of her hair tickled his forearm. 'Dyan is still free! He told them. He is ... frightened. Whenever he comes, frightened! Now they argue with each other. It's dangerous to be near. Many of us flew away.'

'What will the dragons do?'

'Vyan went to his forges,' said the red-haired one.

'So did Tzi-Shu!' said the other, edging closer as though competing for his attention. 'I was in the space beneath. Her feet moved fast. You can't go up and watch her. She doesn't allow it. Most of them don't.'

Eric said, 'Forges. What does that mean?'

'You are the Pilgrim!' said the blue-haired Invia.

'Yes, I am. Will you answer me? What does it mean that the other dragons went to their forges?'

'We do not say,' said the red-haired one. 'Walkers don't know these things.'

'Forges means they'll make things, doesn't it?'

'Of course they will *make* things,' said the blue-haired Invia. 'Silly walker!'

'The *byaskhan* seek you,' said the other. Eric understood this whistling sound to mean war mages. 'We don't like them.'

'Me either. What things will the other dragons make?'

'They are in a hurry,' said the red-haired one.

'Your drake is strange,' said the other. 'He's been touched by Vyin too. We'll watch you. It's interesting. We—'

At the sound of Loup stumbling outside, both Invia were gone with a rush of wind and beating white wings. Loup, shocked, stared at Eric with an open mouth, waiting for an explanation.

'You look like you're my dad and I brought two strange girls home,' said Eric, laughing.

'Inferno's charred *dick*! Why didn't they kill you?'

'I wondered the same thing. I asked them if I was Marked; they said I'm not.' Eric frowned. 'Then for some reason I debated the point with them.'

Loup sent an arc of piss flying over the ledge and into the sea of fog. 'I hope you had a mule's share of sense to keep your mouth shut.'

'Kind of shut.'

Loup listened to Eric's account of the conversation. He said nothing other than, 'Sleep, lad. More flying tomorrow. The castle will be in sight soon, if you're still sure we should go there.'

And with another full day's flight – the Invia keeping their distance, little specks playfully darting through the higher clouds – they made camp with the castle visible in the distance, gleaming as though reflecting a white sun.

For one fleeting moment as they stood gazing from their high perch, the light played a strange trick, spearing painfully into Eric's eyes and leaving the impression of the huge building shifting positions the way a person does in sleep.

Loup turned to him, studied his face, then said, 'I saw it too, lad. I saw it too.'

THE WARRIOR'S REDEEMER

1

Sharfy's hand rested on his knife's handle. He watched Anfen's sleeping body – though *sleeping* hardly seemed right: *almost dead* was more like it. Thin, starved, the rise and fall of his chest hardly perceptible.

Now it was decision time. Part of him made the strong case: knife him. Take that armour, take his weapon. It's the armour that gets us into 'the quiet' or just whatever it really is. I can use that sword every bit as good as he can. Almost as good, anyway . . .

It would be like knifing a friend on the battlefield who'd been cut so his guts were in his lap, in too much pain to live for another pointless hour or two. Maybe deep down he'd be thankful. The Sharfy of years past would not have baulked. If he made it to a city – if there were any cities still standing and free enough to live in – he'd retire off what he could get for that magic gear. Retire? He could probably buy a whole city for himself. Mayors themselves would fork out big for that gear.

Decisions, decisions.

Today they'd continued a long winding march only to stop for a break in the very place they'd left just four days ago. The temptation to kill Anfen had lingered at that moment too. It had been a great uneven circle through bad country with no goat-track, let alone paved road. Loose stone on climbing ground rife with pits and holes. Anfen sick and starved all the while, never once explaining what they were doing or where that damned purple scar of his came from, the scar which still wept blood now and then. It went right the way round, like his whole head had been cut off!

Breaking long silences, Anfen had ranted, raved. Some of it outright crazy-man babble. About how his 'redeemer' would show up again. His redeemer would tell them their task. His redeemer would this, that, the other.

Sharfy crouched, and was a breath away from drawing his knife when Anfen groaned and stirred. Shit, he thought, stepping back. He went off road and pissed on a tree.

Anfen sat up, hugged his knees, rocked back and forth like someone sick as death. 'I must not take us back there too many more times,' he said, his voice a harsh croak. 'We must not meddle.'

'Back where?' said Sharfy.

'Back into the quiet.'

'Yep. The quiet. I thought maybe that's what you meant.' Sharfy shook his cock dry. 'So. How does that armour work anyway? Do you just think about the quiet and you're there? Is that how? Why not just tell me? I won't take it off you or anything.'

'We should not go there at all. We should not be here in this corrupted country.'

Sharfy shut his eyes. 'So. You don't say. We shouldn't be here, huh? You know, I thought that a couple of times. I thought maybe we could be in an inn somewhere. Or something.'

'We can know no purpose until my redeemer comes.'

I'm going to do it, Sharfy realised with a measure of relief to have the matter settled. Next time he sleeps, he's dead.

It didn't take long. Anfen stood up, staggered a few paces then collapsed in a puff of dead leaves. Sharfy drew his knife, crouched by the body, rolled it over, held the blade to Anfen's throat . . .

And for a minute or more he looked down at his gaunt face. He willed his hand to do it but it suddenly wouldn't move. Shit, he thought again, dropping the knife in the dead leaves.

He dragged Anfen – how light he was – back away further from the road, laid a pack under his head, cursed his name and then shut his own eyes, not caring that neither of them was taking watch. They had already relied on luck for far too long to do things differently now.

2

Sharfy woke from nightmares to the sound of something falling to the ground beside his head. Broken there were two stretched pieces of what had once been a man, and still looked like a man, only warped, pulled out of shape as though made of rubber. He touched one piece by accident as he scrambled to his feet. It was light and hard as set clay.

'A near thing,' said Anfen, lordly and triumphant with his weapon drawn. 'It had you. Two of them, Sharfy. Look behind us. That one had you in its time dance. And more of them come. Here in the quiet, they can't hurt us. Draw blade! Draw the blade you yearn to use.' Anfen laughed madly.

Sharfy drew his blade and followed Anfen through the twilight. Looming around them were people twisted out of shape, bent and stretched, far taller than they should be. They moved clumsily, at times seeming not to touch the ground with their feet. One of them turned to regard him, looking into him with eyes horribly conscious, its mouth twisted open and stretched out of shape. Arms stiff and curved up, it moved spastically as though trying to wade through water. Sharfy could not look it in the eyes for long.

Anfen cut it down, cut them all down and left none for Sharfy to kill. Fine by him. The beings did not fight back, did not so much as shuffle away; their eyes just followed the swing of Anfen's sword. He cut the last one apart and crouched by the stiff severed pieces, breathing heavily. 'They serve some purpose, Sharfy, I come to suspect.' He gazed around for more of them.

'Huh! That's crazy. How do you figure? Just monsters.'

'They are changed by something from the foreign side. Whatever it is, it negotiates with *our* side. Our reality makes half the change. Do you see? They must serve a purpose here, give some benefit.'

'Shut up, Anfen. Just fucking shut up with that talk.' Tears of anger threatened to come but he held them off, throat burning. He hadn't cried in the slave farm when his friend was beaten to death by guards right in front of him; he wasn't going to cry now.

Anfen did not seem to have heard. He stalked through the woods, back toward the road, seeking more of the beasts, but there were none around. Off through the trees were occasional scattered glowing forms of spells cast long ago, or perhaps yet to be cast, with more still in the sky far above, faintly gleaming. Some were so huge they must have been cast by dragons, and were still waiting for shapers to reach them and weave them into reality.

Sharfy remembered then the Otherworld sky, vast and black, where distant scattered lights gleamed like diamonds falling into a pit of unimaginable size. Around the fire one night Eric had called them 'stars', explaining their presence to Siel in words making less than no sense while Sharfy listened in. He now saw that 'stars' were really spells cast long ago in that place before its magic dried up, like written orders left lying around for smiths, still waiting for hands to hammer them into existence.

An animal shriek pulled him out of his reverie. It was hard to believe the sound came from Anfen, who staggered drunkenly past Sharfy and back toward the Great Dividing Road, a look on his face ghastly for its sudden happiness. Sharfy pursued him, thinking he had found more Tormentors to slay, and wondering why that grim business should be such a joy to him.

But there were no Tormentors. Ahead of them was a white glow like that of a ghost. Anfen staggered close, dropped his sword and fell to his knees. Only after a minute or more of staring could Sharfy make out a shape in the misty light of a man sitting rigidly on horseback. Both horse and rider were larger than they should have been. The man spoke quiet words. Anfen listened, body shaking as he wept, reaching out to touch the ghostly figure.

Sharfy dared not go closer. Then words carried to him: 'Come and fetch your master's sword, squire, as you wish to do.'

I'm no squire, Sharfy thought. I'm a veteran. Never led an army but seen as much war as him. But he did as told, holding the sword's handle out for Anfen, who did not take it.

'I may go no closer to the castle than here,' said the apparition. 'Even here, I am nervous – It is too aware of me. You are to witness for me, Anfen. You are a mortal for whom It neither knows nor cares. Through your eyes shall I see what you witness. A change comes to the new growing power, called Vous. I know not yet what he will truly become.'

Anfen said, 'Shall I cut Vous down, my redeemer, before his power grows?'

'You could not. Not even with the weapon I have fashioned for you. And if it could be done, you should not. We Spirits may need him.'

'May, my redeemer? How can it be that one such as you, who can undo a man's death, cannot see this for certain?'

And with that question Sharfy suddenly understood. Anfen's sword clattered from his hand. Valour did not seem to notice. Said the god, 'No seer sees his own path winding through the many futures before him. Not even Spirits. To see is to move them; so they are forever shifting out of sight. To your eyes a thousand tunnels they would seem, stretching before you, each as unlikely as the one that is certain. But the past is one path, clear and certain. In it I see the Spirits with me, defeating once-mighty Inferno. Do you know what he was? What the other Spirits are, what I am?'

'Any word you share, my redeemer, shall be treasured.' With no warning Anfen's arm whipped sideways and struck like a hammer blow at the back of Sharfy's knee. 'Kneel!' his voice roared.

Head spinning, Sharfy kneeled and felt Valour's judging gaze fall briefly upon him, then move away.

Valour said, 'We Spirits are pillars, holding up the skies and keeping the brood therein. Inferno it was necessary for us to break. From afar, the brood sent him mad. A pillar has been missing since: our hold upon them weakened. A new pillar is erected soon, named Vous.'

'Will it stand with you, my redeemer?'

'It may. Or it may harm us. It may be small and frail, or have more strength than Mountain. But the Pendulum swings. Another Spirit may, perhaps one day soon, be called across into the far land to do war, leaving those of us remaining too weak to keep the brood in hold. Anfen. You did well not to slay the mage who makes this come about.'

'Thank you. Oh, thank you, my redeemer.'

'It was hard for you. The mage knows not his purpose. Both Spirits and the brood have used him at different times. As he used you.'

'I suspected this was so, my redeemer.'

'You may slay him when the change is done if that remains your wish, and if your hand is fast enough.'

'Thank you, my redeemer. Oh, thank you.'

'The new Spirit will come forth soon. He cannot remain so close to the great power you call the Dragon – he will be pushed away. It will be then you know the change is done. When Vous comes south and chooses for himself a home in the realm, we others must watch. In time we must decide if he is to be kept, or to be sent to where mad Inferno went. Inferno was not slain, Anfen, but brought low. No more can happen to Vous. Even now, he could not be slain.'

'He has achieved eternal life, my redeemer?'

'If this was his quest's object, he has. There will be much time for him to regret it. We now must part. I give you this advice: you have no true friend among the brood. *There shall be no Favoured.* Listen not to any such tempting promise. Tell your kindred. Go forth now, Anfen. Witness for me. I have no governance of the hand wielding the sword I gave you. That is only yours. Your thoughts are yours, your valiant heart is yours. Your

grief and shame are yours, if cling to them you must. Go now.'
Valour's gaze again fell on Sharfy. 'Serve him well.' Those three
words fell as heavily as slabs of stone.

Sharfy wanted very much to run and hide. Instead he stam-
mered, 'Yes, I will.'

3

Step after step, he followed Anfen back to the castle, which soon
loomed enormous over their heads again, seeming to stare
directly at them like a living beast, as though the living beast
buried somewhere far beneath it could see through these great
stone eyes.

Anfen babbled happily about dragons and Spirits and his
redeemer. The scar from his neck dribbled blood onto his collar,
which was already stiff with it. Sharfy glanced skyward hoping
an Invia would come and kill him. None did.

They did not go back into the quiet, and only once was a lone
Tormentor visible in the distance. Its head swung around to
watch them, and it stalked with its odd gait to where they'd
passed, but it did not pursue them.

Whether it was Vous or something else, there was no denying
a change had come, or else one fast approached. It was as tangible
as a gathering storm, the air crackling with energy. There were
patrols, but they seemed strangely disorganised, rushing along
the roads Sharfy had at last – with great difficulty – persuaded
Anfen not to travel on. There were also floods of refugees, or
what looked like them, heading for some reason *toward* the
castle, not away from it. Almost as though they were all obeying
a summons or had heard some call. From the glimpses Sharfy

had of their faces, they rushed with the fervour of those who have heard that treasure is to be found just up ahead.

As he and Anfen got nearer, as the castle's hugeness became overwhelming, the babble of a crowd's voice carried back to them from its lawns. Gathered there were citizens and fighting men alike, starving and well fed mixed together, in rags or occasional finery, all staring up and talking with excitement.

Far above them, on a ledge overlooking the lawns, their Friend and Lord stood with his arms held aloft, his face turned to the sky, where dark clouds gathered in a swirling mass and lightning lashed about like the tongues of enormous beasts. The castle and the ground beneath it seemed to shiver.

IS SHADOW HERE?

1

The castle shook. Strategist Vashun – the only one to still respond to the Arch's urgent summonses – voiced what the Arch himself wondered, what he could only answer with guesswork to give the appearance of control he no longer had: 'Is this it?'

The Arch stared at him; through his gem he saw deeper into Vashun than the Strategist would realise, and saw attitudes he did not like. He answered, 'Not yet.'

He hoped it was true. He would not be here, if he knew this was indeed the great change.

A high-pitched sound had come from Vous's chamber that morning. The drake caged in the Arch's study had heard it, had whined and writhed and scratched at its cage bars. The Arch had seen a disturbance in the airs, as though something had gone through all the nearby energies like a wave through water. Those exotic airs in jars on his shelf stirred and shifted like they had heard the sound too and wished to answer with a voice of their own, if only a mage were to give them that voice. And he had been sorely tempted to smash the jars and cast something, anything, to oblige them . . .

He'd resisted, instead rushing to the higher floors. The canisters of foreign airs still sat beyond Vous's chamber. They were not ruptured or broken. Inside, Vous writhed and thrashed on his throne. His movements were impossibly fast, limbs blurring. His body was translucent.

The Arch stepped backward, alarmed, for Vous was an instant later standing right before him in the chamber doorway. His face held none of its usual rage. It was a blank mask.

'Friend and Lord?' said the Arch.

Vous didn't seem to see or hear him. Arms aloft, he stepped away from his chamber. Colours pulsed in the airs. There was a low background humming throb, and the castle shivered again.

Slowly, slowly, Vous proceeded to the balcony overlooking the lawns, where he stood with his head turned up to the gathering clouds, as though his raised arms conducted their movement. For hours – sixteen, now – he had waited there and not moved at all. The soaring wind did not even ruffle his hair.

Some call had gone out to the closer cities, the nearby patrols, and all villages within a half-day's march. All who'd heard it answered by coming here, and now stood gathered on the lawns below their Friend and Lord. A sea of murmured conversation and upturned faces waited, and the crowd grew ever larger by the hour.

The Arch and his one remaining loyal Strategist – and not loyal by much, he now knew – waited and watched. Influencing Vous was not a possibility. The options were observe or flee. Staff from the castle had congregated below with all the other teeming masses, all but those mind-controlled ones who stayed at their posts, and would do so even if flames crept up their legs.

'You and I are not called below,' Vashun observed, still cheerful.

The Arch did not reply.

'Some kind of lure. Very potent. Now's not the first time it's gone out, you realise. Some of those people began marching here many days ago. From Kopyn! How'd he do it without our noticing till now?'

The Arch did not reply.

'The windows. They have all gone blank. Did you know?'

'I know,' answered the Arch.

'Have the war mages returned? Any of them? Is there ... sign of the girl? Should she not be back by now?'

The Arch rounded on him, ready to strike the Strategist down with a spell, but he was no longer there. There was an echo of laughter instead. Avridis knew that at last he was truly on his own. Angered beyond any rage he'd known before, a feeling that surpassed any desire or emotion he'd ever felt, he went to Vous's chamber and blasted open the metal cases holding in the foreign airs, wanting only to cause some pain, some harm, with – for the first time in his life – no further hint of purpose or reason. Everything he'd done in this castle, every act of war or torture, even every act of kindness, had served a purpose, until this deed.

The foreign airs, a harsh and luminous red, filtered into the vast winding threads swirling about the castle like the arms of a whirlpool with Vous its centre. The red joined the mix of dark glimmering colours till it was no longer discernible. The disturbance in the airs was almost too subtle to see, but he saw it, and felt a twist of pleasure. Whether this act caused what came next, or whether the timing was coincidental, the Arch, and of course Vous himself, would have no way of knowing.

2

'Is Shadow among you?' Vous breathed, stirring from his pose at last.

Though whispered, the words left his lips and found the ears of every listener below. The wind spoke and asked the same question as it scattered the women's hair, whipped through the trampled grass, tossed about litter, flapped people's clothes – flapped Anfen's and Sharfy's too as they hung back at the very edge of the throng, watching like everyone else. The thunder asked the same question in its deep loud voice, clanging and booming about like a maniac striking a drum. The rain hissed down, demanding to know if Shadow was among them in its babble of many tiny voices. The crowd watching spoke many different things, but each word translated itself, took on the meaning of the words their Friend and Lord had spoken. But no one had the answer. If Shadow was there, he hid somewhere.

'Is Shadow among you?' Vous repeated in a louder voice, a hint of displeasure showing itself. And a warning. The crowd shifted on their feet nervously, several thousands of them pressing in together on the castle lawn, pushing at the steps and the barricades set up to keep them out, the older frailer ones among them crying out weakly in pain.

Upon whom should their Friend and Lord's displeasure fall? They were one entity here after all, as seen in his eyes from far above. The skies darkened and thunder bellowed a threat. Lightning stabbed the higher castle towers and the ground shivered.

Vous's voice became a scream louder than all other sounds. '*Is . . . Shadow . . . here?*' The last word drew out and echoed, shrill and obscene. Their Friend and Lord's face was blazing with hate and rage and fear, eyes huge and gleaming as the beam of his gaze swept through all of them below, like a light searching, searching for Shadow.

Vous's screaming voice was all fear and pain; for now his rage had left him, and was the people's to express. A third of them changed so that their faces were Vous's face, eyes ablaze, the fine chiselled features identical to his, their bodies changing too so their arms were thin like his, their fingers long and delicate like the artist Vous had fancied himself to be, centuries before. All things, he'd fancied himself to be, unique and special and brilliant among all the history of men, the finest of warriors, the deepest of thinkers, beauty and charm to seduce the goddess Wisdom if indeed he deigned to do so (he did not). Yet now on the lawns he was replicated several hundred times. Old women with Vous's head hissed angrily at their neighbours in the throng, 'Is Shadow here?' A thousand chattering words, spoken by those with Vous's face, and alike by those who were unchanged, said, 'Is Shadow here?'

Babbling, babbling, a screeching cacophony of voices demanded to know, while Vous far above them screamed with his jaw hung wide as a wolf's, eyes blasting their light through sheets of rain warm as blood. Anfen grimly watched while Sharfy held his ears, wishing for it to be over, not knowing what he witnessed, only that it was worse, somehow, than anything else he'd ever seen, in all the vast catalogue of death and pain and misery his past held.

Those with Vous's face dug out the others' eyes with their fingers, scratched and bit off their ears, bit their throats, ripped hair and strangled, spilling blood all down their chins. Those being slain screamed, broken by pain out of the spell, while Vous above stared down, still screaming, still screaming. The last sound in many dying ears, his voice. The last sight in many dying eyes, his face, branded into the features of a stranger, or onto a wife's or husband's or son's or daughter's who'd made the journey here to the castle lawns with the very person they now clawed and bit and ate to death. Vous, high above, watched this death he had created with no sign of whether or not he approved or even understood what he'd caused. Anfen watched it silently, not drawing his weapon, and not seeming concerned that any of the fevered crowd would turn their way.

Blood soaked the grass of the castle lawns, churning beneath thousands of stamping feet as those on the edges of the crowd panicked and fled.

3

Shadow was among them. Shadow watched some distance back, fascinated by the strange, beautiful creature standing so far above the crowd. The sight of that being – who glowed with light that seemed to be angelic, whose screaming voice was in Shadow's ears a beautiful song – filled him with a peculiar emotion which shifted, moment to moment, from longing to rage. He wanted to kill that being for no reason he could find, yet he loved him without knowing what love was.

Fear could be seen all through the emanating light around the slender, delicate-looking creature so high above, Vous's own fear, seeping from him and bleeding into the air all around, till it had filled the denizens watching below.

The sense Shadow had watching Vous was far stronger than, though similar to, that emotion which had marked Eric as a point of reference. He wanted to yell in answer to Vous's voice, to sing in harmony with it at the same time as shout it down and blot it out. He did not know what to do. He dared go no closer, though the urge to do so was near overwhelming. His mouth opened wide and he tried to find his own voice to match Vous's screaming, but he could not.

This was the first thing to take from Shadow's thoughts the prison he'd just escaped. How sweet it had been at first, his entrapment in what had seemed a round thin room, spinning about itself. He'd fallen backward through suspended clattering chains of many colours. Their touch was pleasure itself: they scratched itches, quenched thirsts, gave sensual delights of a kind his body had not conceived. He had felt whole there, known peace and contentment, felt free of the need to roam and to learn in that outside place where all lessons so far showed that pain or hollowness was at the heart of all things, or that horrible mess lurked inside each person's pleasing exterior; that the pretty things in the landscape were just *there*. There, in that backward-falling space, it had all been balmed and cured, all dissatisfaction and restlessness. It truly was just what had been promised by the lure that had called him across this world, across countless miles, and had eluded him at the tower when Eric and Siel had tricked him.

But with time the chains had grown hot, till heat and pain overrode all pleasure and each second became a shrieking agony. Every thought and instinct bent toward his being free. He'd been so mad with pain that he did not remember how he had come to be free; he half recalled a cold wind rushing over him as though a tiny door had been opened, and remembered diving toward it ...

And by chance he had ventured here. Now Shadow did scream, a more successful attempt to echo Vous, whose arms now reached up to embrace the storm above him. On the lawns the people swarmed and splashed in blood like Shadow had seen fish do in a river in the wild country, swarming through waters turned to bloody froth as the fish ate the killed animal he'd dropped among them.

At the sound of Shadow's scream those Vous-things nearby turned toward him and went still.

4

As Anfen drew his blade it sang like a rasping metal throat. A burst of silver flame ran from handle to tip and Sharfy recoiled from its ice-cold burn. Even when Anfen had cut down the Tormentors, the blade had never burned with this coldness.

He followed Anfen's gaze and his heart leaped when he saw Eric, the Pilgrim, who in Sharfy's mind occupied the exaggerated place of a dear friend and comrade. He was deeply alarmed to see Eric so close to danger – in fact what was he doing here? Who was he with?

The things with Vous's face had turned Eric's way. So it seemed natural enough to Sharfy that Anfen had drawn his blade and was now moving with some urgency toward Eric, surely with the intent of protecting him. Sharfy drew his own sword and followed, through a shoving mass of people screaming as they fled the Vous-things.

It was soon clear that something was wrong. Eric didn't look right: he looked like a mage's illusion or something, with blurred outlines, and – that noise, that screaming sound! Eric's mouth had gone wide as a beast's; his eyes were dead black holes which seemed both far wider than Eric's face and to fit inside it at the same time. Sharfy recoiled from the sight.

A Vous-thing with an elderly woman's starving body clawed at Sharfy, scratching grooves of skin from his neck and lunging to bite his throat. He yelped and kneed her but she kept coming till he slashed his blade across her midsection. She fell sprawling, still trying to get up despite the guts falling out of her, till she was trampled into the grass.

Sharfy ran to catch up with Anfen, who cut a wide arc through the swarming crowd with a cold flare of silver fire, not mindful of whether he slew Vous-things or their fleeing victims. Sharfy had time in the tumult to wonder if one day Anfen would be back here, hopeless with grief over these careless swipes of his blade and eager to polish more long-dead bones. The crowd swarmed away from his cold silver fire. Sharfy held his sword firm as a Vous-thing ran straight at him and impaled itself. He released the blade, stuck fast in the body, and sprinted until he was practically riding Anfen's back.

'Is ... Shadow ... here?' Vous screamed louder than the peal of thunder which followed. To Sharfy's disgust, many of the dead flopped and twitched as though they'd heard a cry to arms. Trampled, mangled, with pieces of their faces hanging loose, with eyes clawed out, they rose and Vous's face pressed itself into their ruined features. They staggered to their feet.

Anfen had reached the Eric who could not really be Eric. Sharfy had no idea what to think – if it *was* Eric, he was under some curse or evil spell beyond their curing. The Eric-being turned to face them, screamed its emotionless scream, utterly inhuman, the voice of rusting metal or barren turf or Sharfy knew not what. Like that big metal wagon that screamed over the bridge, when we went into Otherworld, he thought.

A flock of Vous-things swarmed toward the Eric-thing. Anfen's arm had surely never moved faster, not even when he was in the cusp of youth. He cut them down and the air was filled with his cold silver fire. More of them swarmed over, realising that the enemy Vous feared and screamed for was here. Sharfy knew then that this was it, the final moment, death had come and it bore Vous's face. Had he time for one last mug of ale to reflect before the moment came, he'd have found it fitting that it took the world's Friend and Lord himself to kill him.

But Anfen cut them down. They came in waves but he cut them down, until there was a massive pile of bodies for the others to scuttle over. And then Anfen's sword did strange things, for he seemed to swing it in a circle about his head and yet, some distance away, the oncoming ones would fall back with limbs and heads sliced off, as though the blade had cut them from a distance. Sharfy with his knife in hand was perfectly useless, could only watch with growing shame Anfen's sword saving him from what would have been a warrior's death.

The Eric-thing watched Anfen too, then it flickered and was on the ground behind Anfen, laid out behind him like a shadow ... like a shadow ...

A moment later Shadow was before Anfen again. One arm was long, thin and bladed. It cut through the air, struck the breastplate Valour had made, and was halted with a shower of sparks. Shadow's sword arm broke and fell away. He stared down at the stump left, hesitant and confused.

Anfen wheeled like a dancer, swung his blade in a wide slashing arc, silver fire tracing the swing through the air. Shadow screamed, a worse sound yet than the one he'd made before, as a part of him was cut away.

As the wound was made there was a blinding flash. A force knocked them all down as though it were a blast of the strongest wind. All the Vous-things and their fleeing victims toppled, Sharfy and Anfen blown hurtling back among them. When the flash of light cleared, up on the castle balcony Vous was gone from sight. The Vous-things got to their feet and sprinted away as mindless as insects. The dead ones who had risen fell back and resumed their interrupted sleep.

5

Shadow streaked blindly across the world, shrieking in pain, his path a drunken zigzag covering miles in heartbeats. He went in a line from the Godstears Sea to the unnamed ranges as though from one side of a room to another, so fast he sent his own senses spinning and almost undid himself by the act; as though by doing something that impossible, he nearly made *himself* impossible. A trail of heat blazed behind him, igniting fires to either side of its path as the world objected to this impossibility.

He paused, waited, recovered his senses. The wound still hurt. He was whole, but the left part of his body seemed to flow like molten silver. With agonising slowness its terrible heat dimmed.

Southward he went just a little slower than before, trails of heat like whip lashes on the world behind him. Though his pain gradually subsided his confusion did not. Why had the man done such things to him?

The mechanics of the situation he grasped; he'd shadowed the man but had not been able to shadow the sword and the armour. The stranger's *wanting* to attack him, that was incomprehensible. He'd toyed with elementals, with Lesser Spirits and other dangerous things. Even the dragon had fled from him! Here a man, a normal soft-skinned man, had wanted to hurt him and had done so – worse than anything else ever had.

But ah, that glorious creature up on the castle balcony, embracing the sky. Was Vous one of the things with which to fill this emptiness? None of these people filled him! Not Eric, not the charm (which called him again, promising sweet balm for his pain). They had all left him unchanged.

What of Siel? He wanted to see her long hair in its twin braids, to watch how the braids swung, to hear her voice, whether it laughed or whether it quavered in fear. Either would sound sweet after this bitter, bitter pain. Where was she? He combed a vast distance in search of her, though he didn't yet know what he'd do if he found her.

INTO DANGER

1

The village Gorb had once called home was deserted, its stores plundered. There was no sign of where the locals had gone, nor why. Their tracks led off in all directions. Most of the cupboards were bare. They scavenged what little had been left.

The half-giant emerged from Bald's old workroom with a few of the Engineer's odds and ends, where Siel waited with Far Gaze in his wolf form. The Engineer Bald crouched in the dirt, picking things out to eat them. 'I told him to stop that,' said Siel. 'I don't think he trusts me.'

Gorb plucked Bald up and put him under one arm and they set out following the wolf, who chose their path by scent. He headed east, for the city of Tanton.

The night's quiet was tense and heavy, as if the gloom to either side of the road were filled with watchful eyes. Now and then Gorb held aloft a piece of lightstone Stranger had enchanted for him, which glowed brighter when he squeezed it. Its beams swept aside a veil of darkness to show roadside fields that had never been settled on, never farmed. Like every place a boot could fall on, blood had been shed here in war. Siel began to wonder if war was man's natural destiny, not an aberration at all but the sole purpose of life, for the entertainment of Valour or some other god. *Peace* was the aberration, she felt, nourishing man with its scant scraps throughout history so that he'd fight on, when the call came again.

The tollways, guard houses, roadside stores and booths they came across all sat empty. Even the message towers were abandoned. Rumour of war had spread and people here had seen so little of it that the thought scared them away. Indeed Far Gaze told Gorb before they left that he'd smelled it coming. A vast army of castle soldiers marched south, men who did not follow Valour's ideals of war. Occasional war-mage shrieks could be heard from the clouds, though the creatures could not yet be seen. There was no knowing if it was part of the large flock the dragon had decimated and scattered, or if they were new ones and part of the invading force.

Far Gaze trotted ahead of the others, his ghostly white coat gleaming. He sniffed the breeze and whined in fear. Bald, tucked under Gorb's arm, muttered nonsense. Siel now found the quiet stifling. 'I wonder where they all went,' she said, thinking of the villagers and of the peaceful life she'd so recently envied. It was a melancholy relief to know it had never been on offer after all.

They could see an occasional redness to the southern sky, but the veil covering the barrier had not lifted. 'Old Nightmare's still guarding the gate,' said Gorb. 'Just saw him going west. He was moving fast. Keeping the stoneflesh from going over. That Pendulum stuff must be true. Don't understand it, myself.'

'Each thing has in its *make-up* an ascribed *value*, you ninny!' snarled Bald, spittle flying. 'Value, weight. Weight, mass. Mass, power value. Anything! A man's worth a million bugs!'

'Bald—'

'Now you will *listen*! I divulge *secrets*! Both halves being of *even* power value in total, a vacuum effect *occurs* if a power value's *traded—*'

'Yeah well, you're smarter than me I guess,' said Gorb, shifting the spluttering Engineer to his other arm. 'Shoosh now, that's why the wolf's growling. He's telling you to shut it.'

Far Gaze had halted, head turned to the south. His low growl grew fierce.

Siel slipped her bow from her shoulder and peered into the incline on the road's right-hand side. She could see and hear nothing in the darkness. 'What is it?' she asked the wolf. 'You growl to scare something off, but you may just draw something toward us! Hush now.'

Far Gaze whined, looking from her to the road ahead, undecided.

'If you scent a path less dangerous, take it,' she said, patting the wolf's side, not knowing how much of her talk Far Gaze could understand. 'We'll follow. If there's danger in all directions, that's our fate and we'll meet it like warriors.'

The wolf heaved a sigh but trotted forward at a quicker pace, almost too quick for them to keep up.

'What's worried him?' said Gorb.

'Choose from a dozen threats or more,' she said. 'My bow has never felt so useless.'

'If it's that dragon again, I can't do much about a dragon. Even a little one,' said Gorb.

If it's that dragon, it's probably not very interested in any of you, Siel thought with a shudder.

'What's that sound, anyway?' said Gorb. 'Maybe that's what got the wolf stirred up.'

'I can't hear anything but our footsteps. Can you describe it?'

'Sounds the way wood sounds when you bend it. Creaks and cracks and groans of wood, that's what it sounds like.'

'I don't hear it.'

'The wolf does. And he doesn't like it.'

2

Gorb had put away the piece of enchanted lightstone since they did not want its light being seen from afar by other things. The road was true enough, and just enough light leaked through the gloom to see their way when it bent and wound. Siel's legs began to tire from the pace they'd kept over the past hour. She still heard nothing but the scuffle and tap of their boots on the road, and Bald's occasional muttering. The wolf whimpered constantly, bounding ahead and turning back to glare at them for their slow pace.

The plains to either side were flat as a dinner plate. Now and then campfires could be seen across the flats, caravans pouring from outcast country and making their way to High Cliffs or Tanton, the last two cities to resist their certain fall. The sight of caravans was heartening somehow, camped in rings for safety from bandits. The wind carried smells of smoke. How tempting to head to one of those campfires and beg a night's sleep under their watch.

'That fire's too big,' Gorb muttered just as Far Gaze halted ahead of them again and growled. 'Look! Whole wagons are burning.'

Shouting voices faintly reached them across the plain. It was as though a battle were underway somewhere in the gloom. The hairs on Far Gaze's back stood on end. He crouched low, his growl fierce.

Siel peered into the darkness. At the very furthest reach of her vision it looked like a wagon was indeed burning. She notched an arrow, wondering who she would be shooting at. Had the castle army reached this country already? Or were Blain's men attacking?

Gorb took the piece of lightstone from his pack with a grunt as though he'd forgotten he possessed it. He squeezed it. It spat out its glow, pushing darkness away from the road around them.

They all recoiled. Standing horribly close to the road was what Siel would have taken for an instant to be a burned tree, if she had not seen Tormentors before. Its obsidian skin glistened in the lightstone's light; its rock-lump eyes stared down from double her height. Its mane, a thick fan of spiked needles, rattled.

Far Gaze ran behind it, growled and yelped as though to draw the thing's attention to himself. With exaggerated sweeping movement its head swung around to peer at him, the stiff limbs of its body creaking. Siel's arrow struck its chest and bounced off broken – she might as well have fired at a wall of stone. Forgetting the wolf, it turned to her. She froze in its gaze, paralysed with horror.

It seemed later, when looking back on this memory, that she stood there staring into its eyes for a moment that stretched out forever. While the thing regarded her, she searched its face, looking for something to understand. A hungry animal that wished to eat her, she'd have understood; a bandit wanting to rape her, a war mage doing its mindless duty for its lords, an enemy soldier raising his weapon: *those* she'd have understood. But not this creature. Something burned in its heart, but whatever it was was utterly foreign.

It seemed in that long-drawn stretch of time, as she tried to comprehend this alien horror, that *all* her understanding broke down, that nothing at all was real, she herself least of all. She was nothing, abstract. That it would now draw her to itself and with its spikes and blades unmake her body, for no reason she had a hope of discerning, all dwindled to irrelevance.

A sound – *thwock!* – and the top part of the Tormentor's face flew away. Gorb had one of Bald's guns out, planted on his knee. He quickly stuffed another sharpened stone down the barrel.

The Tormentor's body turned toward him, arms flailing in the gestures of some surreal elegant dance. Siel watched it with her mouth hung open, still transfixed, until the half-giant scooped her up in his arm.

The wolf whined and ran. Gorb followed with Siel and Bald under his arms, his big strides keeping pace with the wolf, though his breathing was laboured. Siel watched the fields by the road, the whole world jolting heavily with Gorb's steps. Set against the odd distant fire dark shapes were silhouetted, though some were surely tricks of her eyes. She still saw that thing's face, staring, and wished desperately to know its mind. It had not hated her, whether it meant to kill her or not. She was sure of that much.

They ran on. As the first light of day bled through the gloom Gorb staggered, clearly exhausted. Still he kept pace with Far Gaze, who now veered off the road, past a farmstead where a family stood on their porch armed with crossbows and burning brands. They watched two Tormentors stalk across their land some way distant, hardly noticing the new trespassers.

Far Gaze yelped and tore across the sloping fields, faster than Siel had yet seen him run. Gorb stopped, bent double, huffing air. She climbed out of his grip. Over a rise in the ground came eight men on horseback, with almost as many vacant horses in tow. They wore Tanton's deep scarlet lashed with gold; High Cliff's colour, gold, taken after that city was conquered long ago, an insult never forgotten. She knew the figure leading them, one arm in a sling, was Tauk the Strong.

For the sight of his injury her heart rose with hope: here was a leader himself willing to fight and risk his precious flesh, to brave a journey such as this. Some of the Mayor's entourage saw them and gestured in signal language: *Approach if you are peaceful, flee in safety if you are not, we seek no needless fight with you and shall not pursue.* Siel gestured back: *We are friends; do not mind the wolf.*

The men watched with interest as the huge white wolf approached them, whining only to point out it was not growling. A good distance from their alarmed horses Far Gaze lay down and began to shift form, writhing, twitching, convulsing, shedding hair, his bones breaking. By the time Siel and Gorb slowly crossed the rise and joined him, he was almost finished.

'Now you keep quiet, Bald,' Gorb instructed. Bald obliged by falling asleep curled up in the grass.

'This is a sight,' said Tauk, his voice cheerful, though his entourage looked tired and bore wounds. 'A half-giant, a warrioress, an Engineer, and a very ill horse-sized wolf.'

'This is Far Gaze, Mayor. Magician of the Mayors' Command,' said Siel.

'Ah, I know the name. I have met him. No one told me he was a shape-shifter,' said Tauk. 'I'm glad you've lived through the night. For us, it was a near thing. We were singing songs one moment, surrounded by horrors the next. Hail, Siel.'

She blinked in surprise – she'd just once met the Mayor, in a crowded briefing from the Mayors' Command on the night she'd asked to join them. She'd not known he'd noticed her then, let alone memorised her name and face. She bowed low.

Far Gaze had finished shifting and now stood, his body naked and starved. He swayed on his feet, bowed low before the Mayor – though Siel saw the sneer on his face – then noisily threw up.

Said the Mayor, 'Far Gaze, it's good of you to have found me. You must know of the demon beasts that have come in the night. Is this what it appears: a planned invasion from beyond World's End? Or are they sent by more familiar enemies?'

Far Gaze pondered the question at length, then laughed long and loud. The men to either side of the Mayor looked askance at each other. Tauk himself bristled. 'I have lost fine men tonight, personal friends among them. I find no humour. Where is the Pilgrim?'

Siel, mortified by Far Gaze's continuing laughter, quickly said, 'The Pilgrim has left us, Mayor. Flown away on a drake, with Aziel, Vous's daughter.'

The Mayor's face went ashen. 'Vous's *daughter* was in your possession? I see there is much to tell me. Where have they gone, and why?'

'They did not linger to tell us,' she said.

'Then they took our hope with them,' said a rider to Tauk's left. 'And we rode through this foul night for naught.'

Stark naked, Far Gaze sat cross-legged on the ground among the wolf fur he'd shed. He wiped tears of mirth from his eyes but at last managed to speak. 'I smelled much in the night. The wind tells me a huge force comes from the north and crosses the Great Road, still some way distant, but coming. They come to take your city, Tauk the Strong. And then High Cliffs, of course. They bring war machines, siege towers, trebuchets. War mages will come too.'

'Those foul things will be weak in our city,' said one of the men. 'There is little magic.'

'They will use their claws and teeth, and cast at you even if one spell kills them! An army like this has not come to wage death on such a scale since the War that Tore the World. But there'll be far less death than that, for you haven't nearly the force to make a contest of it. They mean to burn and poison the land outside your walls, where your food is grown. Occupying your city is not their instruction. All your people will be killed, their bodies thrown in massive pits. The vanguard of that force will reach your city soon and test your defences. The rest is some way distant.'

The men had been, throughout this, getting angrier and angrier at Far Gaze's glee, which he still did not bother hiding. But Tauk's face showed none of his thoughts.

'Meanwhile death comes from the south,' Far Gaze went on. 'It marches with no purpose and no named enemy. But it marches *north*. Do you understand? What we saw and travelled through on this night was just the scattered edge of it! You know of Strategist Blain's men? The rebel faction he sent, to guard World's End?'

'I do.'

'More than ten thousand men. *They* are the Tormentors we've met! We learned what those beasts are: men changed by poisoned airs from Levaal South, or airs which become poison when they mix with ours. A massive gust of this poison crossed the barrier. Not all Blain's men were changed, but a good portion was. Several thousands! More Tormentors than were used to take and hold Elvury, you can be sure. Did all this fit Blain's private plan? I know not. But it was not the Arch's plan.

'Rejoice, Tauk the Lucky! You will only have to defeat the

castle vanguard. They'll have likely avoided the Tormentor swarm, as I judge your city shall too. But the castle's main force is two days or more behind the vanguard. *They* will not be so lucky. And Tormentors will be an enemy they're ill prepared to fight. Trebuchets, swords and arrows will not do them much good.'

Siel's heart sped as though it understood, though her mind had not yet grasped it. A wave of talk broke out among the men. 'Do you mean to say . . .?' began one.

'I laughed from unexpected joy, from relief,' said Far Gaze, lying on his back with his legs akimbo. 'It is a strange world. For the moment – for the *moment*, mind – you are no longer doomed. There is yet a battle to win against the vanguard force, which itself will test you. Get High Cliffs to send support, now! You must win, for the castle will soon lose most of its strength, as the Arch always meant it to do. But he meant it only after *all* Free Cities were ruins and ashes, and all your people dead!'

'Then we will have won,' one of the riders said sceptically.

'No,' said Far Gaze sitting up, suddenly more sober. 'You'll have survived just one peril. Your prize will be a land crawling with death, and a foreign world to your south about which we know nothing. You are close to the barrier. Vous remains on his throne, a god rising. He will need no armies, and you must hope you no longer matter to him. What's more the dragons in the sky are on the brink of freedom, and they mean death to us all. You won't know peace for a long time, if you ever truly do. For the Pendulum swings. You probably do not know what those words mean, and I doubt my explanations will mean much to you.'

If Far Gaze meant to erase any sign of hope or optimism in

the men, no spell could have done it swifter. 'Will more poison come?' said Tauk quietly.

'Who knows? Forgive my laughter, Mayor, and my one moment's relief, joy, hope. It has been the first I've had in a long while.'

'You are forgiven, of course.' The Mayor stared into the distance, thinking. 'A question. Are you familiar with the spell which shares your name?'

Siel saw intense annoyance run across Far Gaze's face; mages were never pleased to be asked to cast something, even by those who were their allies, friends or commanders. He said, 'I know one version of it.'

'I understand to cast it requires high ground. Take me to such a place, and cast it for me, if you will be so kind.'

'If you ask me to look to the south, beyond the boundary, I will not! A greater mage than I was already corrupted by—'

'Calm yourself, I don't ask that. I wish to look upon these lands. Will you cast it for me?'

Far Gaze spat. 'Nothing would give me greater pleasure,' he said angrily.

'Excuse me, Mayor. Have you Engineers?' said Gorb, who had been itching to speak for a while now.

'We do, as you must know. That one there sleeping, he is one of ours, unless he has acquired those garments in some other way. His clothes come from our city.'

'A tattoo on his foot will reveal his origin,' said another of the entourage.

'He is yours. But you might be happy the village I came from borrowed him,' said Gorb. He held up one of Bald's guns. 'There were two monsters over in that field, back yonder. Got time for a quick show of how these weapons work?'

Tauk said, 'There's no time for that now, and we will not go near those creatures when we needn't. I need to see with my own eyes what the magician has claimed.'

'Of course,' said Far Gaze with a sardonic bow.

'It is no insult, good mage,' said Tauk. 'But a wolf's nose can't be the basis of decisions I must now make. I will see with my own eyes how things have shifted, if indeed they have. Then maybe I will laugh along with you, for a little while.'

3

They rode half a mile east until they came to a suitable hilltop, then sighted a taller one further away and headed there instead, to Far Gaze's silent fury. He and Siel gladly rode on horseback, but the entourage was not mindful of Gorb, who lagged some way behind them carrying the Engineer. They encountered no Tormentors on the steep winding paths through a dense glade filled with ferns.

(As they rode Siel could still not free her mind of the sight of that Tormentor staring at her. What had it seen? Enemy? Prey? Would some other happpenstance mage one day look back from far into the future and see its spiked body swing around with alien grace, hear the rattle of its needles, and wonder the same thing?)

They reluctantly left the horses tied to tree stumps when the path got too steep, then climbed a long-abandoned track through thick foliage and found the highest point they could. 'Ready?' said Tauk.

'Where would you see?' said Far Gaze irritably.

'The land about, as far as you can take me. I have had this

cast once before. It showed me many miles beyond, but the mage cooked himself in casting it. I could not eat meat for weeks after.' Some of the men chuckled.

Far Gaze's jaw clenched. 'A very foolish mage that must have been, not to know certain limitations. I heard a similar tale, in which the magician accidentally cooked the ones he cast upon. Such things can happen. It is a shame.'

'The Mayor meant no disrespect, good mage—'

'Shut up! All crowd in. My version of the spell is cast not on one person but over a small area, so several of you will be cast upon. This was once a hunting spell, used to confuse dangerous animals by ruining their vision. The tribes used it. My people altered it and made it more useful. I will be blind. All of you will have "far gaze". It is safe to speak to me during the cast but do *not* touch me. If you feel any pain, step away and keep your eyes closed till we are finished.' He looked around the glade. There was no sign of recent human activity; the old path was grown over. 'I am troubled – this place is not safe. One of you stand watch. Go! We'll soon be blind to our surrounds. Enough dithering, I cast now. Shut your eyes.'

He sniffed hard for a minute or two, waiting for some ingredient in the airs. His eyes rolled back in his head; he began a low murmuring in a lost tribal tongue, almost a song, his resonant voice pleasant to hear. Seven of the Mayor's men crowded in around him, along with Tauk and Siel, all smelling of the road, Siel acutely conscious of the Mayor's closeness. She hoped he would bump into her, longed for his touch even if it were inadvertent. The road did that too – made one ravenously horny – and she felt some of the other men standing much closer to her than they strictly needed to; the odd brush of a hand or elbow against her butt or hip. Just now she didn't mind that at all.

Soon Far Gaze's voice was like a physical thing touching her inner mind, the feel of it pleasant despite provoking a need to squirm away. It went on for a while, then, as though the touch had hit on some key spot, all in a rush the hill fell away in a spinning lurch, to the gasps and mutters of the men crowding in.

From high above they saw the land they'd just ridden through, with occasional people and wagons moving along the roads. The land off road was dotted now and then with Tormentors, motionless or stalking along. 'Take us further afield, if you can,' said Tauk. 'Hear me, mage?'

'He cannot answer you, but he hears you,' said Siel.

Now whizzing beneath was the country they had travelled overnight, the road winding like a river. More abandoned wagons could be seen on their sides, sometimes in smouldering ruin, goods scattered over the fields, bodies abandoned. No Tormentors were here, aside from the occasional corpse of one broken in pieces.

It was as their sight flew near the Great Dividing Road and travelled along it many quick miles north that the Mayor drew a sharp breath. There was the horde that had been Blain's rebel force. Each one looked small from the height of their spell's vantage point, so that it looked like a repulsive swarm of insects crawling along. 'What compels them onward?' one of the men said. 'Whose order to march do they follow?'

'No one's. They are wild creatures, not thinking ones,' said another.

'Yet look, they all head north as though on some mission, obeying some order. The ones who don't move have been distracted.'

'Nightmare!' Siel said, suddenly realising. 'It must be him, or the other god at World's End, Wisdom!'

'Why do you say this?' said Tauk.

'The gods there were keeping things from crossing the barrier,' she said excitedly. 'Blain explained it to us. The gods must have somehow compelled these things to flee north, away from the barrier, so they would not cross back!'

'Surely neither you nor Blain can claim to know the minds of the gods,' said the Mayor. 'But whether you're right or wrong—'

'Come back!' the watch-man shouted. 'Danger! Come back!'

4

Far Gaze ceased chanting. For a little while the world spun crazily around; there was a sensation of falling from high in the air even though their feet were planted. Each of them came to on the ground in a tangle of bodies. The man keeping watch stopped shouting.

When their sight returned it showed Far Gaze frenziedly hurling rocks at something on the overgrown path behind them. Siel was first to her feet. She reeled back from the lone Tormentor which, with ponderous graceful movements, tore apart the man who'd kept watch. The streaks and drops of blood its hands flung through the air made it seem like a composer making music it alone could hear. The thrown rocks bounced off it harmlessly.

'Stop throwing rocks and fight it!' said one of the men, scrambling to his feet.

'I am not casting combat spells,' Far Gaze growled. 'This is your Mayor's fight. We are here against my wishes and I'll not cook myself for you.'

Four men stood with weapons drawn. They hesitated before the Tormentor, having learned in the night how ineffectual swords could be against their hides. One said, 'Do something, mage, or being cooked won't be your greatest danger.'

A shape crashed through the curtain of ferns drawn about the down-hill pathway. Gorb emerged from the greenery with one of Bald's guns in hand. 'Great plan, leaving me behind,' he said. He crouched on one knee, fired and sent a shot ricocheting over the beast's head, bouncing through the glade behind it. He put another sharpened stone down the gun's barrel, aimed more carefully and with a cracking sound the shot split a cleave in the Tormentor's chest.

It went still for a moment then resumed playing with the almost-dead man in its hands, as if it did not realise it had just been badly hurt. The other men found their nerve and rushed at it. Their swords rang on its back but did little more than scratch it. The largest of them heaved his two-handed blade with an overhead diagonal swipe and cut off part of the creature's foot.

The Tormentor tilted sideways, off balance. It turned the motion into a graceful sweeping reach for the man who'd cut it. He fell toward its spread hands.

'Down!' Siel yelled at the men. 'Stay down! You are in the giant's way!'

They did not get down. Gorb waited as long as he dared for a clear shot then chanced firing again. A part of the Tormentor's head broke off and landed with a thump in the foliage some distance away.

The creature took a few steps then went still but for the curling of its spikes. More sword blows toppled its stiff body over. In the quiet that followed there came the *creak, creak, creak* indicating more of them nearby. 'Hush!' Far Gaze said. 'They're drawn by our sounds.'

'Do something, mage, or you will be named an enemy of my city,' said the Mayor.

Far Gaze looked stunned for a moment, then laughed. 'If I do nothing, no one will live to spread news of your city's new enemy. No one but me, that is – I can escape safely enough. So which is it, Mayor? Do you hate me or love me?'

'Enough!' Siel whispered fiercely, grabbing Far Gaze's arm. 'Help us! This excursion was not my idea either. I am willing to die in battle but not to those things.'

'Oh fine! Everyone, listen. Lie down, stay low. Gorb, come closer.'

'What do you cast?' said the Mayor.

'A spell that would shield us from the sight of men. But some animals can see through it, and it may not work on these creatures. There is no time for my other options. I gamble my life for yours, Mayor. I don't have to do this. Remember it if we live! You are steeply in my debt. You personally, and your city. Do you agree?'

Tauk's eyes blazed with anger. 'I do.'

'Good. I have made your word to me binding and if you lied you are cursed. All of you be utterly still, make no sound.'

They lay flat on their bellies among the long stiff grass and dead leaves. The creaking sounds seemed to come through the trees around them, at times from where the path curved behind. Far Gaze began an urgent chant, till his low murmur sounded like wind blowing through leaves. Cold air passed over them as though blown from the magician's lips. 'Hold your nerve,' the Mayor whispered. Siel did not turn her head to see what had provoked his comment, but she heard the creatures coming. The air filled with their stink. She had an almost overpowering urge to watch them, to glean some scrap of knowledge of the creatures while they didn't know they were being observed. Dust from the ground went in her nose and made her want to cough. *Creak, creak, creak . . .*

Here came one stalking through their midst, by luck not bringing its feet's pointed blades down on any of them. It paused by the corpse of the slain Tormentor. The newcomer was taller than the other had been, its arms so long its finger-blades reached the ground. Its head moved in a fast low swing as it peered at the corpse; its mane of needles faintly rattled. It went still.

Another came. Like black knives the long spikes of its feet sank into the ground close to Siel's face. She tensed, expecting to feel the stab of blades sinking into her. Hold your nerve, hold your nerve, she thought. Did the magician's spell work? They were not invisible to each other, and she could not be certain the Tormentors didn't see them. One of the men would panic and run, she was sure. He would dispel the whole illusion . . .

The two creatures stood close together and went still. *Perfectly still,* Lalie's voice echoed, with an image of the hunters' hall and all its death. She shut her eyes as she all too clearly envisioned the same death spread over this ground they lay upon, her own remains indiscernible among the glistening red.

The minutes stretched out as though they were in the pull of the creatures' bent time. One of the two suddenly shifted, its limbs swinging in smooth arcs, its many hooks and spikes in a flurry of motion as though by these means it spoke an urgent message to the other. It stalked away down the path. The other followed.

Siel felt triumphant sweet relief for just a second, till yet another came from the path behind them. Her skin crawled as she heard it come close, closer, the heavy press of its feet indicating it was the largest of them yet. Then the man next to her hissed through his teeth in pain. She turned her head ever so slightly. One of its long dark legs had planted right beside her, the spikes all down its length curling. Two of its foot's five long blades had gone through the wrist of the man next to her.

Its other toes tentatively explored the ground around it with gentle touches. Then finally, finally the creature's foot lifted and it moved on. She could have kissed the man beside her.

The Tormentor went to where the others had lingered and stood still as stone.

There was noise of more of the creatures coming. Siel sighed deeply. Would the next one walk over her? Would Far Gaze's spell break if their spiked feet trampled him?

Movement caught her eye then: a small hand waving. She heard in clear focus a tapping sound that had been going on for a little while now as though to get her attention. The hand came, it seemed, from the ground. As though . . .

Tii's face popped up. He looked back behind to where the lingering Tormentor now seemed engaged in a silent dance of its sweeping arms and head. Tii couldn't see them through Far Gaze's spell, but he knew they were here. 'Tii!' she whisper-called.

'Hush,' said the man who'd endured the Tormentor's foot. His voice was quiet as a breath but she heard furious anger in it for her speaking after what he'd endured in silence.

Tii had heard her. 'Hole! Back, not far! Come down?' he called.

'Take us?' she whispered as loud as she dared.

'Yes! Big one not fit.'

The Tormentor, if it had heard the exchange, did not react – its slow dance went on. Siel took a deep breath, counted to three, then yelled, 'All of you, up and *run, now!*'

She got up and dashed toward Tii without pausing to see if the others followed. Tii darted off like a rabbit, out of a groundman hole too small for the rest of them to fit through. He dived into a slanted cut in the ground she'd not have seen without him going through it first. She dived in after him, her feet hitting its floor painfully hard.

She rolled away to make room for the others. Gorb's head poked in but his shoulders would not fit. 'Tii! What about the giant?' said Siel.

Tii eyed Gorb nervously. 'Cave, that way,' he said, pointing. 'Go in. Big enough. Meet there soon.'

'I'm going to go find Bald,' said Gorb, 'I left him down the path. They might've got him.'

'Fine, but go! You're blocking the hole!'

Gorb stood aside for the Mayor's men, who slid down the dim tunnel and gazed about as though hardly daring to believe what they saw. The small space filled with their hoarse panting. Tii looked at them pensively as though he'd not expected this many would be coming underground with him. Siel was too relieved to care. She laughed, embraced the man next to her, embraced Tii. 'Why are you here?' she said, crying tears of relief.

'Follow,' he said. 'Follow you from place with water. Never far. Tunnels all beneath. Secret tunnels, big people never find. Found friends, below. They come too. Not far.'

'You followed me all this way? Since the tower?'

'Followed, by stone paths. Deep path.' He tapped the cavern wall. 'Felt you. Felt bad things, near you. But no way up. Stone told us where you came. Hard work to follow. You go fast. Where Shadow?'

Eric, he means where's Eric. 'I don't know, Tii. He's not with us. Can you help us? Can you lead us all back to Tanton, underground? It may be the only safe way for us to get there.'

'I take you,' Tii said, still eyeing off the Mayor's entourage with grave concern. 'These men come?'

'Yes. I know that's uncomfortable for you. But Shadow would want it.'

'For Shadow. I take men to city. Only for Shadow.'

5

Their brief walk through the caverns was the closest Siel had come to happiness in a while now: a rush of relief and joy to be alive. Her head spun with what she'd seen in Far Gaze's spell. Generations had known only inevitable defeat or long and bitter stalemate. She felt she were dreaming. What would her parents think, that this day had come in their daughter's lifetime? Would they feel avenged by her part in making history, or just saddened by all she'd gone through?

'I did it for you,' she whispered, tears coming to her eyes as she imagined them with her now, hearing her. 'I did it all for you.'

If Tii's groundman friends were nearby, they were too nervous to show themselves. Soon he took them to a part of the tunnel he had to widen out for them to pass through. On the other side, Gorb the half-giant waited in a hillside cave. Next to him Bald rocked back and forth on his heels, face covered with his hands. Gorb spoke consoling words. One of the guns was braced on his knee. A small dead Tormentor lay in broken pieces at the cave entrance.

The Mayor touched Gorb's gun barrel very carefully. 'What is this device?' he said.

'Bald made it,' said Gorb. A hint of anger had come into his slow speech. 'I got six more of em in the pack. It's what I wanted to show you earlier. But you rode off, left me behind. It cost one of your men his life. That matter much?'

'Watch your words, giant,' said Tauk.

'Watch yours, human. Your bones break easy; your skin is soft; that sword won't kill me.'

'This is an ally of ours,' said Siel, mortified.

Gorb scoffed. 'Not of mine. His city never did much for my kind. Made it a crime to hunt us. But that didn't stop em. One bribe and the Hunter's free. I'm not loyal to *him*. I could break all these guns. Or I could take Bald and run to some other city. Think a different city would want a look at these guns? They might make a thousand more. Then they'll make war on *him*,' he jerked his thumb at Tauk, 'whether they call him friend today or not. Like he'll do to them.'

'I do not make war on friends,' said Tauk in a gentler tone. 'I can't speak for past rulers of my city. You remain free to go where you will.'

'And not because of some human boss's say-so,' said Gorb.

'Of course. You're invited to come with us to the safety of my city's walls, if you will mind your words. I cannot be spoken to this way before my people.'

'I'll go with those two if they want me.' Gorb nodded to Siel and Far Gaze. 'I'll ask them that in private.'

'I've not decided my course,' grunted the folk magician. Still naked, he sat with legs crossed on the stone floor. 'It is now a very changed world. Leave me alone, all of you. Mayor, some advice. Get back to your city, prepare it for battle, if battle is not already upon it. I'll visit to claim my debt when I am ready. And I *will* claim it. Lives are expensive. The lives of Mayors? More so.'

Tauk's jaw clenched; he didn't reply. He and his men filed out through the cave, back into the tunnels.

Siel picked up from the ground one of the broken pieces of Tormentor Gorb had blasted apart. She had to will herself to touch it, but it was just like holding cool stone. The spikes were slightly flexible. 'The corpses get weaker, but very slowly,' said Far Gaze, watching her with his eyes half closed. 'They stay hard but become easier to cut and break. It is not like any other flesh I know.'

'What are they?' she said, and suddenly tears were in her eyes. Angrily she wiped them away. 'I can't understand them. Not anything about them.'

'The wolf scented things which I now understand. The airs that changed them are not normal, not even in Levaal South. They are like poisonous silt on a river bottom. Something kicked them up, probably the stoneflesh giant that crossed. They settled quickly and sank again. Your friend Tii and his people will need to stay away from tunnels near the Conflict Point, once this poison settles again.'

'Conflict Point,' she repeated, intrigued by the phrase. 'What is this poison? A flung weapon?'

'In effect. But so is a violent storm. Maybe we just got in the way. Maybe it was hurled at us on purpose.'

'Must you abuse the Mayor?' she said.

Far Gaze laughed. 'I have the same regard for him as the giant does. He may be fine as lords of men go, but I have known many polite thieves, charismatic traitors, articulate fools. Barbarians who trouble to scrape the blood from their hands don't much impress me either.'

'He is none of those things!'

He looked at her with renewed interest. 'I see.'

'You see what?'

He chuckled. 'What is your course, Siel, now that the old war is not quite lost?'

She sat and buried her face in her hands. 'I'm tired. I want it to be over, I want to live a different life.'

'Poor child. You've done more than most. But you've seen too much now to ever have peace. The nightmares will always come. Part of you will always trudge through battlefields and the reek of death. There are ways to dull the sting. What of the next few days? Those first.'

'I don't know.'

'Giant?'

'I won't fit in the tunnels,' said Gorb, whose voice had lost its edge of anger and was ponderous again. 'I'm better alone, or hidden somewhere. I'll just wander, or go back to the tower. There's a mage there. I've seen him in the valleys. He spelled the village, made it vanish. He might want strong hands. What about you, wolf?'

'The night has changed everything,' said Far Gaze. 'I'll return to the place we left. If there is a mage there I wish to speak with him. A master of disguise he must be, to have hidden himself from me. I'll get there fastest alone.'

'So you won't go with me, if I choose to go to the same place?' said Siel.

'I don't know, I have not been asked,' he said drily. 'Why do you think I spoke to Tauk that way? We are in the age of mercenaries now that the Mayors' alliance has collapsed. My services are for hire. You may make offers.'

She had to get away from the magician. She felt on the brink of tears again and didn't want him to see her; an old instinct not to look weak before men she fought with. She stumbled outside, heard Gorb call a warning about going out there but ignored it, tripping as she went on the stretched limb of the Tormentor's corpse by the cave entrance.

The glade was quiet and still, with many limp vines hanging from tall woods like braids of hair. There was no sound or sign of Tormentors roaming nearby. The first tentative bird calls sounded the way birds sing after a storm has passed.

She sat on a tumbled piece of stone fallen from the hillside long ago, now covered in moss. Mushrooms grew beneath it. She plucked them – easy food was not to be turned down – and checked their underside for signs of poison, pitching one with odd pink markings into the distance then eating the others.

To be alone, to be not mindful suddenly of danger, seemed a protest, an appeal to the gods or the Dragon or against life itself: let the perils take her. But there was no danger here just now, only a quiet rustle of leaves, branches and vines as a breeze swept through the glade. Her head spun from exhaustion. She could sleep here, and in fact why not lie awhile in the soft grass? So she did, just resting her eyes from the incessant light, just resting ...

6

Shadow watched her, asleep in this glade as if she'd grown out of the forest floor like the other living things. She looked truly beautiful to him for the first time, beautiful because there was no trickery to it: she was just here, just *being*. Her chest rose and fell, pulling in air to keep her alive, which itself seemed a kind of magic, one he was newly aware of. His life did not depend on sucking in air, nor on eating and drinking.

So where was she now, while she slept? The dead ones lay like this too, but their chests did not rise and fall. It would be easy to kill her, and to kill the others in that cave just yonder. Easy as swiping his arm down fast.

His rage had died in the long journey. Though his body was again whole, the pain from his wound throbbed slow and dim, now and then flaring like the man's sword had flashed through him again. For a long time his side had burned like molten silver was stuck to him.

The sword had given him something else, a new and peculiar feeling: fear. He'd known what fear looked like in others, the way their eyes widened, their gasping breaths. Even animals had displayed it. But he'd never understood it.

The other girl still called him. Rather, he was called by that thing she wore around her neck, the little place he knew he'd fall into if he got too near to her. Yet it held the same promise and intrigue as when he'd followed its pull across the world. Soon its pull would again become irresistible, and he would forget, he knew, the necklace's danger.

There was a lure to Siel too, which drew him not as keenly. He pondered the two effects. This lure came from within him, that was the difference. The other pulled at him as would hooks dug under his skin. Every hour, it pulled him with more strength.

Eric had left Siel behind. Why? What had she done to offend him? He shadowed her and learned what she dreamed of: walking through an actual past hidden in this glade; that happenstance magic of hers was confined for the moment to her dreams. Her body revolved in cycles, purging itself. Soon she would have these visions while awake again. She hated having them. Strange creature.

Ah, she was stirring now. Eyes open, sitting up, backing away as he'd known she would, hand quite uselessly going to her knife, face indicating despair upon seeing him. He didn't like that. Why not be glad to see him? What could he do to make her smile and laugh? He kept his distance, spun through the ground from nervous energy, though he knew she didn't like it.

'You dreamed of this place.' He waved an arm about the glade. 'Three women sat about a fire trying to do something to make one of them have a baby. They were going to kill an animal in a way that would make magic happen. But two of them killed the other woman instead. Buried her here.'

'I don't remember,' she said, looking back at the cave where the others sat and talked. She wanted to run over there, he saw.

'I'll leave soon,' he said. A strange and unpleasant emotion went through him. It was pain, of sorts, but not physical. He didn't understand it.

'What do you want?' she said.

He considered the question as best he could. 'I don't know.'

'Where is Eric? And Loup?'

'Away.' He pointed north. 'Far. When I was near them, I knew where they were going, and why. Now I forget.'

'Shadow. Will you do me a favour? Will you forget me too? Altogether, forget me? Pretend I am dead.'

That pain again. 'I'll try.' Then anger. 'I could make you dead. If you want.'

'I don't want that,' she said.

Had he hoped she'd be scared? She wasn't. But she wished he wasn't here. 'I don't want it either,' he said.

'What *do* you want, Shadow?' At the cave mouth the half-giant scanned the glade then headed outside to search for her. She called to him, 'I'm fine. Leave me be for a moment. I'll be back soon.'

Shadow thought again about her question. 'I want to learn things. That's all. What am I? Do you know what I am? I understand things for a little while but then it's all gone. I knew things about the man who cut me, the man with the sword. I even knew why he wanted to cut me. But now it's gone. I knew things about the dragon I saved you from, but it's gone.'

'Anfen? Was the man's name Anfen?'

This seemed to excite her. 'Yes,' he said. He tried to remember what had happened but the order of it all was muddled. The basics: 'I fought him. He cut me. It hurt.'

'He cut you? How?'

'His sword has power to it.'

'Where did this happen?'

He pointed in the direction. 'Far. I fled. Came to see you.'

She chose her words with care. 'You have been tricked before, Shadow. I will speak to you as truly as I can. I do not know what you are. A man named Vous created you. He is your father, not Eric. Why he really made you I can't answer. Maybe *he* can't answer either. But if you will take me to him, to Eric, I will owe you a debt.'

'Why?'

She blinked at him. 'Why what?'

'Why do you want to see him, but never me? We look the same, him and me.'

'No. You don't look the same.'

That bad new emotion came through him like a trickle of poison. It was as if she had cut him the way the man's sword had. If she would cut him like this, why shouldn't he cut her back? This was a kind of duel now; she'd made it so. He didn't know how to use the invisible weapons she used, the pain she invoked just with words and a look on her face. He was growing dizzy with pain.

And she watched him coolly, not reacting even as he made his eyes go wide as pits, sucking her into them. His jaw fell wide too; sounds came out of it designed to scare her. The men and half-giant, hearing, came to the cave mouth. She fell toward him, but still a look on her face said she was perfectly willing to meet her death here and now, not afraid like the others were, who had known they would die. She did not care that she'd lie here broken and unmoving!

He grew so confused that some vital piece holding him together pulled taut and threatened to break. He screamed a sound of rage, shoved her away into the rock she'd sat on, watching her body bounce hard against it, then fall limp. With great speed he tore himself far away, not knowing if he'd left her dead or alive, broken like something dropped from a tall height, but still beautiful, in the quiet green glade.

THE CASTLE

1

Eric had a dream that Siel was dead, so convincing he was shocked when he woke in the snug little drake den, enveloped in Case's warmth and snoring. There'd be no more sleep. He was left to wonder if the dream had been her spirit saying goodbye. It had been so convincing that tears pricked his eyes.

Aziel had forgotten her pride – rather, set it down for a moment – and lay huddled close to him as though he could protect her from what she saw in her nightmares. He thought it likely she saw Shadow, still. And he wondered why she forgave him for looking like Shadow, when Siel hadn't.

When daylight came, Eric stood at the cave mouth and gazed at the white dragon-shaped castle they would surely reach today, if Case flew there directly. The airs about it took his breath away when he willed himself to see the magic in them: giant cartwheeling arms of colour turned slowly in the vague shape of a star, so big its upper points surely scraped the sky's white roof.

He guessed at what it was: power gathering itself about the god being made, the god named Vous. And my fate is tied up in his, Eric thought, startled as though this were a new idea. In a way it was new; he had tried to believe it was indeed sheer chance that made it true, but suddenly other possibilities invited him: he really was some kind of saviour, had been all along, a hero from the comics he'd once escaped into after a hard day at the office. It was no accident he was here in Levaal after all . . .

That was absurd. But wasn't all the rest of it just as absurd? He sought for mundane memories of his old life to dispel it all, evidence for the case his being here was all coincidence. But he could find nothing to do it. His mind was blank, as though that old life had never happened, or had been a dream, now murk slipping like sand through memory's fingers.

Loup stumbled past him through the cave's mouth, sent a spray of urine over the ledge, rocking back and forth on his feet as if he felt himself immune to the gravity wishing to pull him into the abyss beneath. It had become quite apparent he was proud to have a powerful urinary stream at his age, just as he was proud of the fit torso so eagerly displayed with all its peppering of white hair. Dick in hand he grinned a toothless grin at Eric as if to say, *Impressive, no?* then gazed at the distant castle. 'Spirits have my guts! Look at those airs!'

They both watched the slowly revolving star-arms without speaking. Now and then thin streams would flit from elsewhere in the sky and join up with the larger mass of powers; others would break off as though the streamers of colour were living things leaving a nest.

'No good's going to come of this at all,' sighed Loup. 'Ah well, let's get it done. We were never going to live forever, lad. Most don't choose their time either, but we have. Today's the day. Ready to fly, Case old man? Ready, Aziel? You're going home, girl. So are we, back to where we came from before our time in these prisons our bodies really are.' He wiped a tear from his eye and tapped his chest. 'Going to miss it in this cage. Up, Case old man. Time to fly.'

The drake got up, yawned, stretched its stiff wings with a sound of leather creaking, then lowered for them to sit upon his back. Aziel – as she'd done every morning – shooed the men out of the cave and spent ten mysterious minutes in there alone before emerging on Case's back.

The drake leaped into the sky and flew them toward their deaths. Whether that destination lay just around the bend as Loup suspected, or was indeed still some way distant, the castle seemed to approach at an equal pace.

They flew high enough that the Great Dividing Road was only just in sight. They passed over the villages set aside for a select Favoured elite of loyalist workers and retired veterans, but as Case took them down a little they saw a curious lack of order below. The country about the castle should have been teeming with people and vehicles; yet the Road and the terrain about it were bare of anything but spot-fires burning and the littered dead. Patrols and guards were nowhere to be seen. The few people they saw moved as though frantically fleeing a battle.

'There!' said Loup, pointing at a group running across a field, converging on a fleeing man with a bundle in his arms. He had nowhere to run and they swarmed over him, his cries faintly reaching them. Loup patted the drake's rump. 'Take us down, Case old man, we have to see what goes on here. This country's the most peaceful and orderly in all the Aligned realm, or should be. Take us down, old man!'

The drake tilted forward, descended, and Aziel shrieked as in clearer detail they saw the attackers were wet with the dead man's blood. But it was their faces which made Eric want to join her in crying out, for it was Vous down there, a face Eric recognised with a jolt from the ghostly figure appearing in his bedroom, some time back. In his mind echoed: *You are Shadow ... last sight, last sound ... my face, my voice ...*

A group of Vous-things scattered from the drake's descent. A handful remained and turned their heads up. Eric felt their glaring eyes meeting his. One had the hunched body of an old woman, her torn dress bright red. Another was in army garb; a sheathed sword hung by his leg which he'd neglected for the use of fingers and teeth.

The drake set down in the grass and huffed a few breaths in an attempt to summon a menacing growl, but it sounded more like a wheezing fit. Aziel crouched behind him, hiding from the Vous-things' view.

The Vous-things fanned out and approached them with hesitant steps, hands limp by their sides, blood-slicked faces blank and vacant. When they got within a dozen paces, Case belched a glut of orange fire.

'Eric, speak to em,' Loup murmured. 'Vous made Shadow from you. He made these things too. Speak up, lad. Let's see what they do. It'll help us understand better what's going on.'

Eric clambered off the drake's back, 'I am here,' he said.

The Vous-things went still – even the swirling wind which howled around them did not ruffle their clothes or hair.

Loup gasped at something he saw in the airs. Eric focussed on them too: a long groping strand from that mass orbiting the castle had wormed over and now moved like a finger above each of the Vous-things, as if briefly debating on one to select. It lingered about the dead man the others had partly devoured. The dead legs twitched, the torso heaved in an effort to sit up before collapsing again. The strand of airs moved to the former soldier, through whose eyes poured a gleam of yellow light. Eric raised the Glock at its chest. High-pitched noise garbled in its throat. 'My daughter returns,' it said.

'I'm not here,' said Aziel through tears. 'Tell him it's not me.'

'Forget your daughter,' Eric said.

'Who brings her?' said the Vous-thing sadly.

'It's who you have waited for.'

'I have waited for myself.'

'You have waited for me,' Eric said.

'I once dreamed of creating beauty,' it said with quiet regret.

'You did. You created your daughter. She has beauty. I bring her to you. I am the one you have waited for.'

'My face. My voice.'

He swallowed. 'I am Shadow.'

The Vous-things hissed. The daylight dimmed. A noise like a whirring machine began from the Vous-thing which had spoken. Quiet at first, the noise built until within it a thousand voices shrieked, babbling panic and rage. It slowly built like a storm about them.

Loup crouched down beside Aziel. The ground heaved, making the castle itself seem to tilt for a moment as though it would fall forward upon them. With a noise like an enormous exhaled breath the five Vous-things lifted up, spun through the air with surreal speed and were drawn back toward the castle, the yellow points of their glaring eyes locked on Eric's own until they were gone.

Stillness fell again like an oppressive weight. Their ears rang.

Aziel covered her eyes with her hands and wept. 'Up, Case,' said Loup urgently, gazing about the countryside. He perched her on the drake's back and he and Eric scrambled on before Case took to the sky, through gusts of powerful wind flying laterally about the castle's face. They were close enough now that windows could be made out on its side like staring lifeless eyes.

'That wasn't my father,' said Aziel.

'It's not your fault,' said Eric gently. 'Your father is ill. He was ill long before you were born. We're going to cure him. I'm not from a "rebel city", I'm from Otherworld. You can help me, Aziel. Where should we go to find him?'

'My bedroom. I'll know the way from there.' After a minute she added, 'And when you say cure him, I know what you really mean.'

'And that upsets you, even after what we just saw. Do you think there's anything else to be done for him?'

'Maybe not,' she said, voice thick with tears. 'But you leave Arch alone.'

'We can't hurt him, neither of us. We can't hurt your father either. I don't know what we can do. This is a leap of faith.' He laughed. 'And it's a big leap. I've read of quests before. People usually have something specific to do, however hard it is. Or they have some weapon to use. We're not even that lucky. I'm going to go and confront a god or a wizard or both, and I'm armed no better than a policeman.'

The gun's weight in its shoulder holster felt reassuring, nonetheless. When clouds permitted sight of the ground beneath, it was strewn with the dead. Loup told him for at least the hundredth time – and for the last time – that it was not too late to go back, but Eric barely heard the words. He willed himself not to see the wildly behaving airs and their storm of colour, but could tell from Loup's gasps and murmurs how intense the sight became as they plunged into the star-arms' outer orbit. The air seemed to fizz with energy, making their hairs stand on end. A part of the swirling mass – Vous's consciousness, or at least a part of it – had noted them, and watched them come.

They were among it now. Eric willed himself to see the magic again and found they were immersed in sickly colour. Each breath drew it into his lungs, spirals and threads of gleaming mist, the power of it making him dizzy. More than that, he felt Vous's direct gaze from somewhere nearby, which barely comprehended anything it fell on, but now had fallen on *him*. Sadness poured through the air, infinite sadness. Eric went dizzy, saw oceans of tears turned to blood in a heaving tide, saw a hundred years of forlorn dreams, a barren forest of dead grey husks where all life had departed, the sound of weeping, weeping, weeping . . .

He fell from Case's back, but it seemed more as though he'd been pulled by strong hands. The air held him as cold water would have. But he was caught in a rip, with no volition of his own. It twisted him around so that before his eyes one moment was the dome sky-roof gleaming white; the next, the ground far below strewn with dead; then the castle big as a planet or a god or he knew not what. He felt sick, dizzy, felt himself a question being pondered by a mind of utter insanity. *I am no threat to you*, he suddenly, belatedly wanted it to know. *Look how you toss me about on the winds! I am an insect. I am nothing. I am about to die alone. As It wills.*

But he was not alone. Aziel was in the air beside him, her face alight with absolute terror, the scream on her lips lost in the turbulence of the wind.

Something carried them both forward until the castle windows were right before them. War mages shrieked nearby like birds of death. He grabbed for Aziel's hand and felt her grip on his, tight with panic. The castle itself seemed to draw them in, just as it had tried to do in his crushed scale vision at Faul's house, when the eyes of mighty Vyin had gleamed through the opening of his prison like two trapped stars.

Do they watch me now? Eric wondered, and somehow he knew they did.

A DISCOVERY

1

Blain's walking stick thumped the base of a tree, a rare expression of rage usually evident only in a deep scarlet pulse through his gown, and simmering in his face of course. With disgust he tossed the charms and wards salvaged from Thaun's body so they fell at Kiown's feet: a ring which made him tolerant of flame and extreme cold; an earring ward – quite powerful – to disrupt hostile spells; and two others whose function Kiown didn't yet know, so he didn't dare wear them to find out. Now was clearly not the time to ask Blain about them either.

Kiown watched the Strategist, wondering for how long loyalty to him was required. The abuse was getting tiresome, and the sulking did not bespeak of a steady hand on the reins. 'Bitten in half!' Blain raged. 'I should have protected him: such assets aren't fodder. Should have used *you*, rat-gnawed bastard.'

Blain's staff lashed toward Kiown's shin. He jumped nimbly so it struck the tree behind him then stepped beyond the range of Blain's swing. Assault by staff was tolerable, could even indicate a certain warped affection, but if Blain started using magic it was time to run, or sneak a blade between his ribs. 'I feel I've earned my status, Strategist,' said Kiown.

'Some say that of you, but I've not seen you do much useful yet.'

Kiown reflected he was probably lucky Blain hadn't seen him hacking at the tower's tender parts as he fled during the war mage attack. He said, 'You didn't see me slay Anfen.'

Blain ignored it. 'Ugh! Envidis off south minding an idiot. Evelle a dragon's whore. It wasn't supposed to *keep* her! Thaun bitten in two, and now I'm stuck with the green one, the sapling.'

'Do you have a plan, Strategist, or am I witnessing it?'

'Don't be clever with me, you shit,' said Blain, but now he sounded more tired than anything. He slumped with his back to a tree, staring forlornly at the tower, where the wizard's tall silhouette could still be made out at the window behind golden light, facing their direction. The whole building looked to be an extension of him, or rather he looked to be one of the living place's inner organs. 'Yes, you sense me still,' muttered Blain. 'Go ahead, pass a sleepless night wondering what I'm up to out here. Ugh! And that's my best revenge. How low I've fallen.'

'Who is he, anyway?'

Blain answered irritably, 'Domudess is his name. I remember him. Not a master when I saw him last, hardly a face worth remembering, back then. Errand runner! So long ago. Don't know how much power he really has now, but there's cunning there at least. Useful cunning.' Blain sighed.

'Your plan, Strategist?'

'No plan! We're fucked. Alone with our wits. We came to make allegiances. Rejected by everyone. Oh, it's understandable. I'd have betrayed them, but only after much mutual advantage. That's what they wouldn't grasp. They really believe in their own purity. Idiots. Play the game! Think I want to rule over a corpse of a world? They would, because of principle! Idiots.'

A rare glimpse into his inner heart, Kiown thought with wry amusement. He climbed up a tree trunk and took a seat on its sturdy branch, which creaked under his weight. Blain looked around wildly, mistaking the sound for a Tormentor.

The Strategist stood and leaned heavily on his walking stick. He said, 'A long way back to the castle. You want a plan? Let's go there and hope by some miracle the fool's been killed, that our Friend and Lord – whether the Change has happened or not – sees us for the long-suffering loyalists we are. May he pet and feed us, his poor starving dogs. You like the odds, whelp?'

'If the Change has occurred, our Friend and Lord will not be there. Or so I understand, Strategist.'

Blain waved the line of conversation away. 'Let me think!' He muttered, 'The others won't trust me; Avridis gone, they'll rush to fill the vacuum like I mean to. So far from it all, here in the south! I've made poor moves. Curse it. The mayor, Tauk. Worth a try with him? Promises and knowledge are all I have to offer him. He's about the only card left, short of going over World's End to chance what we find. Someone else has probably grabbed Tauvene's leash by now ...'

Kiown went higher for a vantage point of the surrounding country. He leaped to a neighbouring tree, up on a branch that bent alarmingly with his weight. He dropped his sword to the ground, steadied himself, gazed around. The charm in his ear made his night vision exceptional – how he'd missed it when undercover, not daring to use any charms under the distrusting gaze of Loup.

Just a way over was the clearing where the dragon had brought Evelle. Perhaps the beast had been aware of him even as it did whatever it did to her. She was a warrior, to subject herself to that so fearlessly, he had to admit ...

Rustling noises a few trees over. An Invia's bright white wings curled about its body, which was obscured by the tree limbs between he and it, so that the wings were all he saw. He hung out at an angle to get a better look.

Indeed it was an Invia. So far south? Very peculiar . . .

He half slid, half dropped to the ground again. Blain's robe flashed scarlet with anger at having his meditation disturbed. 'Magpie,' Kiown whispered.

Blain looked shocked. 'Where?'

Kiown stalked the short distance through the woods to where he'd seen it. Why was the creature here? Was it following the Minor dragon about? In any event, he had a thing to prove to Blain about being a 'sapling'. He'd never hunted a magpie before, aside from scraps when undercover, when the creatures had gone for Anfen. They were not easy game by any measure. But they sometimes – just rarely – bore treasures that made the risk worthwhile.

He unwrapped from his boot a vial of spell-effected poison strong enough to knock out a half-giant, carefully poured its flickering deep red liquid into the hollow tip of a throwing knife, then crept with utter silence to the tree base while Blain hobbled behind him.

A ghostly whistle sounded in the tree above with a rustle of leaves and creak of branches as the Invia noticed the 'walkers' beneath. It was possible, he knew, that it could glean his intentions from his aura, so he had to be swift. Adrenaline poured through him. Killing it and bearing a Mark of course was not the objective . . . stealing from one was not strictly wise either. But the poison had a charge in it made to blank a half-giant's mind. With luck it would work on an Invia too.

'Not like that,' Blain snapped at him when he saw the knife.

'Don't poison it, idiot! Stand back, I have an enchantment known to—'

But Kiown was pulled taut as a bow string and barely heard him. Up through a web of branches the Invia peered down at him with eyes of brilliant green. It all depended on this throw, but Hunters did not miss. He hurled the knife. With a shriek of surprise and pain the Invia thrashed for a second then dropped heavily through the lower branches to the ground. The knife had struck flush into the underside of its thigh.

'You had better hope it didn't break its neck!' Blain hissed, enraged. 'Getting stalked by these things is the last thing we—'

His words fell short, for he saw what Kiown had just seen. A glimmer of dark metal, a flicker of light gleaming across it. Kiown and Blain exchanged a quick glance, then Kiown reached for it, his hands clasping on something cold, which clasped him *back*.

His vision blacked out – he staggered backward. A surge of hot power flushed through his body. His delighted laughter filled the woods as knowledge poured into him. Blain cringed away.

ACKNOWLEDGEMENTS

I'd like to thank Rebecca Taubert of Sunshine Design (sunshinedc.com.au), Katrina Lewry, Tim Jones, Jo Mackay (keep those phonecalls coming, please), Tom Flood, John Berlyne, Ken, Kirsty Brooks, Melissa S, and everyone at HarperCollins but especially Steph, Monica, Jordan and Kate. Also my gratitude goes to George Grie, whose wonderful artwork inspired some of this book (in particular 'Habitat for Humanity', on which I based the wizard's tower).

TURN THE PAGE FOR AN EXTRACT FROM
WILL ELLIOTT'S NEXT NOVEL

WORLD'S END

Book I of the Pendulum Trilogy

1

THE CHANGE

In the doorway of Vous's throne room the Arch Mage leaned upon the forked point of his staff. The odd flash of lightning from outside sent his shadow madly dancing on the floor behind him. His thick curled horns dragged his head down.

Vous was a long way from the young aristocrat of centuries past, lusting madly and without under standing for the very power enveloping him now. A long way even from the tyrant who, with his own hands, throttled out lives rather than share that power. Losing Aziel may have been what burned out the last old shreds of himself; but he had no thought for his daughter now, no memory of both the grief and pleasure with which her sad song had filled him, as it drifted faintly up through his high window each day.

Still the Vous-things scuttled over the lawns far beneath, blood-smeared and mindless. Vous had no thought for these creations either; nor any for the drake in the sky ahead battling the winds with Aziel and the Pilgrim on its back. When she and Eric fell into the sky, when they were drawn by his power through the air towards his balcony . . . even then, Vous did not see them. The human part of his mind was gone, subsumed by something larger.

Vous's body split into several aspects. Some ran through the castle to the lower floors. Only one remained out on the balcony with its hands splayed to the sky. The Vous before the Arch Mage seemed to float just above the carpet, its thin electric form turning slowly, like a dancer making letters with his curved arms and hands. How thin and fragile the translucent body appeared. As if his skin were thin glass which one flung stone could shatter. A swishing windy sound filled the air, in conversation with itself.

'Friend and Lord?' the Arch Mage whispered through dry lips. Vous did not seem to hear, but the Arch did not dare speak louder.

The split canisters of foreign airs lay like popped-open seed pods on the ground. He'd thrown them into the chamber in a fit of emotion and did not understand why nothing had happened when they'd burst apart. He did not understand much of anything, any more. The foreign airs should have poisoned the hidden dimension where spells were made manifest, should have changed the entire world and all of history.

A part of him locked away and hidden from sight knew it had been his last desperate play in the game called power. A still deeper part of him knew that the dragons had used him from afar all along. All along, he'd had masters he never even knew he served.

As the Arch Mage watched Vous, four Strategists watched the Arch Mage. Four men ancient in years, hunched and broken by the magic their bodies had abused. They were as dead-looking as statues of burned wood and bone bent into mean shapes; each was dressed in finery but was now only distantly human. It was as though the wars they'd made and the terrible pleasures they'd indulged in had slowly twisted their very bones. Now and then their hunching shoulders twitched, or their shaking hands would convulsively strangle the staffs they held. Their wheezing breaths filled the silence like whispering snakes.

Vashun — the tallest and thinnest of the Strategists — had stowed the real canisters of foreign airs for transport to his hiding place in Yinfel City, where he had a very good use for them. Those the Arch had flung into Vous's chamber had in fact been filled with ordinary air. The Arch had thought in his arrogance he would rip holes in the past, changing all of reality like a child spilling a bowl of his most hated meal across the table. *Now* Vashun understood why Blain had left the castle while the rest of them were caught in furious squabbles with each other. Clever old Blain!

There are no friends close to a throne. Like the other Strategists, Vashun knew that today was his last within the castle. They all now knew that the Arch Mage had been the one who'd brought down the Wall at World's End. Despite this, Vashun's mood was light. And he sensed humour in the others too, as they watched Vous dance gaily beyond the Arch Mage's outline in the doorway. For power is a game, however seriously played.

So intently was Vashun watching the Arch, enjoying his confusion and suffering (with a skeletal leer uglier than death, bathed in the blooming lustful red of Vashun's Strategist robe), that he hadn't noticed the other Strategists make their discreet exit. It would soon be quite unsafe to stand this close to a god being born. Already the airs were performing in ways he'd never seen, the wild plumes seeming like life forms unto themselves, curls of misty colour flung from wall to wall. 'Arch,' Vashun said gently, placing a long thin hand on the Arch

Mage's shoulder. 'It would seem the Hall of Windows has things to show you.'

The Arch Mage slowly turned to him. On his face — one half like melted wax which had cooled again — was the look of someone lost in strange country. Ah! Vashun sipped of his pain and found it exquisite. There was more to come, much more. 'Come, Arch. There have been . . . developments.

In the war. I suspect you will find events, shall we say, surprising.'

Like a servant given instruction, the Arch Mage hobbled along behind him. Vashun filled the silence with chatter of the books and accounts, and other everyday matters of the castle's running. Each word of it was a careful needle in the Arch's flesh, for it was all over and both of them knew it.

They paused before a non-magical window overlooking the Road-side lawns. Down there a large pile of bodies was heaped, the slain Vousthings which had run rampant through the crowd during the wilder moments of Vous's change. The rogue First Captain stood in their midst, small with distance but recognisable, his sword drawn. Anfen raised his head as if he somehow knew which window they had come to — and perhaps he did. Both wizards fancied he saw them there. A glint of piercing light shone up from his armour to spear into their eyes. 'Who do you suppose he is here to see, O Arch?'

'All of us.'

'Ah. I wonder, who will he visit *first*? O, to know the grim man's mind.' Vashun could not contain it — he wheezed with helpless laughter for a minute or more. 'But ah, your pardon. Maybe he can be stopped. There are . . . how many war mages in the new batch?'

'Many hundreds. Many hundreds more roost in the lower holds.'

'How many do you suppose we'll need? For *one* errant First Captain? He is rather, shall we say, formidable? Brazen too, mm. A little power to that sword, that armour, I'll venture. How many war mages, Arch, to kill a lone man?'

The Arch Mage shrugged and leaned more heavily upon his staff.

'Well, why don't I send them all? Just to be sure. Besides, the new ones are overdue for their first flight.' He got no argument. Vashun whistled for a servant (who was a long time coming, since most had quite wisely fled), and gave him the instructions. Vashun would *not* allow that First Captain to end the Arch Mage's torment swiftly and mercifully with a sword. The very idea was heinous.

He and the Arch Mage walked on to the Hall of Windows, Vashun's long spidery strides making no sound, the Arch's clattering hobble echoing more than usual in the empty corridors. Vashun knew what they would see in the Windows, and he believed the sights bore no deception this time.

Sure enough, across the screens were the ruined bodies of men from the force they'd sent south, sent to conquer the last few Rebel Cities. The ground was wet with blood over many miles. Supply carts and war machines of all types were ruined. Tormentors stood like peculiar tombstones over these fields of death, their dark spiked bodies bright with blood. Now and then, one or two would sway or move their arms with peculiar grace, body language the handlers had never managed to interpret or understand. 'I had no idea you created so *many* of these, Arch,' said Vashun mildly. 'My memory fools me, these days. I recall a strange dream, where we spoke of "controlled release at strategic points". And only to slay the *returning* forces. *After* their fighting was done. Yet, behold! Thousands. Loose about the realm, with not all cities yet subdued. Nearly every Window boasts of the creatures. Thousands of them. Enough to wipe out an army. As it were. You are a master of discretion, Avridis.'

'These ones aren't ours,' said the Arch Mage dismissively. As if this meant the creatures hardly existed at all.

Vashun came closer, making his customary sniffing noise, which neither of them noticed any more. He had learned to discern the scent of many kinds of fear and suffering, and longed now for this new untried flavour: Avridis Sinking in Defeat. He said, 'How do you tell, O Arch? Are "ours" given collars? Brands? Saddles, castle colours to wear? It would appear these beasts have rescued the southernmost Rebel Cities.'

'The Windows lie. Vous said so. The Windows lie.'

Vashun reflected upon this. He did find it curious that the Windows revealed these sights at this time, as though they shared his own delight in the Arch Mage's failure, and wished to rub his nose in it. There did indeed seem some *consciousness* at work in them, a thing he'd never considered before.

'So, the Windows lie. A relief to know it, O Arch. For if they were showing the truth . . . well! It would mean we have nothing left, nothing against the arms of three or four Rebel Cities. Do you suppose our position may have weakened a fraction? Or am I missing something, O Arch?'

'Here!' Avridis spun, a triumphant red gleam in his eye socket's gem. He stood before a Window which showed Tanton under siege.

'You have found an honest Window?' Vashun enquired, moving closer to look.

'As planned. The city is besieged. The war is ours, you paranoid fool.'

Vashun examined the Window's scene, shown from high

above. A good number of the castle's forces surrounded Tanton's high walls, but no siege towers or trebuchets had arrived.

'Just the vanguard. Where are the rest?'

'The vanguard will be enough, even if they are all we have. Vous is ascending. Don't you feel it? We have created a god! Vous will not forget his enemies when he steps forth from the castle. He will clear the realm of those Tormentors, whoever made them. He will bring Aziel back to me, and she shall be next to ascend.'

'An historic day, then.'

'You don't believe it?'

'I think the Windows here invite us to leave the castle, O Arch. We must find a place to hide. Just as the schools of magic were made to hide, long ago.'

'I shall not leave. Never! You truly feel we have *lost*?'

Vashun let a silence draw out, which answered the question perfectly well. The gem in the Arch Mage's eye socket gleamed red and twisted around. A tear fell from his other eye. Vashun watched it slide down the wrinkled skin with utter astonishment. It's Aziel, he marvelled. She did nothing to him, yet she has broken his mind.

Distantly there began a shrieking chorus as the war mages were roused and given their task.

'Easy, Case old man.'

Loup tried to wrench the drake's head but Case kept straining into the wind towards the castle. So much wind! So much chaos and magic and colour in the air he could barely see Eric and Aziel. They'd been pulled from Case's back towards Vous's balcony, but something else had grabbed them and now drew them skywards, to the dragons' sky caverns. They seemed to float slowly and serenely amidst all the turbulence, as if whatever pulled them up wished to do it with the utmost care. Their feet vanished, sucked up into a fat mass of high cloud. They were gone. Loup was too busy trying to control the drake to be sad about it yet, but he knew it was probably the last time he'd see Eric in this lifetime. (And Aziel too most likely, but he'd shed no tears for that . . .)

The drake moaned in protest and spat a gout of orange fire with a sound more like a belch than a roar. 'I said, easy!' Loup yelled above the wind's howl. 'Whatever's taken them up there in the sky, *it don't want us*. You know as well's I what took em. Dragons! Go on, keep trying. Feel that air push back at you? You ain't invited, silly old man. Don't go whining and burping fire at *me*. Away! Off south; I know a place to keep us a time. She who lives there, she loves critters with wings.' Loup was uneasy at the thought . . . Faul the half-giant also loved holding a grudge.

Still the drake strained to follow Eric. 'Listen here!' Loup yelled, clutching one of its ears tight in his fist. It was stiff as boot leather. 'Let em go, you fool sky pony. There's mighty great *dragons* up there! You might not be fraid of *me* when I'm mad but what about them? Turn us around right now, old man, or I'll rip this ear off.'

Case wheeled about, but Loup did not think it was because of what he'd said. More likely it was due to the sight which took his own breath away as much as it evidently frightened the drake. The skies grew dark with moving shapes. From hundreds of the castle's windows, war mages poured, and an orchestra of deathly shrieks rose over the winds. The sound was a nightmare Loup would not forget. Case may have been aided by the wind, but Loup had never seen him fly so fast.

'See that?' Loup murmured to himself, looking back over his shoulder. 'Was like kicking a stump full of flying bugs.' He realised he was still clutching the poor drake's ear. He let it go, patted Case's leathery neck. 'Stay calm, old man, don't tire yourself. They're not following. We don't matter much, not you and me. Be glad of that. Nothing wrong with that.'

Anfen and Sharfy saw the same thing.

Far above where they stood on the castle lawns, Vous had become like a statue with arms splayed. He was naked and his body brightly glowed. His scream no longer carried above the tumult. He no longer conducted the lightning and clouds with sweeps of his thin arms — now they were open as if waiting for an embrace from something in the sky.

Beings fled around them. Some were people, the last few of those from the castle's lower floors to avoid the Vous-things' massacre. Most of the Vousthings too had fled, although now and then they came close in groups of two and three, blood and filth smeared on their clothes and faces. Their eyes burned with light.

It was up to Sharfy to brandish a weapon at them and frighten them away. Anfen, it seemed, was done with fighting. Anfen's strange blade right now appeared no more than a length of normal steel, bloodied with more deaths than Sharfy had been able to count. The sword had not a single notch down its edge. Its tip gouged the dirt by Anfen's spattered boots. Sharfy gazed with powerful longing at the sword which could cut foes from afar. How he thirsted to wield it! He'd be a king. He'd march up through the castle gates, slay the Arch, slay Vous, make the world better.

Here came two Vous-things now, threading through the

corpses, their Friend and Lord's face hungry, sneering, atop a feeble old woman's body. Sharfy waved his sword at them, but only one fled. The other ran with thrashing arms right at Anfen, who didn't bother to even look at it. Sharfy stepped towards it, blade raised, and let the horrid thing skewer itself. Only as his hand made contact with its ribcage, the blade poking clear through the back of a plain dress, did the creature seem to notice him, its baleful eyes peering into his, breathing a warm breath of rot into his face. The moment drew itself out for a long time.

Those eyes were two long tunnels of light, with a small writhing thrashing shape at their very ends. The tiny shape was Vous, he saw: Vous's body convulsing in a small bare room. It took effort for Sharfy to look away.

The Vous-thing fell from his blade and slumped to the ground. He wiped blood from his hand. Some kills in battle one kept in mind like the favoured page of a story, to retell many times. This was not one of them. The Vous-thing stared up at him, hotly, hatefully, as its last two breaths shuddered out. The light of its eyes extinguished slowly.

Serve him well, echoed the god Valour's words in Sharfy's mind. *Serve him well.* 'Just did,' he muttered to himself. 'How many times now? Saved his life. Kept him fed. All pointless.' He wiped his new sword on the grass. He'd taken it from a fallen Elite guardsman: a fine blade, well balanced, though he'd shave a fraction of the weight off if he could. He said, 'Anfen. What's Valour want us to do now?'

'Witness.'

Sharfy wanted to weep at the vagueness of it, but the single-word response was more than he usually got to his questions. He sat down on the soft lawn and gazed up high at the balcony where Vous stood with arms extended to the storming sky. Mad, he is. Everyone in this world. Me too? Must be. Look how I lived. Could've had a little farm. Tended a field, kept a herd, married. Pa wanted a fighter. Grandpa too. They got one. 'Will you kill the Arch?'

Anfen dropped his sword to the ground as though by answer.

'S'that mean you won't? Come on, bastard. Talk. They'll kill us. Right on the grass here. It's where I'll die. I can take it. You can talk to me at least. Not expecting any thanks.'

Sharfy's hands tensed on his sword as two Vousthings came near.

'Is Shadow here?' said one, then the other.

'Off south,' Sharfy answered. One of them snarled; both scurried away.

Sharfy was surprised to feel Anfen's palm on his shoulder. 'The Arch doesn't matter,' said his captain, voice hoarse from the battle cries that had torn from his throat. 'I understand now. Why speak of him? He was used. He never mattered. The spells only ever cast *him*, Sharfy. That's how it really works.'

'Not true. And you know it. We fought im. He knew what he was doing. All on purpose, all planned, everything he did. He knew what war is. Knew how to kill, make men slaves.'

Anfen sat down on the grass beside his fallen sword. 'He did not use his power, the power used him. From where did the power come? That stuff mages see in the air, what is its purpose? Does it have no life or intention of its own?' Anfen began to say more but a coughing fit cut off his words. At the end of it he spat blood.

Mad, mad, mad. Everyone. 'We can't sleep here for the night. Unless we're going in there.' He nodded at the castle steps nearest to them. 'But I know this. I might find a bed and some drink in there. Put my legs up, relax. Then some old commander will come. Make me march to World's End, probably. Without pay. He'll polish some bones. All cos a god told him to.'

At that moment the wind died down. A cry issued from Vous that was like the long note of a beautiful eerie song. All Vous-things in sight went instantly still with their heads raised.

Overhead a red drake flew, its wings labouring into the powerful wind. Two of the drake's riders fell free, but somehow didn't *fall*. Instead they floated on the air, just as debris floats on a river, their bodies drawn towards Vous. 'Looks like Eric,' Sharfy remarked. Then it occurred to him that it might actually *be* Eric, and his heart beat fast. Who the woman was, he had no idea. But when the drake's body angled forwards, he saw clearly that Loup was on its back. 'Loup!' he yelled, loud as he could. 'Down here!'

But his voice was drowned out by the high deathly shrieks of a thousand war mages. They poured from scores of the castle's windows, blackening the skies like great streaks of shadow.

'They come for us,' said Anfen mildly. 'Farewell, Sharfy. My redeemer has willed it.'

'What? No! Get us in the quiet. They can't see us there.'

'Let it end. I am tired.'

'Give *me* that armour then. Quick, before they come.'

Anfen made no move to do so. Above them Eric and the woman had got nearly halfway to the castle when they changed direction. Steadily they floated skywards, away from Vous. Two Invia flew wide circles about them as they were carried higher and higher, until lost from view in thick clouds.

The war mages were soon close enough that the yellow gleam of their slitted eyes could be seen through faces of twisted ropy beard. As one, the mass of them shifted direction and flew up, in pursuit of Eric and Aziel. From a distance it looked as though the flocking mass of them assumed a formation of an arm and fist rising from the castle to strike skywards. Vous's beautiful sung note grew mournful, as if he were sad that Eric and Aziel were no longer coming towards him.

Sharfy knew he'd live, for the moment at least. He also knew he owed Anfen no thanks for it. 'If that was really Eric,' he said, 'that's the last of him. Never seen that many war mages. We have to get under cover. They'll come back. Fuck you and your redeemer. Stay here and die.' He left him sitting there without a moment's pause, nor the faintest hint of guilt or regret.

Anfen stared up at a high castle window, and did not appear to have heard or noticed.

THE
Pilgrims
WILL ELLIOTT

Book I of the Pendulum Trilogy

Eric Albright is leading a normal life until a small red door appears under a train bridge near his home. Then a ghostly being wakes him in the dead of night, with a message from another world: *You are Shadow*.

In Levaal, the world between worlds, the dragon-gods grow restless in their sky prisons, and the Great Spirits struggle to contain them. Vous, the world's Friend and Lord, simmers in madness as he schemes to join the ranks of gods. He and the Arch Mage have almost won their final victory over the Free Cities. A dark age dawns.

But Eric and his friend Case are now Pilgrims, called to Levaal for a battle more ancient than the petty squabbles of men. And they will learn why some doors should not be opened ...